DEEPE

MORE . . .

TOTAL SURRENDER

Best Sensual Novel of the Year
—*Romantic Times* Magazine

"Cheryl Holt is something else again. I was totally blown away by *Total Surrender*, a tale both erotic and poignant. Sensational characters, and a very compelling read that readers couldn't put down unless you're dead! It's also the dynamite sequel to last year's *Love Lessons* . . . Don't miss this author. She's a sparkling diamond."

—Readertoreader.com

"Cheryl Holt scores big with *Total Surrender*. Following in the erotic path set by Robin Schone, Lisa Kleypas, and Catherine Coulter, she taps into secret fantasies tied closely to a romantic love story."

—*Romantic Times Book Club*

"A lush tale of romance, sexuality, and the fragility of the human spirit. Carefully crafted characters, engaging dialogue, and sinfully erotic narrative create a story that is at once compelling and disturbing . . . [A] story that is sizzling hot and a hero any woman would want to save."

—*Romance Reviews Today*

"A deliciously erotic romance . . . the story line grips the audience from the start until the final nude setting, as the lead characters are a dynamic couple battling for *Total Surrender*. The suspense element adds tension, but the tale belongs to Sarah and Michael. Cheryl Holt turns up the heat with this enticing historical romance."

—*Writerspace*

MORE
~ THAN ~
SEDUCTION

Cheryl Holt

St. Martin's Paperbacks

MORE THAN SEDUCTION

Copyright © 2004 by Cheryl Holt.

ISBN: 0-312-99283-1
EAN: 80314-99283-5

Printed in the United States of America

St. Martin's Paperbacks edition / September 2004

St. Martin's Paperbacks are published by St. Martin's Press, 175 Fifth Avenue, New York, NY 10010.

10 9 8 7 6 5 4 3 2 1

. . . As the Season moves into full swing, most of Fashionable London will be content with the various activities in Town. However, for those seeking diversion from the ordinary, several of London's premier hostesses will have their summer homes open in Bath. With such refined entertainment in the offing, the small metropolis promises a delightful escape for relaxation and restoration.

Of course, while convalescing in the country, every discriminating lady will wish to visit Mrs. Anne Smythe's Healing Spa and Bathing Emporium for Women. Guests are encouraged to let their hair down—so to speak—and rumors of the fun to be had are too naughty and too delicious to mention here.

Needless to say, no gentlemen are allowed!

"Mrs. Magpie's Snippets"
London Gazette, May 1813

1

"I can't help you, Lady Eleanor."

Anne Paxton Smythe stared at the elegant noblewoman sitting across from her, hoping she seemed courteous but firm. She struggled to exhibit a serene smile, but could barely keep from fidgeting.

It was folly to refuse an aristocrat's request, and she had to wonder if she was putting herself at risk, if all she'd achieved would be rent asunder simply because she'd stood her ground.

From the instant the exalted lady's coach-and-four had rumbled up the lane, Anne had been wary. She'd recognized that nothing good would come from the visit, and now that an outrageous entreaty had been tendered, she could tell that her intuition was on the mark.

Assistance was out of the question.

"At least hear me out," Lady Eleanor cajoled.

"You can't change my mind."

The warm June breeze fluttered the curtains, and a titter of feminine laughter wafted in an open window. The voices were sultry and relaxed, and they conjured images of summer nights, of lovers, intrigue, and romance.

Uneasy, Anne shifted, praying that her guest hadn't heeded the sounds, but they were difficult to miss. Over the years, she'd grown accustomed to the odd articulations, had listened to so many strange utterances that she didn't notice the occasional outburst of pleasure. Yet, to anyone else, they might appear peculiar, disconcerting. Downright lustful.

She blushed. "As I was saying . . ."

The giggling came again, from very nearby, and she glanced up as a naked female tiptoed by on the outside walk. Like a forest nymph, her hair was down, and her voluptuous breasts were exposed to the afternoon sunshine. A second woman, as naked as the first, darted along behind.

Extremely dismayed, Anne peeked at Lady Eleanor, but her chair was positioned so that she couldn't have seen.

Praise be! There was no way she could explain the spectacle, and the last thing she needed was to spur the prim, proper paragon into a swoon!

Exuding calm, she rose. "Would you excuse me?"

"But I just arrived, and I—"

"I'll hurry." She departed before Lady Eleanor could command her to stay.

Placid and graceful, she slipped out, but once she was down the hall, she ran to the rear door. Her friend and aide, Kate Turner, was trimming flowers in the garden, unaware of the indecent romping. After much frantic pointing from Anne, Kate nodded in comprehension and meandered down the shrub-lined path to confront the recalcitrant duo.

Nude gamboling in the yard was not permitted!

"Check their picnic basket for me," Anne hissed. "If you find any wine, they've had enough. Confiscate it!"

Intoxicating beverages weren't allowed, either. Despite how her patrons insisted that spirits added to their enjoyment, Anne couldn't relent. Many were overwhelmed by the invigoration they experienced while bathing in her hot springs grotto, and she had to keep a tight rein on all behaviors, lest the merriment spin out of control.

Rumors were rampant as to the beneficial qualities of the water—that it was mysterious, magical—and she didn't dare encourage further obfuscation or distortion.

She went inside, even as she pondered whether Kate would have the gumption to seize the liquor. Kate was efficient, pragmatic, gifted at many tasks, but she wasn't adept at dealing with Anne's affluent clients. Kate steered clear of the snobs and society types, while Anne had to welcome and politely interact with all of them, if she wanted to put food on the table.

At the door to the receiving parlor, she slowed, took a few deep breaths, and the delay gave her a chance to assess Lady Eleanor. She was a regal beauty, with a pleasingly plump figure, big blue eyes, and fabulous blond hair that was pinned up in an intricate chignon. Her skin was smooth, pearly white, the kind that the very rich could afford to maintain with expensive creams. Her sapphire gown was constructed from an expensive fabric that crinkled and shimmered when she moved.

In comparison, Anne was dowdy and drab, garbed as she was in her gray, functional dress, her starched apron. Water had splashed on her skirt, and there were stains on the hem. While her brunette hair was braided and bound, heat and sweat from hours of toil had caused several strands to fall.

Hard work, a healthy diet, and her petite frame had combined to thin her torso. Next to the stunning, buxom noblewoman, she felt gaunt, too skinny, underfed. Her body was unfashionably tanned from too much laboring in the sun, her hands rough and chapped from an excess of chores. Her business was thriving, and cash was available for frivolous lotions and pampering, but there was never an idle moment in which to indulge herself.

She was constantly busy, and gazing upon Lady Eleanor made her feel tired and decrepit.

Lady Eleanor had traipsed to the window and was gaping out, wanting to determine what had drawn Anne away. Luckily, the scandalous pair was no longer visible. Anne couldn't conceive of what lies she'd have had to concoct if Lady Eleanor had espied them.

If only Lady Eleanor had advised in advance that she'd be stopping by! Anne could have prepared, could have locked the gate and declined to admit the bevy of unrestrained bathers.

Well, there was naught to be done except to conclude their discussion and send the stubborn female on her way.

As she entered the salon, Lady Eleanor spun around, embarrassed at being caught snooping, but she covered her lapse well. Anne gestured to the chairs, and they seated themselves, once more.

"Now then," Anne began, "where were we?"

"We were talking about my brother, Stephen."

"Ah, yes." The infamous Captain Stephen Chamberlin. Man-about-town. Libertine. War hero. Why would such a distinguished knave have his sister traveling about the countryside and making solicitations on his behalf? Had he no manners? No shame?

"He was wounded in Spain."

"Was he?" Anne queried blandly. The rich and powerful had no monopoly on the miseries of warfare. Her own brother, Phillip, had almost been killed at Salamanca. She refused to show any sympathy for the Chamberlin family.

"Did I mention that our father is Robert Chamberlin, the Earl of Bristol?"

Four times, already!

"You did." But Anne wasn't impressed by the earth-shaking news. She wouldn't give two pennies for any lord in the land, and if Lady Eleanor was planning to shock or dazzle by alluding to her sire, she was preaching to the wrong choir. Anne couldn't care less.

"So if you're worried about my ability to remunerate you for his treatments, I can assure you that you'll be fully compensated."

"It's not the money."

"What then?"

Anne had so many reasons that she couldn't tabulate them all. Primarily, she couldn't have a male on the property. What would her clients say? What would neighbors think of the impropriety?

The nearest large metropolis was Bath, which drew multitudes who sought convalescence. The most wealthy and influential personages in England made regular pilgrimages, but many of the feminine celebrities preferred the privacy of Anne's farm.

The ancient Roman bath, which she and Kate had renovated, was a godsend, a priceless boon, and she wasn't about to spoil everything by having Captain Chamberlin on the premises. No matter how badly he was hurt, she couldn't risk her livelihood.

"My visitors are all female," she clarified. "It wouldn't be fitting."

"Are you afraid you'd lose customers?"

"I'm positive I would."

Lady Eleanor opened her reticule, retrieved an envelope, and passed it over. "I don't know what income you earn, but this should more than offset any costs you might sustain."

Anne peeked inside, amazed to spot a stack of what had to be hundreds of pounds. "This is too much. I couldn't—"

"That's for the initial six months," she interjected. "If it takes you longer to get him on his feet, I'll double the amount."

Anne closed the seal on the small fortune and tried to

return the pouch, but Lady Eleanor wouldn't accept it, so she laid it on the table between them.

"Please, Mrs. Smythe. I'm begging you."

She was distressed, convinced that Anne could successfully intervene, which left Anne terribly uncomfortable. Her true name was Anne Paxton, and the surname of Smythe was false. She pretended to be a widow, for reference to a deceased husband gave her legitimacy, and quashed questions about her background and skills.

In reality, she was a fraud, a twenty-eight-year-old spinster, who'd nursed her ailing mother, then Widow Brown, through their final illnesses. Her depth of medical knowledge was no more extensive than the assorted methods she'd developed through trial and error. To observe Lady Eleanor desperate, pleading for her assistance, mortified Anne.

She couldn't help Stephen Chamberlin. Save for a few tinctures, dietary modifications, and bathing in the grotto, she hadn't the faintest notion how. Nor did she want to tend a spoiled, arrogant aristocrat. The very idea had her stomach roiling.

"What you're asking is too difficult for me to consider."

"How could I make it easier?"

"You can't. If you feel he could benefit from therapeutic waters, there are spas in Bath. Any of them would be suitable."

"I couldn't parade him into a public establishment!" Anxiety creased her brow, and she searched through her bag, once again. "Look at him. This is how he used to be."

She handed over a miniature, framed portrait of Stephen Chamberlin. With dark hair, and mesmerizing blue eyes, he was the most handsome knave Anne had ever seen. He was attired in his military uniform, the red of the coat adding a dashing flare. Smug, conceited, overconfident, he was ready to challenge Napoléon all by himself and win.

Foolish men and their foolish fighting!

Phillip had been dapper and gallant, too, when he'd marched off. She'd implored him not to go, to stay with their father at Salisbury where he'd be safe, but he hadn't listened any better than Stephen Chamberlin. They'd both been mangled and maimed, leaving the women in their lives to deal with the aftermath.

She didn't want to be affected by his plight, yet she scrutinized the picture, wondering about the man, the soldier, intrigued even though she didn't wish to be.

"He doesn't look like this anymore," Lady Eleanor proclaimed. "He was always such a proud peacock, so vain about his appearance. I couldn't let anyone behold him as he is. That's why I thought your farm would be best. It's so quiet here, so isolated. He'd have the privacy he needs to heal."

Just then, laughter sounded from directly outside, and Lady Eleanor whirled around. At that exact moment, the breeze ruffled the curtains, and she was able to view a naked woman flitting by.

"Oh dear . . ." she murmured.

"Pardon me," Anne said, gnashing her teeth, and she rushed from the parlor, down the hall, and out the back, where she glimpsed the bare bottom of the interloper as she scampered into the pool. She hunted for Kate, who—the traitor!—was nowhere to be found, so she had to handle the situation, herself.

A dozen customers were lounging, on the rocks and on the banks surrounding the pond. They were slothful members of the *ton,* whom she didn't know, but Lady Carrington had recommended them. Not wanting to offend, Anne had permitted their visit but, hoping to dissuade them, she'd suggested an exorbitant price, and without hesitation, they'd agreed to pay it. Feet submerged, their hair rolling off their shoulders, their breasts thrust out, they were arrayed like a band of frisky mermaids.

There was a certain element who enjoyed the naughtiness

of the out-of-doors, who liked the wantonness of loafing in the altogether, who reveled in the prospect of being detected, although the opportunity for discovery was slim. Her acreage was fenced, the grotto shielded by thick ferns and bushes.

They also wanted to be able to brag that they'd been at her facility, which was currently all the rage. Incessant gossip abounded: that Anne was a sorceress with restoratives and remedies, that she could cure anything from insomnia to feminine ailments, that her hot springs had special characteristics not possessed by the other spas in the vicinity.

There were even claims that the water had a sexual energy, that when a woman immersed herself in it, she was overcome by lustful urges and insurgent passions.

Anne didn't attempt to quell the scuttlebutt. She was in commerce, and owned the home and the acreage she'd inherited from Widow Brown. With her mother dead, and her father estranged, the legacy was all she had in the entire world, and she would do whatever it took to succeed.

Insolent and disdainful, the promiscuous group watched as she approached, and she champed down on her irritation. There were bottles of wine and expensive goblets strewn about on the grass. Several were empty, evidence of their imbibing, which would account for their nude treks around the house.

She loathed them, but they had money and could purchase her services, which provided her with the leeway to treat the poor who couldn't, so she trod a fine line. She had to be fawning and deferential, but she was in charge, owner and operator, and she couldn't have them running roughshod over her.

"Ladies," she called, "you're flouncing about in the yard. I reviewed the rules with you. Once you're finished in the dressing cottage, you have to remain in the pool area. You can't be traipsing about the property. Especially unclothed. You *must* wear your bathing costumes at all times!"

"But it's so much more fun to go without," one of them responded. She was Camilla Warren, a young, snooty widow, whose elderly husband had recently died, but she didn't seem to be in mourning.

"I have a guest, and you're disturbing our discussion."

"Yes, we saw," Camilla replied. "Is it Eleanor Chamberlin Dunworthy?"

"No," Anne fibbed.

"Really? I could swear the coach has the Bristol crest on the side."

"You're mistaken."

"Is Stephen with her?"

"I have no idea about whom you're speaking."

Lady Camilla stretched, arching up, smoothing her palm across her breast, her stomach, intending—Anne was convinced—to startle and dismay, so she evinced no reaction. In the years she'd managed the emporium, Anne had seen it all, and nothing surprised her anymore.

"I hear that Stephen's gone mad as a hatter." Camilla glanced over at her companions. "Wouldn't it be amusing to learn the truth for ourselves? What tales we could tell, hmm?"

A malicious chuckling rippled through the group, and Anne had to bite her tongue to contain a snide remark. Who were they to jest over Lord Chamberlin's condition? He'd fought for God and country. The least they could do was show some respect.

"If you disregard the rules again," Anne warned, "I'll have to deny you privileges."

"You wouldn't," Camilla pouted.

"I would." Anne met Camilla's calculating stare with one of her own, and the harridan was easily cowed.

"Oh, all right," she grumbled. "We'll behave."

"Thank you."

Anne turned and headed toward the house, and behind her, Camilla grouched, "Spoilsport."

The others snickered, but Anne kept on. As she climbed the stone pathway and rounded the hedge, she literally bumped into Lady Eleanor, who had followed, curious as to what was occurring. From her pallor and blatant anguish, it was obvious she'd eavesdropped.

"Come with me!" Anne commanded. "Don't grant them the satisfaction of witnessing your distress."

Anne ushered her inside, poured her a glass of sherry, then sat patiently, waiting while she sipped.

"He's not mad!" Eleanor insisted once she'd finished it. "He's . . . he's . . ."

Tears surged and began to fall, and Anne couldn't bear them. She didn't want to pity Lady Eleanor and her brother, didn't want to be saddened or swayed, didn't want to be apprised of what afflicted him, wouldn't display any concern, wouldn't commiserate, console, or comfort.

Yet, she caught herself inquiring, "What *is* wrong with him?"

"He was terribly wounded. In the legs and back. With saber slashes, as well as pistol shots. His limbs are still attached, but he can't walk, when there's no reason he can't. The doctors say it's as if he doesn't want to get better."

"Perhaps he doesn't. You can't force a person to improve if he's dead-set against it."

"But he's only thirty! Should I throw up my hands? Give up? Give in?" She swallowed, shaken. "The quacks advising my father are demanding to cut off his leg! If he attacks his physicians again, my father will send him to Bedlam!"

Anne shuddered. She'd been in the asylum, on a dreadful occasion, when she'd rescued Kate after Kate's husband had had her committed. She'd never wish such a penalty on man or beast.

"He wouldn't," Anne contended.

"I saw the papers on his desk."

"You could have misunderstood."

"I didn't," she asserted. "Do you have a brother, Mrs. Smythe?"

"Yes."

"Would you let your father do such a thing to him?"

Anne wanted to snort in disgust. As if her *father* would ever have cared enough about Phillip to expend the effort! "No, I wouldn't."

"Then, help me!" More tears flowed.

"Oh, Lady Eleanor . . ."

Anne sighed, heartsick and discouraged. She'd ceaselessly been too kind, too compassionate. It was her greatest failing, and Lady Eleanor's plea nettled her, making her want to assist, despite her reservations. Eleanor kept injecting their brothers into the conversation, which weakened her resolve. She had a soft spot for Phillip, and couldn't conceive of sitting by if he was in trouble.

Her determination was waning when she noted Camilla Warren's carriage pulling out of the drive. She and her friends were chatting gaily, waving and blowing kisses to the Bristol footmen attending Eleanor's coach.

The ruckus had Anne snapping to reality. She couldn't get involved in the Chamberlin family's problems! Particularly when their father, the Earl of Bristol, was about to dispatch one of his three sons to Bedlam. It was a no-win situation, in which she dare not intervene.

"That bunch is why I have to decline," she pointed out. "You observed what they're like. Some of my customers are a bit wild, just as some are very ill, but they're all women, and this is an establishment where they can relax and be themselves. He simply couldn't be here."

"I've heard stories about you," Eleanor implored. "You're a healer. You're aware of remedies and methods that others aren't."

"The stories aren't true," Anne confessed. "I have some rudimentary nursing skills. There's nothing exceptional about what I do."

"Everyone talks about you."

"Trust me: my acclaim vastly exceeds my abilities."

"The water in your grotto," she prodded, trying a different tactic. "They say it possesses a magic power that isn't found in the other hot pools."

"What they *say* is a fallacy, Lady Eleanor. It's just water. It bubbles out of the rocks. That's the only mystery."

For a lengthy, painful minute, Eleanor studied her. "You could cure him. I can see it in your eyes. You could do it. Please! Save my brother for me."

"I can't. I'm sorry."

"I'll give you anything you ask. There must be something you've always wanted. Something you need."

"No. There's nothing."

Defeated, her shoulders slumped, and she stuffed her envelope of cash into her bag. "If you change your mind—"

"I won't."

She held out a piece of paper, and Anne took it, recognizing it as the directions to Bristol Manor. As if she needed to be informed of the route to the estate! She couldn't have resided in the area since she was three and not known.

"I'll be there—with Stephen—through the end of September."

"Don't count on me. Find someone else."

"There is no one *else*," she declared. "I've searched throughout the country. You were my last hope."

The comment cut Anne to the quick, and she pressed her lips together, lest her undisciplined tongue make an offer she couldn't fulfill. Lady Eleanor rose and left, without a farewell or backward glance, and Anne was rooted to the floor. She lingered, listening to the tread of the lady's slippers as she exited and trekked down the walk.

There was a protracted murmuring of voices—an apparent argument—a slamming door as she climbed into the conveyance, much creaking and jingling of leather and harness as she prepared to depart. The vehicle rumbled off, the magnificent horses clopping in a perfect rhythm as they promenaded in a circle and journeyed toward the road.

In grave despair, Eleanor approached the coach and Stephen's friend, Charles Hughes, leapt to attention. He was handsome, in a rough way. Stout and wide, strong as an ox, tough as nails, he reminded her of a pugilist at a fair. With his reddish hair, green eyes, and windburned skin, he exuded a masculinity that might have attracted many women, though not an experienced widow such as herself.

At age thirty-two, he was three years younger than she was, but he seemed so much older and wiser, and he made her nervous. She stiffened, bucking up to insulate herself. When in his presence, she felt smaller, immature, less confident.

While she'd spent her twenties married and engaged in frivolous pursuits, he'd been a career soldier, roaming around Europe. He'd traveled with Stephen, and though neither of them ever discussed what had actually happened in Spain, Eleanor suspected that Stephen wouldn't be alive had Charles not been by his side.

As it was, Charles had lost a hand, not in the battle, but in medical treatment after it ended. He had a hook strapped where the absent appendage should have been, which enhanced his air of danger and authority, and it was discreetly tucked into his shirt, his arm resting on his stomach. His valor and maiming ensured that he would be on the Bristol payroll for as long as he was inclined to stay. Though the men in her family had many faults, they were loyal.

"Well?" he demanded without preamble.

"She said no."

Good, was his unspoken response, and he queried, "Now what?"

"Is he still passed out?"

Charles's lips thinned to a tight line. He hated it when she referred to any of Stephen's bad habits. "Yes."

"Let me see."

Charles opened the door of the elegant vehicle, and she peered into the dark interior. Slumped against the squab, dirty, unkempt, stinking to high heaven, her once-beautiful, dynamic, charismatic brother snored in peaceful oblivion.

Bile rose in her throat, and she turned to Charles. "Take him out. Leave him on her stoop."

"What?"

Behind them, the driver and footmen tensed.

"You heard me."

"Have ya gone daft, woman?" As Charles's temper flared, his native Scottish brogue poked through.

"She's a kind person. She'll help him."

"I thought she refused you."

"She'll relent."

"Are you insane? What if she doesn't?"

"I won't have him at Bristol, where my father will permit those sawbones to remove his leg."

"The earl will calm down."

"If that's what you suppose, then you don't know my father very well."

Charles was so angry, he was trembling. "I won't let you discard him here, like a sack of rubbish!"

"Take him out, Mr. Hughes."

"I won't!"

Charles occupied a strange position in their household. Though he was technically a Bristol employee, he answered to no one but Stephen, and he couldn't be ordered about. A man of lofty morals and principles, he'd quit before he'd obey a command that went against his better judgment.

She glared at the footmen, who didn't dare defy her. "Carry him out, gentlemen."

Near to a mutiny, they bristled, but ultimately, the driver stepped forward to comply with her edict, as Charles shoved him away.

"I'll do it," he bit out, and he reached in and gripped Stephen around the shoulders. With only the one hand, he was awkward, and the other men vaulted forward to lend their support.

They hauled him up the walk and laid him down, and he didn't flinch or make any motion to indicate that he noticed what they'd done. He slumbered in serene indifference.

The men came toward her, and Charles muttered under his breath, "Crazy shrew."

"Did you say something, Charles?"

She stared him down, evincing an arrogance and rage she never showed to others. He met her look but prudently held his tongue.

In the current heat of the moment, it wouldn't do for either of them to spew remarks they might later regret.

Charles lifted her into the coach, and the others readied for departure. None too soon, they were away. The horses were maneuvered around, and as they were about to exit the yard, Mrs. Smythe ran out the door, screaming and running after the carriage as though she might catch it and yank it to a halt.

"No, you don't!" she wailed. "No, you bloody don't! You can't do this to me!"

Eleanor leaned out the window. "I'll return in a month, to learn how he's doing. Write to me at Bristol if you need anything."

Clasping her reticule, she retrieved the envelope of money she'd brought. She flung it out, and it landed in the dirt at Mrs. Smythe's feet. Her expression of wrath and scorn was wrenching, and Eleanor couldn't abide her disdain, so she settled inside and shut her eyes.

This is for the best, she persuaded herself. *It is!*

She offered up a prayer. For Stephen. But for Mrs. Smythe, too.

∾ 2 ∾

Stephen awakened in a dark room, unsure of where he was or how he'd come to be there. The only fact he knew with any certainty was that he wasn't in his suite at Bristol Manor. He'd spent the preceding few months in hiding, demanding a privacy that wasn't afforded, and battling the incompetent fiends his father hired in the guise of medical practitioners.

In a prior period of his life, he might have been startled by the strange surroundings, might have leapt to his feet, ready to fight or flee. Now, he was simply muddled, his head throbbing, his bones aching, his fatigue grave.

He took stock of his environs. The bed upon which he reclined was comfortable, the mattress soft and cushy. The quilt smelled clean, a sheer contrast to the fleshly odors emanating from his person.

His vision adjusted, and he could see a rocking chair, framed pictures on a white wall, a vase of flowers on a dresser. The furnishings were modest, the decor plain, yet it was cozy, welcoming.

Turning onto his side, he peered out the opened window, and an invigorating evening breeze blew over him. In the distance, thunder rumbled with the approach of a summer storm.

The moon was up, the golden orb shining down on a quiet, manicured yard, the rolling hills beyond. Off to the left, he could detect a barn and cottage. To the right, the lawn sloped, a stone walk winding to a stretch of hedges and large shade trees. He could hear water gurgling, as though there was a stream nearby.

Had he been here before? Or had it been a dream?

Motion caught his attention, and he narrowed his focus, gazing through the shadows. At the end of the pathway, there was a break in the shrubbery, and he could observe a woman rising to her knees, then her feet.

She was naked! And wet! Water sluiced down her pale skin. She was bathing in an outdoor pool. Unclothed! Not a stitch of fabric covered her.

How outrageous! How shocking! How marvelous!

Pretty, with a heart-shaped face, high cheekbones, and full mouth, her hair was long, ebony, hanging past her waist and deliciously curled. Wide at the shoulders, thin at the waist, then wide again at the hips, she was slender, yet curvaceous, her torso shaped to accentuate her feminine gifts, to capture a man's eye and hold it.

Her breasts were ample, inviting, the centers dusky and distinct, the nipples erect and pointed. Her tummy was flat, her legs lanky and lean. At the top of her thighs, her enchanting puss hinted at the delights shielded within.

She was flawless, bewitching, ethereal, and in his disordered state, he wondered if she was an apparition. Out of some suppressed, buried need for companionship, had he conjured her up? Was he pining away, subconsciously mourning the loss of his masculine drives?

He thought he'd come to grips with what had happened, with his deformities and impairments, but apparently not. She made him rue and regret in a fashion he hadn't previously.

He'd always adored women, the taste, scent, and feel of them, and a smile flitted by as he recalled a ravishing mistress, a Sunday afternoon, scones and wine on the table by the bed, the sun shining in . . .

Was the temptress before him a hallucination? A delusion evoked out of misery and desolation? He didn't think so. She seemed very real.

Though he was a gentleman by birth, nothing about his character indicated genteel tendencies. Without a flicker of remorse or chagrin, he spied on her, and it was obvious this wasn't the first occasion she'd bathed outside. She was relaxed, at ease, unperturbed by the circumstances.

During his tempestuous interval as a libertine in London, before he'd joined the army, he'd wooed and seduced and debauched, but in all his philandering, he'd never run across a female who was so complacent with her body, her nudity. It was thrilling to view her, and he couldn't look away. Like the worst, most pathetic voyeur, he watched, cataloging her every move.

She retrieved a bar of soap, and proceeded to wash. Raising her hands, she lathered them, then stroked the bubbles downward, under her arms, round and round her breasts, her stomach, her thighs. She scrubbed between her legs, the bar passing over and over her sheath, then she spun about, showing him her delectable backside, the cleft of her dimpled ass.

Feet braced, bum pushed out, she was bent over, open, splayed wide, revealing every risqué inch of her privates. He'd never witnessed such a carnal sight, and he pictured himself dallying with her, advancing on her from behind, seizing her flanks and entering her with a languid thrust.

She dipped into the pond and rinsed herself, then she clambered out, her skin white against the thick foliage. Sexy, alluring, she scrambled onto the grass and picked up a towel, sensuously caressing herself with it. Arms up, breasts jutting out, she dried her shoulders, bosom, belly, legs, the towel descending in enticing circles, then she swathed it around herself. The fabric fell to her knees, and she secured it by tucking a corner at her cleavage. The wrap made her appear wanton and untamed, like a native savage.

His strength gave out, and he flopped onto his pillow, his destroyed torso sinking into the mattress, and he reached down, his fingers at his crotch. A withered stump, his cock lay on his leg, limp and useless as a noodle. Nothing. No blood pounding. No flesh swelling. Not so much as a pulsing vein.

How could he evince no reaction? How could the lusty display leave him unaffected? From the night at age fifteen when he'd swivved a tavern wench at the Bristol harvest festival, he'd been a randy, robust fellow. His partners raved over his size, his prowess, his stamina, and ability to satisfy.

Where had his manly aptitude gone? Why couldn't he feel anything? How could he gawk at such a beauty and be indifferent? Masculine instinct, of its own accord, ought to stir some response, no matter how tepid.

Fatigue set in, and he drifted away, finding it easier to slumber than to deal with reality. He had no answers to the questions that plagued him, could make no sense of the odd failings of a body he no longer recognized. It was simpler to drift, to disregard and neglect.

Sometime later, a noise woke him, and she was standing over him, clad in a thin robe. The belt was loosely cinched at the waist, the lapels baring her to her navel, the globes of her breasts teasing him from behind the material.

She smelled like roses, and her hair was still damp, though she'd brushed it. The tresses curled around her hips.

On espying her, he experienced such a wave of peace and tranquillity that he speculated as to whether the serene, snug place was heaven. Perhaps he'd finally died, as he'd been hoping.

"Are you an angel?" he asked.

"No." She chuckled.

"Are you sure?"

"Very."

He was desperate to know for certain, and he slipped a hand inside her robe. Her skin was warm and smooth, and he cupped her breast and petted the nipple.

His crude, disrespectful touching didn't seem to bother her. She tolerated the naughty gesture, staring him down as if he was a nuisance, as if she'd expected nothing more, and he was furious that she noted none of the physical attributes—the blue eyes, the muscled anatomy—over which his lovers had always gushed. Calmly, she nabbed his roaming extremity, and deposited it on his stomach, and she was so casual about it, he might have supposed that strange men fondling her was a regular occurrence.

She grabbed a knitted throw off the end of the bed, and tucked it around him, muttering, "Lord, you stink! We'll bathe you tomorrow, before we send you home."

"I don't want to bathe," he complained. As if he'd permit her to see him in the altogether!

"It will make you feel better."

"I don't want to feel *better*. I wish to be left alone."

"Your wish is granted, Your Majesty." She strolled out.

"What's your name?" he bellowed, but she kept on. He repeated the query, and when she didn't reply, his rage escalated. "Where am I? Who brought me here?"

Why didn't she stop? How dare she ignore him! Didn't she realize who he was? Didn't she recognize his family? With the snap of his fingers, the slash of a pen, he could ruin her!

Incensed, defenseless, he clasped his pillow and flung it after her. It crashed into the dresser and knocked a figurine to the floor, and the clatter had her stomping back in.

"I am Mrs. Smythe," she proclaimed. "Your sister, Lady Eleanor, has abandoned you at my *Healing Spa and Bathing*

Emporium for Women. It is near to Bath and many hours' ride from Bristol Manor. This is *my* business, and *my* residence, and you are not welcome. I intend that you will be on your way to Bristol as soon as a carriage can be arranged." She snatched up the figurine and repositioned it on the dresser, then she marched toward him. "Now, do be silent. I have a tedious schedule tomorrow, and I need my rest."

All tenderness absent, she snagged the pillow and stuffed it under his head. "If you toss it again, you'll sleep without it."

She flounced out, grumbling as she went. "Impossible, blue-blooded, arrogant, pampered . . ."

The epithets trailed off, and he listened as she strode up the stairs, as she trekked to the room above him and climbed into bed.

Embarrassed and contrite, he exhaled and peered out the window, studying the stars.

So . . . Eleanor had delivered him. To a *women's* establishment, operated by a fussy, authoritarian, nudity-flaunting witch. If he hadn't felt so miserable, he might have laughed.

What had Eleanor been thinking? That he could be restored at some . . . some bathhouse? That a rude, cheeky commoner was the answer to his prayers?

He tried to remember earlier in the day, but due to his over-imbibing, he had scant recollection of anything past dawn. She'd accomplished his kidnapping, but how? Charles must have abetted her. Had she convinced him? Or had she commanded his assistance?

Well, the cantankerous Mrs. Smythe had promised to evict him, and if she didn't, he'd contact Charles to fetch him. He wasn't about to remain with his persnickety jailer.

Uncomfortable, aching, sweaty, and parched, he craved a stout brandy, a splash of laudanum, and he fell into a fitful doze. When he awakened, it was morning. His joints were throbbing, his hands shaking, his mouth dry as a desert. He was much too sober, when he couldn't bear to be coherent. He'd rather dawdle in his self-imposed void where nothing signified.

Glancing around, he searched for a bell he could ring to summon a servant, but there was none to be had.

Outside, down by the pool, Mrs. Smythe was aiding a frail, elderly matron in a wheeled chair. Various peculiar images floated through his mind—of his viewing her in the nude, of his massaging her breast—and he couldn't decide if the memories were genuine or fantasy.

Whichever they were, they had him unsettled, jittery, and yearning for something he couldn't define. He didn't want to be lucid! Didn't want to be brooding over Mrs. Smythe and what might or might not have transpired between them. Most of all, he didn't want her attending to someone else, and he grew illogically irate.

Mrs. Smythe was correct: He was spoiled, querulous, and downright despicable. He hadn't always been thus, but after events in Spain, which had transformed him into a different person, he couldn't determine how to act. The gods had played a cruel joke, raising him with everything—good looks, charm, notoriety—then swiping it all away. As they'd proven, he wasn't strong, he couldn't carry the burdens they'd forced him to assume.

He was being exceedingly cross and juvenile, but he couldn't abide that she was neglecting him, and he banged on the windowsill and shouted at her.

"Mrs. Smythe! Come here!"

She froze and whirled around, as her patient panicked at hearing his male voice. Toppling her chair, she leapt into the water, her unflattering swimming costume billowing out behind.

"Was that a man?" she inquired of Mrs. Smythe. "Is there a man inside?"

"Don't be silly," Mrs. Smythe soothed. "I wouldn't have a

man about. You know that. Would you excuse me for a minute?" An employee took over the therapeutic session with the invalid, then, her own fury evident, Mrs. Smythe stalked to the house, and he waited, as a door slammed, as she rushed in his direction.

"Are you insane," she snarled as she strutted in, "scaring that poor woman as you did? Have you forsaken all decency and civility? Or are you simply an unconscionable boor by nature?"

"I needed you."

"Well, so does Mrs. Goodman. She's dying. You're not." If she stuck her snooty nose up any farther it would have rubbed on the ceiling. "At the moment, her affliction takes precedence over your imperious whining."

She'd told him, hadn't she? Did she hate all men, or just himself? As they were scarcely acquainted, he couldn't fathom what he might have done to offend. Perhaps he'd insulted her when he'd been intoxicated. Not that he cared. Eleanor had transported him to the blasted facility against his will, and Mrs. Smythe would rue the day she'd agreed to board him.

"I require a stiff whiskey—bring the entire bottle—and a hefty dose of a soporific. Whatever you have available is fine."

"For what do you need a narcotic?"

"I'm in pain."

"Pain promotes healing."

"Balderdash. Go get them for me," he pronounced. "And I'm ready for breakfast. Three eggs. With ham. Thickly sliced and fried."

As if he hadn't spoken, she said, "I advised your sister that this was exactly the reason I wouldn't treat you."

She'd refused Eleanor?

The idea nettled, making him eager to stay solely to annoy her. He was famous. Infamous. The whole country was groveling at his feet. What was the matter with her?

"You decline to help me? Me? Captain Stephen Chamberlin? Decorated hero of the Crown?"

"I have a thriving business," she stated. "For *women*. Mrs. Goodman's reaction was typical. There's no place for you."

"You will *create* a place."

"No."

"Yes!"

"Aren't you a bloody piece of work?" she chided, shocking him with her bold cursing. "You aristocrats believe you can do whatever you please, to whomever you please. You and your sister are positive I will exhaust myself, merely because of who you are. Well, you can think again!"

She started to leave, and he worried she might never return. "I need a bell, so that I may signal you."

"If I gave you a bell, you'd be jangling it constantly, and then, I'd have to kill you. I'm not inclined to commit murder. Not even yours." She tromped to the door. "I'll be back with your breakfast in a few minutes, Your Royal Assness."

He relaxed, wearied by their argument, but titillated, too. In his world, as the third son of the Earl of Bristol, he was plagued by lackeys, by hangers-on and sycophants. People jumped to do his bidding, to pamper and coddle, and in his current condition, their hovering left him feeling as if he couldn't breathe.

It was refreshing to have her sassing him, to debate and match wits. She wasn't in awe, wasn't concerned that he was an exalted Chamberlin son, didn't seem to be aware that he was the champion of Salamanca and many other battles. How exhilarating to interact with someone who didn't cast that carnage into his face every two seconds!

She was coming, and he lay very still, memorizing her gait. Carrying a tray, she entered and approached, balancing it as she pulled up a chair.

"Can you sit?" She showed no lingering animosity over their quarrel.

"Yes."

"Would you like to?"

He nodded, and she set the tray aside and arranged the pillows, then she gripped him under the arms and dragged him up. Her strength, compared to his weakness, made him ashamed.

"You're skinny as a rail," she mentioned. "No wonder your sister brought you to me."

He blushed, detesting that she would comment on his physique. Once, he'd cut a dashing figure. He'd been firm and fit, but no longer. Injuries had shriveled his anatomy till he resembled a dried-up old crone, rather than a vibrant, robust rogue.

"Are you a nurse?"

"Of sorts."

"You heal people?"

"They heal themselves, with God's help. I don't have much to do with it."

A novel notion, and it sparked a glimmer of optimism he'd not felt in ages. "Could you cure me?"

"Probably. If you wanted to be cured."

Another interesting concept. "You don't even know what's wrong with me."

"I don't need to know." Shrugging, she took two small glasses off the tray, holding them out.

"What's this?"

"Hair of the dog."

He gulped the amber one, which he assumed to be brandy, and it was. Then he swilled the other, shuddering at the bitter tang, but his headache and trembling eased instantly.

"Laudanum?"

"Yes."

"It's not nearly enough."

"You need to wean yourself."

"I have no desire to taper off."

"That's certainly your choice, but while you're here, you shan't receive larger doses." She lifted the napkin off the plate. Except that it wasn't a plate. It was a bowl. Of oats. A pitcher of cream. A crock of berries. And tea.

He loathed tea. He abhorred oats. He needed a manly meal. "I ordered eggs and ham."

"So you did."

"Do you ever listen to anything others say to you?"

"Not when they're being foolish."

"What's *foolish* about a hearty repast?"

"You're incapacitated and trying to recuperate. You must adjust your diet."

"What the hell do you know about nourishment?"

"Obviously, more than you"—which was true, but he deplored her snippy, superior attitude—"and watch your language."

"You don't."

"My home, my privilege."

What an impertinent wench she was! He liked her, liked her brazen style, her insolent tongue, her sharp wit, and he was amazed that he did. Since he'd left the army, he hadn't met a single soul whose company he enjoyed.

His stomach grumbled, and begrudgingly, he grasped the spoon and dug into the gruel, though as he sampled it, he decided that *gruel* might be too harsh a word. It was fresh, hot, and he ate every delicious bite.

"The tea." She motioned to the cup.

"I despise tea."

"Mine will make you feel better."

"I don't want to—"

"I know, I know," she interrupted, waving away his protest. "You don't want to feel *better.*"

To his consternation, she didn't debate the benefits of recovery, or plead with him to try harder. She was the only person in months who hadn't deluged him with idiotic advice, unwelcome enthusiasm, or unbidden recommendations as to what he should or shouldn't do.

She couldn't care less as to how he proceeded, and the fact that she exhibited such scant regard bothered him enormously.

He stared into her eyes. They were a stunning green, as verdant as the grass in the yard, and she matched his steady look, so serene and unwavering that he shifted uncomfortably. She peered far inside, as though she could delve to his very core and see the petty fears and secrets that were buried there.

He was reluctant to have her discern so much, and he glanced away, unable to abide her scrutiny. Reaching for the tea, he swallowed it down. Sweet and heavily flavored, it appeared to be a mixture of honey, apples, and oddly, flowers.

"A magic elixir?" he mocked when he'd consumed the last drop.

"Yes." Smiling, she offered nothing further, and he pondered whether she was joking, or if she really imagined it to be a mysterious concoction possessed of hidden powers.

"Is the carriage ready? Will I be going soon?" Strange, but now that it might be time, he wasn't in any hurry. What was there for him at Bristol? A dismal sickroom? Whispering servants? Fretting family? Whining physicians?

"I'm hoping to borrow one from a neighbor."

"You don't have your own?"

"It's a gig, for quick trips to the village, but you'll need more space."

"And your neighbor's is bigger?"

"Yes, and he's the type who'll be incredibly flattered to escort you."

"A man of good sense."

She snorted. "But he's out today. So it may be tomorrow, or the next, before you can actually depart."

It was on the tip of his tongue to tell her to send someone to the livery in Bath. She could utilize the Chamberlin name to rent a finer coach, with promise of payment once they arrived at the estate, but something—lunacy? boredom? intrigue?—forestalled him.

"So I'm stuck with you?"

"Yes, you lucky fellow."

He barked out a laugh, which surprised him. He couldn't remember when he'd previously expressed any merriment, and his voice sounded rusty from disuse.

"Do you come by your caustic temperament naturally?" he queried. "Or is it honed through years of practice?"

"It must be ingrained. I've only ever displayed it for you."

"I doubt that. You're much too proficient with your cutting remarks."

"I aim to please." With his victuals devoured, she removed the tray and set it on the dresser, then she stood, all business, any hint of joviality tucked away. "If you're to spend another night, you'll have to bathe."

"In your pool?"

"Yes."

"I don't wish to."

"So you've said, but I won't have you stinking up my house. As it is, I don't know if I'll be able to launder your stench out of the blankets. You're quite foul."

The slur was so deftly thrust, and so ruthlessly delivered, that he couldn't respond. He'd never been so thoroughly insulted. Before the war, he'd been a dapper chap, with a fashionable wardrobe and fastidious grooming. Now, his hair was ragged and snarled, and he never shaved. There didn't seem to be any point.

As to hygiene, whenever he lowered his trousers, his doctors would cluck and wail about his wounds infecting, about amputations and other extreme medical operations. The prior week, one of the bastards had shown up in his room with a saw, prepared to do the deed. Charles's adamant presence—and cocked pistol—had prevented the dolt from continuing.

He could profit from a stern washing, but there was no way in hell he would disrobe for her. No way in hell he would dip into a lagoon she used to treat aged invalids.

She clutched his shirt. "Let's get this off."

Frantically, he gripped at the lapels. "No."

Exasperated, she scowled at him. "Hear me well, Lord Chamberlin, and understand that I am serious: If you do not agree to wash yourself, you will be deposited out in the barn. With my horse, and my cow, and my chickens. Is that your desire?"

"You would put me out in the . . . the . . . barn?"

"Without an inkling of remorse."

He was aghast. She would do it! She would! She'd lodge him with the animals. To what a wretched precipice he'd descended!

Despite all the humiliations he'd endured so far, he'd never been more mortified. "Why do you hate me?"

"I don't *hate* you. I just don't like your kind."

"My *kind*?"

"You aristocrats. I've tolerated tyrannical behaviors from you people all my life, and I'm sick of the lot of you. Now, I deal with you on my own terms. I refused your sister, and she dumped you on my stoop. You're a burden I don't want, but you're hurt and weary, and though you've been forced on me, I will tend you until you leave. All I request in return is that you take a bath. I'm not asking for the moon. Don't be so difficult."

"Eleanor left me on the stoop?"

"Yes."

The information was too depressing. For an eternity, he glared at her, a thousand morbid thoughts careening through his head. Why couldn't he have died like so many of his comrades? Why had he been spared? Was this as low as he would fall? Was it possible to plummet further?

"I'll fight you if you try," which he deemed an amazing threat, considering how decrepit he was.

At his visible fury, she eased down on the bed, sitting close, leaning in, and he calmed, just from having her near.

"Tell me what's wrong."

"I'm so tired," he admitted, and a single tear dribbled down his cheek. She swiped it away, and he deemed it the rarest, most humane thing anyone had ever done for him.

"Of course, you are. What is making you so afraid?"

How had she guessed that fear was his primary motivation? Until that moment, he'd barely acknowledged to himself that he was scared witless.

What if he never improved? The question taunted him. He comprehended that he should merely be grateful that he was alive and proceed accordingly, but he was vain and proud, and worries kept tormenting him: What if he was forever maimed? He was supposed to marry, to start a family. How could he go to his bride, incapable of carrying out his husbandly duties, of siring the children she would be eager to have?

"I'm terrified that I'll never mend," he confessed aloud. He pressed his hands over his face, the heels digging in, and she clasped his wrists, pulling them away so that he had to look at her.

"This is a good place, Stephen. You're safe. You can rest, and you don't need to fret. Everything works out precisely as it's meant to. It's all ordained, so you can let your anxiety flutter away." She linked their fingers. "Let's get you in the pool. When you're finished, your problems will seem less formidable."

His resolve was weakening. "I don't know . . ."

"I'll come in the water with you. You won't be alone."

He was exhausted, powerless to be firm against her gentle insistence, and she took his silence for acquiescence.

"Can you walk, at all?"

"I can stand." It was another brash revelation. At Bristol, he'd let them believe he was crippled, and the more he'd contended he was, the more it had appeared to be true. "But I couldn't make it to the pond. I don't think I could make it to the door."

"My assistant, Kate, built a wheeled chair for me. I'll fetch her, and she can—"

"No! I don't want her to see me. I don't want anyone to see me. Just you."

"All right. Lie back and relax. I'll remove your clothes."

Cursing himself for a fool, he settled onto the pillows. She was so determined, and he was so depleted. It was easier to let her win than to argue. After all, it was only a bath. It wouldn't kill him.

Plus, he was convinced that if he waffled, she would put him in the barn with her cow. While he'd braved many indignities since departing Spain on a stretcher, he didn't anticipate he could survive that one.

He sighed. "Just this once."

Her smile lit up the room.

~ 3 ~

"You can't do this," Kate Turner declared.

"Of course, I can," Anne insisted.

"It's not fitting."

"Why?" Anne asked, though she already knew the answer.

"You're a maiden."

"A very old one," she wryly pointed out. Though she was twenty-eight, she felt more like eighty-eight.

"Be that as it may," Kate scolded, "you can't be undressing a man. And you certainly can't bathe him! What will people say? What will they think?"

"No one will find out."

"Don't be too sure. Even the best kept secrets have a way of leaking," which was too true, considering that Camilla Warren had espied the Bristol coach, and Mrs. Goodman had heard a masculine voice. Any person with half a brain would figure it out.

Anne studied her friend and smiled. Kate was different from other women. Tall, big-boned, and burly, her blond hair cropped short, she was two years older than Anne, and she could pass for a man and often did, wearing trousers around the property when they were by themselves. She was creative with her hands, could build or fix anything, and she was very strong, and thus, a perfect assistant.

After her horrid marriage to a vile, vicious—now thankfully deceased—husband, Kate was levelheaded, able to deal with any situation, which was a benefit at the spa. The very sick and the very rich were their customers, so strange incidents were wont to occur.

It was hilarious to have her nettled over Captain Chamberlin's presence, over his effect on Anne's virtuous condition. There was nothing typical in how they'd chosen to live their lives, and normally, Kate wouldn't have questioned Anne's decision, so she assumed that Kate's innate distrust of males had elevated her concern.

Kate was rolling up her sleeves. "Let me do it for you."

"How would it be any more appropriate for you than me?"

"I'm a widow. A *real* widow."

Anne chuckled. In every fashion, she was a fraud. She wasn't a nurse. She understood naught of medicine. She had no healing powers. She'd never been married, having left for six months at age twenty to care for a dying auntie, and returning with the false yarn firmly in place. Even her gold wedding ring was fake. The list of prevarications that made up her world was lengthy and always enlarging.

"I won't swoon if I view him in the altogether," Anne vowed. "I promise."

"It's not your *swooning* I'm worried about." Kate gestured toward the rear bedroom, where they'd lugged and heaved Captain Chamberlin the prior afternoon. "I've listened to the gossip about him. He's a cad, through and through. If you start taking off his clothes, there's no telling where it will end."

"You believe he'd rape me?"

"There'd be no force necessary. Under all that stink and

bodily hair lurks a tempting, handsome libertine. You'd ruin yourself willingly. Then, where would we be?"

Anne laughed again. As if she'd surrender her chastity to an overbearing, pompous, wealthy aristocrat! She'd learned her lesson, and learned it well, from watching what her father had done to her mother. There'd be no nobleman's wooing for Anne, no starry romance or pining away, no bastard child growing in her belly.

And as to his being handsome! Hah! Those mesmerizing blue eyes, and all that dark hair, hinted at an intriguing scoundrel, but he was thoroughly hidden. With that scruffy beard, and tangled mane, that emaciated torso and anatomical stench, he looked like death warmed-over, like something rotten the cat had dragged in.

"Don't fret, dear Kate. Nothing will happen. He's tired and sick, and he needs our sympathy. I almost wish . . ."

"Wish what?"

"That he'd stay for treatments. We could help him. I'm positive."

"Lord preserve us!" Kate grumbled, and Anne shooed her out.

"Lock the gate for me. Don't let anyone in for the next two hours. And make yourself scarce. He doesn't want you to see us."

"What if he falls, and you can't lift him?"

"I'll fetch you. He claims he can walk, so I should get him in and out of the pool without too much trouble."

"A likely story," Kate muttered, as she grabbed her hat and gloves, and lumbered out the door.

Anne sighed and went to her bedchamber, donning a discreet bathing outfit. It was baggy and dropped to below her knees. Her legs and feet were covered with stockings, though she wouldn't wear shoes, and her arms would be bare, but she could muddle through. If any embarrassment was to be had, it would be Lord Chamberlin's.

At least she'd send him home smelling better than when he arrived!

She descended to his room, and he was dozing, the laudanum and tea making him drowsy. As she evaluated him, she pondered what it would be like to have once had so much, to have been the talk of London, a rake and a rogue, and supposedly the most attractive, most notorious bachelor in the kingdom, then to have lost it all.

He wasn't a Romeo now. He was worn and haggard, ill, but not dying. Not yet, anyway. The moribund had an odor about them that, for some reason, she could detect, but it wasn't perceptible in him.

Sensing her, he opened his eyes and scrutinized her costume, and he grinned. For a brief second, she noted an appreciative masculine gleam and was graced with a glimpse of the scoundrel he had previously been. How sad that he couldn't muster the strength to permit that hale fellow to emerge.

The scamp had a suppressed randy streak. He'd proved as much the evening before, when she'd checked on him as she was retiring. She'd been surprised by his being awake, which had given him the chance to fondle her breast with his naughty hand.

She was baffled by that caress. While she'd been apprised of the antics couples engaged in when they were alone, no man had ever touched her intimately. She'd been kissed exactly once, at age fifteen, when her mother had allowed her to stroll with a boy at the harvest fair.

Other than that sole occasion, she'd had rare contact with men. Save for her brother, who'd departed at fourteen for employment by their father at Salisbury, her life had been filled with women. When she was a tiny girl, her mother had taken a job as Widow Brown's companion. Anne had been raised on the property, had been taught to read and write at the widow's kitchen table. Had tended her mother through a protracted, fatal illness, then had done the same for Widow Brown, who'd died with no kin, and who had bequeathed both the farm and the house to Anne.

By transforming her legacy into the business she had, she was surrounded by and associated only with females.

She didn't know anything about men, how they behaved, or what they wanted, so she wasn't certain why Captain Chamberlin had been so brazen, and when it had been occurring, she'd been so shocked that she hadn't reacted.

But throughout the remainder of the endless night, she'd ruminated over it. Her skin had burned where he'd petted her, and her breasts felt fuller, cumbersome, her nipples erect and throbbing till dawn.

Restless and aching, grouchy from lack of sleep, she'd somehow found the courage to face him, and she'd been delighted to discover that he didn't recollect the incident. Thank heavens! If he ever mentioned the scandalous episode, she'd expire from mortification.

"Are you ready?" she asked.

"No."

Perching on the mattress, she began unbuttoning his shirt. He didn't help or hinder her efforts, and she was relieved. She was determined to wash him, and if he'd resisted, she might have tied him to the bedposts.

"Won't your husband object to your bathing me?"

"My husband?" She was temporarily confused, but she hastily regrouped. "I'm a widow."

"How long has it been?"

"Many years." Her reply was deliberately enigmatic, for she wasn't inclined to discuss her purported spouse, though she did have a complete tale to tell if pressed.

"How could that be? You can't be a day over thirty."

"Do I look that bad?" She took a quick peek in the mirror. "I'm only twenty-eight."

"Oops. Sorry. My flattery skills are a tad rusty."

He was silent as she finished with the buttons and tugged the hem out of the waistband of his trousers. She started to draw the lapels off his shoulders, as he struggled to sit up, but she pushed him down.

"Let me do all the work."

"It's awkward."

"Shut your eyes. Concentrate on something else, on something pleasant."

He did, and soon, an enormous smile creased his cheeks, though it was mostly concealed by his unruly beard.

"What are you envisioning?" she queried.

"You. Without any clothes."

"Captain Chamberlin!" She blushed from the top of her head to the tips of her toes.

"Sorry," he apologized again, but he didn't seem very repentant.

"It won't do you any good to distract or fluster me. I'm going to do this if it kills me."

"You've made that very clear."

"So don't be difficult."

"I'll try not to be."

She scowled at him, and a smile still curved his lips, and she suspected that mischief was his ingrained nature. Very likely, he thrived on rascality, and no doubt, had he been healthier, he'd have been impossible to tolerate.

Not intending to be dissuaded, she yanked at his shirt and tossed the fetid garment on the floor. He was rail-thin, and he was bandaged everywhere, the wrappings dirty and gray. Where he wasn't bandaged, she could see spots where he'd been sewn, the stitchwork ragged and crudely accomplished. Some of the scars had healed while others, though they'd been inflicted months earlier, were red and inflamed.

No wonder he couldn't get back on his feet!

"Dear God in heaven, what happened to you?" she murmured.

"I was shot a few times—"

"Shot!"

"—and stabbed."

"They filleted you like a fish!"

"They tried," he quietly admitted. "They didn't succeed."

He held out a swathed arm for her to unbind. "No," she decided, "we'll remove them in the water. It will be easier."

Unsettled, her fingers went to the placard of his pants. They were laced at the front, and she commenced with the tie, when he stopped her. "Must we take them off here? Can't we do it down at the pool?"

"It'll be less taxing if you're lying down."

Because he'd lost so much weight, his trousers were very loose and simple to dislodge, and she pulled them down his hips, baring his stomach, his abdomen, but as his manly hair poked out, she halted.

This was so much more complex than she'd imagined it would be! It was one thing to bluster to Kate that she could waltz in and strip him, but it was quite another to actually do it. Another inch or two and his privates would be revealed.

She was no stranger to male anatomy. After all, she'd had a younger brother, but she'd heard that the masculine appendage grew bigger, just as a body did, and that the sight was too abominable for a maiden to view.

He was staring at her, waiting for her to proceed, and she was flummoxed, nervous, so she reached for the knitted throw and arranged it over his lap. If he had any opinion as to her abrupt burst of modesty, he had the courtesy not to voice it.

She dragged his pants over his toes and forced herself to glance down.

His right leg was intact and hardy, though there was a bullet wound above the knee, but his left leg was as bandaged as his upper torso. The dressings were soiled, and they smelled putrid.

"How long has it been since your wraps were changed?"

"I don't recall. I wouldn't let those crazed sawbones near me. The only remedy they ever rendered was to bleed me. The only advice they offered was to cut off my leg."

The incessant razor slashes, inflicted to drain the ill-humors, marked his arms. What petty tortures he must have endured! So he'd lain in his own filth, refusing any assistance. What a tragic tale!

"Would you rather die than lose your leg?"

"Yes. Wouldn't you?"

She supposed she would. "I realize it's a radical notion, but some medical people have begun to suggest that cleanliness promotes recuperation and stems infection. Was there no capable doctor at Bristol?"

"They were all fools."

She could picture his cadre of physicians, fussy, arrogant, clumsy buffoons, hovering over him and bellowing orders. He wouldn't have been a submissive patient, so the Chamberlin household must have been in a constant state of upheaval and strife. It was no surprise that his sister had been at her wits' end.

She'd borrowed one of Kate's billowy nightshirts, and she tugged it on him and adjusted it around his waist so that the hem would fall when he stood. The bagginess of the garment attested to his frailty. It hung on him like an enormous tent.

"My bathing costume?" he smirked.

"Unless you'd rather be buff naked."

He blanched. "The shirt will be fine."

"I have my wheeled chair in the hall. Can you make it that far?"

"We'll see."

"I'll go slowly."

She guided him to his feet, and he tottered, so she folded herself around him. Except for the kiss her beau had bestowed at age fifteen, it was the nearest she'd ever been to an adult man, the single occasion she'd hugged one.

Her breasts were crushed to his side, her feminine parts to his thigh. It was an electrifying experience that rattled her nerves and jumbled her insides, causing butterflies to swarm through her stomach, but she didn't have time to daydream or fantasize. If she wasn't cautious, she'd drop him on his skinny arse. What a mess that would be!

They took clumsy steps but, without catastrophe, they made it to the chair. Though it was a distance of a few feet, he was sweating, trembling from the modest exertion.

She draped a blanket over him, which had him grousing. "You're handling me like an ailing grandfather. Why not shove me into the corner and ignore me?"

She grinned. As if she could *ignore* him! He wasn't the sort one could neglect. He was too overbearing.

"Quit complaining," she shot at him. "I don't want you catching a chill."

He was so sickly, so depleted, that the slightest modification of condition could lay him low. He wouldn't be strong enough to fight off an ague.

Utilizing the clever ramps Kate had constructed, she maneuvered him to the pool.

"Can you swim?" she inquired.

"For God's sake!" he snapped. "I wasn't always an invalid."

"Don't bark at me. Your sister will be furious if I let you drown."

"As if she'd care," he grumbled, sounding defeated.

Clutching his shaggy hair in her fist, she tipped his head back. "She cares. Don't ever think she doesn't."

They were so close. She could detect the individual whiskers of his beard, the flecks of black in his blue eyes. It seemed she could read his mind, could sense his bottled-up fear and fatigue, anger and frustration, sadness and melancholy. She

knew things about him she had no way of knowing, understood details for which there was no accounting.

Flustered, she moved away. "Let's get you in."

"Is it deep?"

"From knee-high to chest-high, depending on where you
are. And there are rock benches carved into the edges. Under
the water."

Glancing about, she wondered what he thought of her
grotto. It was an ancient place, a trick of nature. The
Romans—at least she believed it had been the Romans—
had hewn the stones and blocked the spring to create the
pool. At the far end, the water trickled over a dam and meandered to an adjacent stream, where it flowed away.

Surrounded by shrubs and trees, it was secluded, quiet.
Enchanted, too. As a girl, she'd been convinced that fairies
whispered, their voices concealed by the rushing current,
and she'd spent thousands of hours tiptoeing and searching
under leaves, trying to unearth the elusive pixies, but she'd
never been lucky enough to stumble upon one. Even though
she was twenty-eight, she still swore that they resided in the
ferns.

Bracing herself, she gripped his wrists as he teetered to
the first stair. He doused his foot, then his calves, soaking his
bandages and wetting his nightgown.

As the water climbed to his waist, she hugged him again
and led him so that he was sitting on the rocky shelf. He
couldn't speak, and there were tears in his eyes.

"What is it?" she frantically asked.

"Hurts . . ." he managed to grind out.

Of course, it would! At being so anxious to carry on,
she'd disregarded the obvious. She spread his legs, and
snuggled herself between them, flattening her torso to his.

"Focus on me," she coaxed, wishing she could absorb his
pain. "It will pass."

"Jesus . . ."

"Breath in," she directed. "And hold it. Now, let it out."

He repeated the process over and over, then he embraced her, his good arm clasping her with all his strength. His face was buried at her nape, and for a lengthy period, they were melded together. She could perceive the illness in him, could feel his fever, could hear his heart beating too rapidly.

Gradually, he relaxed, his muscles flexing, his pulse moderating. His arm slackened, and she pulled away. The encounter grew intimate, their lips an inch apart, and she felt so much like kissing him that she frightened herself.

She wasn't some hussy, some coquette practiced in the art of seduction. She wasn't even sure *how* to kiss him, and the realization brought a blush to her cheeks that had nothing to do with the temperature of the water.

As she was a natural caregiver, her affection was produced by the fact that he was suffering and she couldn't stand to witness it. She invariably became more attached than she should to people who were in distress.

Positive that his musings were a far cry from hers, she couldn't help smiling. If she pressed her mouth to his, he'd probably be so aghast that he'd have a seizure.

Just as she'd rationalized her emotions to the point of absurdity, he dipped down and kissed *her*. It wasn't stormy or tumultuous as she'd envisioned in her female fantasies, nor was it as passionate as it might have been had he been more robust.

As if she was cherished and fine, his lips settled onto hers, and she held herself very still, letting the perfection of the moment surge over her. The birds sang in the forest, the brook rippled, and it was the sweetest, most thrilling thing that had ever happened to her.

Much too soon, it ended, and she was so disappointed! She'd been kissed by Stephen Chamberlin! The most infamous rake in London! The great hero of the Crown! She was giddy with excitement, and she yearned to shout the news aloud, but she squelched her euphoria, plummeting to the reality of what she'd allowed. Of who he was and who *she* was, and the gravity of what they were about.

She wouldn't deny how precious it had been, though. They shared an affinity, one that had no rhyme or reason behind it. It was a bond she'd never previously experienced, a connection that perplexed her. Why did it exist? What sparked it? There were no explanations.

"What's your given name?" he queried.

It was so odd that he'd deigned to kiss her before he knew.
"Anne."

"Anne, would you . . . would you . . . let me stay? Would you heal me?"

"Oh, Captain Cham—"

"Stephen," he countered.

"I can't, Stephen."

"I'm begging you."

"No."

She recognized how hard it had been for him to make his request. He was proud, and she suspected his vanity was ninety-nine percent of why he wasn't recuperating. He couldn't abide failing.

Peering into the water, at his legs, she noticed that the bandages were coming loose, and she busied herself with unraveling the cumbersome strips and tossing them on the grass. His nightshirt was in the way, and she drew it over his knees to where she could fuss higher up.

As she tugged on a tangled ribbon of fabric, her hand bumped his phallus. Soft and limp, the appendage was drooped at his crotch. It didn't feel menacing or ominous, as she'd pictured it would be.

She peeked at him, relieved to find that he paid her no heed. He was inspecting the pond, taking stock of the landscape, and it dawned on her that he hadn't noted what she'd done.

Had he no sensation in his sexual anatomy? What an intriguing discovery! What effect did the deficiency have on his attitude and behavior?

Opening his nightshirt, she pushed it off his shoulders so that it was wadded over his lap. She unwound the bandages on his arm and chest, then she seated herself behind him, so that his back was nestled to her front, his rear burrowed to her loins, her thighs cradling his own.

Their position was lewd, indecent, and she wasn't certain how to handle the situation except to forge onward, to pretend that there was nothing unusual transpiring, yet, detachment was impossible. When she moved, her breasts rubbed him, and her nipples reacted, constricting into spiky buds that had to be poking him like shards of glass. Though he hadn't perceived her brushing his phallus, he had to be conscious of her nipples, but she couldn't decide what to do about it.

Shamefully, the friction felt phenomenal, so she kept him right where he was.

"I'm going to wash your hair. Can you dip down and wet it?"

"Yes."

He complied as she grabbed for a bar of rose-scented soap she'd left on the bank. She scrubbed vigorously, creating a fragrant lather.

"I'll smell like a damned popinjay," he griped.

"Better than a barnyard mule."

"A low blow, madam!"

She had him rinse, and by then, exertion had fatigued him and he rested against her shoulder. They sat, cuddled together, and shortly, he dozed off. Within minutes, though, he awoke with a start, rigid and taut, ready for action. He blinked and blinked, unable to recall where he was, then awareness dawned, and he shuddered and exhaled, reposing, once more.

"Dreaming?" she probed.

"Yes." He offered nothing further, and she speculated as to what dreadful phantoms haunted him.

He gazed at the pool, at the shrubbery and blue, blue sky, then he rotated, balancing on his hip so that he could look at her.

"Why won't you let me stay?"

Gad, it was so difficult to say *no* when he was so close. He was serious, intent, pleading.

"I just can't." She wasn't willing to discuss what her father had done to her mother all those years ago, wasn't disposed to elucidate as to why she held aristocrats in such contempt.

"You've refused, but you won't tell me why."

Stunning her, he kissed her again, another light grazing of his mouth to hers, then he trailed a finger down her cheek, across her lips.

"Stop doing that."

"I can't resist. You're so pretty."

While she was scarcely an ancient hag—she resembled her beautiful mother too much to believe otherwise—no man had ever said such a thing to her before. Her idiotic heart pounded. "And *you* are an unmitigated flatterer."

"You make me yearn to get well. It's the first time I've wanted anything in so long."

"The drive is inside you, Stephen. You don't need me."

"But I can't return to Bristol. I really think I might die there. I feel it so strongly."

"You don't give yourself enough credit."

"I wasn't always such a weakling. After Salamanca, I . . . I . . ."

"You were at Salamanca?"

"Yes."

She frowned. She'd known that he'd fought in Portugal and Spain, but she hadn't reflected much upon the information, not surmising how it could matter. Yet her brother, Phillip, had nearly been killed at Salamanca, and it had never occurred to her that Phillip and Stephen might be linked through their military service.

A name popped into her head, mentioned often by Phillip with awe and affection. *Captain Steve*. Of the tens of thousands of British men who'd answered the call to arms, what were the odds that he and Phillip would have crossed paths?

"Were you with the One Hundred and First?"

"That was my regiment."

Praying it wasn't so, she ventured, "You must be acquainted with my brother."

"Who is he?"

"Phillip Paxton."

"You're joking."

"No."

He studied her, then remarked, "You *are* a Paxton, aren't you? I can see it around your eyes and mouth."

"You saved his life."

Embarrassed, he glanced away. "I wouldn't go that far."

"I would. Don't be so modest."

Phillip had related bits and pieces of their story, but it had been enough for her to glean what a terrifying, bloody rout it had been. Though he'd been reticent about his combat adventures, there had been one fact he'd proudly proclaimed: Captain Steve had been his friend. And had saved his life.

Could she do any less?

Besides her loathed father, Phillip was her only living relative. As a girl, she'd worshipped the ground he'd walked upon. Due to their banishment from Salisbury—her father's exalted estate—as youngsters, they'd been inordinately attached, and she loved him more than anything.

Stephen Chamberlin's valor had ensured that Phillip came home from Spain. If she'd had an entire century to try, it was a gift that could never be fully repaid, and a resounding determination seized her. She would help Stephen, because

he'd helped Phillip. Though he was of the same class as her
father, Edward Paxton, and represented everything she abhorred, there was no other option.

"I've changed my mind," she told him.

"About what?"

A smile lit up his face and quirked his cheeks. Dimples
lurked under his beard, and she was taken aback, for she was
provided another glimpse of the radiant man he'd been before the war, and it made her nervous, had her questioning if
she truly knew the ramifications of what she was planning.

"I'd like you to remain for a while."

"Really?"

"Yes."

He nodded. "Thank you."

"You're welcome, but it will be strenuous. You'll have to
do what I say without complaining."

Looking devilish, he grinned. "I can't promise I won't
fuss occasionally, but I'll try my best."

It would be an arduous journey, and she wondered if he'd
succeed. But he'd begun. He wanted to improve, and as
she'd learned through extensive experience, in the healing
process, mental attitude was most vital.

She slipped from behind him and circled around. "I want
to flex your legs under the water. To loosen them up. Then
we'll go inside, and I'll fix you some more of my special
tea."

"I can hardly wait," he grouched.

Laughing, she reached for his ankle, and bent his knee.

∿ 4 ∿

Eleanor Chamberlin Dunworthy stood by the window of her room in the rather seedy inn where they'd been forced to tarry on their return to Bristol Manor. A wheel on the coach had started to rattle, then wobble, and Charles had instructed the driver to pull off to the side of the road.

None of it was his fault, and he'd taken the only logical course, but his decree had instituted a string of irritating events, and she was chagrined to acknowledge that she'd petulantly complained about each and every one of them.

She'd had to wait for another carriage to ferry her to the inn, had had to dawdle in the main parlor until the sole chamber deemed appropriate for her exalted self was cleaned and aired.

By then, it was dark and too dangerous to travel, so she'd sent a messenger to Bristol, explaining what had happened, and that they would be back soon. She'd been vague and breezy so that her father wouldn't worry, or foolishly come searching for them.

While she was thankful to have a loving family, and was grateful that she'd had a place to hide after the scandal surrounding her husband's death, there were times at the estate when she felt so stifled that she was afraid she might begin screaming and never stop.

Her father was a tyrant—kind and well intentioned, to be sure, but a tyrant nonetheless. He dominated his four children, as he did his tenants and everyone else.

At age seventeen, she'd wed Harold, against her father's advice, just so she could escape his hovering, the result being that she'd chosen a person exactly like him, though Harold had had a cruel streak her father had never possessed.

Harold had been dictatorial, jealous, arbitrary, and she'd been worn down through thirteen miserable years of marriage. He'd never let her forget that she was incompetent, particularly at her marital duties, and he'd insisted that if she'd tried harder, if she'd relaxed more, she'd have conceived a child, and he wouldn't have had to suffer through the humiliation of a barren wife.

He'd been killed, supposedly for a gambling debt, although whispers abounded that it had been in a duel over a lover. She'd never been apprised of the sordid details, but after his affairs had been settled, she'd crawled home to Papa, mortified that she'd had no other options.

She hated being a woman! Hated relying on men, and having to plead with them for every little thing. At age thirty-five, she was filthy rich—her inheritances held in various trusts—yet she'd never been able to so much as purchase a new dress without checking first with a man to see if it would be all right.

She thought about Mrs. Smythe, the widow who ran the bathing emporium where she'd left Stephen. Mrs. Smythe was modern, independent, and she was making her way in the world without some male relative lording it over her with his unwelcome criticisms and harangue.

What she wouldn't give to have such an unfettered existence! To do what she pleased! To go where she pleased!

Why, she wouldn't be surprised if the intrepid Mrs. Smythe had her own bank account!

She tried to imagine herself strolling into a financial establishment, plopping her ledger in front of a cashier, and requesting a withdrawal. In cash!

The concept was so outrageous, and so disreputable, that she chuckled.

A sharp rapping sounded on her door, and she had no doubt it was Charles. There was nothing reserved about him. Every step he took, every gesture he made, was bold and emphatic, and for some reason, the assertiveness of his knock annoyed her.

Usually, she was placid and congenial, but for the past few days, she'd been an absolute shrew, and poor Charles Hughes had borne the brunt of her ill-humor. He'd accepted her cranky mood with a patient grace, and had dealt with her as effortlessly as he dealt with everything, which had her even more furious. Just once, she'd like to elicit a response from the staid, resolute oaf.

The previous night, the inn had been full, so there'd been no room available for him. She'd anticipated that he would sleep in the barn loft with the footmen, but despite her orders to the contrary, he'd camped on the floor in the hall, saying that he couldn't leave her unprotected. The result, of course, was that she'd tossed incessantly, worrying about him on the other side of the wall.

Since dawn, he'd fussed with the broken wheel and the blacksmith, visiting occasionally with progress reports, and at every meeting, their mutual lack of slumber had been apparent in their testiness. Though she couldn't pinpoint why, he rubbed her the wrong way, and when they were both so fatigued, he was like a burr under her saddle, inducing her to be cross and cantankerous.

Evening was upon them, and she knew he'd inform her

they were still trapped, that they couldn't depart till morning or maybe later, and she was so relieved, though she'd never admit as much to a single soul. She was in no hurry to return to Bristol. Without confiding in anyone, she'd whisked Stephen away, and she wasn't eager to argue with her father and brothers as to what she'd set in motion.

It had been so refreshing to traipse off, without benefit of her maid, and only Charles and her trusted footmen as her retinue. Her furtive journey was flagrant, out of character, and it was so marvelous to be on her own and making her own decisions.

She couldn't recollect when she'd ever committed so frivolous an act. Perhaps it was the glorious weather, or the lazy summer afternoons, that had inflamed her passionate need for a change. Or it might be her advancing age. With each subsequent year, she was more dissatisfied with the direction her life had taken.

Why did she have such paltry accomplishments to show for her three and a half decades on earth? No husband. No children. Nothing and no one to call her own.

Restless, unhappy, she was constantly wishing she had the nerve to do something shocking, something reckless, yet she was away from Bristol, free and unencumbered, and all she'd done for the past twenty-four hours was sit and mope, catching sporadic glimpses of Charles as he'd traversed the stable yard.

When had she grown so timid? She was at a public inn, not loafing on the moon. Why couldn't she trot outside, walk about, chat and mingle, as any less-inhibited, less-restrained female would do with ease?

She was so tedious. So boring. So dull and routine. No wonder she was so alone! Who would want to shackle themselves to such an insipid creature?

Charles knocked again, anxious that she hadn't answered. She stomped to the door and yanked it open.

"What now?" she irascibly inquired.

"I've brought your dinner." His reply was equally acerbic.

Two maids followed him in, carrying trays, and placing them on the small table, then curtsying and scurrying off, but not before casting several suggestive glances at handsome, rugged Charles.

Obviously, they were interested in him in a sexual fashion, which intrigued her. She'd heard that there were women who relished the sorts of unpleasantness her husband had regularly perpetrated on her, but she couldn't understand why.

She'd performed her duty whenever he'd demanded it of her, and she'd struggled to enjoy it, but she'd always been left with a lingering disappointment, and with a fervent hope that it would end quickly and without a great deal of humiliation for either of them.

The food smelled delicious, and she realized that she hadn't dined since breakfast. She gawked at the covered containers, and Charles asked, "Do you need me to dish it up for you?"

His tone implied that she wasn't capable of doing it herself. "I'm not helpless."

His frown indicated that he believed otherwise. Was that how he saw her? As inept and incompetent? The notion was aggravating, and she briskly lifted the lids from the pans. There was a hearty stew, fresh-baked bread, cheese, apples, and pastries for dessert.

She arranged a portion for herself, then peered at him. "Will you join me?"

"I couldn't possibly."

"Why not? There's enough for an army."

"It wouldn't be fitting."

"So? I won't tell if you won't."

"Yes, but you're the lady of the manor, and I'm . . . I'm . . ."

He couldn't elucidate what he *was*. Stephen's friend, certainly. His champion and defender to her father and the doctors. He was also an excellent horseman and assisted in the stables though he wasn't an employee. His lack of a hand gave him trouble and made it difficult for him to do steady work.

"You're what?" She was curious to learn how he'd describe himself.

"Your brother's servant."

"Under the circumstances, a triviality, I assure you." She gestured toward the food. "What will you have?"

"Nothing, thank you."

He was going to be churlish. Well, she could trump his vexation. "I command you to dine with me."

"I've already eaten, milady."

At her insistence, he referred to her as Eleanor, and the fact that he'd just addressed her as *milady* attested to how he was smarting from their ceaseless bickering. From the moment she'd confided her plan for Stephen, he'd been in a state, contending that she'd gone batty.

"Fine," she imperiously proclaimed, "you will keep me company while I sup."

Pouring two glasses of wine, she handed him one, and he took it without argument. Then she started to sit, and he rushed around the table and held her chair. There was scant space to maneuver, so he was very close, and as typically happened when he was near, her senses reeled.

She could feel the heat emanating from him, could detect the manly aromas of horses, tobacco, and fresh air, on his skin and clothes. But there was another scent that was musky and unique, and she suspected she'd delved to his very essence.

She tipped back to thank him for his courtesy, and he was gazing at her so intently that she shivered.

He always evaluated her as if he wanted to say something important, and at times, it appeared as though his regard was libidinous, that he was assessing her with masculine appreciation.

Which was ludicrous. If he thought about her at all—and she was positive he didn't—he likely pondered why she was such a dreary, snippy widow. A widow whose lush figure was beginning to droop, and whose striking blond hair was sprinkled with strands of silvering gray.

He moved away, seating himself on a chair by the door, so that she was alone at the table. She busied herself with her meal, trying to ignore him, but the silence was oppressive, and she couldn't abide it. She peeked up to find that he was sipping his wine and scrutinizing her with a fiery glimmer.

She needed to break the ice, but also to raise the question that plagued her. "Do you think Stephen is all right?"

"No."

His curt retort wounded her. "Why?"

"Mrs. Smythe is a quack."

"You didn't meet her!"

"I didn't need to."

"She seemed perfectly normal to me."

"As if you could heal someone with a bit of hot water and a different diet! She's naught but a charlatan, preying on people who are desperate."

His criticism hurt, and she scowled at her plate. Stephen's kidnapping was one of the few assertive, brave things she'd ever done. How dare he discount it!

"We'll see, won't we?" she snapped, and she offered up a prayer for some divine intervention. Stephen's recovery aside, she yearned to prevail, merely so she could flaunt Mrs. Smythe's skill at the overbearing, dictatorial men in her life.

"I'm sorry, Eleanor," he apologized, noting her fury. "I shouldn't have said what I did. I wish your Mrs. Smythe enormous success."

"Shut up, Charles."

She ate without speaking, each scrape of her spoon across the china inordinately loud. Her temper escalated until she was fuming. Gulping down the last of her wine, she glared over, ready to give him what-for, only to discover that he'd fallen asleep.

Wasn't that just like a man! She was eager to quarrel, and he was dozing! Exasperated, she shook her head. Perhaps she wasn't destined to have a smooth, functioning relationship with any male of her acquaintance.

Striding over to him, she gripped him by the shoulder, and he lurched awake.

"I'll be going now," he told her, flushing with embarrassment.

"You're exhausted. Take a nap on my bed."

"Are you mad?"

"I won't hear otherwise."

As he'd spent the night on the floor, he probably hadn't had a wink of sleep, then he'd labored all day to repair the carriage. The stubborn lummox! She positioned herself in front of the door, so that he would have to pick her up to exit.

"Eleanor!" he groused.

"I won't let you refuse."

Her suggestion was outrageous, scandalous in the extreme, and she couldn't explain what was driving her.

"Lie down!" she decreed.

He studied her, the bed, her, the bed, gaping at it so longingly, that she smiled.

"Maybe for a few minutes," he relented. "But you can't tell anyone."

"As if I would."

Woozy and muddled, he rose and stumbled over, pitched onto the mattress face-first, and in an instant, he was slumbering.

She seated herself at the table and adjusted her chair so she could watch him. Nibbling at the leftovers, she appraised his thick, reddish hair, his broad shoulders, narrow waist, muscular thighs, making the languid journey over and over.

Her husband, Harold, was the sole man with whom she'd

been physically familiar, and compared to him, Charles was so hard, so robust. She speculated as to the body hidden by the clothes. What would he look like naked? How would his torso vary from Harold's?

When she noticed that her wicked mind was conjecturing as to the size and shape of his privy parts, she was stunned. She was relishing the clandestine episode much more than she ought.

Careful not to disturb him, she put the trays in the hall so the maid could remove them without knocking. Dusk came and went, the sun sinking on the horizon, the yard and taproom quieting. She drank a glass of wine, then another, and another, until she was quite giddy.

Still, he didn't stir, and she was growing tired herself. The tasty supper, coupled with the excess of spirits, had her drowsy. She considered nudging him, advising him to leave, but she didn't have the heart.

Why not just lie down with him?

The query rang out, and was so fiendish and so diabolical, that the devil, himself, must have been perched on her shoulder and nagging her to transgress. Before she knew what she was about, she was tiptoeing over, and she climbed onto the mattress, stretching out, with him on one side of her, and the wall on the other.

When she'd been in the bed by herself, she'd deemed it adequate and plenty large, but with him in it, too, there wasn't enough space. He simply took up more than his share.

Scooting around, she tried to get comfortable, to relax, when he shifted, his arm resting across her waist. She stiffened, surprised and puzzled over what to do. It hadn't occurred to her that he might touch her.

Or had it? Had that been her plan? Was she attracted to him? Had the multiple goblets of wine lowered her inhibitions so that her true sentiments were bubbling to the fore?

After the groping and pawing she'd endured from her

husband, she'd sworn she'd never submit to a man's urges again. Yet, she was so lonely! So starved for human contact.

Charles dragged her closer, so that her breasts were crushed to him. Their proximity had a strange, exhilarating effect on her anatomy. Her pulse pounded, her skin prickled, her nipples tightened into painful buds.

"Ah, my darlin' Meg," he murmured, "you feel so good."

"Meg!" She punched him in the ribs.

He snorted and jumped alert, blinking to orient himself and realizing where they were.

"Eleanor? What the hell?"

He had her pinned to him, and down below, she could distinguish his loins. He was aroused! She kicked him in the shin. "Let me go."

"What are you doing?"

"Trying to sleep," she contended, "since you wouldn't wake up and depart."

She continued to struggle, but he wouldn't ease his grasp so that she could regain some dignity by slipping away. Instead, he lifted a leg and draped it over hers, further increasing the intimacy.

"Do you have any idea how long it's been since I've lain with a woman?"

"No. And I don't want to know! Don't you dare tell me!"

He rolled onto her so she was trapped. They were wedged together, and they fit perfectly. He was flat where she was rounded, lean where she was plump. A clump of his rusty hair flopped down on his forehead, and he appeared dangerous, menacing, determined.

"I guess you've missed having a man in your bed. Have you decided I'd do in a pinch?"

"I've *decided* no such thing."

"It would serve you right if I proceeded."

"Hah! As if I'd let you!"

"Do you assume you could prevent me? You're not some

innocent girl! You're a widow, for God's sake! It's risky to flirt. I'm not a gentleman. I could take you without batting an eye." He halted, assessing her. "Or maybe that's what you're hoping will happen. That way, you can swive your lowly soldier with a clean conscience, then afterward, you can persuade yourself that it wasn't your fault."

She opened her mouth to protest, when he stroked her breast, cupping it, tweaking the nipple so that it ached and throbbed.

"Unhand me," she declared, but without much vigor. Early on in her marriage, her husband had massaged her breasts, but he'd quickly lost interest. The lascivious caressing had fascinated her, and Charles was so adept!

"No. I've been yearning to do this."

He had?

He kissed her, and she'd meant to resist, when it dawned on her that she wanted this to transpire, too, and had for an eternity.

She wrapped her arms around him, anchoring him to her, as he stuck his tongue into her mouth! The move both astonished and delighted her. He tasted like the wine they'd been drinking, and she reveled in the novel sensation. Harold's kisses had been a wet, sloppy affair, usually initiated when he was very foxed, while Charles's were all passion, hunger, craving. It was everything about which she'd ever fantasized, and he swept her away on a rising tide of carnality she'd never previously experienced.

Without her being aware, he'd released the top buttons of her dress. The bodice was loose, and he slithered his fingers under her corset and chemise so that he was fondling her bare breast. He massaged it, stroked and petted it, in a fashion she'd never imagined, until she was writhing with agony and wishing he'd desist. It was so stimulating that it hurt.

He abandoned her mouth, and traveled down her neck, dropping to her cleavage, when astoundingly, he tugged on her gown, exposing her bosom. Bold as brass, he sucked on her nipple, his teeth nipping and biting at it.

The exploit stirred a fever in her blood. She wanted . . . wanted . . . she couldn't describe what, but she was wild and reckless, ready to commit any incautious act without regard to the consequences.

Much too rapidly, he was inching up her skirt, raising it past her knee. Soon, her privates would be revealed, and she knew what would come next. He'd unfasten his trousers, and impale her with his masculine rod.

Was she prepared to fornicate with him? Fully clothed, with scarcely a word being exchanged between them?

Her circumspection was clouded by a combination of the liquor, the isolation, and their odd situation, and she was about to order him to stop, when he reached the vee between her thighs.

She wasn't sure what she'd expected, but it wasn't the tender, nimble rasping he'd instigated. He was hardly touching her, brushing so lightly that the palpation was a petty torture. Her torso responded, her hips flexing, striving to enhance the pressure. Her reaction embarrassed her. In her old age, had she become promiscuous? Wanton?

His fingers dipped inside her sheath, plunging in, stretching and widening her, and his manipulations felt so spectacular! An itch she hadn't known needed scratching! She was slippery, saturated, her loins weeping, and she was abashed at being so out of control. She thrust in a furious rhythm, grappling toward an elusive goal that remained beyond her.

Was this desire?

Augmenting the tension, he tightened his lips on her nipple, as his thumb flicked out and jabbed at a sensitive nub she'd never noticed. She hurdled over a cliff of pleasure. Blinded by the exhilaration, she flew through the air, and she cried out. Loudly! He muffled the sound by capturing her mouth in another torrid kiss.

She was soaring, ascending, the delectation never seeming to end, then gradually, the tumult waned, and she floated to earth. With great trepidation, she peeked about, terrified that her blindness might be permanent, and she was relieved to note that it wasn't!

As she reassembled, it occurred to her that she'd had an orgasm. Her very first! She was stunned. Harold had claimed she was frigid, that she'd driven him to other women because she was such a cold fish.

Not having any frame of reference to refute his charges, and being too mortified to discuss them with anyone, she'd believed every insult he'd spewed.

He'd been wrong!

A glow started, a tiny spark that grew and grew, until she was warmed all over by the glorious discovery. She wanted to shout the news to the heavens, to giggle with glee, to clap her hands in merriment.

Charles pulled away, courteously lifting her bodice and lowering her hem.

"Is that what you needed, lass?" he asked. "Are ya feeling better?"

Generally, his Scottish brogue was barely distinguishable, but now, it was distinct and clear, emphasizing their differences, and she wondered if he wasn't doing it on purpose.

He sat up, straightened his apparel, then cool as a cucumber, he stood. Was he leaving?

She wasn't certain what she wanted, but she'd supposed they might at least chat or snuggle. With more than a bit of longing, she recognized that she'd always wanted to cuddle with a man, but his actions and detachment made their behavior seem so impersonal, so tawdry.

"Where are you going?" she managed. She was sprawled on the mattress. Her hair had fallen, her tresses flowing across the pillow, and her cheeks were flushed from exertion and excitement. She had to look worse than a demimonde courtesan.

"I thought I'd try flirting with the tavern girls. If I'm lucky, I'll talk one of them into a tumble." He rubbed his phallus, pressing at his obtrusive erection. "I find I could use a spot of fun myself."

It was the cruelest remark anyone had ever uttered in her presence, and she was crushed. She and Charles weren't friends exactly, but he was habitually cordial and polite, and she'd foolishly, romantically presumed that the moment had been as splendid for him as it had been for her.

She was devastated. Could he really stroll out, bound for the taproom and the strumpets who worked there?

While she didn't aspire to much vanity, she had her pride, and she wasn't about to let him see how deeply he'd wounded her.

"Don't let me keep you."

Acknowledging her dismissal, he nodded. "Good night, Lady Eleanor. Be sure to lock up behind me."

With that curt farewell, he strutted out, departing so swiftly that it was as if he'd never been there, at all.

As the silence settled around her, she propped up on her elbow and peered at the door. Ultimately, she forced herself out of bed and turned the key in the lock. Her knees were weak, her body trembling, and she staggered over and flopped down on the mattress, rolling to her back and gazing up at a crack in the ceiling.

Oh, how would she ever face him in the morning!

Humiliated, ashamed, confused, more forlorn than she'd ever been, she cried herself to sleep.

~ 5 ~

Anne stood on the stoop, trying to be gracious, but privately gnashing her teeth. Even on her best days, her neighbor, Willie McGee, was difficult to tolerate, but with how harried her life had recently become, she hadn't any patience to abide his swaggering and braggadocio. She needed a polite way to get him moving, but he was regaling her with details of his latest criminal conquest, and he wouldn't shut up.

He was fascinated by law enforcement, by transgressions and felons, and he fancied himself as a sort of unofficial petty magistrate, a rural Bow Street runner, who was the sole barrier between peace and anarchy in the Bristol area.

Though he owned the adjacent property, and earned a stable income from farming, his passion was the pursuit of lawbreakers. He was forever chasing after culprits, seizing them, and delivering them to various judicial entities. In the pasture behind his house, he'd even built a small gaol, where he incarcerated offenders prior to transporting them.

Citizens purchased his assistance for a fee, and he provided a beneficial service for those who hadn't the resources or time to prosecute wrongdoers themselves. Still, rumor had it that he employed unscrupulous methods, that he could be bribed to manufacture evidence, that he wasn't beyond charging an individual on false facts if the money offered was sufficient.

She didn't believe the chatter, mostly because he seemed harmless, more boast than substance. He liked to impress with his narratives of valor and danger, but how many of them were actually true was open to debate.

At age forty-one, he wasn't maturing very gracefully. He was bald, his skin swarthy and pockmarked, and he didn't bathe much, which was nauseating when she was so fussy about individual hygiene.

He stunk, and his clothes needed a thorough laundering.

He was short, not much taller than herself, but his shoulders were broad, his arms and thighs beefy, and he was very strong, so he appeared much larger than he was. A bachelor, who lived with his shy, spinster sister, Prudence, he was an odd duck, with peculiar hobbies and a quirky character.

When Lady Eleanor had first dumped Stephen in her lap, Anne had deemed Willie the perfect choice to convey Stephen to Bristol Manor. He had a large wagon, with an enclosed bed that he used to convey outlaws, and Stephen could have reclined in the back for the journey, so she'd sent him a note, asking him to visit, but now, with how events had untangled, she rued contacting him.

"I'm sorry I bothered you, Willie," she said, eager for him to go. "I had a client who needed a ride, but he—that is, *she*—found another carriage."

Willie was no fool, and he noticed the slip of speech. "Oh, Anne, don't tell me you've considered having a man on the premises."

"I'd never do anything that idiotic," she lied.

"Good. This is a conservative community, and you need to maintain your reputation. It's bad enough that you're operating this place by yourself."

"What do you mean?"

"People talk, Anne. And what they say about you isn't always kind."

A master at innuendo and insinuation, he was constantly hinting that he'd been apprised of the *real* story, the secrets to which others weren't privy, and she refused to react. Very likely, no one had uttered two words about her, and she wouldn't give him any fodder for the gossip mill. Besides, by passing herself off as a widow, she quelled speculation about her independent conduct.

"I'll keep your advice in mind," she blandly agreed.

Puffing up, he stuck out his chest, convinced that he'd made an important point. "Have you reflected on the discussion we had last week?"

Had she! She could barely repress a shudder. "I told you, Willie: I'm flattered that you think so highly of me, but I'm not interested in being wooed." He scowled so she added, "My decision has nothing to do with you personally. I'm simply satisfied with my situation, and I have no desire to marry again. It would be cruel of me to lead you on."

"But it's not natural for a female to be so self-reliant. So self-supporting. You need a husband's guiding influence."

Several scathing remarks were on the tip of her tongue, but she kept them stuffed inside. If she'd had any fond feelings for him—which she didn't—his condescending attitude would have drowned them.

Calming herself, she inhaled a slow breath, held it, let it out. "Thank you for being concerned about my welfare. You're a dear soul to worry. I appreciate it."

Intent on hurrying him along, she sauntered down the walk to his gig. He had to join her or be left standing by himself in the doorway. Prudence was waiting in the passenger seat, quiet and meek as usual, but she was perusing the grounds as though she yearned for the temerity to hop down and stroll about. Willie wouldn't let her explore or venture inside.

The few occasions Anne had invited her, Prudence had declined, and Anne was certain that Prudence would be incurring her brother's wrath if she violated his dictates. Just once, though, Anne wished Prudence would show a little backbone, but then, Prudence had to suffer Willie round-the-clock. It was probably easier to remain tractable.

After another irritating exchange regarding Anne's autonomy, the McGees were off, and she lingered in the drive, relieved to see them go. With mixed emotions, she returned to the house. Due to Stephen's taking up residence, her affairs were in chaos, but how could one man instigate such upheaval?

She had him swimming three times a day, which disrupted her schedule, and everyone else's. His privacy and her reputation were paramount, so she'd postponed appointments with her ailing invalids, and she'd had to rebuff many wealthy customers, because she couldn't have Stephen crossing paths with any of them.

Camilla Warren, and her unruly friends, had endeavored to cajole admittance, but Kate had sent them packing to Bath, where they had spread tales of their inhospitable welcome, which had induced flagrant conjecturing as to the reasons.

Rumors abounded that she had an illustrious guest on the premises, the identity varying from an ill Italian countess, to a vacationing American heiress, to the Queen herself. Kate had been to the village, and she'd been peppered with questions from merchants who were wondering if there was anything special they could furnish to make Her Majesty's stay more enjoyable.

From the moment Eleanor Chamberlin Dunworthy had pulled into the yard in her fancy coach, Anne had known that she was in for trouble, and she'd been correct. She didn't regret fostering Stephen; she merely wanted matters to calm, so that she could reestablish some of the routine on which she depended and thrived.

Stephen was demanding as a newborn babe, his road to recovery bumpy, and he was a terrible patient. Placid one minute, angry the next, he was never content with his progress, and unable to accept defeat or failure. Now that he was determined to mend, he expected instant health.

She devoted all her energy to him. If she wasn't helping him in the pool, she was cooking his food. If she wasn't cooking his food, she was serving it to him. If she wasn't serving it to him, she was keeping him company.

When she managed to sneak away, she couldn't concentrate on any topic but him. She was exhausted, weary, the oil in her lamp scarcely lit, yet she wouldn't trade her experience.

His presence made her . . . happy. Yes, that was it. Where before, she'd imagined that she'd had an adequate and pleasant existence, she'd been deluding herself. She hadn't been happy.

Something had been missing, and until he'd arrived, she hadn't recognized it. He made her pine away, had her fretting over what might have been, and what could be, instead of what was, and she couldn't believe she was imprudent enough to hunger for more than she had. The cards had been dealt at her birth, and she couldn't alter who or what she was. She'd been a smart girl, had grown up to be a pragmatic woman, and at an early age, she'd resolved never to lament her fate.

As she'd watched, her mother had faded away, shattered from having loved the wrong man, an aristocrat she couldn't have wed in a thousand years, and Anne had reaped a valuable lesson.

She understood her place, had been resigned to her circumstance. But Stephen Chamberlin had transformed her view of the world.

She wanted to be more than a spinster, wanted a serenity that ran deeper than what could be gleaned from running her

own business. The tangible aspects that had sustained her—
the walls of her home, the dirt in the yard, the water in the
pond—seemed cold comfort.

Much to her surprise, she wanted a man in her life, and
not just any man, but Stephen Chamberlin. The notion was
so depressing! Had she learned nothing from her mother's
plight? Had she no better sense?

He was so far above her, so out of her reach, that he was
like an angel in heaven. She could worship him from a distance, but could never have him for her own. Her father's
despicable behavior toward her mother had guaranteed that
fact.

Yet, she aspired to be Stephen's equal, to meet him on
common terms. His sister had hired her to care for him,
which created an association of employer and employee, and
she chafed at her subservient position, but there was naught
to be done.

She'd agreed to tend him, and she would, but she would
have to tamp down on her feelings. Stephen didn't have a
lock on vanity. She was proud, herself, and she wouldn't
evince the slightest hint that she was enamored.

Marching inside, she filled a bowl with hot water, grabbed
some towels, and proceeded to his room. He was on the bed,
and he assessed the items on her tray, frowning when he saw
that they weren't food.

"I'm hungry," he grumbled.

"A good sign that you're recuperating."

"I must have something to eat besides gruel. I'm a bloody
human being, not a bird!"

She laughed. "Are we a tad grouchy this morning?"

"My head's throbbing."

"I'm reducing your amounts of laudanum." She'd been
weaning him off the vile stuff, the liquor too, and she hoped
to have him free of them when his sister next visited, though
it would be no easy chore.

"I could use a stiff drink."

So could I, she mused, smiling. It was eleven o'clock. He could try the patience of a saint. "No. You had a dose with breakfast. You shan't get more for a bit. I'm not about to send you home a drunkard and an opium addict."

"I'm neither one," he huffed.

"You couldn't prove it by me."

"I can do without them. I'll show you."

"I'm sure you will."

"I'm itchy when I don't take them."

"Your body has cravings, but they will abate. Give it some time."

"I don't want to give it some *time.* I want to be cured now."

"I realize that."

He motioned to her tray. "What have you there?"

"I plan to cut your hair."

"The devil you say!"

"And you're going to shave." He shot her a mutinous look, and she threatened, "Or else *I* will shave you. It's your choice."

"I'm partial to my hair and beard. I'm not ready to lose them."

Trophies of his illness? she speculated. *Or a shield to hide behind?*

She picked up the sharpened razor, flicked her thumb across it. "Don't argue with a woman who's about to hold a blade to your throat."

"Witch," he muttered. "Seat me in front of the mirror. I demand to observe every snip."

She situated a chair, then guided him into it. Though he hadn't noticed, his strength had increased. The therapeutic sessions were having a remarkable effect, as were the nutritious broths and teas she'd been forcing down him.

If only his mood would rectify accordingly!

Gripping his wild mane, she whacked off a hunk. He

complained, and she punched him on the shoulder. While she was no coiffeur, she was no bungler, either. She'd had plenty of practice on Phillip when he was a boy. But that had been before he'd turned fourteen, proclaimed himself an adult, and hied himself off to toil in their father's stables. She hadn't seen much of him after that, but she still recalled how to barber.

"Where's Phillip these days?" he asked as though he'd read her mind.

"Back at work."

"At Salisbury?"

She stiffened, irked that he would so casually mention her father's estate. "Yes."

"How's his leg?"

"Mostly healed. It occasionally causes him trouble. He limps."

"Did you nurse him?"

"I did my best."

"That's my girl."

He patted her hand, which flustered her. What did he mean by his *girl*? He sounded sweet on her, possessive, as though they were connected. Was he fond of her? More than fond? The very idea made her pulse pound.

"He's your father's stable master, isn't he?"

"Yes," she murmured.

"How is Edward? I haven't seen him in an eternity."

Edward Paxton. Earl of Salisbury. The father she loathed. Stephen Chamberlin knew him well enough to refer to him as Edward.

Of course, he would! They traveled in the same circle. They were probably bosom buddies, and the prospect aggravated her beyond her limits.

"I wouldn't know how Edward *is*," she answered, inexplicably distressed by the question. "He doesn't deign to inform me as to his welfare."

Angry, she combed through his snarled, uneven tresses, not aware that she'd been so sensitive on the subject. Being very rough, she tugged and jerked.

"Ouch!" he snapped at a particularly vicious yank. He peered at her over his shoulder, scrutinizing her.

"I hurt you. I'm sorry."

"For what?"

"For bringing up your father. Phillip spoke of him warmly. I thought you were . . . were . . ." He trailed off, grasping there was nothing he could say that would be appropriate.

"We're not close," she managed, tears suddenly swarming.

"Do you want to talk about it?"

Talk about it? To him? The legitimate, lauded, acclaimed son of an earl?

How could she explain a lifetime of fury and anguish? A mother who'd died of a broken heart? A father who'd cast them off like so much rubbish? If she'd had an entire year, she couldn't have vented it all.

"No," she mumbled.

Linking their fingers, he pulled her around the chair, snuggling her onto his lap even though it was painful for him, and he brushed one of his light, dear kisses across her lips.

"Don't be sad," he coaxed.

"I'm not."

"I can't bear it when you're not smiling."

He kissed her again, lingering, the embrace enhancing to a level it hadn't before. She relaxed into him, enjoying the moment, but as she raised her arms to wrap them around his shoulders, the rear door opened, and Kate came into the house. Anne jumped away from him as if he'd gotten too hot to handle.

"Kate?" he inquired. He'd met Kate, and appeared to like

her, had even permitted her to assist them once when he'd fallen, and Anne couldn't lift him by herself.

"Yes."

Because of Kate's cautions when he'd initially arrived, she hadn't found the courage to confess her burgeoning affection, or the intermittent kisses and caresses they'd shared.

Our dallying doesn't signify, she told herself, as she intended to insist to Kate should her flirtation ever be discovered. *He'll be gone in a few weeks.*

He held on to her hand, cajoling a smile from her.

"Will you tell me about Edward someday?"

"Perhaps," she equivocated, not sure she could voice that much sorrow aloud.

"And would you be kind to my hair?" he chided, changing the mood from somber to teasing. "I have quite a lot for a man my age, and I'm vain about it. I don't need you ripping it out, strand by strand."

"I'll try to accommodate you, Your Royal Highness."

"I can't have you adding baldness to my problems."

She rolled her eyes, and he chuckled.

As she aimed the scissors, he persisted with griping over every clip and pare, and she hated to admit that even his grousing thrilled her. Pitifully, she was smitten, enthralled, captivated, but she ignored him and kept on. Dark locks drifted to the floor, and she was struck by the intimacy the activity generated. It hadn't seemed overly familiar when she'd done it to Phillip, but with Stephen, it had the same effect as their being in the water together.

She was behind him, his shoulders leaned on her chest, his head nestled between her breasts. The arrangement was naughty, improper, and it allowed for bodily contact she wouldn't have attempted or sanctioned in a different environment.

When had she grown so brazen? Why did she torture herself with such proximity? When she was with him, she couldn't stop touching him, and she pondered how he must view her.

Did he find her loose? Wanton?

Whenever a physical interlude occurred, he acted as though it was normal conduct, so he provided no clues as to his thinking, and amazingly, she didn't care what his opinion might be. She was unable to keep her distance and had ceased trying.

It was exciting to riffle about, and she fussed and trimmed much longer than necessary, just so she could stretch out the encounter. But she couldn't loaf forever, so she combed through the mass, then offered him a small mirror.

"Well?" she queried.

"You've missed your calling. You should be running a tonsorial parlor instead of a bathing establishment."

"I'm a woman of many talents."

"Yes, you are."

He gazed at her, and her stomach twisted in knots. She'd heard stories as to how winsome he was, and she'd suspected there was a rogue lurking under all that scraggle, but it was frightening to have that man emerging. In light of her sheltered upbringing, she had no experience or aptitude for dealing with someone of his magnificence and charm. He simply took her breath away.

Busying herself, she dipped the towel in the water, and pointed to his beard, though she didn't confide that she'd never shaved anyone before. The news had to be more than a sick fellow could abide.

"Would you like me to do it?"

"You'd better. My hands are too shaky."

"You're very trusting."

"Hah! I'll be watching your every move."

With the scissors, she lopped off the length, then she retrieved the towel, wrung it out, and draped it across his cheeks and chin, pressing it in place. She didn't know if she was proceeding correctly, but she imagined if she continued with sufficient aplomb, he wouldn't guess that she was incompetent.

She picked up the razor, studied it, studied him, then gnawed on her lip. She wasn't sure how the blade fit to the skin, and she approached, twisting it this way and that, trying to figure out where to start.

"Give it to me!" He yanked it away, just as she would have nicked him. "You've no idea what you're doing, do you?"

She thought about lying, then laughed and shrugged. "No."

"Lord, keep me safe from bossy females!" He still had the mirror, and he passed it to her. "Hold this so I can see, and set the bowl and soap where I can reach them."

His commands furnished her with a hint of what he must have been like in the army, ordering about the poor young men who'd served under him. A virtual terror, no doubt! How had Phillip stood it?

For many minutes, she dawdled, tilting the mirror, lathering, or swabbing away whiskers. Little by little, his features were revealed, until he wiped off the last of the residue.

"Well? How do I look?" Grabbing the mirror from her, he preened. "Am I a handsome dog, or what?"

He grinned at her, and she gawked in dismay. Was he handsome? Like a seraph painted on a church ceiling!

She didn't want him to be so attractive! She wanted him to be ordinary, plain, common. It wasn't fair that he should be gifted with so much. Couldn't he have at least one flaw? No wonder he was so impossibly arrogant!

Declining to stoke his vanity, she clutched his chin, assessed him, and blandly announced, "I suppose you'll do."

"I'll *do!*" he barked, feigning affront. "I'll have you know that there are ladies in London who have swooned upon observing my pretty face!"

I'll bet they have! she reflected miserably.

"If you're fishing for compliments, you won't get any from me. You're entirely too pleased with yourself as it is."

"And *you* are a sassy, impertinent wench."

"Someone needs to keep your head out of the clouds."

"You're jealous," he jested. "You can't stand to be reminded of how everybody loves me."

"Oh, spare me your egotistical drivel!"

Rolling her eyes again, she did everything she could to hide her true reaction, for he was right. She detested considering his existence outside her farm. In the brief period he'd been with her, she'd come to think of him as her own, as if he belonged with her. She couldn't bear to remember that he was hers for just a short while, that she was healing him so that he could carry on as he had before they'd met.

She would only play a tiny role in what would be his lengthy, fruitful, eventful life, yet he'd already begun to mean everything to her.

How attached would she be if he stayed a month? Two? Six?

What a void he'd leave when he departed! What would she do with herself?

She had to rein in her fascination and fast! She couldn't let him have such dominion over her emotions, couldn't permit her bewitchment to rule. Nothing good could ensue from her budding fondness, and she refused to be desolate and bereft after he'd gone.

"How are you feeling?" she inquired, desperate to assert some control, to push their association to the more disparate level, where it had to remain.

"Terrific."

"You're not fatigued?"

Full of mischief, he evaluated her, commencing at the top and traveling downward, across her bosom, waist, crotch, and legs. "I'm eager to bathe in the pool. Go fetch your bathing costume." He halted and wiggled his brows. "Better yet, don't fetch it. Let's swim in the buff."

At the indecent suggestion, she blushed such a bright red that she was surprised she didn't burst into flames. "We most certainly will not."

Embarrassed, she bustled around, tidying the room.

Was this the sort of thing he ruminated about during his boring hours of convalescence?

The bounder!

While she washed in the nude every night—by herself!— she couldn't frolic so decadently with him.

Or could she?

Unbidden, several lusty, lewd images flashed into her mind. She could picture the two of them, wet, slick, hot, their torsos rubbing together.

The vision was so realistic, and so stirring! Was that what she wanted? Was she hoping for something so risqué to occur?

"I'll go don my bathing clothes," she primly stated, "but I intend to keep them tightly buttoned!"

"I won't promise that I shan't try to remove them."

Would he? What would it be like to have him undoing her bodice, baring her breasts, her stomach, her bottom? Her heart raced, her nipples throbbed.

If he attempted to perpetrate such nonsense, would she stop him? She didn't believe so, and the realization scared her to death. Where was she going with him? She knew she should tread carefully, but some insane, wild part of her didn't plan to be cautious.

What had happened to her? Deep down, was she a Jezebel?

"If you can talk about merrymaking in the pool," she admonished, "you must be much improved."

"I'm definitely *better,*" he declared, and he raked her with such an ardent look, that she felt as if she'd been scalded.

Whirling away, she rushed to her bedchamber, almost running to escape him, but also, to put on her outfit as rapidly as she was able.

What did she propose? What did he?

The prospects were so titillating and so terrifying that she couldn't wait to learn the answer.

Stephen lounged in the soothing water, studying the grotto, the wall of rocks, the dam that formed the pond. Sun had set, and the gloaming was upon them. The sky was indigo, and the evening star twinkled on the horizon.

He shut his eyes and offered up a selfish wish. For a return to full health, to some semblance of how he'd carried on before disaster had laid him low.

A week previous, he'd have deemed such aspirations impossible, the yearnings of a desperate man. He wouldn't have dared to trust, and he couldn't explain how so much could have changed so fast.

It was all because of Anne Paxton Smythe. She had a curious manner, an attitude that precluded his languishing or declining further. She was so sure he could improve, and so adamantly opposed to a different conclusion. Her obstinacy had ignited a spark of optimism that couldn't be doused.

While he couldn't marry or sire children, there were other ways to lead a long and fruitful life. He could forge a new path, could locate diverse avenues to contentment. It was nothing short of a miracle that she'd brought about such a complete and utter transformation. He wasn't positive how she'd done it, but he wouldn't question the Fates that had compelled Eleanor to drop him on her stoop.

Behind him, he could hear her puttering about, arranging towels, soap, and her other accouterments. She labored so diligently, was so focused on his recovery, and he didn't know how she found the energy to keep going.

She'd instituted an exhausting regimen of diet, arm weights, and leg movements. The eccentric female had even ordered him to daydream about things he would most like to do when he was better. It was a peculiar method of therapy, and in the beginning, he'd resisted, bluntly telling her it was a stupid idea. But now, he spent his every leisure moment concentrating on pleasurable activity. A walk on the beach. A ride on his favorite stallion. Making love.

Clearly, his ability to copulate was gone and wouldn't be restored, but he wouldn't lose hope, and it was easy enough to fantasize. Over the years, many beauties had graced his bed. He'd been the toast of London, an unrepentant cad and libertine. So he had plenty of recollection to stir his reveries, but he also had Anne, herself.

Each night, she relished a quiet, relaxing swim, and like the worst voyeur, he watched her. He scolded himself, appreciating that he shouldn't stare, that he should roll over and ignore her, but he couldn't forgo the naughty delectation.

He would never again entice a woman to philander, because he couldn't risk having her learn the extent of his war injuries. In his social circle, such news would sizzle like a wildfire, and he couldn't abide such a public humiliation.

His sojourn at Anne's emporium might be the sole occasion he'd ever have to gaze upon a nude female, and if it was to be his last opportunity, he wasn't about to pass it up. The furtive sight was an unexpected boon, a divine gift of sorts, that allowed him a final glimpse of a prior road fading away.

She wasn't aware that he had an unimpeded view of the

grotto, or maybe she believed he was sleeping, so she was oblivious to his spying on her. She always looked so sad and forlorn, and he wondered what thoughts induced her melancholy. Her farm? Her business? Himself?

Smiling, he discounted the foolish assumption. If she reflected at all, it was likely on her deceased husband, and more and more, the notion disturbed him.

She never spoke of her spouse, and he'd never been rude enough to pry, but he often pondered the lucky fellow who'd snagged her. Had he realized how fortunate he was? Had their marriage been one of joy and passion? Or had it been tame, a marriage of convenience, contracted for property or money?

He didn't like contemplating that man, didn't like being reminded that she'd once belonged to another. Their many intimacies made it seem as if she was his, and had never previously shared any of her unique qualities.

She appeared to cherish him, as evidenced by her visiting him in the wee hours, tucking him in, or checking his fever. Her tender ministrations had him feeling special, precious, and they tugged at something deep inside, an empty spot he hadn't recognized to exist.

Since he'd arrived home from Spain, it had become apparent that he wasn't close to anyone, except perhaps Charles and Eleanor. He could count on one hand the number of supposed friends who'd called on him at Bristol, and a couple of those—he was convinced—had stopped by to determine his condition so they could spread juicy stories in town.

He was disconsolate, isolated, and Anne filled a wretched loneliness.

In a few minutes, she would join him, would exercise his limbs and wash his body. She went about her duties with the utmost professionalism, but it was difficult to be with her and not want to misbehave.

Something was going on between them, something

dramatic and sensational. He was so very attracted to her.
To her comeliness, certainly, but to her personality, as well.
He admired her intelligence, her character, her sense of humor. His emotions toward her were much more intense,
much more extreme, than any he'd ever felt for another,
and after spending so much familiar time with her, he
imagined it was just as well that he'd never have a wife, for
he couldn't fathom being embroiled in a typical aristocratic union. A detached, conventional marriage held no
appeal whatsoever.

As she'd finished her chores, she entered the pool, gliding under the water so that it lapped at her bosom and shoulders. She was dressed in her blue-striped bathing costume. It
was baggy and frilly, with abundant ruffles across her bust to
conceal it once the fabric was saturated. Still, he was sporad-
ically granted a hint of breast or nipple, and the fact that he
observed so carefully, anticipating an indiscreet peek, was
the best indicator of how quickly he was improving.

She swam to the other end of the pond, her outfit poofing
with air over her shapely rear. He wished he could coax her
out of it, which he considered the height of optimism for a
chap in his feeble state.

If he got her naked, what—precisely—did he propose to
do with her? Would he merely ogle her, like some aging,
perverted reprobate?

She came toward him, and he grabbed her wrist, and
pulled her near.

"Are you ready to begin?" she asked.

"Not yet." He snuggled her onto his thigh, and she fell
forward, her chest pressed to his own.

He was attired in a nightshirt, but it was a thin, summery
garment, and so was her apparel. When the two pieces were
moistened, and their torsos melded together, it seemed as if
they had nothing on. Her breasts reacted to the indecent contact, her nipples growing rigid and poking at him.

What would she say if he confided how he spied on her in the dark? He almost spilled the beans, but sanity prevailed, and he bit down on a confession. It was a lascivious secret he wasn't prepared to reveal. Maybe he never would.

"What is it?" she inquired, her pretty green eyes searching his.

"I'm mending so rapidly." He didn't add how thrilled he was, or how afraid that it was a chimera, that it wouldn't last.

"Yes, but don't forget: you'll have reversals. You can't be discouraged. Healing isn't a straight line, where you continually advance. It's more like a meandering stream."

"No, I'm better. I can feel it on the inside."

"And I can see it on the outside."

"Why is it happening so swiftly?"

"I've told you: it's all in your mind. You've decided to recover."

"I think there's something about this pool."

She laughed "It's just water, Stephen."

"And your potions and recipes are magical, too."

"Absolutely." She laughed again.

"Why did you invent them?"

"They were created out of necessity. I nursed a widow—I inherited this place from her—as she died a slow death. So did my mother. The doctors and apothecaries were so incompetent that I was forced to make up my own remedies."

"But how?"

"Trial and error."

"It has to be more than that. You're so proficient. Why?"

"I have no idea."

"Are you a witch?"

As if he'd poked her with a stick, she lurched away. "That's not funny."

She tried to escape, but he now had enough strength to keep her from leaving. "I was joking."

"Were you? Not long ago, they burned women at the stake over such idiotic comments."

"They don't anymore."

"Don't be too sure they wouldn't. You could destroy my business, with such a dangerous innuendo."

Could he? He hadn't realized that she could be so vulnerable to public opinion. "I'd never let anyone harm you."

"You wouldn't be here to prevent it, would you?"

Too true. There would come a day when he would be revived, and he would have to depart, which was so depressing.

Where would he go? To Bristol Manor, to reside under his father's authoritative influence? To London, to sponge off friends?

As he'd had no prospects for earning an income, he'd intended to marry Felicity Babcock, mostly for her wealth, but the problems with his genitalia guaranteed that he couldn't take up with her, or with any other. It would be fraud to wed when he couldn't beget children.

So what was his plan?

He yearned to stay with Anne, forever, and he had an hilarious vision, of the two of them, elderly companions swimming in her hot pool. Was that how the rest of his pitiful life was to pass? Would there never be more?

"I'm a fool," he apologized. "Don't be angry with me."

"I'm not."

Quickly and easily, their quarrel was terminated. He liked that about her, liked that she was feisty and assertive, that her temper could flare, then wane as promptly as it had ignited.

Relaxing, he nestled with her, resolved that by their next encounter, he would wear only drawers, or perhaps nothing. If he was to be celibate after he left her, he wasn't about to refrain from having their naked skin merged.

She was leaned against him, smiling and studying him.

"What?" it was his turn to ask.

"Does it ever seem to you as if we were acquainted before you came here? As if we'd met?"

"Yes, I've been pondering the same."

"I know so much about you, that I have no reason for knowing. Why do you suppose that is?"

"We share an affinity," he clarified, and he speculated again as to the relationship she'd had with her husband. If she didn't comprehend any more than this about males and females, it must have been very tepid.

"What causes it?"

It was the type of magnetism that produced searing sexual affairs, that generated uncontrollable ardor, that had couples racing to folly and ruin, but he didn't say as much.

"Some people are naturally close. There's no explanation. It's one of the great mysteries of the universe."

"Does that mean that *I* am a great mystery?"

"No." He tapped the tip of her pert nose. "It *means* that you are a brazen, bawdy wench and much too impertinent for your own good. You're lucky I'm an invalid, or I'd show you how rash you are, being here with me."

"Rash . . . hmm . . ." She mulled the word, as if applying it to herself, to see how it fit. "I don't believe I've ever done anything *rash*, and I'm twenty-eight. Maybe I should indulge myself."

He shook his head. This was another pathetic example of how his fortunes were running. He was alone, in the dark, with a gorgeous, wet, alluring woman, who was practically begging to be ravished, and he couldn't do anything about it.

Or could he?

While he couldn't be aroused, *she* could be. At least, he could enjoy that portion of it. She was a randy widow. Why not revel with her?

"Maybe you should," he concurred.

She wrapped her arms around his neck, her lush mouth hovering at his own.

"Kiss me," she ordered.

For an instant, he was frozen, frightened to obey her command. Anymore, he was a coward, scared of so many things he used to take for granted. Was he reduced to being too terrified to kiss a woman?

He understood that she was demanding more than what he'd instigated prior. She craved heat, and fire, and he wanted to give them to her.

Jolting himself out of his asinine stupor, he captured her lips, as it vaguely occurred to him that, when he failed to generate an erection, she would deduce he couldn't. At the moment, he wasn't concerned. Later, he'd fret over humiliating rationalizations and justifications. For now, he would rollick and play, would luxuriate in the very essence of her.

He stroked her shoulders, her back, and she responded to his every move, imitating his gestures, though it was with an odd curiosity, as if she wasn't positive she was proceeding correctly. A captivating mix of innocence and boldness, she touched him everywhere, but with a perplexity that belied her experience. She was hesitant, wavering, yet fearless—all at the same time. The incongruity drove him wild.

It was almost as if she'd never philandered before, but he was too enamored to slow and allow her to acclimate. She made him feel whole, complete, and he wasn't about to desist.

He wanted her hair unbound, to have the lengthy mass floating free as it did when he spied on her, and he jerked off her cap, yanked at the combs and pins, and tossed them onto the grass.

His fingers went to her outfit, undoing the buttons, until he was able to slip under the material. She was warm, slippery, and inch by inch, he peeled the garment away, revealing her chest, her bosom. Braving the final distance, he dragged at the bodice until her breasts were bared, though concealed by the water. He filled his hands with the plump mounds, and he thumbed her nipples, making her groan and writhe.

"You're so beautiful, Anne," he coaxed. "Let me look at you."

"This is wrong," she managed on a tortured breath.

"I don't care. Do you?"

Her confusion evident, she scrutinized him. He was so attuned to her that he could read her tormented thoughts: She was ablaze, and desperate to progress, but she was chafing over morals, stigma, and reputation.

"There's no one here to see," he cajoled. "There's just us."

"That's what has me worried. I like this too much. I want this too much."

A wanton! Who wasn't too coy to admit it! How absolutely divine! He laughed. "Are you afraid that I'll discover how lustful you can be?"

"Yes." Even in the dim moonlight, he could detect her blush.

"I've never considered an excess of passion to be a bad trait in a female."

"You wouldn't." She glanced around at the empty yard, then she assessed him, so bewildered, so precious in her consternation, then she shrugged and chuckled. "Why not? Who's to say I can't?"

"Who, indeed?"

She fairly leapt into his arms, initiating a kiss of her own, that was much more torrid than any he'd bestowed. He met her with an equal amount of relish and elation, a renewed energy coursing through him. He might be debilitated, might be exhausted and weary, but he had the stamina to make love to her. For some strange reason, the water imparted the necessary vim and vigor.

He toyed with her breasts, as she fussed with his night-shirt, loosing the tie at the front and drawing it off so that she could push it around his hips. He aided her as much as he could, shifting about so that it was shoved lower, so that it came loose from his legs and drifted away.

Nude, balanced on the smooth rock ledge, his body was exposed, with no fabric to act as a barrier, and he wanted her in the same condition. He wrestled with her costume, tug-ging it past her waist, her hips, until she was as naked as he.

Their embrace grew more spirited, more enthusiastic, and he lured her nearer. The pond made her buoyant, so it was easy to lug her around, to position her where he wanted her. He spread her legs, her thighs on either side of his, so that she was over his lap.

Her breasts were pale and glimmering, the tips erect and pouting for attention. He buried himself in her cleavage, snuggled between the rounded orbs, licking at the droplets pearling on her skin.

Her back arched, her muscles tensed, she gripped his head, urging him to feast. Perched as she was, her hair flow-ing, her splendid torso displayed, she resembled a pagan goddess, a mythical Valkyrie.

He nipped and bit, nuzzled and suckled, until her nipple was raw and extended, then he burrowed to the other and latched on.

She was clutching at him, her nails digging in, and he reveled in the sharp sensation. It had been so long since he'd felt a woman's rising desire.

He guided her loins to his stomach. Though he had no manly rod for her to press against, no hardened phallus for her to mount, she needed to flex. She was on the edge, ready to fly to the heavens, and the slightest provocation would send her over.

How he yearned to penetrate her, to be joined with her

when she fell to pieces, but the interlude was so enchanted that he refused to lament what couldn't be changed.

He swept his hand downward, tangling in her silky feminine hair. She was splayed wide, open, and he slid two fingers into her sheath. She stiffened, as if surprised by the exploit, but she hastily adapted, rubbing in a furious rhythm. His thumb found the nub where her pleasure was centered, and he flicked at it.

"Oh, God," she moaned. "What are you doing to me?"

"Let go, Anne," he beguiled. "Show me how much you need this."

He took her nipple, forcefully sucking at it, and she quivered with ecstasy, her womb clasping in spasms.

Making no attempt to shield her reaction, she cried out and soared higher and higher, the orgasm never ending, and so intense that it seemed as if she'd never previously had one. He was thrilled by her potent response, charmed by her lack of inhibition.

As she began to calm, he nestled her at his nape. She purred and stretched like a lazy cat, and he smiled, treasuring how wonderful it was to hold her through the aftermath.

Would she be embarrassed by her raucous performance, or would she take it in stride? Was she always so vigorous?

He regretted that he hadn't had more to contribute to the foray. What would it be like to be a man by every definition of the word, to have his sexual capacity restored, and Anne his paramour?

"You are so wicked," she said, and she was grinning, too, her mouth curved and happy at his neck.

"I don't deny it."

"I can't believe I let you do that to me. If I were a Catholic, I'd have to spend a month on my knees, begging for forgiveness in the confessional."

"Perhaps two."

"Perhaps more." She pulled away and stared up at the sky. "Have you ever imagined becoming someone else? That you could snap your fingers, or swallow a magic powder, and you'd be transformed?"

"I wish it all the time," he stated, thinking of his mangled body.

"So do I."

It was a peculiar admission. He'd pictured her content, with her farm, and her grotto, and her business. To what more did she aspire? How would she alter her affairs if she could? Who would she like to be besides herself?

She gazed at him so profoundly that he was unnerved. Her expression was a mixture of adoration and fondness, with a sprig of hero worship thrown in, and it settled uneasily on his shoulders. Dalliance was more vehement for the woman, and she was appraising him as a virgin might after her first excursion into carnal territory.

Her blatant affection troubled him. A year or two earlier, he'd have perceived himself as so far above her station that he wouldn't have bothered to learn her name. He'd been that much of an arrogant prig.

Circumstances had brought him down a few pegs, but he had nothing to offer her, not in a fiscal way, and not in a personal way, and the fact that she might be developing an affinity depressed him. She was so rare, so fine, and in comparison, he felt so inadequate.

With the waning of her passion, he was fatigued. He kept trying to accomplish more than he was able, starting tasks that he hadn't the vitality to complete.

She noticed immediately. "I've tired you."

"I've tired myself."

"I'm sorry. I was having so much fun that I—"

He put a finger to her lips, silencing her. "Don't ever apologize for what happens between us when we're alone like this."

"I won't—as long as you promise we can do it again."
She wiggled her brows. "Very soon."

He was delighted by her candor, by her unabashed sensuality, and he hugged her as tightly as he could. "You are so good for me."

"And you, for me."

Was he *good* for her? How could he be? What had he to contribute that was in any fashion beneficial or essential? He'd been dumped on her without warning, had done naught but grumble and complain, had to be fed and washed and hauled about. He was an enormous burden she'd willingly assumed, though he hadn't figured out why she would.

How could he possibly be an advantage to her?

"Let's move you inside," she said, "before I have to summon Kate to carry you."

"By all means, let's do." He gave a mock shudder. He'd met her burly, competent, no-nonsense assistant and avoided her at all costs.

He watched as she retrieved their clothing. The garments were heavy, sodden, and it was much more difficult to put them on than it had been to strip them off. They didn't speak, and she didn't look at him, and he couldn't decide if she was chagrined or simply disconcerted by the ardor that had flared.

She hadn't tried to instigate any libidinous conduct on his end, hadn't touched or stroked his phallus, and she had to have realized that he hadn't spawned an erection. Nor had she commented on his dearth of ability. He was grateful for her reticence, and he hoped that she wouldn't raise the subject later. He had no thoughts he could share, and he couldn't devise any method for discussing the situation without making an utter fool of himself.

When she had them presentable, she helped him stand, and like the cripple he was, he clutched her arm. As she escorted him out of the water, he peered around, at the shimmering pool, the thick shrubbery, ruminating on how magnificent it all was.

But as she guided him onto the bank, his legs buckled, and he was so very weak. He saw months—nay, years!—of barely maintaining, of not being capable of doing for himself, and he whispered a short prayer.

Please, Lord, he implored, *let there be more for me than this.*

Taking the smallest, slowest of steps, he allowed her to lead him into the house.

7

Anne hovered over Stephen, knowing she should leave his room, but unable to force herself to go.

She yearned to confide that she'd never been with a man before, that she'd just had her first experience with desire, but by claiming to be a widow, she'd painted herself into a corner. Over the years, she'd told so many lies that she almost believed them herself, sometimes forgetting that there'd never been a *Mister* Smythe.

Stephen thought she was an accomplished matron, when in reality, she was a sheltered virgin. Passion had been a nebulous concept, pondered during those infrequent moments when she'd wondered what it would be like to have a husband.

He'd shown her such fantastic pleasure that he had her questioning the choices she'd made in her life. Her mother had often counseled as to the wages of sin, how a girl could be led astray by a handsome fellow, and Anne had embraced the admonitions.

As a result, she'd forgone marriage, telling herself that she was happy with her feminine surroundings, but now, she wasn't so sure. He'd scratched an itch that she hadn't realized was plaguing her, and she pined to swim naked with him again. As soon as he was up to it, she wanted him to unveil more of the secrets of the flesh.

Stephen Chamberlin was a sorcerer who had transformed her into an unrestrained slattern. How could she slow this rush to recklessness that had her greedy to try any nefarious conduct he might suggest?

At that very second, if he asked her to fornicate with him, she'd eagerly agree, when she wasn't even positive as to what the deed involved. Twenty-four hours earlier, the notion would never have occurred to her, but suddenly, she couldn't wait to discover the joys of carnality.

She sighed, debating how to make a gracious exit. From the instant they'd stepped out of the water, she hadn't opened her mouth, for fear that she'd begin to babble like a ninny.

"Are you feeling better?" she inquired, deeming it an innocuous query that could nudge them to the firm ground of healer and patient.

"Yes. How about you?"

Though he was depleted and drained, maimed and mangled, he had the energy to smirk in a thoroughly masculine fashion. He was preening! Devil take him! He was half dead, but had only sex on his mind!

"You are an unrepentant libertine, Captain Chamberlin."

"I am at that." His laugh was a low, enticing rumble that rattled her.

"You'd likely seduce the Blessed Virgin if you had the chance."

"She wouldn't be nearly as fun as you."

Rolling her eyes, she attempted to appear irritated, but she didn't succeed.

Oh, it was hopeless! With his wry humor, and cocky manner that charmed and enthralled, he was so different from how she'd imagined he would be. He was smart, clever, and she was falling head over heels, so much so that she'd shed her outfit and romped with him in the nude, and pathetically, she felt no guilt or shame over what they'd done.

She was her mother's daughter, all right! The poor woman was probably spinning in her grave!

He started to speak, and she silenced him. "You should rest. Let's get you out of this wet shirt and lay you down."

It was tricky business, undressing him, while striving not to see anything that ought to be concealed, but after their rollicking, she had no desire to be cautious. Their lusty interplay created the impression that he belonged to her, that his body was hers.

She untied the laces at the front of his nightshirt and drew it off. Goose bumps prickled on his arms, and she reached for a blanket and draped it over him.

In a huff, he shrugged it off. "Don't treat me like I'm a decrepit grandfather."

"I don't want you catching a chill."

"I'm fine."

Continuing, she moved the shirt downward, assessing every inch of his torso as she went. Previously, her evaluations had been analytical, like a scientist carrying out an experiment, but after their frolic, her interest had changed.

He was too skinny, but she intended to fix that, and was already building him to a more robust condition. Despite his lack of bulk, she could picture what a dashing figure he'd been before he'd been wounded.

Brawny and broad-shouldered, his chest was coated with a matting of hair. It was thick across the top, then it thinned as it descended, narrowing into a line that pointed to his loins, guiding her to iniquity—in case she couldn't locate it herself!

Normally, this was the juncture where she'd have placed a towel across his lap, but on this occasion, she didn't bother. They'd leapt far beyond the spot where privacy mattered.

Kneeling before him, she lowered the nightshirt farther,

revealing his belly, his abdomen, his phallus. Limp, harmless, it dangled between his legs, with no apparent purpose, and the fact that it hadn't stirred since his arrival—not even when they'd been naked in the pool—underscored her suspicion that he had no sensation in the extremity.

She had no capacity for conferring over male sexual organs, had scant comprehension of how the rod functioned, or what she could do to fix his problem. For once, she was at a loss, and she shifted him around, lifting one hip, then the other, to work the garment free so that he was unclothed.

If he suffered any discomfort from his nudity, she couldn't detect it, so she feigned nonchalance, too, acting as though she stripped men all the time.

He smiled the crooked smile she cherished. "I'm not much to look at anymore."

"No, you're not."

"I wish you'd known me before. I was such a gallant rogue."

"I'm sure you were impossibly handsome, and impossibly vain about it."

"I was."

Chuckling, he pulled her close, snuggling her to him. While he was mostly dried off, she still wore her wet bathing costume, and her hair was soaked, but he didn't seem to mind.

"Stay with me," he whispered. "I want to hold you till dawn."

Hadn't she just been thinking the very same? That it would be marvelous to tarry? Yet, she could contemplate no more dangerous proposition. She ignored his tempting words, refusing to let them sink in and take root.

"I can't," she forced out, endeavoring to sound cheery.

"Don't say no."

There was a peculiar gleam in his eye, of tenderness and regard, but something more, as well, something she couldn't interpret, and she was crazy enough to presume that it was affection. Was he growing attached, as was she?

How thrilling! How terrifying!

"You need your beauty sleep," she teased.

"I *am* more tired than I realized," he conceded, "and I need to regain my strength so I have the stamina to flirt with you tomorrow."

"Bounder."

"Always."

He kissed her, a sweet brush of his lips to hers, then she balanced him against the pillows, hoisting his legs onto the mattress. She perched on the edge, studying him.

An intimacy had been forged between them, and there would never be a better opportunity to broach the delicate topic of his impotency. She wanted to hash it out, to delve into the dilemma, so that she could ruminate over a remedy.

"I must ask you a question."

"Go ahead."

"Don't be angry."

He scoffed. "As if I could be *angry* with you."

"It's personal."

"As I'm lying here, buff bare, I don't believe it could become more so."

How to phrase it? She had limited terminology, and she blushed. "I've noticed that . . . that you're . . ."

"I'm what?"

Her fingers slithered down, to his navel, to his tummy, and she wrapped them around his phallus. He displayed no reaction, not so much as a twitch.

"Can you feel me?"

For an eternity, he glared at her, and he was so tense that she worried he might snap in half. He shimmered with fury, and it was his turn to blush.

"Yes."

"But nothing happens?"

"No."

With blatant curiosity, she scooted down, inspecting and caressing the pliant appendage. She hadn't seen one since the days Phillip had been a boy, before he'd gotten too old and too modest to have his sister helping him wash. Though Stephen's was much bigger than Phillip's had been, she couldn't envision it being rigid enough to penetrate a woman.

She explored, cradling the two dangling sacs, while she persisted with stroking his droopy member. It wasn't so much a stroking, as an examination of the yielding skin, the more firm crown. Her attention was focused on his lap, so she was surprised when he pushed her away.

"Stop it!" he commanded.

"Stop what?"

"You're touching me as if you're some kind of coquette. As if you can make it hard. You can't."

"I didn't mean to upset you."

His rage was scarcely controlled, his shame disturbing to witness, but at least the forbidden subject was out in the open. They could talk about the situation and decide what to do—if anything.

"Is this another of your injuries?"

"Would you shut up?"

"It isn't an impairment from before the war, is it? I assume you could develop an erection prior, and I need to find out if—"

"I will not discuss this with you!"

He stared out the window, not meeting her gaze, and she leaned nearer so that he couldn't avoid her. "Look at me."

"No."

"I understand this is difficult for you."

"No, you don't. You couldn't."

"Is this why you haven't wanted to improve?"

Incensed, he scowled at her. "How did you know that?"

"I told you before: I'm aware of things about you that I

oughn't be." She rested her palm on his cheek. "Your functioning may come back."

"Like hell it will."

"It might. As the remainder of your body heals, this might, too."

"Have mercy! Please be silent!"

"And if it doesn't, you can have a full life."

"Spoken like an idiotic female who has no bloody idea what she's saying."

"It's true. You will—"

"I can never marry!" he shouted. "I can never have a family. I can't pledge myself to a woman. What type of existence is that?"

"Maybe there's someone out there who would figure having *you* was enough, that she could forgo children, if she had you. Many would consider it a fair exchange."

"Name a single person."

"Me," she asserted, and she kissed him on the mouth. "You're worth having, my dear Captain Chamberlin. You're worth fighting for."

"You're mad."

"I want to attempt a physic that I've been—"

"No! None of your broths, or your alchemist concoctions. I forbid it."

"You can't *forbid* me. It's my own damned house!"

Clutching her wrists, he squeezed harshly enough to leave bruises, and he gave her a firm shake. "What will it take for you to listen? You'll raise my hopes so high, but when you can't deliver, I'll be crushed. If you prepare me for a miracle, and then, you can't bring one about, I won't be able to bear it."

He shoved her away, and she frowned at him with a significant amount of consternation. "I've never claimed to work miracles."

"You certainly pretend quite well."

"I just want to rub some lotion on you. We won't declare that it has a defined restorative purpose. I simply think it will feel good."

"What sort of *lotion*?"

"It's a balm I devised for Widow Brown. Her joints used to swell, and she'd be in such agony. I made a salve, out of ground mint and other herbs. It relieves many aches and pains, and I want to massage you with it every night."

He gulped, flaming a brighter red. "On my . . . my privates?"

"Yes."

"Do you . . . you . . ." He had to swallow twice before he could continue. "Do you believe it could help?"

"It's soothing. That's all I contend." The yearning in his voice was distressing, so she flashed a wicked smile. "If you're searching for a magic solution, you should concentrate on my hot springs."

"Why?"

"My clients insist that the water has erotic tendencies."

"Utter nonsense!"

"I swear it! They maintain that a quick swim has them racing home to their husbands, and demanding the men exercise their marital rights."

"You're joking."

"I've always ignored their gibberish, but after my antics outside, I'm not so sure I doubt them anymore." She placed her hand over his heart. "Let me."

For a long while, he assessed her, his anger having faded into resignation. He shrugged. "What the hell? How can I refuse? I may be impotent, but I'm not dead."

"I'll go fetch the ointment."

She rushed to her room, and shed her damp clothes, opting for a robe and nothing else. A week prior, she wouldn't have dared such brazenness, but Stephen Chamberlin had bewitched her, had effortlessly goaded her to conduct she'd never have risked before she'd met him.

On her way down, she detoured to the pantry and retrieved her arthritic cream. When she returned, he appeared calm, but there was an intensity about him that was scrupulously banked. She seated herself on the bed, and dissolute fellow that he was, he loosed the belt on her robe, and tugged at the lapels, so that her center was revealed to her navel.

He dipped into the jar and held a glob to his nose. "It smells delicious. Is it edible?"

"I don't see why not."

He dabbed it on his tongue. "Not bad."

"Roll over."

"I thought you were going to rub it onto my genitals."

"Your back, too."

Probing for an ulterior motive, he scrutinized her, then he rotated as she'd requested. She crawled on top of him, her thighs spread, her loins over his buttocks. The positioning was decadent, scandalous, but she didn't care. Jolted by the impropriety, she lowered herself, but she declined to reflect on what was transpiring.

Cupping the liniment, she smoothed it across his scarred, healing torso.

"This will tingle."

"It already is."

"Just relax."

Commencing at his shoulders, she dug into his muscles, circling down and down to his waist, and she scooted off, her crotch on his thighs, so that she could knead his buttocks. Clasping and molding the curved mounds was so naughty, and so thrilling, that she could barely breathe.

Throughout her life, she'd dispensed many massages, but they had been performed on seriously ill or dying females, so she hadn't grasped that manipulating him would be so different, that the mere act of touching him would titillate and arouse beyond measure. The caressing had her aching to do so much more, to accomplish feats she couldn't describe.

She wanted him to render the same pleasure he'd managed in the dark, swirling water. Could it happen a second time? And so soon? Disgracefully, she prayed that it was something he could effect with regular frequency.

She patted his rear. "Roll again. Onto your back."

Coming up on an elbow, he glared at her. Her legs were open, her thighs splayed, her hair unrestrained, and he shimmered with male admiration.

"You're fortunate that I'm incapacitated."

"Why?"

"Because if I was able, I would ride you as a stallion rides a mare."

On her recognizing the sexual comment for what it was, the world fell out from under her. The indecent remark sucked her further into an eddy of lewd craving and confusion.

He spun over, and she focused on her ointment, scooping some out of the jar and applying it to his flaccid cock. She wasn't certain where or how to utilize it, and she was dabbing it around the base of the shaft, when he stopped her.

"Do it as if you're fucking me with your hand."

She had no idea what he meant, and as he deemed her to be a widow, she couldn't ask, so she was relieved when he folded his fingers around hers and began pumping up and down, showing her what to do.

"My balls," he ordered. "Put some on my balls."

As she slathered it across the two sacs, he jumped. "Easy, girl. I can feel what you're doing, even if I can't grow an erection."

So . . . the sacs were more delicate than the phallus? From the way he'd lurched, she guessed they were, so she fondled them gently, as if they were a pair of precious eggs, and he reposed onto the pillows.

Deciding she was finished, she queried, "How is the cream?"

"Warm."

"We'll use it every evening."

"Do you promise?"

"Lecher."

"Absolutely."

The jar was balanced on the mattress, and he daubed the lotion across his chest, his slender, devious finger going round and round in seductive circles.

"Suck my nipple," he commanded, drawing her to him.

Though he guided her down, she went without resisting, wrapping her lips around the tiny nub. Were a man's breasts as sensitive as a woman's? What did the action feel like, when it garnered no accompanying response down below?

"Harder," he coaxed, and she increased the pressure, using teeth and tongue to add stimulation.

He urged her to the other nipple, and as she played, he directed her hand to his cock, swathing it around the shaft, spurring her to restart the stroking motion.

Finally, he pulled her away, and he untied her robe, tugged it off, and pitched it onto the floor. They were lying together, blissfully naked, and he reached for the salve but, surprising her, he smeared it on *her* nipples instead of his own. The heat sank in and inflamed them so that they throbbed with each beat of her heart.

He spread the minty balm over her tongue, then into her sheath, the warmth flowing up to her womb. She was afire, inside and out, a burning whirl of agitation and excitement.

Dragging her down so that she was over him, he suckled her, an exploit that was even more tantalizing with the hot unguent inciting her private parts. The lotion stirred her until she was a writhing ball of ecstasy and agony. She hurled into the conflagration, spiraling with an ardor that was much more electrifying, and much more potent, than it had been in the pool.

As she drifted down, he was holding her, and he kissed her sweetly, tenderly. She was astonished by how readily she'd succumbed, by how freely he accepted her conduct as appropriate and normal. Did all adults comport themselves with such abandon? Was she the only one who hadn't been apprised that they did?

"What a gem you are," he murmured.

The dear utterance was poignant, profound, and she couldn't reply. Was he implying that he'd enjoyed her licentious display? That she was skilled at it?

She wanted to laugh. Up until he'd been plopped into her life, she'd never suffered an erotic moment, so how could she be adept at carnal activity? Such lustfulness couldn't be part of her inherent nature. Could it?

"You rest now," she said, and he studied her as if he yearned to say something, and she was so terrified that he would.

Her wishes were jumbled, her desires chaotic, and she couldn't bear it if he expounded on a burgeoning fondness. What did she want? What did he? At that instant, she was too befuddled to know, or to discuss it rationally.

He saved her by shifting them so that she was spooned to him, his front at her back, and lazily, he draped an arm across her waist.

"Stay with me," he pleaded, once more.

"For as long as I am able," she relented.

He hugged her and, after a lengthy quiet, inquired, "What was your husband's name?"

"My husband?" She caught herself and lied. "John."

"Did you love him?"

"Yes," she fibbed again.

"How lucky he was."

She was too nervous to augment the fabrication, and he was content to let the matter drop, and she listened as his respiration evened out, as he fell into a deep slumber. It was the sole occasion she'd ever lain with a man, and she struggled to catalog every detail so she'd never forget, but her thoughts were in such disarray that she couldn't relax.

Sneaking out of the bed, she donned her robe and went outside, hoping the fresh air would soothe her body and clear her mind.

The grotto beckoned, and she wandered to it, dipped her toes, and without thinking, she stripped and waded in. Floating, she let the current convey her to the end, then she swam to the other, repeating the journey.

Jittery, feverish, discomfited, she couldn't decide what to do with herself. Stephen had unlocked a Pandora's box of want and need. The Anne Paxton she'd always been had disappeared, and a wild, reckless female had taken her place.

Baffled and confounded, she pined for so many things she couldn't identify. In a torrent of misery, a muddle of uncertainty, she exited, drying herself but not bothering to put on her robe. Naked, alone, she walked to the house.

Willie McGee lurked in the bushes beside Anne's pool. She was undressed, her nipples poking out into the darkness, taunting him with the forbidden.

He was fascinated by her. By night, she frolicked in the pond, as comfortable with her nudity as any harlot would be. But by day, she passed herself off as a chaste, virtuous lady, and the dichotomy drove him mad. Was she whore or matron?

With scant effort, he could leap out, push her against the rocks, and have his way with her. He'd seize her from behind, perhaps even sodomize her, and throughout the episode, he'd whisper his name over and over so that she would realize it was he, that he was in control and could do whatever he liked.

He would gag her so that she couldn't cry out and alert her Amazonian assistant, Kate. Kate had abnormal manly tendencies, and he conjectured about the two of them, about whether Anne didn't cater to a more aberrant behavior, the type Kate would relish.

Though both women claimed to be widows, Willie had his doubts. He liked to picture them romping together in the water, kissing and caressing each other. He imagined himself vaulting out of his hiding spot, arresting them for their illicit transgressions, and incarcerating them in the gaol he'd built in a pasture on his farm. He'd shackle Anne to the wall, would use every technique at his disposal to coerce a confession of her most deviant misdeeds.

Ages ago, and by accident, he'd stumbled upon her nocturnal indecency. His property was a short distance from hers, and on an evening when he'd been tense and edgy, he'd gone out for a stroll and found himself in her yard. She'd been finished with her swim and brushing out her wet hair. Moisture had glistened on her skin, and she'd looked slippery, exotic, like a siren risen up from the sea.

At the time, he'd considered joining her, but he'd hesitated, and for his reticence, he'd been rewarded with regular prurient exhibitions. Whenever he was home, and had no felons to tend, he crept through the woods to seat himself in her shrubbery.

She had no clue that he watched her from the shadows, and he liked that she wasn't aware. The furtive peeping left him excited, agog.

His hunger for her had developed into vicious realities, with his frequently acting out his fantasies against the female prisoners he detained. Feeding his insatiable, incorrigible passion for rape, he forced them to assume the role Anne Smythe would ultimately perform.

He liked to hurt women, to have them beg and plead for mercy. Their terror made him feel strong, invincible. He had a knack for dishing out punishment, and he thrived on bringing to heel those who were weaker than himself.

His malicious methods had been learned from witnessing how his powerful father had dominated his foolish mother. She'd feared and obeyed the imposing tyrant, and Willie wanted others to show him the same deference. His mewling sister, Prudence, comprehended who was her lord and master, but Anne had never viewed him as capable and impressive, and the fact that she wasn't fawning or adulatory, that she refused to be subservient, had him furious.

With sincere intent, he'd tried to befriend her, to court her, to bind her to him in a proper fashion, but she couldn't be ordered about as his sister was. She never heeded his advice or followed his counsel.

He'd offered to marry her, an honor she'd tossed in his face, and he wasn't about to graciously suffer such an outrageous slight. By fair means or foul, he *would* become her husband, and he had great plans for her. And her land.

After their wedding, he would own her mysterious hot springs that were reputed to have aphrodisiatic effects. Only a chap with his stellar business acumen could perceive of the most beneficial ways to utilize the facility. The spa would make him very, very rich, would provide him with decades of obscene, licentious, degrading entertainment.

When he finally took the extreme step of ravishing her, it would be carefully plotted so that she would have no chance of escape or rescue, and no opportunity to evade his scheme. She would be his, and so would her farm.

She stood and strutted to the house, and with a manic gleam in his eye, he observed her retreating figure. Her delicious ass swayed, the muscles in her legs rippled, and he envisioned himself rushing up behind her, tackling her onto the grass and defiling her.

The notion was so tantalizing that he had to grip a nearby branch to prevent himself from doing something stupid.

Patience, he exhorted. *All in good time.*

He tarried, wondering if she would light a candle in her bedchamber, so that he might steal further glimpses of her, but she didn't.

Provoked, titillated, ecstatic over her looming subjugation, he slinked away.

8

Charles Hughes crept into the elegant salon at Bristol Manor. The earl, Robert Chamberlin, Lord Bristol, stood next to the hearth, by his very presence taking charge of the room. Luckily, it was just the earl. The other two Chamberlin brothers, Michael and James, were in London, which evened the odds. When the Chamberlin men ganged together, they were an indomitable wall of resolve, so it was much easier to breach their defenses individually.

Still handsome at age fifty-five, the earl had comfortably donned the mantle of wealth and power that birth had bestowed. He wielded his authority for maximum effect, certain none could decline to obey his dictates, and about the estate, it was oft remarked that going against him was like sailing into a hurricane. He made others tremble in their boots—or their slippers, as was the current case.

Eleanor confronted him, appearing tiny and fragile, which was an illusion. She was a tough nut, imposing in her own right, and Charles couldn't understand why she let her father intimidate her. Perhaps, it was habit, ingrained after many decades of bending to the earl's will.

Well, Eleanor might be cowed, but Charles wasn't. He'd

spent his life in army camps, with members of the aristocracy as his superior officers, and with the exception of Stephen, he'd rarely met a nobleman who'd been worth the respect they thought was their absolute due.

As far as he was concerned, Robert Chamberlin was a pompous blowhard, and Charles wasn't about to have him chastising Eleanor. Not when Charles could deflect any anger toward himself. He didn't imagine she would welcome his assistance, but he would give it anyway.

After their escapade at the inn, they hadn't spoken, and he'd avoided her like the plague. Any encounter would have been awkward, and he'd been terrified that she'd want—in an irritating feminine fashion—to dissect what had happened between them.

For an eternity, he'd secretly lusted after her, though he'd never have dishonored her by letting her discover his attraction. He was the orphaned, penniless, maimed son of a soldier, and she was so beyond his reach, that it was ludicrous to hope he might have a chance at her, so he'd been royally shocked to have been invited into her bed, and even more amazed to have dallied with her.

As he'd suspected, she was hot-blooded. His confirmation of her sexual nature had left him so titillated that he'd yearned to ravage her like a wild animal, but he'd managed to restrain his basest impulses and had fled before he'd humiliated both of them.

Since then, he'd remained hidden, a weakling who'd finagled his schedule so as to never be in any spot where he would stumble upon her. While he might have once been a valiant warrior, a brave and fearless leader, with Eleanor Chamberlin Dunworthy he was a coward.

"Where is Stephen?" the earl was barking. "I've asked you the question in ten different ways, and I don't have a straight answer."

"That's because I don't know," she claimed.

"You're lying; I can tell." Lord Bristol had been off the property when they'd kidnapped Stephen, and he'd returned to find that his disabled, critically injured son had vanished. He was furious. "I have it on good authority that you absconded with him. A veritable platoon of servants saw you. Now, where is he?"

"If I don't confess, what will you do? Paddle me?"

"Don't think you've gotten too big for a spanking."

Would he really do such a thing? Gad, she was thirty-five—three years older than himself—and a widow, who'd been married for over a decade. Did the earl regard her as a child? Would he treat her like one?

Charles didn't believe her father would resort to physical punishment, but he couldn't risk it. He stepped forward.

"If I might interrupt—"

At the sound of his voice, she whipped around, incensed and dismayed. "No you may not, Charles. Begone!"

"Of course, Charles." Lord Bristol greeted him as though Eleanor hadn't spoken. "Come in, come in."

She bristled at the slight, and Charles was baffled by how her family never noticed the fire bubbling inside her. He'd observed it the first time they'd talked, and he constantly wished he could figure out how to ignite her fuse. Just so long as she blazed in his direction!

"I heard you were wondering as to Stephen's whereabouts."

"How are you involved in this fiasco?"

"Actually, sir, Stephen was frustrated with his recovery, and he requested that I aid him in traveling to a facility about which he'd read."

"A facility?"

"Yes."

The earl waited and waited, intending that Charles supply the name and location, but Charles was silent, and Lord Bristol fumed, aware that he could order Charles to disclose the information, but Charles would refuse, embarrassing all of them. He wasn't a retainer, so he couldn't be fired for insubordination, and he couldn't be commanded to stop being Stephen's friend. He could be compelled to vacate the premises, which he'd do in a trice if such a demand was made, but then the earl would have to explain to Stephen why his mutilated companion had been sent away.

Bristol sputtered, striving to discern how to proceed. He was incredulous, confounded by Charles's admission, as well as his behavior, and he inquired, "Stephen wasn't happy here?"

"He felt he would have a better prospect for recuperation with a new group of doctors. I handled all of the details. Lady Eleanor had naught to do with it."

Eleanor shimmered with ire, enraged that he would interfere, that he would assume the blame and steal her thunder, when he'd been opposed to the plan from the very beginning.

She opened her mouth to protest, when the earl queried, "So it was your doing?"

"At Stephen's behest."

"Well, then . . ." As his excuse for anger had been quashed, the earl's temper fizzled. "You know where he is?"

"Yes, sir."

"It's a reputable establishment?"

"Of the highest quality." Charles had no idea if his appraisal was accurate. Mrs. Smythe's farm had looked tidy and well run, but he hadn't interviewed her, and he didn't trust Eleanor's assessment. She was too distraught by Stephen's condition to be impartial.

"Are you in contact with him?"

"Yes."

"You'll keep me posted."

"Certainly."

Charles accepted the remark as his cue to leave, and he slipped out, not eager to loiter when Eleanor was in a snit.

Hustling to the dining hall, he gobbled the last bites of a supper he'd abandoned when he'd been notified that Lord Bristol was about to upbraid Eleanor in the library.

He went outside, enjoying the fresh air and the gloaming, and he wandered through the stables, checking that the horses were settled, before returning to the manor and his room on the third floor. Due to his vague position in the household, he couldn't reside in the attic with the servants. Stephen had insisted he be furnished a grand suite on the second floor, but he wouldn't have slept a wink in that bloody king's bed up on its pedestal.

After one peek at the ornate apartment, he'd opted for less, and it had been a good choice. Functional and modest, it was the sort of chamber that would have been provided to an undistinguished guest, and it was situated at the end of a deserted corridor. No maids walked by, no visitors bumped into him, and he was next to the rear stairs so he could come and go without being detected.

He undressed, which was an arduous task with only one arm. Stephen had offered him a valet, but he couldn't have tolerated some queer bloke yanking his trousers on and off, so he'd declined. He washed, another difficult endeavor, then he crawled between the clean sheets. As he'd been born on a battlefield, and had grown up following the drum, he never took for granted such amenities as a soft mattress. Smiling, he gazed out the window. Dusk had faded, the stars were twinkling.

A board creaked in the hall, alerting him that someone was approaching, and he tensed, listening, and determining that it was a female. Was it a housemaid? Sneaking down for a tryst? Several had hinted at an interest, but he'd kept his distance, not wanting to curry displeasure with his host, should Lord Bristol learn that he'd been trifling with the employees.

His caller halted outside his door, and his curiosity spiraled. She hesitated, and he watched, intrigued as to whether she'd enter. Ultimately, she found the courage to spin the knob, and as she did, he was hard as stone. It had been ages since he'd copulated, and he wouldn't be adverse to a tumble. As she prowled in, he scooted up so that he was resting against the headboard, and he blinked and blinked.

Eleanor! What the devil!

What did she want? To fight? To philander? He wouldn't argue with her, and he wouldn't fornicate. He had his pride after all, and if he so much as touched her, she'd grasp how smitten he was, and he wasn't about to reveal his enamoration.

She was attired in her nightclothes, a slinky, shiny negligee and robe outlining her curvaceous form. Her blond hair was down and brushed out. Sexy, bewitching, desire incarnate, she tempted him to all manner of debauchery.

"Get the hell out of here," he hissed. "Before you're caught."

"No."

"Are you mad?"

"Very likely."

Carrying a candle, she set it on the dresser and advanced on him. She was in a fine state, still seething after their appointment with her father, and he was reminded of the myriad of reasons he'd lived his life surrounded by men.

He sighed. "Lighten your load, darlin', but make it quick. I'll not have your ruination on my conscience."

"Lighten *what* load?"

"Whatever lambaste you're about to level. Let me have it."

"How dare you treat me like a . . . a . . . child!"

"I've never—"

"Did I ask for your help?" She was shouting, though in a whisper. "Did I? Am I such a namby-pamby that I can't

confer with my own father without you sticking your male
nose into my affairs? What do you suppose? That I'm ten
years old and I can't possibly survive without your control-
ling every breath I take?"

She was a far cry from ten. With no corset to conceal her
shape, he could see her breasts, the erect nipples jutting at
the thin fabric. He'd viewed them before, had fondled and
suckled, and he'd acted as chivalrous as he was able, but he
couldn't force himself to be so noble a second time.

Reaching out, he clutched her wrist, the gesture stem-
ming her tirade.

"Let me go!"

"No."

She struggled, but he wouldn't release her, so she lashed
out with her free hand and slapped him across the face. He
wasn't as nimble as he'd been previously, and he couldn't
prevent the blow. The whack reverberated in the quiet space,
freezing them both.

Horror-stricken, she pressed her fingers to her lips, appearing as if she might be ill. "Oh, God . . . oh, God . . . I'm
sorry. I'm so sorry."

"I'm not a gentleman. If you hit me again, I'll hit you
back."

Pulling with all his might, he flipped her onto the bed. He
had lost much of his maneuverability, but his legs were as
strong as ever, and he kicked out from the blankets, rolled
her, and locked her in place beneath him. She pushed and
encountered bare skin, and her eyes widened with shock.
She hadn't realized that he was nude, and suddenly, she was
being pinned down by a very naked, very irate, very provoked male.

He wasn't positive what he intended to do with her—
scold her? paddle her? make love to her?—and he studied
her, wishing he could utter something profound, but she

curbed any comment he might have made when she swallowed, shuddered, and started to cry.

He couldn't bear to witness her distress! Couldn't stand that he might have caused her any anguish.

"What's this?" he soothed, and he dipped down and kissed her, lingering, tasting the salt of her tears. She was too dejected to explain her upset, and he nestled her to his chest until she'd calmed. Her body went limp, as though she'd deflated with the effort of sobbing.

Brimming with hurt, she chided, "Why don't you ever talk to me anymore?"

"What do you mean? Of course, I *talk* to you. Whenever I can." A lie, which they both knew. After using her so badly at the inn, he'd been too chagrined to interact.

She peered at him, and her mottled cheeks broke his heart. "No, you don't. Since that night when we . . . when you . . ." Too shamed to refer to the ignominious event, the tears flowed again, and she buried herself at his nape, so she could hide her mortification.

"I'm not loose," she contended, "if that's what you've been thinking."

"I never imagined you were."

"That was the first time . . . the only time . . ."

Was that what this was about? Was she hurting over the aftermath of their aborted assignation? He'd flayed himself, rationalizing his conduct to the point of absurdity, but he hadn't paused to wonder how she'd weathered the ordeal. Obviously, not well.

What had she expected? He couldn't begin to guess. She couldn't have anticipated that they'd developed an affinity, or that they'd established a relationship that could be disclosed.

It had been a moment of temporary insanity, a wild, incautious romp that neither of them had foreseen or sought. It had just *happened*. She was a widow. Surely, she understood that insignificant dalliances occurred with alarming regularity.

Had she hoped for it to be something more?

He wouldn't presume that she might have. The concept was preposterous, but thrilling, too, and his pathetic spirit enlivened merely from his pondering it.

"Don't humor me, as if I was a baby, Charles." She nibbled at his neck, the sensation hurling a lightning bolt to his groin. "All my life, those around me have been convinced that I can't care for myself. I'm so weary of being coddled, and I can't abide it from you."

Was she implying that she had a fondness for him? That she had tender feelings? To what end?

He let her words sink in, but couldn't reply, for he didn't know what to say. Should he tell her she was being foolish? That she was stupid to fancy him? Should he send her away? Warn her never to return?

He couldn't. He wasn't that honorable. Forlorn, isolated, he was alone in the world, and there was such enchantment in holding her. If she was willing to venture all, to be with him despite the consequences, then he wasn't about to discard the gift she was anxious to bestow.

"I wasn't being condescending," he said. "I simply can't tolerate your father berating you. Why do you let him?"

"It's his way."

"I won't allow him to speak down to you ever again. I swear it."

He sealed his vow with a stormy kiss, and he couldn't keep a moan of delight from escaping. Initially, she was reticent, timid about her participation, but she rapidly shed her reserve, her busy fingers tracing his shoulders, his back, though she couldn't muster the courage to go any lower. She was both bold and cautious, her gestures tentative, as if she'd never frolicked before, and a niggling suspicion dawned.

Yes, she was a widow, but what kind of experience had

she truly had? He'd heard gossip about the lout to whom she'd been married. The physical side of their union must have been less than satisfying, and the prospect intrigued him. Was she a budding flower, ready to bloom?

He clasped her hand, and guided it to his cock. It had been so long since a woman had touched him there that he nearly spilled himself like a callow boy of fourteen. Staring at the wall, he let visions of Spain fill his mind, concentrating on anything but her, until the fierce urgency passed.

As he'd surmised, she had no idea what to do with his aroused member, and he had to show her how to stroke him, but she was an avid pupil, and swiftly, he was at the edge.

"I have to be inside you. Now," he told her. "I'm too eager. I can't wait."

Rotating to his back, he situated her on her haunches so that she was hovered over him and straddling his lap, her knees cradling his thighs.

"Remove your robe."

She glared at him, then acquiesced, the silky material slithering off, so that she was clad solely in her skimpy negligee. The two tiny straps barely contained her full breasts, and he plucked at her nipple, pinching it, making her squirm.

"This, too." He indicated her nightgown. He wasn't about to fornicate with her when she was clothed. If he was going to hell, he would enjoy the trip. "Take it off."

She blushed. "I can't."

"I want to look at you."

"No . . ."

"We're not in your husband's bed," he crudely broached. "I won't have any barriers between us."

The mention of her spouse embarrassed her, and she glanced away. "It's too awkward for me."

"Have you never been naked with a man before?"

She shook her head, incapable of admitting it aloud.

What a strange marriage she must have had! Only an oaf would have declined to feast on her lovely flesh. "I'm bewitched by your beauty. I always have been."

She was stunned. "You have?"

"Do it for me, Eleanor." He nodded at her negligee, wanting it gone, but she didn't budge. "I'd undress you myself, but it's difficult with my arm as it is."

After the sawbones had amputated his hand, his amorous pursuits had been altered. It was strenuous to stabilize himself, then to massage or caress. For them to achieve any pleasure, she would have to assist, but considering her limited carnal tutelage, perhaps it was for the best. She'd have to be more aggressive, would have to take the lead, which would increase her confidence.

"I don't have the slightest notion how to begin."

"Slip off a strap. Let it drop down." She did. "Now the other."

He tugged the fabric away from her bosom, her breasts swinging free. The garment was pooled around her waist, and she wiggled out of it.

Nervous, bashful, she withstood his brazen scrutiny. She was perfectly formed, wide at the shoulders, small at the waist, wide at the hips, her sweet puss covered with a dusting of blond hair.

"Do I please you?" she demurely asked.

Didn't she recognize how ravishing she was? What sort of cruel buffoon had her husband been?

"Oh, aye." He let his Scottish accent flow over her. "I'm verra pleased."

He tipped her so that her chest was melded to his own. The contact was electrifying, shooting through him, making him pine and hunger as he never had.

Though clumsy, he fondled her between her legs. He toyed until she started to respond, until she was straining and writhing, then he took his cock and centered himself.

"Ease yourself down." She was confused, not comprehending what was required. "Ride me," he instructed. "Like this."

Entering her, he prodded in, giving her more and more, until he was impaled to her womb. She was tight as a virgin, but regardless of any discomfort, she was enthusiastic to attempt whatever he demanded, and as he flexed, she assumed the rhythm. Her modesty vanished, and she rode him hard, fast, relishing the naughty position.

In his titillated state, the stimulation was too much, and his desire spiraled out of control. He'd meant to extend the conclusion, but he was beyond delay, and he gripped her thigh, halting her.

"What?" she snapped, irritated by the interruption.

"I need to come."

"You stopped to tell me that?"

Flushing bright red, he was shamed by his infirmity. His inability to love her as she deserved had him feeling half a man. "I don't have the leverage to lift you off me."

She frowned, not understanding, then his intent dawned. "You don't want to finish inside me?"

"We daren't risk making a babe."

"It's of no import," she flippantly replied.

A child was of no *import*? "It is to me."

"Don't worry about it. Keep going!"

She tried to continue, but he wouldn't cooperate. He couldn't remember when he'd last emptied himself inside a woman's sheath, and he wasn't about to break his habit for her. With the whores in the soldiers' camps, he'd purchased French kisses, to avoid the pox, but also to quash any possibility that he might unwittingly sire a babe, the result being that he'd leave it to rot in some brothel.

He was behaving badly enough without impregnating her, and he'd never degrade her by requesting an oral gratification.

"Promise me you'll move away," he decreed through clenched teeth, "or we're done right now."

She leaned over and tapped him on the chin. "I can't have a child."

"Why would you think that?"

"I'm barren."

"Who told you such a thing?"

"For pity's sake, Charles, I was married for thirteen years."

"So? How can you be sure it wasn't your husband?"

"Everyone knows it's the wife's fault."

"Not me."

It was rumored that her spouse had philandered with any female who'd raise her skirt, and even with some who wouldn't, but he'd never heard that the cad had left any bastard children behind, though he didn't suppose there was any way on God's green earth he could point out such a coarse fact.

He settled for a more crucial question. "What if you're wrong and you wind up expecting?"

"I won't." She laughed, but without humor. "Trust me."

Like a skilled courtesan, she pushed backward, pressing down with her hips, having discovered how she could control the whorl to fulfillment. Her mons was flattened to his belly, and she manipulated herself into a frenzy. In a matter of seconds, an orgasm flooded over her.

With her soaring through the universe, he couldn't desist. He pumped into her, once, twice, thrice, and he joined her in a fiery wave that never seemed to end. He hadn't planned to commit such a reckless act, but he hadn't been able to restrain himself, and with her weight squashing him down, he couldn't prevent what was transpiring. At the moment, he didn't care.

There was danger and excitement in spilling himself. A primal urge drove him, and he wanted to mark her as his

own. Madly, he hoped that he'd planted his seed so deep that
she *did* become pregnant. He yearned to bind her to him, to
have them forever attached. If there was a child, there would
have to be a resolution, an outcome besides a brief, torrid,
secret affair.

At his surge, a haunting groan escaped from her, and he
grabbed her and kissed her, silencing the sound. Though his
room was in a vacant corridor, he couldn't chance that someone might stroll by.

The embrace went on and on, throughout the ascent to ecstasy and down, and as her climax waned, she slumped onto
him, her delicious torso melting with satisfaction. They were
tangled together from head to toe, and though he'd just copulated to high heaven, his cock was impaled, prepared for
another go-round.

He reveled in the quiet, in the opportunity to cuddle. For
him as a soldier, sex had been a simple commodity to pro-
cure, but the encounters had been speedy, rough-and-tumble,
pennies paid for services rendered. He'd forgotten about
this . . . this companionship, where the aftermath was the
most precious part.

Studying the ceiling, he decided that he hadn't really
lived until this instant. His heart seemed to swell until it
didn't fit between his ribs, and he felt content, complete as
he'd never been.

Was this love?

He exhaled a heavy breath. What should he do? He
wasn't foolish enough to envision a future with her, nor
could he imagine skulking around in her father's house, fornicating in the wee hours, while praying they wouldn't be
caught. Yet, if she crawled into his bed, he wasn't such an idiot that he'd refuse her.

His mind whirred with the prospects for tragedy, the likelihood of disaster, but he couldn't be sorry for what they'd
done. For so long, he'd watched her from afar, had dreamed

and fantasized. His reveries were now a reality, and he wasn't about to ignore such a stroke of luck.

What if this was the only rendezvous they ever managed to seize for themselves? If it was, he wasn't about to miss out on any aspect of the adventure.

He rolled them, not pulling out of her, so that she was on the bottom, and he could gaze into her exquisite face. The rigidity of his phallus hadn't diminished, and awkwardly, he balanced himself on his arm and commenced anew.

She rippled with surprise. "You can do it again? So soon?"

"I can do it all night, if you can keep up with me."

"You're joking."

"Not about this." He thrust more vigorously. "Never about how much I want you."

"Show me."

"I will."

She smiled at him, her affection shining through and washing over him. Did she feel the same sense of connection as he? What did it portend? Where could it lead?

"It's different, isn't it?" she queried.

He realized that she meant it was distinct from what either of them had ever experienced prior. "I always knew it would be."

"I'm so glad."

"So am I." Suddenly shy, he queried, "How long can you stay?"

"Till dawn."

He was relieved that she wouldn't immediately sneak out, for he couldn't have let her go. Holding her close, he increased the tempo.

~ 9 ~

"Your sister has come to visit you," Anne bit out. "She's brought along your fiancée."

"Felicity is with her?" Stephen couldn't believe it.

"How sweet that you remember her name."

"Dammit," he cursed, flopping onto the pillow.

"My feelings exactly." Spinning on her heel, she left.

"Anne!" She continued on, which infuriated him, so he shouted, "Anne, get back here!"

The curt command had the desired effect. She whirled and stomped into the room, slamming the door behind.

"Be silent!" she scolded. "I have customers taking the waters."

"I don't care."

"I won't have you upsetting them."

"Don't you dare walk out on me!"

"Don't you dare order me about!"

"Let me explain."

"I'm an intelligent woman. I'm cognizant of the definition of the term *fiancée*. I require no clarification."

"I'm not engaged," he pathetically claimed.

"You insult me with your lies."

"I'm not!"

"Shut up, Stephen." She stormed to the wardrobe, yanked it open, jerked trousers and shirt off the hooks, and cast them toward him. "They await you in the front parlor."

"I was betrothed but—"

"I don't want to hear it!"

"I couldn't be a true husband to her. You know that, so I—"

"I said: I do *not* want to hear about it!"

She rushed out, and though he bellowed to her over and over, she didn't reappear. Momentarily, he saw her at the grotto, calming the ruffled feathers of those in the pool. His petulant outburst ensured that there was no question of a man being on the premises, and they were craning their necks, trying to peer inside so as to identify who it was.

Bitter, acrimonious, he struggled to control his temper, to quell the fast pounding of his heart. For the past month, he and Anne had spent every minute together. They'd grown closer than any two people ought, yet he hadn't confided about Felicity, hadn't told Anne much of anything about his life in the outside world.

His tarriance at her farm was a precious idyll, a respite from reality, and he despised having others interrupting his bucolic reverie. He liked to pretend that he'd always been at Anne's house, that he had no obligations beyond her fence, and he was incensed that Eleanor had sought him out, though why he'd deemed she wouldn't was a mystery. Of course, she'd check on him. She'd sworn she would, but he'd discounted the possibility, shoving it out of his mind, so that he could wallow in his illusion, where he didn't have a nosy sister, or a prying family.

Heavy footsteps sounded in the hall, and he recognized them as Kate's. Without knocking, she peeked in. "Mrs. Smythe says you'll be needing my help."

He'd instructed Anne not to let Kate attend him, so he

was angry at both of them. As he was attired solely in a pair of Phillip's old drawers, the scars on his chest and arms were visible, and he hated having Kate observe them.

"I'm not up to greeting any guests. You may tell them to go."

"Tell them yourself, your *lordship*. I'll leave you the wheeled chair."

She, too, marched off, grumbling about his being an ingrate. Was there no one in this asylum of females who had any respect for male authority?

Like a brat having a tantrum, he deliberated on lying in bed forever, and declining to speak to Eleanor and Felicity. Yet in light of how obstinate Anne could be, if he didn't meet with them, she wouldn't either, and they'd remain for hours, expecting him to emerge.

He wanted them gone! Wanted them ejected, then banished from the property.

In a snit, he rose and clumsily donned his clothes. He'd regained an enormous amount of energy, so he was able to complete the task himself. Earlier, Anne had shaved him, and with his hair trimmed, he didn't resemble a wild savage, but on the inside, the turbulence still raged.

He would relish having a few words with Eleanor, where he would relate what he thought of her tyrannical orchestration of his kidnapping. As to Felicity, she was the last person on earth he wanted to see. He'd explicitly apprised her that he didn't consider them to be bound, that she was shed of him, but she persisted with tromping around London, his ring on her finger. Whenever anyone inquired as to the status of their betrothal, she vehemently and publicly denied any dissolution.

In his current state, she was a fool to have called on him. How many times did he have to spell it out?

Initially, she'd captured his fancy with her chatty nature, her upbeat attitude, her unflagging enthusiasm. Plus, she was rich, with an inheritance from her grandmother. Only a moron would have failed to snatch her up, and as a third son, with a military career as his option, he'd chased her until she'd caught him.

Love had played no role in his offering for her, but he'd liked her amicable style, her blithe disposition, and he'd been eager for the wedding. But after Salamanca, after traveling home more dead than alive, he couldn't tolerate her quirky habits.

The pleasantness that had once attracted him now scraped his nerves raw. She was so young, so naive, and she was so blasted cheery. The two occasions she'd trekked to Bristol, he'd been so aggravated by her optimistic blather that he'd directed Charles to bar her from his sickroom.

A split was for the best, and he'd been positive that he'd persuaded her. Was the accursed girl deaf? Stupid?

He wasn't about to marry her! How often and how loudly did he have to assert as much?

He limped to the hall, and as Kate had promised, his invalid's chair was parked nearby. She was leaned against the wall, her arms crossed over her chest. Probably, he could have hobbled to the parlor on his own, but he wouldn't embarrass himself by seeming weak, so he sat, and she approached—without comment, praise be!—and pushed him down the lengthy corridor. She rolled him over the threshold, then vanished, forcing him to confront his guests alone.

They were dawdling by the window, staring toward the grotto, and they turned in unison, agape with astonishment.

Was he that changed? He hadn't realized it.

"Stephen, my goodness!" Eleanor exclaimed. "Is it really you?"

"What the hell are you doing here?" he snapped in response.

"Don't be surly. And curb your foul tongue! I won't stand for it in Felicity's presence."

"Did I ask her to come?"

"No, and you didn't ask me, either. But we've arrived, and I demand that you be civil."

Felicity hesitated, thrown off guard by his gruff behavior. When they'd been courting, she'd never witnessed this side of him, and his irascible constitution was an indication that the individual to whom she'd been pledged didn't exist.

"But I'm glad I braved the journey, Stephen," she chirped. She flounced over—there was no other way to describe her saunter—and she knelt beside him. "I wouldn't have missed viewing this wonderful improvement for all the gold in El Dorado! I just knew you'd get better! I just knew it!"

He gnashed his teeth. Everything about her irked. She was so annoyingly perky, a trait that had previously charmed him, but now rankled. Their ten-year age difference had seemed insignificant, too, but had enlarged to a monumental hurdle. After his experiences in Spain, he felt a thousand years older.

"Go home, Felicity," he bluntly advised. "Please!"

As if he hadn't spoken, she gushed, "With you recuperating so rapidly, we'll be making wedding plans before the summer is through. Won't we, Eleanor?" Nervous, she peered over at his sister, seeking her support.

"There will be no wedding," he interjected before Eleanor could reply with an absurd remark that would fan Felicity's flames of fantasy.

"Nonsense," Felicity chided. Gripping his hands, she squeezed tight. "I told you I'd wait, for as long as it takes. Did you suppose I didn't mean it? That I'd forsake you in your hour of need?" Her blue eyes were steady, her blond ringlets bouncing with resolve. " 'For better or worse, in sickness and in health.' That's what the vows say. I'm not so fickle that I'd cry off over a few minor injuries. Give me some credit, Stephen."

He was pondering a scathing rejoinder, when boot heels clicked in the hall, and Charles entered.

Save me, Stephen mouthed to his friend over the top of Felicity's head.

Charles grinned, his old self poking through, as if he too was much recovered. Mischief glimmering about him, he contemplated strolling out, abandoning Stephen to his fate, but they'd been through too much, and Charles couldn't desert him.

"Lady Felicity," Charles interceded, "I'm sorry to disturb you, but we must be going. One of the horses is having trouble, and we must be off to the village so the blacksmith can examine him before it grows any later."

Thank you! Stephen mouthed, once more.

You owe me, Charles retorted.

"Of course, Mr. Hughes," Felicity acceded. It was impossible for her to act any other way than sweet-tempered and affable, but after fraternizing with Anne, Stephen couldn't bear such tractability.

She stood and patted Stephen on the shoulder. "Buck up, my dear soldier. I'm thrilled to have you so hale. You've made my heart rejoice."

As she promenaded out, she left a trail of floral perfume, and they were frozen in place until the door was shut behind her.

"Don't bring her again," he informed Charles.

"As you wish."

"You are such a barbarian," Eleanor scolded. "You're lucky she's so kind. If I were her, I'd have let you rot in your misery. It would be no more than you deserve, you brute."

"Did I solicit your opinion?"

"No, but there it is. And you won't hear me apologizing for my absconding with you. Not only do I intend to commend Mrs. Smythe, but I shall bestow a hefty bonus upon her."

He'd figured that Anne was treating him for money, but he detested having her care for him as a fiduciary obligation.

Her attentions ought to be based on affection. "How much are you paying her?"

"Obviously not enough."

"How much?" he barked.

"None of your business." She strutted over and kissed him on the cheek. "I'll visit you in a fortnight, and don't even *think* about telling Charles to refuse to assist me. If he does, I'll come by myself."

She waltzed out, but not before the briefest pause next to Charles. Their eyes met and locked. Stephen couldn't observe her face, but Charles's was visible. He was gazing at her with a manly hunger that was so potent it sizzled between them.

What was this? He'd been away from home for a month. Had this been fermenting, with himself too incoherent to notice? Or was it recent? Had Charles seduced Eleanor? Or had Eleanor seduced Charles? He couldn't imagine Charles doing something so spontaneous or out of character, and Eleanor had been a widow too blasted long, so it was likely at her instigation.

If they weren't already lovers, if was merely a matter of time before lust won out. What then? Had either of them thought beyond the itch in their loins?

Eleanor broke the torrid assessment, and glared at Stephen over her shoulder. "I'll be back in two weeks," she reminded him.

"I can hardly wait." Stephen oozed sarcasm, but in reality, he would anticipate seeing her. It had been an eternity since he'd been excited about anything, and he regarded his enthusiasm as a sign of his improving condition.

"Why don't you use the interlude to find your manners?"

"If you don't like my *manners,* stay away."

"Maybe I will. I certainly can't claim to enjoy the company."

She stomped off, while he and Charles tarried.

"You look terrific," Charles mentioned. "I guess Mrs. Smythe's not the charlatan I'd been fearing."

"I'm not sure what she *is*," Stephen replied, "but she's not a quack."

"I hope you're not angry with me about your being transported here. Eleanor was bound and determined to do this, and if I'd declined to aid her, she'd have found someone else."

"I realize that. She's much too bossy."

"You won't catch me arguing the point."

"I believe she should marry again," Stephen hinted. "She could benefit from guidance by a man who's not afraid to stand up to her."

"Yes, she could."

Stephen said no more. He wouldn't be so crude as to inquire whether they were having an affair, but he'd planted a seed in Charles's head. It would never occur to Charles that he might be a suitable husband for her, and after her first debacle of a marriage, Stephen wanted her to pick someone honorable and devoted, loyal and true. She could do no better than Charles Hughes.

The comment was also a warning. If Charles was philandering with her, he ought to be planning on matrimony. Stephen wouldn't tolerate anything less. Due to Charles's common antecedents, his father and brothers would be an obstacle, but Stephen could persuade them. They'd helped her with her choice before, and it had been a disaster. What did any of them know about selecting an appropriate mate for her?

"How long will you remain here?" Charles queried, changing the awkward subject.

"Until I can walk out on my own."

Actually, he yearned to reside with Anne forever, but once he was healed, there'd be no reason to linger. Though much of the luster had dimmed, his other life beckoned.

"Should you need me, send a messenger. I can be here within a few hours."

"I won't need you."

"I'll return with Eleanor, to check in."

"If you bring Felicity, I'll have to kill you."

"Hah! Threats from a cripple."

"I won't always be incapacitated."

"God willing," Charles murmured, alight with friendship and fealty.

Stephen stared at him, so much gratitude bubbling around inside that he worried he might break down and cry like a baby.

"Be off," he commanded, wanting Charles to go before he embarrassed himself. "Give me some peace. There are enough crazed women in this house, without your ushering in more to plague me."

"So Mrs. Smythe hectors you, does she?"

"Constantly."

"I'll have to compliment her."

With a smart salute, he strutted out, and Stephen dawdled in his invalid's chair, listening to the carriage as the driver and footmen made ready. The horses pulled away, and he felt more alone than ever, which aggravated him. The entire day, he'd been more stressed than usual, and Felicity had exacerbated his irritation.

He had to converse with Anne, to explain about Felicity, but he was in no mood to clarify the relationship. Still, he was eager to be with Anne, which meant he would have to expend some of his limited energy to locate and pacify her.

Loitering in the parlor, he expected Kate to come for him, but she didn't. Anne had several maids, but he'd been adamant that they not help him, so now, when he needed them, they were conspicuously absent. Impatient, exasperated, he lumbered about and started down the hall, where he succeeded in jamming the chair into the wall, so he hobbled to his room and lay down.

Where was Anne?

Out at the grotto, numerous women frolicked in the pool. They were giggling, laughing, and splashing. One of them was in the shallow end. She was naked, her voluptuous breasts on full display. Another lounged on the rocks, revealing her dimpled, bare bottom.

Hadn't these people heard of bathing costumes? What was it about the pond that spurred them to indecency? Why did Anne let them cavort in the nude?

Normally, he'd have been delighted by the spectacle. He was only human, after all, but their prurient loafing kept him from searching for her.

He saw her approaching the swimmers, her functional gray dress drab against the colors of the abundant shrubs and trees. Ignoring him, she chatted with the group, and he became more annoyed. He was being churlish, but he couldn't quell his ill-humor. What if he'd collapsed? What if he was dying?

Limping, he went to the rear door, then out into the yard. Naked women be damned! He would have a private moment with her!

"Mrs. Smythe!" he called. "I would speak with you. Now, if you please!"

Her back was to him, and she halted, her ear cocked as if she couldn't make sense of the sound of his voice.

"Mrs. Smythe!" he repeated.

She whipped around, her horror evident, but before she could spew any outrage, a female popped up behind her.

"Stephen Chamberlin," cooed Camilla Warren, "as I live and breathe!"

He could scarcely stifle a groan. Of all the rotten luck! His prior fiancée and his prior paramour! On the same afternoon! What were the odds? What would Anne say? What would she do? Commit murder, perhaps?

"Yes, Camilla, it's me."

Many of her cohorts were with her, loose hussies of the *ton,* and they floated nearer. Like a slippery eel, one slithered onto the bank and stretched. She arched up and ran a palm across her belly and thigh.

Not to be outdone, Camilla slinked over, rested her forearms on the grass, her breasts pressed together to accentuate her glorious cleavage.

"I've been dying to stop by Bristol Manor," Camilla declared, "but I didn't think I ought."

His father and hers were enemies, and when he was younger, Stephen had begged to wed her, but both men had refused the match, and he'd ended up relieved by the decision. She'd married another, had been widowed straightaway, so he'd had plenty of subsequent opportunity to sample her charms. She was clever and beautiful, amenable to any sexual antic, but she was also cunning and vicious. Had she visited Bristol, his father would have chased her off with a stick.

"Probably not."

"Especially with that fierce Scotsman guarding you."

Charles loathed her. "He can be difficult."

"Couldn't you have told him to let me in?" She slid her tongue across her ruby lips. "For old times' sake?"

The other women tittered, and Anne flushed. "You shouldn't be up, Lord Chamberlin," she admonished. "Let's get you inside."

Camilla studied them, much more interested than she should be. "It's been rumored that you were terribly injured, darling. Is Mrs. Smythe making you all better?"

Her associates shimmered with curiosity, as Anne glanced around. Three of them were now posing on the lawn, while he pretended not to notice, and her fury was palpable.

"Ladies! You forget yourselves! Into the water! At once! Captain Chamberlin! Into the house!" Spinning him around, she gripped his elbow so hard that he winced. "Kate! Kate!" she shouted toward the barn, and Kate appeared, wiping her hands on a soiled rag. "Lady Camilla's appointment is over. See to it that she departs. Immediately!"

As though he was a recalcitrant toddler, she dragged him inside, towing him much faster than he could walk. She hauled him to his room, deposited him on the bed, slammed the door and the window, then whirled around.

"Your mistress?" she hissed. "Your mistress is out there in my pool?"

"I have no mistress."

"Oh, shut up!" She grabbed a brush off the dresser and threw it at him. "You despicable wretch!"

"Calm down."

"Are you mad?" she shrieked. "How dare you flaunt yourself in front of my guests! Do you have any idea of the damage you've wrought?"

"I wanted to talk to you."

"Well, I don't want to talk to you!" Pacing, she peeked out the window to discern if Camilla had obeyed her dictate, but she was arguing with Kate and hadn't budged. "What is it with you aristocrats? Do you suppose that you can ruin my business? I've worked all my adult life at this enterprise. How could you do this to me?"

"Do what?"

"Gossip will spread that I'm operating a lewd establishment, some sort of debauched bathing facility, where you and your female companions can romp in the nude!"

"I wasn't *romping* with them."

"This tale is so juicy. Will anyone pause to ensure that the details are correct before they're disseminated?" She shuddered. "I'm not about to end up in Willie McGee's little gaol on a public obscenity charge!"

"Who is Willie McGee?"

"My neighbor, who revels in arresting people. And the charges don't have to be true."

"I'd never let him harm you."

"How would you prevent it? You'll be off in London— where you don't have any fiancées *or* any mistresses!"

"I'll be here for a while."

"No you won't," she muttered.

They glared at each other, an expanse as vast as an ocean dividing them, and a chill crept down his spine. "What are you saying?"

"You'll have to go. Today. I can't afford such risks."

"But I don't wish to leave."

"Did you hear me asking what you desire?"

"No."

"Then be silent." She moved away. "Lady Eleanor can't be too far down the road. I'll have someone ride and fetch her."

"Anne—"

"A maid will be in to pack your things." She frowned at him, no hint of fondness apparent.

"Just like that?"

"Yes. Just like that."

"But we're . . . we're . . ."

What were they? He couldn't describe their acquaintance. Friends, certainly. Lovers, in a lopsided fashion, with himself unable to fully participate in any carnal activity.

He couldn't envision Eleanor's arrival, getting in the coach and traveling to Bristol Manor. His world seemed inextricably bound with Anne's, and he didn't feel as if he belonged anywhere else.

"We're what?" she goaded, echoing the question that was ringing through him.

"Friends," he answered, deeming it a safe response.

"So?"

So, indeed. "You mean everything to me."

"Do I? You have a funny way of showing it."

"I came outside because I missed you. Is that a crime?"

"No, you did it because you were demanding attention, and I wouldn't oblige you. You're like my father, naught but a spoiled child."

"I'm nothing like your father," he felt compelled to maintain.

"You're exactly like him. You're selfish. You're overbearing. You believe you're God's gift to mere mortals. I can't abide that type of arrogance." She opened the door. "I'll have Kate keep you posted on your departure. It may be tomorrow before we can arrange it. Make ready."

She left. Without a fare-thee-well, a hug, or even a pat on his shoulder.

Stunned, he listened as she trudged down the hall, then climbed the stairs to her room. The floor was quiet, then she went to the bed and lay down, the frame creaking with her weight.

As if he could force his thoughts through the wood, he stared at the ceiling.

Don't do this to me, Anne, he pleaded. *Don't send me away from you.*

Would she? Could she?

Bleak, exhausted, he reclined and closed his eyes, needing to regain his strength so that he had the stamina to fight her. Despite her edict, he couldn't return to Bristol.

Strangely, his sentiments where she was concerned had become entangled with his health, the two connected in a manner he daren't sever. He sensed it to the marrow of his bones. She was a part of him, a portion of the whole, and splitting from her would be akin to chopping off an arm or a leg. If they separated, he'd never recover.

He'd hurt her, had angered her, too. She labored under burdens he didn't understand, had to worry about hazards he didn't comprehend. As a nobleman's son, he was insulated from social peril, never having had to deal with the situations that harried her, so he had to be more sympathetic to her plight.

She'd called him arrogant, spoiled. Was he?

Yes, he was embarrassed to admit, but he could change. For her. For her, he could do anything.

He'd always been adept with the ladies, and he would have to use his renowned silver tongue to soothe her. There had to be a way, and he was determined to find it. He couldn't leave her. Not yet.

~ 10 ~

Anne sat at the desk by the window in her room. Night had
fallen, and she stared out at the stars.

The letter she'd penned to Lady Eleanor, requesting that
she retrieve her brother, was before her. She couldn't muster
the resolve to dispatch a messenger, so she'd procrastinated,
and the delay had ensured that delivery would be postponed
until morning.

Despite their bitter quarrel, she couldn't do anything to
hasten Stephen's departure. Yet, she couldn't have him wreak-
ing such havoc. Once he left, she would be shattered, and her
spa had to be thriving so that she could immerse herself in
her work. She would need to slave away, not allowing herself a single second in which she could rue or regret their
affair.

Having spent the day hiding and grappling with her unruly emotions, she was restless, unaccustomed to inactivity.

The pool beckoned, as did the quiet darkness. When she
swam, her adversities were never too difficult to handle, and
her worries floated away, so she stripped off her clothes,
donned a robe, and tiptoed down. Sneaking out, she ignored
the lure of Stephen's door. She couldn't face him, not when

she was so confused, so perplexed about what she wanted.

As she inhaled the refreshing air and strolled across the grass, Kate exited the barn, where she'd been toiling at one of her mechanical projects. Anne had skipped supper, claiming she had the woman's headache, but Kate had been dubious as to her suffering any ailment.

"Are you feeling better?" Kate queried as she approached.

"I was never under the weather."

"I didn't think so."

"How is our illustrious guest?"

"Fed. Bedded down, but surly as an old goat. He summoned you a hundred times over." She glanced toward the house. "From the instant his sister pulled into the yard, we knew he was trouble."

"Yes."

"Will you let him stay?"

They'd been acquainted since they were girls, since Anne's mother—a disgraced trollop with two bastard children—had moved in with Widow Brown. It was useless to conceal her thoughts. "Would you suspect I was mad if I said I can't bear to make him go?"

"Oh, Annie . . ." Kate sighed and patted a consoling hand on her shoulder. "Nothing good can come of your attraction."

"I know."

"Then there's not much for me to tell you, is there?"

"No."

"Are you in love with him?"

Was she? She mulled the question, trying to decipher her wild swings of sentiment. As she was hopelessly devoted, insanely attached, what other word besides *love* could describe her condition?

"I suppose so."

Gently, Kate pointed out, "He'll leave soon. Whether you cast him out, or he goes on his own."

"I never presumed he'd do anything else."

"Even if he considered remaining, his family would pressure him into it."

"His fiancée, too."

Kate was aghast. "He's engaged?"

"She was the younger one who visited with Lady Eleanor."

"Oh, Lordy, Lordy."

"And I'm smitten regardless. Aren't I pathetic?"

"You're destined for heartache."

She gazed at her friend. As an adolescent, Kate had had a beau, but her parents had forbidden the marriage, had plighted her instead to a sadistic, perverted swine. He'd beaten and abused her, and when she'd defied his tortures, he'd committed her to an asylum.

But occasionally, if she was waxing nostalgic, she'd refer to her first swain.

"Was it worth it?" Anne queried.

"Worth what?"

"You were in love, and the ending was painful, but at least you have your memories. Do you wish it had never transpired? That you'd never met him?"

Wistful, Kate smiled. "I wouldn't have missed it for the world. It was the only really grand thing that ever happened to me."

After Stephen had gone, would Anne say the same? "I can't *not* do it, Katie."

"I understand."

"I'm so weak of character. Don't be angry with me."

"Ah, girl," Kate scolded, "as if I could be *angry* at you for finding some joy in your lonely life." She started toward the barn. "Just remember: He could abandon you with a babe nestled in your belly. You should probably decide up front if that would be a blessing or a tragedy."

Currently, pregnancy was an impossibility, but it might

not always be. As his health improved, his functioning could return. What if it did? What about a babe?

It wouldn't be such a terrible dilemma. With her being out in the country, and away from so many meddling neighbors, there were fewer people to judge, many methods by which to ease a child into her existence without creating a huge scandal. She'd have a piece of Stephen that would be forever hers.

The notion was thrilling and scary, but she didn't need to chaw over it. Such a dire prospect would likely never be a problem.

"I'll ponder it," she replied.

Kate nodded. "By the way, I ran into Prudence McGee in the village. She's been feeling poorly, so I suggested she take the waters."

Prudence was Willie's shy sister, and Anne winced. She didn't want to have any reason to be in closer contact with him.

"How could Willie approve?"

"We can have her over when he's out of town, and he won't be any the wiser. He'll never have to know."

Secrets had an irritating habit of leaking out, but Anne wouldn't contradict an invitation Kate had extended, for she rarely made any. If she'd asked Prudence, it was important to her.

"It matters to you?"

"Prudence needs it."

An incentive Anne couldn't discount. "Be cautious."

"I will."

Kate went off, and Anne trudged to the pool. She tarried on the edge, dangling her feet. The cool breeze chilled her, so she shed her robe and dipped into the pond. Lounging on her back, she dawdled until she was overheated, until she was wrinkled like a prune, then she waded over and reached for a towel, rubbing it over her skin, but the solace she typically attained was absent.

She shuddered.

Behind her, the trees and shrubs loomed, ominous and sinister, as though they held a thousand eyes, and she sensed that she was being observed, which was silly.

Her property was isolated—securely fenced!—and there was no adjacent farm within comfortable walking distance. If the grotto's location had been otherwise, she'd never have risked bathing in the nude.

The quarrel with Stephen had her distraught and unsure, and she peered toward the house. The window to his room was open, and it dawned on her that he might be able to see her from his bed.

Had he been watching her? Was that why it seemed as if someone was spying? If so, why did she perceive such menace? Such danger?

Like a talisman, he lured her inside. For hours, she'd dodged him, had intended to evict him, but she couldn't. She needed him as she needed water to drink or air to breathe. If he was insolent, pompous, imperious, she didn't care. As an earl's son, he represented everything she despised, everything she hated, but it didn't signify. The fact that he was betrothed meant nothing, that he kept a beautiful mistress meant nothing.

She was eager to continue on, to debase and shame herself for any tidbit of affection he might toss in her direction, and a novel thought occurred to her: was this how her mother had felt about her father? Anne had deemed her mother a ninny who'd fallen for a man she could never have, who'd gone to her grave pining for him.

Anne was prepared to make the same mistake, to forge ahead to a predestined bad ending, but she was unconcerned as to the result. When Stephen left, and she was alone, there would be plenty of opportunity to mourn, but not now. Not when he was so near, and waiting for her.

Frantic to be with him, she struggled into her robe, and rushed across the lawn. In case he was asleep, she crept in, but even in the shadows, she could discern that he was awake. He was undressed, on top of the covers, a blanket across his loins, and he glittered with a strange fire.

"Come to me," he decreed.

She raced across the floor, and eased down as he clutched her around the waist, pulling her to him.

"I'm sorry," he said.

"So am I."

"Forgive me."

"I have."

"Don't send me away."

"I won't. I can't."

He initiated a steamy kiss, their tongues sparring, and he took her hand, guiding it to his crotch.

He was hard! His phallus erect and prodding at her, he wrapped her fingers around it, and began to flex.

Shocked and surprised, she tried to grasp what this portended. The questions she'd been posing to herself, about fornication and babies, had to be answered.

"When?" she sputtered, more perplexed than ever.

"A while ago. It just . . . just happened."

She pushed the blanket away and had her initial glimpse of an aroused male cock. It was so big! She knew that it was supposed to fit into her sheath, but she couldn't figure out how. Huge, red, and throbbing, it had thick, ropy veins that beat in a rhythm with his pulse, and it extended out toward her.

Stroking him, she slid up and down, her thumb trailing over the oozing crown. "Does it hurt?"

"Only in a good way." Laughing, he flexed again.

She punched him on the shoulder. "I *mean:* does it hurt on the inside?"

"No. I feel perfectly normal."

The body was a mystery she'd never unraveled, and she wouldn't try to explain the event. She'd suspected that his manly capacity might return, and it had, so he would spur their intimacy to the next level. Was she ready? Was he?

"Touch me," he commanded, sounding strained and anxious. "Don't let go."

He clasped her hand and lowered it to his loins, once more, applying pressure when she didn't squeeze tightly enough. Rooting under her robe, he found her nipple and suckled as he hugged her with all his might, the tip of his phallus rubbing her belly.

After several thrusts, he went rigid, taut as a bow, and a haunting wail escaped from him. His seed spewed out, a fiery pile seeping between them. It was hot, sticky, a glue binding them. Gradually, his lust abated, and he slowed, then stopped. His respiration ragged, his heart thundering under his ribs, he crushed her to him.

She was stunned, both by how swiftly his desire had escalated as well as how rapidly it had peaked and waned, and she wasn't certain how to react. She hadn't realized that a man could spill himself without being impaled in the woman, but then, most facets of carnality were a puzzle to her.

Down below, he was still hard, and she speculated as to how he could have the energy to maintain an erection. Perhaps with the quickening of his ability, he was like a fountain bubbling over, and he would be in a savage rush to copulate as often as he was able—if for no other reason than to prove to himself that he could.

With his ardor demonstrated so vividly, she had no idea how to proceed, and as a purported widow, she couldn't bumble around. She clambered off the bed, relishing the excuse to do something concrete so that she could avoid thinking about what would come next.

She grabbed a towel and wiped at her stomach and his
own, and when she was finished, he pitched it on the floor,
and drew her to him.

"I'm randy as a lad with his first girl."

"I can tell."

"I could frolic with you all night."

She chuckled. "You're an optimist."

"Want to see me try?"

"I'll *let* you philander, but not until you tire yourself."

Nestling with her, he murmured, "My dearest Anne, how
did I ever get along before I met you?"

He rotated them so that they were spooned together, and he
yawned, his muscles drooping. The sexual display had him
much more weary than he cared to admit. He yawned again.

"I'm going to nap for a few minutes."

"All right."

"Don't you dare sneak out."

"I won't."

"If you do, I'll have to find you. You wouldn't be so cruel
as to make a cripple climb the stairs to your room, would
you?"

"No." She laced their fingers. "Close your eyes. I'll be
here when you wake."

Within seconds, he was slumbering, his breathing steady,
his torso a heavy, relaxed presence behind her. She relaxed,
too, wallowing in the luxury of tarrying with him.

She was glad that he'd nodded off, for his fatigue gave
her the opportunity to ruminate over her choices. After he'd
rested, he'd take her virginity, and she couldn't imagine saying no.

What benefit was her chastity anyway? It had served no
purpose for twenty-eight years of her life, and after he was
gone, she couldn't fathom how it would be of use. After
knowing him, she couldn't cavort with another.

This was her one and only chance to love and be loved, to

experience all the ecstasy a man could bring to a woman. She wasn't about to pass it up.

Peaceful and content, she drifted off and dozed, too.

Stephen roused as dawn was breaking. A rooster crowed, and a sliver of light was visible on the horizon. As Anne had promised, she hadn't left, but was snuggled with him, her lush hair scattered across the pillow, her arms and legs tangled with his own.

His cock was stiff with morning passion and wedged to the cleft of her shapely ass, and he heaved a sigh of relief. He'd worried that his nocturnal stimulation had been an aberration, a fluke.

Grinning, he conjectured as to what she must have thought of him the previous evening, when he'd acted like a barbarian. He'd suckled her breast, thrust a few times, and emptied himself all over both of them. It was as if his months of loathed celibacy had created a dam in his loins, and it had burst so vehemently that he hadn't been able to exhibit any finesse.

Likely, she was pondering what sort of erotic partner he'd prove to be, and he intended to show her.

She was cuddled to him, and he massaged down her arm, her flank. He'd never awakened with a paramour before. His prior trysting had been more expedient, usually based on luck and location. Sleep was a private endeavor, and he couldn't abide sharing his bed, hadn't wanted to endure the awkwardness of rising.

But with Anne, he couldn't wait to observe her as her eyes fluttered open, as she recognized where she was, as she smiled just for him.

He dipped down to toy with her nipple, as his fingers rambled down, to her stomach, her navel, her mons. He slipped them inside her, and instinctively, she flexed, her hips responding with an eagerness that thrilled him.

"Mmm . . ." she purred. "What are you doing?"

"I'm having my way with you."

She was warm, fragrant, drowsy, and as he gazed down at her, a profound wave of emotion swept over him. Bliss. Serenity. Affection.

Near to love, he mused, cherishing how he felt complete and whole when he was with her.

He abandoned her breasts and traveled down to her abdomen, so that he could burrow his cheek in the silky pile of hair shielding her mound. Scooting off the mattress, he balanced on his knees, and he draped her thighs over his shoulders, widening her, exposing her soft, pink core.

Leaning in, he parted her with his tongue, and she stiffened and came up on an elbow.

"Stephen?" She was scowling.

"Did your husband never pleasure you like this?"

She gave him the strangest look. "No."

"Lie back. I'm going to taste you."

"Taste me?"

What kind of oaf had she married? How could he have declined to know her so intimately?

He delved in, and she flopped onto the pillow, her complaint forgotten. She was wet, ready, his manipulation of her nipples having aroused her, and in seconds, a powerful orgasm shook her.

As she bucked and writhed, he pinned her down through the tumult, then, lingering and exploring, he nibbled up her torso.

Finally, he arrived at her mouth, savoring the tang of her sex on his lips. Her legs were spread, and he centered himself, his cock pulsating, impatient, and he had to be in her.

Reaching down, he traced the crown across her, and he prodded in the smallest inch.

"Stephen, I—"

"I can't bear it that another man had you before me." He

pushed in a tad farther. "When we're together, I won't have you remembering him. From this moment on, think only of me."

She was assessing him with consternation, and what appeared to be alarm, but he couldn't understand why she was nervous. He hadn't inquired as to how long she'd been a widow. Perhaps, it had been a lengthy interval, and she was unsettled as to how it would go. Or perhaps, it had occurred recently, and she was anxious about commencing anew. Or it could be that she wasn't promiscuous, that it went against her grain to fornicate when she wasn't married.

What they were about to do was morally inappropriate, but he couldn't prevent himself from proceeding. He wanted her so badly, all his life it seemed now. How could such fervent desire be wrong?

"Stephen," she repeated, "there's something I need to tell you. Something that I should have—"

"It will be all right," he interrupted. "Don't be afraid."

"I'm not afraid. It's just my—"

"It will be wonderful."

He scrutinized her, surmising that she was frightened, and he wished he knew what was the matter so that he could allay her fears.

Had her husband abused her? Had her carnal interludes with him been ghastly?

He wasn't about to discuss her dead spouse! Not when he was partially sheathed inside her.

"Put your arms around me," he instructed. "Hold me tight."

"Please. I'm not positive what—"

A gentleman would have delayed, would have soothed and cajoled her into acquiescence, but the sad fact was that he was beyond restraint, beyond the spot where he could withdraw. He *had* to have her, had to finish it. There could be no debate, no chatting or comforting words.

"Hush," he chided.

He flexed, once, again. She was tense as a virgin, and perverted as it sounded, he grew even more titillated. It seemed as if he was her first.

Gripping her hips, he steadied her, then he thrust hard, harder, and burst through.

He sensed the rip, the rush of her maiden's blood, and he frowned, confused as she arched up and cried out. Mentally, he comprehended what he'd done, but physically, he was past hesitation. He couldn't stop.

His pulse pounded through his veins, his seed surged, and after several brisk penetrations, he started to come.

"I can't . . . can't—" he ground out.

Whatever else he might have said was lost in the ripple of ecstasy that washed over him. He spiraled higher, higher, the exhilaration never ending. The torrent was so intense that he worried his heart might quit beating.

Would he die in her arms? In the throes of the most exquisite rapture he'd ever encountered? What a way to depart the earth!

The maelstrom waned, and he became cognizant of his surroundings. He was poised on his elbows, hovering over her, and she watched him with equal amounts trepidation, horror, and a shy joy. A sheen of tears made her eyes sparkle like diamonds, and he brushed a kiss across her lips.

"Why didn't you confide in me?"

"I couldn't work it into the conversation." Tremulously, she smiled. "I tried to warn you, there at the end, but it was a little late for confessions."

"It was a splendid gift, but I don't believe I'm worth it."

"I wouldn't be too sure."

He studied her, and so many details were clear. "You've never been married, have you?"

"No."

"Why all the lies?"

"It's easier to be a widow. Easier to run a business. Easier to give advice and be taken seriously."

She was correct. Unwed, she wouldn't be allowed to have accounts at the shops in the village, wouldn't be able to advertise her services. Men wouldn't have permitted their daughters or wives to frequent her establishment without a more mature, respected widow as the proprietor.

"I was very rough. I didn't know. I'm sorry."

"I'm fine."

With his ardor subsiding, he was weak, shaky from the exertion, and he pulled out of her. She winced, and he felt like the lowest cad.

"Next time will be better. It won't hurt."

"It didn't this time. Not really."

"We'll bathe in the pool, to relieve the tenderness."

"That's a good idea."

She peered at him, her fondness and regard visible. Was she feeling the same connection he was? He'd never been so happy, so at peace.

Why couldn't this be the circle of his life? Why did his universe have to extend beyond this room, and this glorious woman?

She rested her palm on his cheek. "I'm glad it was you."

"So am I."

"Let's snuggle till the sun crests the hills."

"I'd like that."

Nestling her to him, he drifted off. In his dreams, he was certain he heard her whisper, "I love you, Stephen."

He smiled.

11

Kate stood by the fence that separated Anne's farm from Willie McGee's. It was very late, and Anne had retired, though with the shenanigans going on in the small bedroom at the rear of the house, Kate didn't suppose she was sleeping.

Stephen Chamberlin was a sin any woman would gladly commit, and Anne hadn't been immune to his charms. She was a passionate individual, her nature hot-blooded and emotional, and Chamberlin had easily lit her fuse.

"Good for you, Annie," Kate murmured to the dark night. Eventually, her dashing Captain would leave, no matter what he might promise, or how fervently she might crave that he stay, and Kate hoped that Anne wouldn't be too devastated in the end.

She'd have to discover for herself how little value his word held, how strong the pull of his society would be.

Kate adored Anne and had from the day they'd met, when they were both girls. She knew Anne better than anyone, and after Chamberlin was gone, Kate would protect her, would cherish her, and, if there was a babe, would shield her from scorn.

Without a doubt, if Chamberlin planted a seed, he wouldn't be around to see it grow. But Kate would.

She'd always had feelings for Anne, but early on, she'd recognized that they were different in ways she didn't comprehend. It was something inside of her, something Anne didn't share and never would. After much searching, she'd determined that there were others in her predicament, and they agonized over the same deviant urges.

Anne was aware that Kate had once been in love, that she'd had a grand amour, but Anne wasn't aware that it had been with a female. Kate had had her own aristocrat, an earl's wife who'd often traveled to Bath on holiday. Kate had been twenty, and her friend thirty years older.

The liaison had lasted almost three years, persisting even after her parents had forced her to wed. Her husband had detected her wicked propensity, and in punishment, had nearly killed her, then shipped her to Bedlam.

Kind, devoted Anne had made her sole trip to London, had used all of the money bequeathed to her by Widow Brown to bribe the guards and garner her release, and she'd hidden Kate while she recuperated.

Soon after, her husband was murdered. The idiot had been bent on earning some fast cash off of Kate's immoral predilection, so he'd tried to blackmail the earl over his countess's sexual bent. Shortly, the buffoon had found himself on the wrong end of a highwayman's pistol.

Kate hadn't mourned his demise, but in the process, she'd learned an important lesson. She rarely indulged her hunger for intimacy, despite how lonely she became. She had her job, her relationship with Anne, a roof over her head, and food to eat. A woman needed no more than that to be happy, yet she couldn't stop wishing that she would encounter someone as forlorn as she was herself, that she could have a lifelong companion.

They could reside in the old cottage behind the barn.

Perhaps a widow with children, so Kate would have young-sters to watch over, too. She was at her best when she was car-ing for others, but she never had the chance. In her fantasies, it was such an appealing picture, of herself, part of a real family.

Footsteps sounded on the path, and she paused, waiting, as Prudence McGee appeared out of the shadows. As usual, she was somberly garbed, as drab as a Puritan at a funeral. Kate was positive that Willie compelled her to attire herself so modestly.

He was an odd duck, a loudmouthed bully, who reminded Kate of her deceased spouse, and she imagined Prudence had endured many tortures in living with him. It was a sad world, when women had to be perpetually tied to such un-worthy villains, and in her prayers, Kate always gave thanks for the freedoms she'd been granted. She had her own salary, her own room, and could come and go as she pleased. There was no one to order her about, tell her how to dress, what to say, what to do.

Prudence approached, looking fragile and frightened, which was understandable. Very likely, her resolution to uti-lize the spa was the only exotic, brave, independent thing she'd ever done. She had to be scared witless.

"I received your message," Kate mentioned.

"I was so worried that you wouldn't be here."

They'd decided that Prudence would send notes to Kate, but that Kate wouldn't reciprocate. Prudence couldn't gam-ble that Willie might intercept any communication, and her adamancy had Kate troubled as to what penalty Willie might be prone to wield should Prudence disobey him. Would he beat her? Starve her? Or might he instigate something even more sinister?

Did her desire to interact with Prudence justify the risk to her safety?

Just then, Prudence smiled, and Kate concluded that any moments they stole for themselves were a gift.

"Your brother is gone?"

"For several more days. The magistrate asked him to transport some prisoners to Portsmouth."

Willie's interest in law enforcement regularly occupied him, and Kate was awhirl with calculating how frequently they'd be able to meet in his absences. Would there be sufficient occasion for romance to bloom?

In Prudence, she'd sensed a curiosity, an eagerness to explore, so her complaints of weary bones and sore joints had given Kate the excuse to suggest a therapeutic session. There was no more appropriate tonic than a soak in Anne's grotto, and Kate suspected that the bubbling water might stir another sort of excitement that Prudence hadn't known she craved.

She offered her hand, and Prudence grabbed it. Together, they sneaked toward the pond.

Prudence was forty, her brunette locks streaked with gray, but her face was unlined, smooth and supple, so she seemed much younger than she was. She was tiny, thin and fragile as a bird, and beside her, Kate felt like a hulking oaf.

Before venturing out, she'd donned her swimming outfit, a worn, baggy gown that would hug her torso when moistened, but as they tromped through the woods, it billowed around her, making her feel even larger than she was.

She led them to the building she'd constructed, where customers removed their clothes. It was simple, containing benches, shelves, and hooks. While a few of the looser hussies from the city liked to romp in the nude, and proceeded despite Anne's rules to the contrary, the overwhelming majority wouldn't dream of being naked.

Prudence hesitated. "What are we doing?"

"You have to change, and I've dug up an old nightshirt that you can use as your bathing costume."

"How very considerate. I hadn't grasped that it would be required."

"You oughtn't be caught lugging one around."

"No, that definitely wouldn't be a good idea." Anxious, she peered into the dark space. "Well then . . ."

Kate went in and lit a candle, the dim glow illuminating the area, and Prudence entered behind her.

"Do you need assistance?"

"No. I can manage."

"I'll be right outside."

Apprehensive, Prudence studied the pool. "Is it deep?"

"No. It's very shallow, except at the far end, where it would be up to your neck. But we don't have to go down there."

"I never learned to swim."

"And you don't have to now. You can kneel, or there are places to sit on the rocks. Don't fret."

"Will you get in with me?"

"Of course. I wouldn't let you try it alone."

Satisfied that she'd be safe, she closed the door. Kate tarried, impatient and testy. Though only a few minutes had passed when Prudence emerged, it seemed to take forever. Kate had judged her size correctly, and the nightshirt fit well, flowing over her frame, and hinting at a shapely figure. Her breasts were small, the nipples alert and poking at the fabric.

Lest she embarrass Prudence, she glanced away.

"Is Mrs. Smythe abed?"

"Yes." *But she's not sleeping!* Kate mused to herself.

"Are you sure she doesn't mind that I'm here?"

"She said it was fine, but that we probably shouldn't tell Willie."

Prudence chuckled and evaluated the pond. A sliver of moon was shining, the surface glimmering, and it had to appear intimidating. Kate extended her hand again, and Prudence took it.

"We'll go slow. Don't be afraid."

"I'm not. Not when I'm with you."

Shy and pretty, she peered down at the grass. Kate squeezed her fingers, then maneuvered her down the carved steps. Kate immersed herself first, then guided Prudence as she waded in to her ankles.

"Oh, my!" she gushed with delight. "It's so warm."

"Yes. Come further."

Kate held tight as Prudence descended. The water lapped at her waist, her feet anchored on the ground.

"Dip down," Kate instructed. "Go ahead. I've got you."

Prudence went down, and Kate joined her, so that they were on their knees, and face-to-face. The current surged around them, and Prudence giggled. "I hadn't realized it would be so . . . so . . . refreshing. I'm so buoyant."

Her bodice was drenched, her bosom molded by the material, which when wet was nearly transparent. Kate fought the urge to gape, or to confide how enchanting she was.

Instead, she stated, "Sink in farther. To your chin."

Prudence complied, swishing her arms and reveling in sensation. There was a new sparkle about her. "It's dangerous, isn't it? The water, I mean."

"Why would you say so?"

"It makes me . . ." She paused, pondering. "Reckless, I guess. And wild. As if I'm being incited to do something I've never done before. Do I sound silly?"

"Many have claimed it has that effect."

"Do you think I might take my hair down?"

"Certainly."

"Would you help?"

"Yes."

Prudence turned, while Kate shifted onto a ledge that served as a seat. She gripped Prudence by the hips, and snuggled her in, so that she was balanced between Kate's legs as she extracted the combs and pins.

"Lean on me," Kate persuaded, and carefully supporting

her, she tipped Prudence so that she was on her back. At the odd position, Prudence tensed.

"Relax," Kate assured her. "I won't let go."

Prudence's eyes were shut, her respiration lethargic, and Kate caressed her thighs, her stomach. Unable to resist, she cupped her breast, the mound soft and pliant as she played with the nipple.

Throughout, Prudence remained at ease, submitting to the tender petting. Kate thought about kissing her, either on the mouth or on the breast, but she was too nervous to push. In the future, there would be plenty of time for more. They didn't need to rush.

After a protracted interval, Prudence lowered her feet so that she touched bottom. Her bashfulness had vanished, and she brazenly assessed Kate.

"I should be going."

"All right," Kate agreed. "We'll retrieve your clothes, and I'll walk you home."

They exited, and on the bank, Prudence stopped to wring out her hair.

"I feel so strange. So invigorated. Is that normal?"

"Yes. It's a combination of the percolating water and the heat."

"Rumor has it that it's more than that. That the spa is possessed of mysterious properties."

"Balderdash." Kate used the response Anne insisted upon. They could never contend that magic was afoot, or next they knew, they'd be tarred and feathered and run out of town.

Prudence had grown bolder. "Would you dry me?"

"I'd like to."

They stared at each other, and a world of perception flickered between them. Prudence proceeded to the changing room, and Kate followed, trembling with eagerness.

Modesty abandoned, Prudence clutched the hem of her

drenched nightshirt and tugged it off. The candle was still lit, and Kate could see all: her pert breasts, her slender waist, her curvaceous hips.

Kate gulped and fumbled about, then seized a towel and dropped to her knees. Starting at Prudence's shoulders, she fluffed it down. At her breasts, she massaged in leisurely circles, round and round her nipples. She sank to her tummy, her privates, her legs, but as she spun her so that she could dry the rest, she glared, then frowned.

Prudence had bruises from a strap across her back and buttocks. They were over a week old, faded to yellow, but visible.

She traced the welts. "Willie did this to you?"

Prudence deliberated, then admitted, "Yes."

"Why?"

"Our cook burned his eggs."

"Why did he whip you and not her?"

"He beat her, too, but I supervise her, so he considered it my fault."

"Oh, Pru . . ." Wrapping her arms around Prudence, Kate hung her head in dismay, as Prudence linked their fingers. Frozen in their spot, they contemplated the enormity of what had been acknowledged.

Prudence broke the moment. "Let's get me dressed."

Kate rose and fussed with buttons and laces, and in case a servant happened to observe Prudence sneaking in, she did a quick braid of her hair.

They hiked through the woods toward Willie's farm. At the boundary, they scaled the fence and continued on to the edge of the trees. Willie's house was situated in the spacious yard beyond.

With Willie's violent tendencies confirmed, she was terrified to let Prudence depart. Yet, she couldn't ask Anne to shelter Prudence, and if they tried, Willie could show up and forcibly remove her.

What power did three unmarried women have against a man?

"If you're ever in danger," Kate inquired, "you must contact me straightaway."

"We have a stable boy," Prudence said. "He likes me. I assume he'd come to my aid, but it would be hazardous for him. Could you pay him?"

"Yes. If you ever need me, send him. I'll find a way to assist you."

Prudence gazed at her as if she wanted to confess so much more, but they both required opportunity to think, to plan. Surprising Kate very much, she raised up on tiptoe and kissed Kate on the lips, then fled.

Kate watched until the rear door opened, and Prudence slipped inside. Then, with a heavy heart, she trudged away.

Lady Felicity Babcock paced on the verandah that circled her mother's mansion. It was stuffy inside the ballroom, and guests were wandering the gardens, so her smile was firmly affixed. Her mother's fetes were all the rage, with people begging for invitations, so the cream of society had flooded to the residence, and she couldn't bear that someone might espy her and speculate as to whether she was despondent.

There'd been so much slander about Stephen, and the status of their betrothal, and she declined to instigate further discussion. With no one having seen Stephen in such a long while, gossip was rampant—that he was mad, that he'd lost limbs, that he'd been struck deaf, dumb, or blind, or all three combined—and no matter how vehemently their families denied the lies, they kept circulating.

Inside, the music ended to a smattering of applause, and she could barely keep from charging in, commandeering the stage, and shouting at the crowd. Didn't they recognize genius when they heard it? Couldn't they discern when they had a virtuoso in their midst?

Her dearest cousin, Robert, had labored for months, or-
chestrating the dancing for the soiree, but the members of
the *ton* scarcely noticed the prodigy behind the tunes.

Others didn't understand how he struggled with his art,
how he suffered in creating his symphonies and sonatas. It
embarrassed him, having to degrade himself by writing and
performing for money. As he'd mentioned so often, he
couldn't achieve his full potential when he had to work for a
living. She ached for him and wished she could help.

If only she'd met Robert before Stephen!

When Stephen had proposed, Robert had been studying
on the Continent, and he had returned later, after Stephen
was gone. He'd run out of funds, had been destitute and
pleaded for her family's support.

Had their paths crossed earlier, there would have been no
courtship by Stephen Chamberlin. With Stephen away at
war, and Robert abiding in her mother's home, he'd been a
daily companion who'd charmed her until she'd been smitten, enamored to the point of excess.

If she'd had the authority, she'd have given her entire fortune over to his control so that he could use it to bolster his
talent. She had the most splendid vision, of the two of them
sharing an Italian villa, on the shores of the azure Mediter-
ranean. Robert could spend his days composing, and she
could be his rock, his foundation, a silent witness to his musical gift, a stalwart friend, a confidante. She could . . .

Her mother's voice boomed, announcing the start of the
buffet line, and Felicity jumped, mentally lashing herself for
her untoward rumination.

How could she pine for another while Stephen was wast-
ing away? He was a hero, England's champion, his name
reverently whispered by an admiring citizenry. He'd nearly
sacrificed all to King and country, yet she lamented being
stuck with him.

Oh, she was so fickle, so ambivalent and selfish!

Down the patio, Robert crept outside as everyone else was wandering in to dine, so she strode to the gazebo, their secret meeting place. Being affianced, she had much more freedom than she needed, so there was no chaperone about to dissuade her or urge caution. She hurried to be with him.

As she raced up the stairs of the decorative building, he was already there, and she was thrilled anew by how beautiful he was. With his blond hair, blue eyes, and pink cheeks, he was pretty, in an almost feminine way. A few inches taller than herself, he was slender, small-boned, and not a masculine sort. He'd never excelled at sporting events or exhibited aggressive behaviors.

In every fashion, he was the exact opposite of Stephen Chamberlin, and the more acquainted she was with Robert, the more she realized what a grave mistake she'd made in plighting herself to Stephen. When Stephen was hale, he was so manly, so virile and robust, and he possessed no appreciation for poetry, art, or music, which were the topics that consumed Robert. Robert needed her, needed a strong woman to look after him. He stirred her female instincts to coddle and care in a manner Stephen never could.

Stephen was too independent, too self-reliant. Even while lying at death's door, he hadn't called for her a single time. Where was the romance in that?

Robert bussed a chaste kiss on her cheek. Once prior, he'd attempted the same—but directly on the mouth!—and she'd shied away and scolded him. She wasn't the type who would sneak around, dallying with another whenever Stephen wasn't present.

Yet, at the same juncture, she was irritated that Robert had so easily acquiesced to her edict that they not embrace. She viewed their amour as a Grand Passion, the kind about which poets waxed on. If he felt a heightened ardor, wouldn't he be overcome by desire, despite her requests to the contrary?

Just once, couldn't the blasted man grab her and kiss her senseless? Did he have to be so accursedly polite?

"Felicity, darling, how I've missed you."

"I'm so glad to be home."

"Sit with me."

He gestured toward a bench that was shielded by the shadows, and she hustled to it. After her recent trip to Bristol, she was desperate to confide the details.

For months, Stephen had refused to speak with her, claiming the engagement to be over. He'd insisted she disseminate the news that he was crazed, crippled, and thus, their betrothal terminated.

She'd wept and prayed and deliberated as to whether she should agree, but in the end, she couldn't forsake him. Her mother had explained how he was hurting and angry, but would recuperate, and when he did, she would be waiting, loyal, dependable, and delighted with the match she'd settled upon.

"How was your journey?" Robert queried.

While they endeavored not to talk about Stephen, he was like a large African elephant, tromping around between them. "He's traveled to a private spa. Lady Eleanor took me to visit."

"And . . .?"

"He's very much improved."

"No," he muttered, sounding irked.

"Yes." Unable to abide his disappointment, she glanced away. Was he hoping Stephen would die? No one could be that cruel. "I was very pleased!"

"Well, of course you were." Solicitous, he patted her wrist and stroked her glove. "You love him. It's only natural that you'd be happy."

Did she love Stephen? Her fortune had guaranteed that she could marry whomever she wanted. Stephen had seemed a stellar choice. Handsome, dashing, spirited, and fun, when he'd escorted her about, she'd felt like the luckiest female in England. Decked out in his military uniform, he'd been so gallant, and the other girls had been so jealous.

"It was marvelous to see him so healthy."

"So he'll fully recover?"

"I'm positive."

At the notion of Stephen's successful convalescence, Robert appeared ill, and she was confused as to her sentiments. Stephen's rehabilitation would mean the termination of her relationship with Robert. After all, she couldn't be newly wed, but mooning over an old admirer.

Still, she could never wish Stephen harm, could never be satisfied with his malingering. She wanted the best for him. She really did, but her decisions were jumbled.

She yearned, she didn't. She'd grown attached, she shouldn't have.

What she wouldn't give to return to her initial season of parties, where life had been merry and gay, and there had been no wounded, tormented soldier to cloud her horizon!

Suddenly, Robert seized her hands, squeezing tight, and he raised them to his lips. "Tell me there's a chance for us!" He gazed at her, his fervor making her heart pound. "I can't bear this . . . this . . . uncertainty, where I can't be sure if you'll ever be mine!"

"Robert!"

"My sweet, if we are torn asunder, I don't know how I shall survive it. I truly, truly don't."

Stunning her, he leaned in and kissed her, and she let him. He pressed her backward, so that her chignon was crushed to the lattice, and his mouth ground against hers, their teeth clinking together.

Was this manly ardor? Had he finally been swept away by lust? He tipped her farther, so that she was reclined on the bench, and he came down on top of her, a knee draped over her thighs, the other on the floor.

He continued with the mashing of their lips, and she tried to relax, tried to succumb as was expected, but she couldn't muster any enthusiasm.

It was so awkward, so uncomfortable. While his eyes were closed, hers were open, and through the rose arbor she stared out at the sky, finding it absurd that she was counting the stars.

He reached to the front of her gown and caressed her breast through the fabric. Her married friends had hinted that her future husband might fondle them, so she wasn't shocked or revolted, but though Robert's touch was interesting, it didn't generate so much as a ripple of excitement.

Perhaps she had on too many layers of apparel.

His fingers slithered up, and just as he would have glided them under her bodice, voices murmured nearby, and they froze. A couple strolled past on the walk, and frantic, they scrambled about, straightening their clothes and hair.

"I'll wait for you forever, darling!" Robert vowed at her ear. "Forever!"

Felicity frowned, and stood, relieved that it was too dark for Robert to observe her expression. Why had there been no spark? No fire? Had they been doing it correctly? As it had been her first genuine kiss, she was no expert, so she couldn't say. Maybe she didn't know how to feel feminine passion, or maybe it took more time.

Calming herself, she clasped Robert's arm, and they promenaded out of the gazebo, acting as if they were innocently exploring the garden. Felicity stayed with him till they were inside, then, more confused than ever, she pleaded fatigue and rushed to the ladies' retiring room.

~ 12 ~

Camilla Warren loitered in the shade, moving farther and farther away from the horde in the pool. They were frolicking with their usual abandon, so they didn't notice as she disappeared toward the house.

With the recent sighting she'd made, having determined that Stephen was on the property, Mrs. Smythe's Bathing Emporium was packed elbow to elbow, as the more risqué ladies of the *ton* flocked to the country to catch a glimpse of the popular hero. Or more likely, they were hoping *he* would catch a glimpse of them. In case he peeked out his window, they were naked—as she was herself—and taking turns lounging on the grassy banks.

The loose hussies! They were a bunch of sexual vultures. Who were they to come sniffing around Stephen? He was hers and always had been.

Earlier, Mrs. Smythe had walked down the lane toward a neighbor's, a basket in tow as if delivering tonics. The hulking assistant, Miss Kate, was in the barn, absorbed with chores, so there was no one about with authority to stop Camilla, and a few minutes were all she needed to accomplish her task.

She slipped inside, pausing as she adjusted to the dimmer light. By her calculations, Stephen's bedchamber was close by. She could steal in, chat, and depart without anyone being the wiser.

Her estimate proved correct, as she found Stephen's room to be the first on the left. It was small, designed for use by a cook or scullery maid, and she stepped in and shut the door. He was sleeping, unclothed, a sheet draped over his loins, and she studied him, imprinting every detail so that later, she would be able to recount what she'd witnessed.

Eager for a scrupulous inspection, she tiptoed over. Stories abounded as to his injuries and condition, and there'd been extensive discussion as to whether he'd gone mad, but that prior afternoon, he'd seemed lucid enough.

She approached. As she'd noted previously, his limbs were attached, his face unmarked, but without a shirt to conceal his torso, she could detect severe scarring on his arm, a portion of which was bandaged.

The more shocking tales claimed that they'd hacked off his phallus. Wouldn't she be the talk of the town if she could say she'd verified as much for herself!

Curious as to what secrets she'd discover, she lifted the sheet. Contrary to rampant speculation, his manly extremities were affixed, and she couldn't decide if she was relieved or disappointed.

Let's see if they still work! she mused, and she crawled next to him and stretched out.

She couldn't wait to view his expression when he recognized it was she. He'd once told her that he'd never had a lover who could satisfy him as she did. She knew what he liked, how he liked it, when he liked it, and she suffered a thrill, conjecturing as to whether he'd been celibate since their last rendezvous.

Perhaps he was like a virgin, anxious for his passion to be rekindled. If so, she was just the woman for the job!

She snuggled, and though he didn't wake, he smiled as if he'd been expecting her. Reaching down, she stroked him, and instantly, he swelled, the appendage robust and vigorous.

Slowly, leisurely, he flexed, the sensitive crown pressed to her belly.

No, there was nothing wrong with his virile functioning!

Stirring, he purred and murmured drowsily, "Ooh, do that again."

She dipped to his nipple, bit and played as she toyed with him down below.

"You like that, don't you?" Her tone was husky with desire. It was like old times, when he'd been crazy for her.

"You drive me wild, you lusty wench." She giggled and nipped at his shoulder, licking the salty skin at his nape, elated with how matters were progressing, when he sighed and said, "Oh, Anne, you make me so happy."

Anne! Who the hell was Anne? Wasn't that the given name of Mrs. Smythe? A wave of wrath shot through her. So . . . he was cohabiting with the proprietress, was he?

How bloody convenient! Apparently, Mrs. Smythe had many more skills than Camilla realized. A nurse. A dietetic. An apothecary. And a strumpet.

Wasn't Stephen fortunate! The wretch!

Tamping down her resentment, she refused to let him surmise how irked she was by the news.

"It's not Anne, silly." She swatted him on his bare bottom, pretending his gaffe was a funny mistake.

Stephen froze, his eyes flew open. He blinked and blinked as if he didn't know who she was.

"Camilla?"

"Yes, darling, it's me." She affected a credible pout.

He peered around. "How did you get in?"

"I sneaked in, when that Amazon, Miss Kate, was looking the other way."

"You're so naughty."

They were on their sides, only an inch separating them, and she kissed him.

"It's been so long. I've missed you."

Rolling onto her back, she thrust her bosom up and out. He'd always relished her breasts, and he hadn't lost his predilection. He pinched her nipple, and she squirmed with pleasure as he drifted down, to her tummy, her mons. She'd had her maid shave her, and he smirked as he swiped his fingers across her smooth puss.

"That's my Cammie."

"I did it just for you." Grinning, she cuddled even nearer. "Have you missed me, too? At least a little?"

He chuckled but didn't answer. "You shouldn't have done this."

"Nonsense. How could I stay away?"

"There's a reason no one is aware that I'm here. I'm having a private recuperation."

"But surely, you won't deny me visits. Not after all we've meant to each other." Again, he didn't comment, failing to reinforce her understanding that they were a couple.

"I'm afraid you have to leave."

"No!" His erection was in excellent shape and pulsing at her leg. He was very interested in a dalliance. How could he send her packing?

"Mrs. Smythe will be upset if she finds you."

"Why would her opinion signify? You're Stephen Chamberlin. She's naught but a glorified washerwoman. It's none of her affair how you conduct yourself."

At the slur to Mrs. Smythe, he tensed but didn't rise to her defense, which made Camilla feel slightly better.

"I'm a guest in her home, and it's been a rough week. Ever since my identity was revealed, she's been overrun by trespassers, who've been prowling the grounds and attempting to enter the house."

She boiled with fury! Which harlots had engaged in such

perfidy? Every female member of High Society knew
Stephen was hers, and she couldn't bear to be apprised that
she'd humiliated herself by slinking in after many others had
already tried the same.

"You're glad I came." She arched a brow. "I can tell."

She fondled his cock, pleased with how heavy and vibrant it seemed, but he removed her hand and rested it on her
stomach. Then, giving an explicit signal that couldn't be
misconstrued, he lifted the sheet. "Why don't you go? Before we cause trouble for Mrs. Smythe."

"I couldn't care less if we cause her *trouble*."

"Camilla, I don't want—"

She was positive he'd planned to utter something horrid
about their being through, and she was saved by the door
swinging open.

Camilla glanced over her shoulder, ecstatic to observe
Mrs. Smythe on the threshold, clutching a tray laden with
food. Her knuckles were white, and she was so pale, she
looked as if she'd seen a ghost.

Camilla stretched and laughed. "Do you mind, Mrs.
Smythe? We're terribly busy. Put the tray on the dresser, and
you may be excused."

"Anne," Stephen interrupted, "it's not what you think."

"Get out of my house!"

Her voice was low, dangerous. She was seething, goaded
to mayhem, and Camilla hesitated, wondering if it had been
wise to cross her.

"I say!" Camilla blustered. "Must you barge in on us?
We're otherwise engaged!"

Mrs. Smythe raised the tray and hurled it at them. Plates
and silverware flew by, some pieces hitting them, others
sailing past and crashing into the wall with a loud bang.
Camilla shrieked as sticky jam and oozing eggs landed on
her. A pot of hot tea shattered, the spray scalding them.

"Get out!" Mrs. Smythe shouted. "Get out! Both of you!"

"Anne!" Stephen barked, endeavoring to calm her, but to no avail.

She marched over and grabbed Camilla by the arm and hair, clawing so tightly that Camilla winced and cried out. Then the deranged shrew half-dragged, half-carried her into the corridor and to the yard, where she was flung—naked!—out onto the lawn.

"You bitch in heat," Mrs. Smythe railed. "If you show your sorry hide around here ever again, I swear I'll take a switch to you!"

Camilla was sputtering, and she yearned to exude bravado, but it was impossible to exhibit any aplomb when she was bruised, buffeted, and lying on the grass without her clothes. To her horror, everyone was watching the altercation. Agog, they were lined up along the edge of the pond, their mouths flapping in amazement.

"You petty commoner. How dare you threaten me! How dare you touch me! I'll have you jailed for battery."

"You're lucky I'm satisfied with a simple assault!" Smythe gestured toward the assemblage and screamed, "All of you! Vacate the premises! The spa is closed. Indefinitely!"

She spun on her heel and stormed inside.

A stunned silence followed, then one of them tittered, and another joined in, until they were all chortling and pointing. Camilla stood, her rage palpable, and she stared them down, one by one, until the merriment ceased.

She'd been violated and abused, but she wouldn't let any of her associates detect how frightened she'd been. Knees knocking, bones weak, she started toward the pool, when Miss Kate appeared from the barn.

"Where are you going, Lady Camilla?" she had the gall to inquire.

"After that . . . that lunatic attacked me, I need to wash."

"I believe Mrs. Smythe demanded your departure."

"Well, I don't intend to oblige her."

"I'm politely requesting that you comply. If I have to ask twice, I won't be so courteous." Her scorn evident, she glared at the mob. "You have ten minutes to clear out. I'll have your carriages brought round."

Camilla scowled, declining to be intimidated, but the others were hanging their heads like a gaggle of chastised children. To shake them out of their doldrums, she clapped her hands.

"Continue with your swim, ladies. We've paid good money for it," and she walked toward the water, but the crowd kept its wary attention focused on Kate.

"Let's go, Cammie," one of them said, and like puppets, the rest nodded. "It's not worth the fuss."

The group scrambled out, and there was a frantic race to the changing room, where they searched for stockings and rummaged for gowns. Mrs. Smythe's maids were locating hats and dispensing parasols. Camilla ignored them and went into the pool, alone, while Kate scrutinized her every move.

She didn't exit until the building was empty, then, dawdling forever, she donned her clothes. As she strolled to her coach, Kate tagged after her to ensure that she left.

In the drive, her conveyance was the last remaining. The ingrates had fled without her, not wanting to linger after the discord, but also, she suspected, desirous of hurrying to Bath so as to spread stories about the fracas they'd witnessed.

A flush of mortification commenced at her toes and crept upward, heating her cheeks, burning through her stomach. With how she'd been roughed up, her joints ached, her muscles throbbed, and she rubbed the small of her back to ease the tension.

The brawl had been the most embarrassing moment of her life, and she would never hear the end of it. Not if she lived to be a hundred, and she was so furious she could have bit nails in half.

Mrs. Smythe had disgraced her in front of Stephen. In front of her friends and enemies. In front of the entire world.

Camilla never forgot a slight, never forgave a lapse, so Smythe would suffer for her audacity. Camilla vowed to extract revenge, and she was relieved to be by herself on the journey to town so that she'd have plenty of quiet opportunity to reflect on the most appropriate retaliation.

Stephen lounged, observing the bizarre activity outside. Who would have guessed that a ladies' bathing facility could be a breeding ground for such vitriol and commotion?

Considering what had transpired, he wasn't nearly as coherent as he should have been, though he'd certainly perked up after those victuals had been pitched at him.

Anne had been in fine form, and poor Camilla hadn't known what hit her. He'd never seen anything quite so spectacular.

The past few days had been a nightmare, as Anne had been besieged. Every female coquette of the *ton*, every heiress, every rich merchant's daughter, had rushed to the country in order to frolic in Anne's grotto. Ridiculous as it sounded, they were all anxious to flaunt themselves for him in various states of dishabille, and the erotic waters only exacerbated their vamping.

He'd always been a magnet for women, had attracted them like flies, but during his stint in the army, their esteem had exploded. When he'd attended fancy soirees in his uniform, he'd been accosted in alcoves, lured into closets.

Now, with a bravado bolstered by Anne's pool, the interest was extreme. Their antics were eccentric, outlandish, humorous. On his end, anyway. But not on Anne's.

She'd been perplexed over how to handle the burgeoning

numbers. She was too shrewd to reject anyone who flashed a pouch of coins, but the growing swarm had swiftly destroyed her even disposition and willingness to please.

How the hell had Camilla gotten into his bed?

He'd roused from a nap, and there she was, her nipples poking him in the chest, her fingers wrapped around his John Thomas. How could he explain the encounter to Anne? She was already convinced that he had paramours slithering out from every nook and cranny, and it was difficult to deny the perception, what with intruders breaking in, and Camilla acting like a whore.

Sighing, he flopped onto the pillows, listening as she charged inside, as she stomped up the stairs and retired to the sanctuary of her room. She was so fiery, so temperamental, that she might sequester herself for an eternity, and he didn't suppose he'd have many more chances to wheedle out of an eviction.

Rising, he pulled on a pair of trousers, then he went to the hall. So far, he hadn't invaded her refuge, but maybe it was time. He didn't like it that she had a place separate from him, didn't want there to be any aspect about her with which he was unfamiliar.

He limped to the top of the narrow staircase. Her door was closed, and without knocking, he entered.

It was cozily furnished, feminine, with frilly curtains, woven rugs, knitted throws. A corset hung off a chair, stockings draped beside it. She was by the window, peering down on the lawn. Stiff with rage, her fists were clenched as if she might strike him.

"Go away," she said without turning.

"Anne—"

"I can't tolerate any more of this."

He came up behind her and hugged her, but she didn't welcome the embrace, so he nuzzled her neck, gratified by the goose bumps that cascaded down her arms. She might be incensed, but she wasn't unaffected. It was the way between them; their bond was too strong.

"She climbed into my bed, Anne," he announced before she could cut him off. "I was asleep. I swear it."

"Shut up."

"I woke up, and there she was."

"My God, she was caressing you! You were leaned over her, hard as a rock, eager to do the deed. Do you take me for a fool?"

"I thought she was you."

She elbowed him in the ribs, so firmly that he flinched and released her, and she whirled around. "What do you want from me, Stephen? You're recuperating in my home. You're eating my food, and benefiting from my healing skills. You're using my body when it suits you. So what do you want?"

It was a question he never stopped asking himself. What did he want?

He tried to imagine marrying her, uprooting her to the familial estate, but how could she fit in? She wasn't a woman of leisure, like his sister. He couldn't picture her frittering away, drinking tea, sponsoring musicales, and painting tepid watercolors.

She'd be bored to tears. And how would he support her?

Neither of them would feel comfortable, residing under his father's roof and dependent on his charity. The yoke of reliance had chafed, and was the reason he'd joined the army, that he'd proposed to Felicity. He couldn't abide that subservient existence, nor could he drag Anne into it with him.

The other option was to stay with her, to be a kept man, to have Anne the breadwinner, but he couldn't envision himself loafing while she worked herself to the bone. What would be his role? Clerk? Sexual partner? Footman? He was too much of a gentleman—the teachings of his upbringing ingrained and indelible—and too proud to have her providing for him.

As he'd proven, and Anne had insisted from the outset, his presence was an impossibility. It wasn't feasible to have a man about, especially one with his renown and celebrity, yet her business would have to thrive. It would supply their only earnings.

There were no other alternatives, and he had no solutions to offer, but one fact was paramount.

"I love you," he asserted.

"So?"

As it was the sole occasion he'd proclaimed himself, he gaped at her, offended and startled that she'd tossed his declaration in his face. He frowned, then laughed. How fitting that she would disregard his declaration!

After all his philandering, his peccadilloes, and loose conduct, he'd found a female he adored, had confessed as much, and she was unmoved.

"That has to count for something."

"To whom?" she queried.

"To you."

"My father used to tell my mother, on a daily basis, that he loved her. For three solid years, he swore it. He sired two children on her as his proof. Then—poof!—he tired of her and sent us away. I never saw him again, so pardon me if I say that your *love* doesn't signify in the slightest."

A tough nut to crack! He wasn't about to wade into the murky circumstances involving her father, for he didn't presume he could win by going that route. Edward Paxton had behaved badly, but it was the custom of noblemen toward their paramours. Still, Stephen didn't see how he could redeem himself by mentioning as much.

"I don't know what I want from you," he honestly admitted.

"You must have some idea."

The answers were so complex. "I can't begin to decide."

"Why not? It seems simple to me. Are we to marry? To be

together forever? Or are we merely to cohabit until you leave?"

He couldn't lie to her. "Yes, Anne. That's how it has to be."

"Very well." She was hurt, bitter. "I guess I have to determine how far I'm willing to debase myself. Should I let you tarry, while I pine away for the scraps of attention you deign to throw in my direction? Or should I lop you off immediately, like a festering limb, so that I can instantly be shed of you?"

"It's not as wretched as all that."

"Isn't it? If I relent, I'll be forced to share you with all the others who sneak in when I'm not looking. I'm not sure I can be that magnanimous. You matter to me, but it's fairly clear that my affection isn't reciprocated."

"I told you that I love you."

"I heard you, but I don't think the word has any meaning to you. Not deep down. You don't know what *love* is."

Didn't he? Wasn't it this giddy rush he felt when he was with her?

"It's what I feel for you."

"How do you intend to act on it?"

With reality lashing at her, she seemed to deflate, and he couldn't bear that she was so unhappy. "Anne, listen to me." He took her hands in his, but she wouldn't meet his gaze. "If we married, what kind of life would we have?"

"I expect the type all couples have, though I suppose we'd enjoy a tad more passion."

"I live with my father. Could you conceive of yourself residing at Bristol Manor? With nothing to do but sip tea and peruse fashion magazines with my sister? You'd be batty in a week."

"Perhaps I'd relish the opportunity," she defiantly maintained.

"Not bloody likely."

"Why couldn't I? Do you assume that I prefer slaving away like a dog, with so little to show for my efforts? Maybe I'd jump at the chance for indolence, where I could have someone take care of *me* for a change."

"But if you couldn't stand it, what would become of us? I couldn't support you as a husband should. I have no income, and no method of generating any. I can't fathom another tour in the military, so what would I do?"

"Stay with me."

"You're aware of what an infeasible prospect that is." He pulled her into his arms. "I'm here for now, and I'm crazy about you. Can't that be enough?"

"Maybe I need more."

"I'm certain you do, but I've never been the man to give it to you."

What a sorry statement of his situation! He was the son of an earl, an aristocrat, the most famous personage in England, his exploits bandied high and low. Every maiden in the land wished she could have him for her own. But what advantage was there in his repute if he couldn't have his heart's desire? He felt like a spoiled toddler, denied his favorite treat.

Though he hadn't a penny to his name, he was too vain to tie himself to a workingwoman. He was pathetic! A despicable, conceited snob, who would forgo bliss merely because he couldn't figure out how to arrange his affairs. When had he grown so set in his ways? So stodgy and unbending?

Yet, he couldn't envision a different future, couldn't deduce how to achieve another conclusion, and he would never be so cruel as to raise her hopes, only to dash them.

He was with her to be healed, and after she'd finished with him, he'd reestablish himself at his previous pursuits, and he was nearing that crossroads.

What a pitiable creature he would be when that juncture arrived! He would go back to the empty swirl of London parties and frivolous gamboling, while she would be at her farm, busy, content, and fulfilled by her employment.

How fortunate she was to have something she cherished! Something that was satisfying and tangible. He envied her her industrious, fruitful existence, but there was no place for him in it.

"Come," he said, trying to lead her across the floor. "Lie down with me."

"No. Not after you've just been with another."

Sad and weary, she assessed him, and he couldn't abide that he would inflict such sorrow on her, not when he regarded her as so fine and unique. He clutched her and gave her a shake. "Will you get this through your thick head: nothing happened between us."

"Once you're home, will Lady Camilla be your mistress?"

"No."

"But there will be others like her, won't there?"

He flushed. Of course, there would be. A depressing string of them. It was the manner in which men of his society carried on. "Probably."

"And how about Lady Felicity? Will you marry her?"

"Anne, don't torture yourself like this."

"Will you?" she sharply inquired.

"I can't say." Felicity was one in a long line of decisions he'd avoided, but he couldn't evade a resolution forever. "Don't let's talk about it now."

"If not now, when?"

He felt as if she was wielding a knife and pricking at his vulnerabilities. "Never. How can any of it signify?"

"I need to know what you'll do, and where you'll be, after you leave me."

"To what end? To torment yourself?"

"With a bit of *torment,* I'll get over you faster." She walked to the bed and sat down. "It would be so easy to hate you."

He sidled next to her. "You don't mean that."

"Yes, I do."

She glanced out the window, where Camilla was floating in the pool, and in no hurry. The others had fled, and Kate stood guard, a silent sentinel tracking Camilla's activities.

"I know you'll have to depart soon," she said. "All I ask—" Halting, she had to swallow twice before she could continue. "All I ask is that you make your farewell as gently as you are able."

"I promise you I will." He sat, too, and kissed her, tentative and nervous about how she'd receive the gesture, but she didn't reject him. "I'm feeling stronger," he asserted, "and I can manage the stairs. I want to move up here, to share your room."

As if it was beyond her to protest, she shrugged. "All right." Forlorn and disconsolate, she leaned forward and rested her chin in her hands. "I'm the biggest fool in the world."

"No you're not." Eager to proclaim himself again, he draped an arm across her shoulder. "I love you."

"So what?" she responded miserably. "It's cold comfort, Stephen. Cold comfort indeed."

~ 13 ~

Anne rose, the water sluicing off her torso, the cold night air blasting her heated skin. There was a touch of autumn on the breeze, yellow leaves in the trees, and soon, she'd be attending the dance at the harvest festival.

Stephen would be gone by then, and she tried not to feel any regret, but it swept over her anyway.

He was walking across the yard, his strong legs covering the grass in easy strides. Other than a slight hobble in his gait, it was difficult to identify him as the same man who'd come to her in June, weak, sickened, and crippled.

Through diet and strenuous exercise, he'd regained much of his weight, growing whipcord lean, his muscled physique the type a sculptor might carve into a block of marble.

Mental wounds lingered, though they were abating, and his nightmares had lessened, too, and she was idiotic enough to wonder if it was because he slept with her. She wanted to be the reason.

When he'd moved upstairs, she'd been too embarrassed to explain the intimate situation to her servants. She'd had Kate do it for her, and they'd been kind enough to pretend that there was no torrid romance occurring. They went about their duties as though stumbling upon him in the morning, cuddled next to her, was perfectly normal.

Thank God, none of them had quit! If they'd been outraged by her immorality, she couldn't have borne it. She was shocked, herself, by her complete and unconditional fall from grace, but Stephen was like a disease for which there was no cure.

The staff had accepted his presence, showing him the deference they might have had he been her husband. Even the lad who helped Kate in the stable wasn't immune to Stephen's charisma, and like a lost puppy, followed him around whenever he was outside.

He was stockier now, no longer fitting in the wardrobe of Phillip's old apparel in which she'd dressed him early on, so he'd had a trunk of his own possessions delivered from Bristol Manor. The first time he'd donned his finery and tromped downstairs, she'd been so stunned that she'd had to grab a chair and sit down. The cook had been with her, and she'd been so flustered that she'd burned the muffins.

Decked out as he'd been, in breeches and a tailored white shirt, his blue coat setting off the color of his eyes, his hair pushed off his forehead, he'd resembled an angel painted on a church ceiling.

No, she thought, *not an angel.* He was too dark. Too dangerous. *A devil!* That's what he was! A devil with the power to corrupt and seduce.

Currently, he was attired in his robe, a thin, silky garment constructed of an exotic fabric that a friend had brought him from the Orient. He shrugged out of it, and he was naked, his cock partially erect with his anticipation of what would happen once he entered the pool.

As he maneuvered the ramp, immersing himself to his ankles, to his thighs, he kept his gaze locked on hers, and she was so mesmerized that she couldn't look away. At that very moment, she would have done whatever he requested. Jumped

off a cliff. Hurled herself into a pyre of flames. She was so enamored that there was no despicable conduct she would regard as too scandalous.

Smitten, bewitched, she'd been lured to ruin, and she didn't
care. Not about Kate, or her employees, or her customers. Not
about the neighbors, or Stephen's sister and family. She was
hopelessly, miserably, totally in love, and she'd debased herself so often and so thoroughly that she didn't recognize herself as the woman she'd been before he'd arrived.

That confident, autonomous, enthusiastic person had vanished, replaced by a seething, festering malcontent, who
craved things she couldn't have, who dreamed of things that
could never be.

When will you go? she yearned to shout, but didn't. She
never asked about his plans, because she couldn't bear to hear
his answer. He had to have a departure date in mind, but if she
was apprised of what it was, she'd obsess over its gradual,
dreadful approach. It would loom, like a cancerous tumor eating her alive. She couldn't tolerate the anguish of certainty.
Better to have it be a horrid, gut-wrenching surprise.

He floated toward her and sunk onto a stone ledge, reclin-
ing, his arms resting on the rocks. It was a natural seat, either
created by eons of rushing water or carved by the Romans—
she didn't know which—but he appeared to be perched on a
throne.

"Wash me," he ordered, imperious as any king.

Like the pitiful minion she was, her deplorable heart
pounded at having the chance to oblige him.

After fetching a cloth and soap, she swam over. Eager, excited, she couldn't wait to begin, for she knew how it would
conclude. She couldn't get enough of his body, of the carnal
antics he taught her. He was her tutor, she his pupil. He was
her master, she his slave, and she participated in each foray
with the fervor of a prisoner bound for the gallows, proceeding as if each encounter would be the last.

Scrubbing up a lather, she started to bathe him. Commencing at his shoulders, she traced his nape, his collarbone, his chest, his nipples. Leisurely, she circled them, played with them, then she descended, to his belly, to his privates. He was hard, his erection prodding her, and she swabbed him with the cloth, wrapping it around his rod and using the nap to incite him even more.

Rubbing lower, she cleaned his legs, his feet, until she was crouched before him, like a beggar, a supplicant, and she peered up at his dear face.

How had he come to mean so much to her? Why had she let her emotions run amok? Only suffering could ensue, yet she was determined to forge on.

The bathing emporium was temporarily closed to the public, and while she liked to dupe herself into believing that she'd done it for Stephen, the pathetic fact was that she'd reached the greedy decision so that she could have him all to herself.

For the remaining days he would be with her, she could abide no interruptions, no interference, and she couldn't be distracted by such mundane issues as work or chores. With the resolve of a fanatic, she had to fill herself with bits and pieces of him so that after he went, she could feel as if he'd left some of himself behind.

He brushed her cheek, his thumb grazing her lips. It seemed as if he would utter a profound remark, an eloquent and deep declaration that would further confuse her, and have her reeling, but he didn't comment, and she was relieved.

Since that hideous afternoon when he'd claimed he loved her, he hadn't professed as much again, which she deemed a blessing. The attestation had rattled her, had made her anxious to commit any ridiculous transgression, so it was best that he was silent. When he expressed his sentiments aloud, she longed to assume they were true.

He scooted up to a higher ledge, exposing his flanks, his genitals.

"Put your mouth on me," he said. "I want to watch you."

Without hesitation, she complied. Before meeting him, she hadn't grasped that a woman would do such a thing to a man, that she could enjoy it, but when he'd suggested the wicked deed, she'd been avid to try it, and she'd grown to relish the iniquity. It called to the lusty, bawdy side of her character, the one that hadn't existed before he'd burst into her life, and she was wild to indulge.

Snuggled between his thighs, she massaged him, running across the crown, making him writhe, making him squirm. She dipped down, licked him over and over, stroking her tongue up his rigid length. Arriving at the tip, she laved it, teasing it, and he became more tense, more strained.

As she opened wide and took him inside, he hissed with pleasure, and he thrust, giving her more and more, until he was impaled. She reveled in the ribald act, titillated by how primitive it was, how electrifying. The universe was reduced to its basest elements. There was just him, and her, the dark night, and his rhythmic motions.

He persisted far past what she would have guessed was his limit, until his cock was throbbing with its need for release, and he pulled her away and slid down into the pool.

She pouted at the loss. "You never allow me to finish this way."

"You're not ready for such crudity."

"Why don't you let me be the judge?"

"No." Which meant he considered the matter settled.

As with all facets of their relationship, his dictatorial attitude rankled. She was too independent to obey his orders with any grace, and he was so used to issuing them that it was second nature.

"Turn around," he commanded.

"No. I want to—"

"You talk too much."

He was beyond the point of delay or discussion, and she gleaned some satisfaction in comprehending that she'd goaded him to the edge. Gripping her, he spun her, an easy task with her being so bouyant. She grappled for purchase as he positioned her on her knees, then nestled himself to her bottom.

"Do you have any idea how aroused I am when you take me in your mouth?" He slid three fingers into her sheath, provoking her with smooth, slow caresses. "I like to see you, with your breasts bared, and the moonlight glistening on your skin."

"Make love to me, Stephen," she implored, her voice unsteady and weak, and sounding nothing like her usual, confident self.

Chuckling, he leaned in, biting her earlobe, inducing her to thrash against his hand, but he had her pinned between himself and the rocks so that she could scarcely move.

"Do you like that?"

"Yes, yes," she whimpered, detesting how he could get her to plead and beg.

"How about that?"

"Ohh . . ."

"Should I stop? Or continue on?"

"Don't stop."

With a few deft flicks of his thumb, he goaded her into a powerful orgasm. She soared to the heavens, quivering with ecstasy, her body convulsing. For some reason, dallying in the water made their ardor more vehement. No doubt, it was because the naughtiness of doing it in the out-of-doors tickled her perverted soul. She'd fallen so far from the straight and narrow that it was embarrassing to realize how low she'd stoop. There was no lewd, lascivious exploit that was beyond her.

The spiral peaked and waned, and he was behind her, his

phallus stubborn and insistent at her core. He inserted the tip, taunting her, leaving her desperate, impetuous, and he laughed, preening over how proficient he was at spurring her to a deplorable state.

"God, I adore how you come."

"Take me now," she beseeched.

"Should I?" Pretending scant interest, he declined to confer the relief she craved.

"Stephen!"

He ran his palm up and down her back. "You're so impatient."

"I hate this torment!"

"Tell me how much you want me."

"No."

He penetrated an inch, another. "Tell me that I'm the one. The only one you'll ever have."

"No." Testy, petulant, she wouldn't stroke his male vanity. "After you go, I plan on having dozens of lovers. Hundreds of lovers!"

Clutching her to him, he sheathed himself, and her breath caught as he filled her. "There'll be no one but me!"

He was determined to have her agree, but she wouldn't. Let him stew! He was returning to his doting harem. "I'll have as many as I please. I'll—"

He cut her off, refusing to listen to her assertion, even though they both knew she was boasting. After him, there could never be another.

"Only me!" he repeated, biting her shoulder, and she was trapped and couldn't shake him off.

"You're a cur, a brute, a . . . a . . ."

He started flexing, entering all the way, then withdrawing. Brutal, methodical, his hips slammed into her like the pistons of a huge machine. She was splayed, her bottom slapping his thighs, her shins scraping on the stones. In the morning, she'd be bruised and scratched, but she didn't care. Whatever he asked to do, she would permit, however he demanded his gratification, she would acquiesce.

She was his captive, his vassal, imprisoned by his look, his touch.

His thrusting grew more aggresive, then abruptly, he halted and came. His cock pulsated inside her, his seed spewing out in a fiery torrent. She nearly wept with the rapture of it, the savagery of it. How remarkable, that she—an unpretentious, ordinary female—could propel him to such a drastic condition.

His orgasm went on and on, having no end, as he spilled himself with great relish, and she hung her head and rode the wave with him.

He descended, dragging her with him so they were in the pool. He was imbedded in her, his erection not subsiding, and she reached over her shoulder, cradling his face, his cheek, and he kissed her palm.

"I'm going to die in your arms," he murmured.

"Do you think so?"

"I'm quite sure of it."

Pulling out of her, he scooted onto the rocks, and he took her with him, spreading her legs and easing her down onto his phallus. He kissed her so sweetly that a sheen of tears flooded her eyes.

"What will happen to us, Anne?"

"I don't know."

"How will I persevere without you?"

Don't go! she wailed to herself. *Don't forsake me!*

But she understood that he would. There was no place for her in his world, and no place for him in hers. There was only the present, the next few days or weeks, each passing with a terrifying swiftness.

They had discussed a future, once, that horrid afternoon,

and he'd humiliated her by maintaining that she could never fit in, and she was too proud to beseech him to view their dilemma from a different perspective.

They could succeed, they could find a way—if he truly wished to—but she kept silent. She'd never beseech him to choose her, to stay with her, when he was so adamantly opposed to the notion. Some entreaties couldn't be uttered aloud, some things weren't meant to be.

She embraced him, burying herself at his nape, where she could be soothed by his scent. Already, he seemed to be slipping away, his form less distinct, as if he was fading.

A strange sense of menace and loss crept over her, and she shuddered, the dread of his departure looming like a dangerous, dark hole. She felt as if a thousand demons were out there in the shadows, watching her, waiting for the moment she would be alone, so that they could rain havoc down upon her.

He hugged her. "Are you all right?"

"Yes, just sometimes . . ." She shuddered again and glanced into the thick shrubbery. Lately, there were occasions when she perceived a threat from whatever was out in the woods, though she couldn't explain why, and she shook off her anxiety.

She was being ridiculous. She was merely disconcerted about their imminent separation, and the worrying had her jumpy.

"Sometimes . . . what?"

"I'm being silly. Don't mind me." Smiling, she couldn't have him presuming she was distressed or apprehensive. In the short period remaining, she intended to be as happy and content as she was able, and she wouldn't dampen their joy.

Needing to lighten the mood, she balanced on her knees, riding him, as he surged inside her. They were at their best when they were together like this. Their outside problems dissolved away, the pending anguish ceased to exist. There was just the two of them, unfettered, isolated, seeking the ultimate bliss.

He tipped her forward, her breast in his eager mouth, and he suckled, his tongue playing wicked tricks on her anatomy, igniting the spark that would whirl into an uncontrollable frenzy.

She arched her back, giving more of herself, and she stared up at the stars.

I'm yours, Stephen, she vowed. *Yours forever.*

No matter where he ended up, no matter where the road took him, no matter the sorrows or woes he endured, there would always be one person who loved him beyond imagining.

She closed her eyes and let desire sweep her away.

Willie McGee seethed with fury.

He'd heard the rumors that Stephen Chamberlin was recuperating at Anne's farm, but he'd discounted the gossip, for he hadn't wanted to believe that Anne would be so reckless. Her decision to nurse Chamberlin was unnatural, perverted, so he couldn't fathom why she'd have acceded to such a disastrous ignominy.

How dare she be promiscuous! How dare she be wanton, loose with her favors! With Chamberlin, of all people!

On a daily basis, Willie interacted with the upper crust of society, and he loathed them. They were arrogant, rude, and they scorned him, when they noticed him at all. Usually, they pretended he was invisible, convenient when he was needed to sort out criminal mischief, but unnecessary for any other purpose.

Chamberlin was everything Willie was not. Rich, tall, handsome, he was celebrated by the nation, lauded by royalty and commoners alike, and he probably had a woman around every corner. How revolting that the insolent swine would deign to corrupt Anne!

She was over his lap, reveling in the foul deed like the whore she was. She cried out in passion, and Chamberlin let go, too, spilling himself inside her, and taking no steps to avoid impregnation.

Sickened by the sight, Willie lurched away and barreled into the woods, his head pounding with rage.

He'd been inclined to marry Anne. To honor her by selecting her to be his wife. Oh, the agony of learning she was a Jezebel! Scant more than a prostitute!

Weak, shaking, his legs were wobbly and barely capable of conveying him to his own property. As he climbed the fence, he forced himself to slow, to calm the wild beating of his heart, to restrain his temper, while he evaluated the circumstances.

Anne had betrayed him, had desecrated their friendship, had shattered his faith in her. She'd shamed him, and it was an insult that couldn't go unanswered, but any redress would have to be sought after Chamberlin was gone. It was obvious that the infamous Captain harbored an affection for her, so Willie wouldn't behave improvidently. Chamberlin was too renowned, his family too powerful to cross.

But once Chamberlin left, well . . .

Willie had many methods by which he could garner revenge.

The grotto would be his, and Anne would be his, though her position would be significantly lowered from what Willie had originally conceived. She was a harlot, and therefore undeserving of respect or esteem, and he would treat her accordingly.

He knew how to deal with trollops. He did so regularly, and it was invariably pleasurable. Anne would pay for what she had done. He simply had to figure out the most fitting manner for ensuring he was adequately compensated.

~ 14 ~

"Marry me."

Eleanor stopped moving and gazed down into Charles's rugged, handsome face. "What did you say?"

"You heard me."

She glared at him with no small amount of consternation. "I could swear you just asked me to marry you, so I couldn't possibly have."

"I am askin', and I'd have your answer."

Her knees digging into the mattress, she straddled him, his cock a rod, wedged inside her. She relished the indecent position, treasuring the control it gave her, the power she wielded. *She* determined the pace, the conclusion. It was up to her to decide how deep to take him, how fast to let him thrust—or not.

When he was on the bottom, he was at her mercy, and in his surrender, she'd soared. She wasn't frigid, as her husband had claimed. Hot-blooded, appealing, she was a woman in full bloom, and she'd found a man whose very touch could send her flinging to ecstasy.

He was patient, solicitous, a generous lover, who'd proceeded slowly, who'd treated her like a virgin learning her

way, and his willingness to indulge her exploration and edi-
fication had charmed her.

Sweetly and methodically, he'd escorted her down the
path of iniquity, making it seem as if what they'd done had
been his idea, when in reality, she was like a child with a
new toy.

How could she have been wed for over a decade and not
know how to please a man? Or how to please herself?

Each day was a celebration, with Charles bestowing another gift. They trysted as if they were lust-starved adolescents, sneaking off and breaking every moral tenet ever
devised. Their wild, unrestrained couplings had her wondering if she hadn't become a bit crazed.

In her daft craving for him, she was growing deranged,
and he never refused to oblige her, though he always cau-
tioned that they were courting trouble. Considering the reckless abandon with which she'd thrown herself into the liaison,
she recognized that it was a matter of time before they were
caught, but she was so heedless to the consequences, that
she often speculated as to whether she didn't hope they'd be
detected.

What then? The question slithered past, but she pushed it
away. If she was discovered in a compromising situation
with Charles, how would her father respond? What would he
demand?

She wasn't sure she cared. In her negligent drive to be
with Charles, she couldn't worry about rectitude, the family
name, her reputation, or anything else. The rest of the world,
and its petty ethics, had ceased to signify.

Rocking across his phallus, she reveled in the smooth
glide of sensation. She was sore, stretched beyond her limit,
bruised and battered from their incessant philandering, but
she couldn't desist.

He had unlocked a well of desire that had to be filled, and
she felt that if she trifled long enough or hard enough, she

would find an elusive contentment that had perpetually been beyond her grasp.

He put his arm across her thighs.

"Talk to me," he urged.

"No."

"Eleanor!"

His tone was scolding, and she detested it when he was unhappy, when he chided or reprimanded. While in his company, she wanted unqualified acceptance. For so much of her life, she'd been advised that she was deficient and defective, and she couldn't bear it when he was disappointed in her, even if it was over a minor incident.

She tried to begin anew, but he wouldn't join in.

"We have to discuss this," he maintained.

"Why?"

"I love you."

"No, you don't." Frantic to chase away the unbidden attestation, she shook her head.

"I'm lying here, with my heart on my sleeve."

"Well, you shouldn't be so indiscreet in blurting out your feelings."

"What the hell is that supposed to mean?"

She couldn't abide his anguished expression, so she studied the wall behind him. "Have I said or done anything that would lead you to presume I might wish to wed?"

He paused, reflected. "No."

"There you have it."

"So . . . I'm not to receive the courtesy of a yea or nay?"

"Nay," she bluntly decreed.

As he absorbed her harsh repudiation, his erection waned. "Then what have we been doing here every night?"

"We've been having enthusiastic sexual relations. There's no reason to complicate the proceeding by interjecting unnecessary sentiment into the middle of it."

"I see."

He was quiet, contemplative, not the type who would declare himself without an abundance of forethought. His hurt was so colossal that she was paralyzed with the enormity of her conduct, and as though it had never existed, his warm regard faded. She yearned to reach out and grab for it, to clutch it to her chest so that it wouldn't be lost to her, but it was already gone.

Her passion for Charles was the only magnificent, splendid event that had ever happened to her, and if he took his affection and rejected her, what would she do? How would she carry on?

Oh, why had he opened this door? She wanted to shout at him. Didn't he realize that she couldn't deal with his emotions? Or her own? She wanted to return to where they'd been minutes earlier, but that place had disappeared.

"May I be apprised of why?" he queried.

"I don't intend to wed again."

"Have the decency," he barked, "to look at me as you say it."

She forced herself to be strong, to meet his gaze. His blue eyes were wide with torment and anger, and she could peer into his soul, could read how terribly he'd been wounded. She'd rather die than harm him, yet she replied, "I'm honored that you asked, but I can't."

"Spare me your apologies."

He pulled away and evaluated her, providing her with a chance to redeem herself or change her mind, but she couldn't furnish the words he needed to hear, and even though she hated herself for it, she made no rejoinder.

Sighing, he rose and went to the chair where, in his haste to couple with her, he'd pitched his trousers. He sat and tugged them on, which was an arduous task for him.

"Let me help you," she offered.

"Don't you dare."

Disconsolate, she watched him struggle, recalling the previous occasions when she'd assisted.

He scowled at the floor. "Is it because of my arm?"

"How could you think so?"

"My background, is it?"

"God, no." She'd had a spouse with the loftiest of antecedents, and the experience had taught her a valuable lesson: lineage was an idiotic measure of worth.

"Are you afraid that I'm after your money? If you are, I can tell you that I don't give a bloody damn about it. You can burn every farthing for all I care."

"It hadn't occurred to me that you might be interested in my fortune."

"Then, what? You're fairly eager to fornicate as long as no one knows. So what has this been about? Was it just a lark for you? A naughty romp with your hired man?"

She was crushed by his use of *was*. He was intimating that the affair was over. "Charles, please."

"Answer me! Why have you been doing this?"

"Because it was amusing and delightful."

"Am I to gather that you'll debase yourself in private, but you'd be too ashamed to claim me in public?"

Was that how he perceived her? Hadn't she shown him, in every way possible, how much he meant to her? How could he discount what they'd shared?

"Can you really believe I'm that shallow?"

He assessed her, and a silence festered, becoming awkward, then painful.

"You'd better leave."

Her heart skipped several beats—literally—but she remained calm. "No. I'd planned to spend the whole night. Like always."

"Your *plans* have been altered."

Sitting up, she swung her legs over the edge of the bed,

her feet dangling. She was naked, and with the sudden tenor of the conversation, she felt vulnerable because of it. She scooped up his shirt and drew it on so that she could be surrounded by his scent. The aroma soothed her, gave her courage.

"Don't do this, Charles. Don't send me away."

"What purpose would be served by your staying?"

"I need to be with you."

"I've fucked you several times today," he crudely mentioned. "That ought to keep you sated for a few hours, until you can persuade somebody else to give you a tumble."

He moved toward the door, and she was positive he would physically toss her out if she refused to go on her own. Desperate to smooth over their rift, she clasped his hand, linking their fingers. "I don't want another lover. Just you."

"No. If I had to explain your behavior, I'd argue that you receive a thrill from degrading yourself with a commoner. Does it arouse you? Is it part of some odd fantasy?" As if he couldn't stand to be near her, he yanked away. "I'm sorry, but I won't play your game. You'll have to find another who will."

"Are you truly convinced that I'm the sort who would lie down with just anyone?" He was too much of a gentleman to voice his opinion, and she started to cry, tears streaming down her cheeks.

"If you suspect that a bout of weeping will make any difference, you've miscalculated. Now go, before this gets any worse."

She couldn't describe why she'd plunged into their reckless amour. Had it been loneliness? Advancing age? Insanity? But the stormy liaison had swept her into a dream state, where nothing was concrete. Stuffy, pompous Eleanor Chamberlin Dunworthy had metamorphosed into someone new and free, who was at liberty to indulge her raucous whims.

The idea that he might cast her aside was too bizarre, and

the strange reality she'd built came crashing down, the rubble pummeling her as it fell.

"I am barren," she choked out, humiliated at having to remind him.

"So?"

"A married man deserves children."

"Have I said I wanted any?"

"You don't have to. It's what all men want."

"Is that what this is about? You think you can't have children, so you won't have me, either?"

"I don't *think* I can't. It's a certainty." She gulped and sputtered, rage and shame flaying her. "I knew it each and every moment of my thirteen years of matrimony."

"And I told you that it might have been your husband's fault and not your own."

"Everyone is aware that it's the woman."

"I'm not, you foolish girl! Don't you have any faith in yourself? In me and how much I adore you? Can't you comprehend that having you all to myself might be enough?"

"You insist as much now, but you're only thirty-two. How will it be when you're thirty-five? When you're forty?"

"I'll feel the same."

"Liar!"

He gripped her by the neck, squeezed tight, and shook her. "I may be many things, but I wouldn't lie to you. Not about this, when it matters so much to me."

"I know exactly how it would be." A flood of bitterness, that she'd religiously kept dammed, finally burst. Surprising him with her fury, she pushed him and leapt away. "When I couldn't produce an heir, what do you suppose my life was like? It's all I heard, day after day, month after month, year after accursed year. How I was inadequate, incapable, imperfect! Then, there were the pitying glances from my acquaintances, the horrid comments, the malicious whispers. Like a valiant soldier, I weathered it all, until I was sick to death, and I will not return to that spot. Not ever again." She took a deep breath, let it out. "Not even for you."

"Don't you dare charge me with the sins committed by your lout of a spouse."

"You're a male. I can't help but compare." She was being ruthless, but she couldn't stop herself. On this topic, she couldn't relent, couldn't compromise.

"What if you're already increasing?"

The question sucked the air from the room. "Why would you speculate on such a ridiculous notion?"

"Your breasts are fuller, your nipples darker."

These were indications of pregnancy? She was so un-schooled! "Nonsense."

"I'm not wrong," he asserted. "You've changed. Your body has changed."

"And you pretend to recognize the signs?"

"Yes."

"How could you?"

"I was married when I was younger. I thought you knew."

He'd been married? The news, heaped on top of their quarrel, was too much. She couldn't abide that some other woman had had him as her own, when Eleanor would only ever have this small portion.

"What happened to her?"

"When I met her, she was a laundress who followed the drum. She died outside an army camp. Giving birth to my son. It was an awfully difficult delivery, and no midwife about to assist me. She didn't survive it."

"Where is your son?"

"He died, too."

So . . . he'd sired a child. If they wed, and she never be-came pregnant, there'd be no doubt as to whose failing it was. His fertility was established.

She was shattered. He hadn't confided in her as to his

wife or his boy, and it was the worst betrayal, making her own plight even more hopeless. Her world fractured into a thousand tiny pieces, her illusions in ruins on the floor around her, their affair ended as surely as if the death knell had sounded.

Devastated and forlorn, she longed to hurt him as much as he'd just hurt her. "Am I to presume the experience makes you an expert on pregnancy?"

"I understand more about it than you." He cupped her breast, impersonally assessing shape and size. "They're bigger," he contended. "When you calm down and reflect on this rationally, you'll realize I'm correct."

"You're spewing rubbish."

"Am I?"

"You're trying to pressure me, to confuse me." Her pulse was pounding so loudly that her ears were ringing. "Well, it won't work."

His exasperation evident, he scrutinized her. "Fine. Have it your way. But if you're expecting, I'll not have you betrothing yourself to some blue blood and passing it off as his. I'd kill you first."

At the cold statement, she blanched. He assumed she could wed another? That she could cuckold a husband, and falsify an infant's paternity? In the period they'd been together, had he learned nothing about her character?

"My decision doesn't have anything to do with you!" she shouted.

"It has everything to do with me!" he bellowed in reply, both of them beyond the point of worrying about detection. "If I had some fancy pedigree, you'd have me in a trice!"

"You imagine that I could spurn you, merely because of who you are?"

"I've suddenly discovered how fickle you can be."

The insult wounded her. Why couldn't he grasp how

terrified she was of matrimony? After what she'd been through, she couldn't conceive of risking so much. She'd rather perish than be that unhappy.

Disoriented and muddled, she felt sick at her stomach, and she needed privacy, needed peace and quiet to sort through her emotions. "I must get out of here!"

"What if you're with child?" His words jabbed like the prick of a knife, but she ignored him and retrieved her night-gown and robe. "Do you actually believe your father will let you gad about the estate until you birth a bastard? You're being crazy."

She had a vivid recollection, of a fight with Harold, when she'd found an earring in his bed that wasn't hers. It had been the sole occasion she'd let loose, and he'd pronounced her deranged, had hit her several times, forcefully enough to blacken both her eyes. Then he'd threatened to have her confined to an asylum should she ever again display such a wild swing of temper, so she never had. She'd stuffed it all down inside.

An inferno burned, a turbulence so potent that she was frightened by it. At that moment, she *was* a bit mad, as Harold had alleged. The past had risen up, like a sea monster, and each of Harold's petty slurs had been rubbed raw. She was inflamed by memories she'd never revealed to another soul.

"Don't *ever* tell me I'm crazy."

"That's how you're acting."

"Sod off, you prig!"

She flung the crudity at him, then raced into the hall. While she was frantic to escape, to run as fast as she could away from him, a tiny, idiotic part of her wished he would call to her, that he would cajole and coax her to return, but he didn't.

At the stairs, she climbed, trudging through the empty corridors of the mansion. Shortly, she was sequestered in her suite. She slammed and barred the door, then she walked to the window where she could gaze out at the bleak night sky.

• • •

Charles marched toward the family dining room, his boots clicking on the polished marble floor.

He'd spent the day away from the property, hiding out and trying to figure out what his plans should be. With Lady Eleanor's rejection of his proposal, it was obvious that he had to withdraw from Bristol Manor, which he should have done much earlier, and would have if Stephen hadn't begged him to remain.

Back then, Stephen had needed him, but after his recent visit to Mrs. Smythe's, it was clear that Stephen would soon be recovered, and Charles couldn't determine what role he'd have. He didn't want Stephen's charity, wouldn't be a burden or a parasite, living off Stephen's limited funds.

There weren't many options for a maimed veteran. A man had only to travel through the streets of London, observing the forgotten cripples, to discern that a dismal destiny might await, but he'd always been lucky. Had always landed on his feet. He was skilled with horses and firearms, at managing people and situations, and despite his deformity, he'd carve a spot for himself.

If the future was grim and depressing without Lady Eleanor in it, he would adapt. Over the years, he'd endured ample agony and loss, and he would persevere, would survive any toil the Fates could throw at him.

He'd known better than to reach so high, had recognized from the outset that he and Lady Eleanor were doomed to a few furtive couplings. Yet he'd dallied with her anyway, hoping he could sway her to love him, and he thought she probably did—as much as a person of her station could love someone such as himself.

He was disgusted. By his folly. By his stupidity. He'd claimed *she* was crazy, but *he* had behaved like a lunatic.

A maid had notified him when the Chamberlins were seated for supper. The earl was present, as was Eleanor and her brother Michael. Stephen was at Mrs. Smythe's, and the third brother, James, was in London, so the pending confrontation wouldn't be as dreadful as it could have been.

Of course, there was the chance that Michael might murder him, that he might simply seize one of those ornamental swords that were hanging all over on the walls and stab him to death. Considering Charles's mental condition, it wasn't such a bad notion. In a matter of seconds, he could be put out of his misery.

He entered the elegant salon. The lengthy table was rectangular, the family a lonely trio at the far end, with the earl at the head, Michael on one side, and Eleanor on the other. A footman hovered behind the earl's chair, eager to assist.

Lady Eleanor immediately noticed Charles, and her eyes widened with surprise and fear as to his intentions. She appeared wan, pale, as if she'd been ill, but he declined to be moved. She'd made her choice, and it wasn't him.

Fleetingly, he wondered what her goal had been in trifling with him. Had she imagined they'd keep on forever? Had she predicted an end point? What had it been?

As rapidly as the questions popped into his mind, he shoved them away. Rumination was a waste of energy. It was impossible to decipher the mercurial woman's conduct, and he wouldn't try.

"Charles Hughes!" Michael greeted him. "How fabulous to see you! I'm told you've been creating havoc with Stephen. My hat's off to you!"

"Have you dined?" the earl interjected, though tentatively, uncertain as to whether he wanted to extend any invitation. "Would you care to join us?"

"No, Lord Bristol. I've come to say farewell"—Eleanor gasped, but he didn't glance in her direction—"and to thank you for your courtesy and generosity over the last few months."

"You're welcome," Bristol said, "but you're leaving? Isn't this a tad sudden?"

"Yes."

"Does Stephen know?"

"I'll stop by and inform him."

"Hmm . . ." Having not wanted Charles on the premises in the first place, the earl was at a loss as to whether he should murmur any regrets.

"However, there's a detail I must discuss with you before I depart."

"What is it?"

He peered at the footman. "Would you excuse us so that we may speak in private?"

The servant gaped at the earl, who waved him away, and the threesome shifted in their chairs, as they waited for him to exit, for the door to close.

"You've interrupted my meal, Mr. Hughes," Lord Bristol commented. "This had better be good."

Charles had assumed that it would be easy to confess, then slink out, but he'd never been adept at atonement. He blushed bright red. "I apologize, but there's no tactful way around this, and I couldn't risk that there might be rumors or innuendo, so I want to set the record straight."

"What is it?" Michael inquired when his father couldn't muster a response.

"For many weeks now, the Lady Eleanor and I have been involved in an intimate affair."

There was a shocked pause, then Michael breathed, "The devil you say!"

The earl arched a brow. "Clarify what you mean by *intimate*."

"We've been having sexual relations."

Eleanor leapt to her feet. "Be silent! I do not give you permission to talk of this!"

"Sit down, Eleanor." Bristol gestured to her chair, and like a scolded tot, she obeyed, her knees collapsing. His furious glare hadn't left Charles. "Explain yourself."

"The liaison was completely at my urging and induce-
ment."

"That is a lie!" Eleanor slapped her palms on the table.
"A bald-faced, despicable lie!"

"What is the lie, Eleanor?" the earl queried. "That the
assignations occurred? Or that Charles was the instigator?"

She was blushing, too, and Charles could feel her staring
at him, endeavoring to compel him to look at her, but he
couldn't let himself be affected.

"From your reticence to answer," Bristol proclaimed, "I
shall infer that the circumstances have transpired as Charles
has asserted."

"I take full responsibility," Charles announced.

"As you should," Michael muttered. "I could kill you
where you stand."

"That is your prerogative," Charles agreed. "Or if you'd
prefer the satisfaction of a duel, I would be happy to—"

"Don't be melodramatic!" the earl snapped, cutting him
off. "As if I'd permit the two of you to duel! And you with
one arm!" Perplexed, he scowled at Eleanor, then at Charles.

"Be assured, sir," Charles affirmed, "that I proposed marriage to her."

"And . . .?" the earl and Michael probed together.

"She refused me"—both men bristled—"so that's the
reason I'm going. I won't have her forced into a union she
can't abide, and I won't stay where I'm not wanted."

"Is this true?" Lord Bristol asked Eleanor. "You've
spurned him?"

She didn't reply but started to cry, and it was the worst
moment for Charles. He yearned to rush over to her, to hug
her and insist that everything would be all right. Her father
and brother were as dismayed as he, none of them able to
tolerate her melancholy.

Quiet tears dripped down her pretty cheeks, and she
gulped for air. "Yes, I've rejected him."

A huge weight seemed to drop into the middle of the room. Charles felt as if it was crushing him, as if his heart was breaking all over again, and they could all witness it happening.

"Can you tell us why?" the earl implored of her, but she could only shake her head.

Charles supplied, "She thinks she's barren."

"Oh, for pity's sake!" Michael griped. "I won't listen to such improper remarks about my sister. Not from the likes of you, and especially not when she's sitting here with us, so I suggest you guard your tongue before I rip it out of your mouth."

"Delicate concerns," Charles shot at him, "require indelicate conversations."

The earl was flustered, having no idea how to deal with his intractable, fractious, saddened daughter. "Charles . . . ah . . . would you have her, even if she couldn't bear you a child?"

"Absolutely," Charles declared, "and I told her so. But I also told her that she's wrong. She's not barren. She's already increasing."

"And you make this allegation because . . .?" Bristol couldn't finish the sentence.

"Trust me," was all Charles would provide, "she's pregnant. She doesn't believe me, but she is." The predicament was sufficiently abominable. He wasn't about to review the sensitivity of her breasts with her father!

"We've heard enough," Michael reproached. "You'd better go."

Charles ignored him and pleaded with Lord Bristol. "I would have your word that you will let me have the babe when it's born."

Michael stood, so angry that his chair toppled over. "You have the gall to issue demands?"

"What will *you* do with him, milord?" Charles strove to be rational. "Have him adopted? Farm him out to a crofter?

Abandon him on the streets of London like a vagrant mutt?"

"Sweet Jesu!" Bristol moaned, pained and appalled.

"I want what's mine. I nearly had a son once, but he and my wife died during the delivery, and I never thought I'd be blessed with another. I might have many faults, but I'd be a good da."

"We're not maintaining that you wouldn't be," the earl countered.

"The babe will be your grandchild. Perhaps the only one you'll ever have. Could you dump him on strangers, never to be apprised as to what became of him?" Surprisingly, he suffered his own surge of tears. "I'm begging you, Robert"—he impertinently used the earl's given name—"swear to me that you'll let me have him."

For an eternity, Bristol mulled, pondering the hideous options, and finally, he nodded. "Advise Stephen as to your whereabouts."

"I will."

"We'll contact you if it's necessary."

"Thank you."

He looked at Eleanor then, but she seemed to not really be there, as if she'd been too overwhelmed and had mentally fled, with the shell of her body remaining behind. Her shape was fuzzy, indistinct, the lines so distorted that she was more a chimera than flesh and blood.

He turned and left without glancing back.

～ 15 ～

"Where will you go when you leave here?"

Stephen held Anne in his arms and pondered her question. The mid-morning sun was high in the sky, but they lazed in bed, unable to break the intimate moment.

Because there were so few choices that appealed, her query had him vexed. His two options were Bristol Manor and the mansion in London, but either place belonged to his father, and while he was fond of the earl and they got on well, he couldn't reside under the man's roof. He had to make his own way. But how?

He had no real skills, and even if he'd been adept at some task or other, he wasn't about to toil at menial labor. He tried to conceive of himself slaving away at a desk as a clerk or gentleman's secretary, but the concept was ludicrous.

The only thing at which he'd ever been proficient was soldiering, but he would never again pick up a weapon. Perhaps he'd join those odd Quakers, would enjoy a simple, pious life, and he'd travel the country, preaching sanity and peace.

He smiled. "I suppose I'll be off to London."

"Do you own a home there?"

"No." If he could somehow have scrounged together the money to purchase one in an acceptable neighborhood, he couldn't have afforded the maintenance or the servants.

"Where will you stay?"

"At my father's town house." How depressing! After all he'd been through, he'd come full circle.

"Isn't it strange, living with him when you're thirty years old?"

Touché. "Very, but I haven't any other alternatives."

"He's rich. Why doesn't he settle funds on you?"

"He's wealthy on paper, but his fortune is tied to his realty, which can't be sold, and what's disposable will ultimately be inherited by my eldest brother, James. It's not my father's to dole out. Besides, I'm not sure I would welcome a huge stipend. What have I ever done to deserve it?"

"You've been one of his sons. That should be enough." Such an egalitarian! "If I had three boys, I'd treat them equally."

"You would, would you?"

"Yes."

He wondered about her having children. Would she? Might she have his? Massaging her stomach, he speculated as to whether he'd planted a babe. If he hadn't, it wasn't from lack of trying, and he was surprised that he'd behaved so recklessly. He hadn't sired a child before, had never fornicated with such abandon, but with Anne, it had been natural to forge ahead. He hadn't considered denying himself.

Secretly, he was thrilled by the prospect. If she was pregnant, there would be excuses for continuing contact, letters, updates, requests for assistance. The fact that his offspring would be a bastard, raised without a father, bothered him, but he declined to contemplate the dreaded possibility.

A more horrid thought occured to him. It had been fluttering around on the edges of his consicousness: What if she had a babe with someone else? What if, after he departed, she fell in love and married? He ought to be glad that she might eventually find happiness, but the notion of her achieving it without him was so distressing that he couldn't reflect upon it.

As he had for weeks, he bumbled about in oblivion, pretending that their affair would last indefinitely, that nothing could interfere.

"How will you keep yourself busy?" she asked.

"I'll lounge and loaf."

She punched him in the ribs. "Just as I suspected, you idle scoundrel."

"Leisure diversions suit me."

"You won't catch me arguing."

"Wench." He swatted her on the rear.

Snuggled next to her, he yearned to cast off his societal shackles, to shed his position like an animal molting its skin. *She* was what he wanted. Her quiet, contented world grew more attractive every day, and when he was being particularly morbid, he flirted with a dangerous, tempting decision.

What if he remained? What would he lose?

Everything familiar! Everything I cherish!

What would she gain? An inept, slothful, unemployable laggard, who had no income, but extravagant tastes. She'd murder him before the first month was out.

A fellow could make himself crazy, wallowing in such pointless rumination, and he sighed and stopped his woolgathering. "And how about you? What are your plans after you're shed of me?"

"I'll work. I'll tinker with my concoctions. I'll bathe ailing women in my pool. It's a fine way to carry on."

At her blithe response, irritation bubbled. Just once, couldn't she evince a bit of sorrow? Couldn't she weep in anticipation of losing him? Or beg him to tarry?

A silly vision flashed, of her down on her knees, clutching

his coat and pleading with him not to go. That's what he wanted, for what he was hoping, to have her desperate and forlorn over his pending egress.

He loathed her cheery, resigned attitude, and it was so depressing to admit that she didn't need him. Except for his capacity in providing an occasional tumble—which she could obtain from any man at whom she batted her pretty green eyes—he hadn't a single benefit to offer, hadn't a redeeming quality, save that he loved her beyond imagining. Yet as his father had oft been heard to remark, *love* and a few pennies could buy you a cup of weak tea.

"Good." He attempted to sound merry. "When I remember you, I want to picture you, puttering around at your projects and making people feel better."

"It's what I do best."

"It certainly is."

Which was another detail he admired but hated about her. Others needed her, needed her skills and abilities and many kindnesses. While she'd closed the pool to frivolous guests like Camilla, she allowed visits from the neighborhood women who were ill or dying.

From his perch in her room, he spied on her as she nursed them. Her energy was unflagging, her compassion bottomless, her optimism infinite. In the beginning, he'd been envious of her patients, irked by their taking her away from him, and his jealousy of those sick souls underscored what a pathetic individual he was, especially after he was recovered thanks to her. He was selfishly inclined to withhold her expertise from others, merely so he could lie around for hours on end, fornicating with her.

When he left, he wanted to whisk her away, too, but with such wretched invalids seeking her help, who was he to abscond with her? Even if she'd consent to run off, her mercy and generosity were coveted by so many, her talent so vital, that he had to believe they were God-given, a divine bounty she used wisely and well, and with which he shouldn't interfere.

In the grand scheme of the universe, he was irrelevant, too negligible to keep her to himself.

He feigned levity. "Will you miss me?"

"Yes, you bounder. Every second." She kissed him on the mouth. "Who will be here to drive me mad? Who will whine and complain and snarl at me?"

"I never snarl."

"Hah!" she laughed. "You are the worst, most demanding patient I've ever had."

"Really?" Had he been that bad? When he'd initially arrived, he was sure he'd been a terror, but he'd been suffering so dreadfully that he didn't have clear memories of their early spats.

"Yes, *really*. You're a nuisance."

"But a sexy one, wouldn't you agree?"

"You're a sexy one, all right. And much too vain for my money."

She stroked his chest, his stomach, his phallus, as adept at carnal games as she was at everything else. She was a temptress, a beautiful sphinx, and he couldn't get enough of her. No matter how often or how rigorously they copulated, he wasn't satisfied.

His fascination with her was a mystery. She was unlike any female he'd ever met, so feminine, yet so autonomous, and the combination had him beguiled. He couldn't restrain himself, couldn't bridle his erotic impulses. She had only to glance in his direction, and he was eager to dally.

Would his desire ever wane? The more he had her, the more he wanted her. There was no limit to his craving.

As he moved over her, their naked bodies connected, and tingles of sensation cascaded all the way down. He kissed her cheek, her neck, his whiskers tickling her, goose bumps flaring down her arms.

At her bosom, he rooted to her nipple, soothing himself, suckling her, inhaling her sweet scent. It was an aphrodisiac that inflamed, that spurred him to repeated acts of foolhardiness.

He went to her other breast, nuzzled and played, reveling in her uniqueness, in the oneness he experienced when they were together.

Nudging her thighs, he settled himself and glided inside. She was tight, hot, and an impression of peace and serenity swept over him. This was where he belonged, where he was meant to be.

She locked her feet behind his back, rocking them to the end, and when he came, he felt so fortunate, so special, so . . . so . . . cherished. It was the only word that applied. As she gazed up at him, her devotion and affection were manifest, and his heart ached at noting how much she cared.

"Oh, my," she breathed as their passion ebbed. "How will I survive without you doing that to me at least once a day?"

She was teasing, wanting to sound light and gay, but her query held a veiled significance. It probed at issues neither of them could bear to address, so he replied in the same breezy tone.

"I've tried my best to plumb your depths." He flexed, still erect and wanting her again.

"I've definitely been *plumbed*." She giggled and stretched. The clock on the mantle indicated the hour was nearing eleven. Her maids were kind; they hadn't interrupted. "What a wanton I've grown to be. I could adapt to this life as a slugabed."

"You're a fast learner."

"I've been observing you."

Chuckling, he pulled out and slid off so that he was lying beside her, and immediately, she sat up, her dawdling over. He thought about coaxing her to forgo her chores, but she wouldn't. She was always busy, always productive. He'd never known anyone who charged on with such boundless determination.

Shuffling about, she dressed herself as he watched. She was so at ease with her nudity, with his presence. It was as if they were an old married couple, who'd performed this ritual a thousand times previously.

Her garments were functional, so she didn't need a fancy lady's maid, and it afforded him an extra privacy he treasured. There couldn't be a husband and wife alive who generated the intimacy he'd found with her, and he'd never achieved anything comparable with his prior paramours.

She let him fuss with her hair, having him brush the lengthy strands, braid it, then hold it while she secured it with combs. It was his favorite part of the morning, and he was saddened with how it flew by.

Much too soon, she was prepared to go about her business, which would leave him isolated and feeling sorry for himself. He was sufficiently restored that he could meander downstairs, could occupy the front parlor, but he never did. He was uncomfortable around her employees, chiefly Miss Kate, and he couldn't figure out what he should say to them, or how he should deport himself.

They respected Anne, even after his reprehensible behavior toward her, yet they were polite to him, and hadn't judged her too harshly. Around them, he felt like a cad of the highest order, so he hid in her bedchamber like the coward he was, though he wouldn't be bored.

Kate had fashioned some weights for him, and he had bending exercises to accomplish, so there were plenty of projects with which to engross himself, but he'd be lonely. In between chores, he'd sit in a chair by the window and, like a lost puppy, would stare out at the yard, hoping to catch glimpses of Anne as she walked by.

"I'll send up some breakfast," she said.

"I'm starving." He gave her a lascivious grin. "I seem to have worked up an appetite."

"Lecher."

"And celebrating every moment of my excess." He lay on the pillows. "Will you eat with me?"

"No. I've lagged too long already, and if I return, I'll never escape your wicked clutches."

"I should be so lucky!"

A maid knocked, and Anne peeked out the door. After a whispered conversation, she had surprising news. "Your friend, Charles Hughes, is here. He'd like to speak with you, if you're up to it."

Charles? Fleetingly, he worried. Was everyone all right at home? "Has my sister come with him?"

"He's by himself."

Which increased his anxiety. "Tell him I'll be down."

"I'll entertain him, so don't rush. Will you need help with your clothes?"

"Be my guest." He held out his arms in naughty invitation, but she ignored him and stomped out, muttering about insatiable appetites and extravagent scoundrels.

Many minutes later, he strolled into the salon, pleased that he'd managed on his own. Anne was nowhere to be seen, and the servants were absent, but Charles had been well tended and was snacking from a tray of goodies.

Charles stood and scrutinized him from top to bottom. "Last I saw you, you looked like an old man. Where's your wheeled chair?"

"I don't need it."

"That's grand, Captain. Just grand."

"Where's Mrs. Smythe?" he inquired.

"Introduced herself, ensured I was fed, then scurried out. I think I intimidate her."

"You alarm most everyone who crosses your path. I'm beginning to suspect that you do it deliberately."

"Perhaps." He smiled, a rare sight. "You're exceptionally hale."

"Mrs. Smythe's skill as a healer is unequaled. What was your opinion of her?"

"She's different than I imagined. Much younger. Much *prettier*. I'd envisioned an elderly crone."

"She's hardly that."

"No, she isn't." Charles scowled. "I'm developing a new theory as to why you've remained here."

"What do you mean?" But he had the answer to his own question. Who could relinquish gorgeous, appealing Anne?

"Will you marry her?"

He sputtered, fumbled about, tried to appear shocked. "Marry . . . Mrs. Smythe?"

"Yes. Or is it just for sport?"

His cheeks flushed, and the temperature in the room felt too hot. Was he so obvious in what he'd been doing? He'd thought himself careful, discreet, and he couldn't fathom how Charles had guessed, but then, Charles was more astute than others. If there was a secret to ferret out, he was the person who could, and now that Stephen's antics had been exposed, he couldn't decide how to justify his misdeeds. They were both adults, so there was no point in denying what Charles had deduced, yet how to account for the unaccountable?

His affair with Anne wasn't a trivial gambol, and he wasn't the type who would capriciously ruin her. At least, he hadn't been before his wounding. Since then, his demeanor and mental processes had been so disjointed, he'd been so unlike his prior self, that it was difficult to predict how he might or might not act. Plus, his sojourn at her farm hadn't seemed real, had been so separate from his other life, that it was easy to pretend the rules of civilized behavior didn't apply.

Where was the harm if they were cavorting like newly-weds? If it was make-believe, codes of conduct were abolished.

Weren't they?

How he hated to have Charles intruding into the fantasy world he'd built!

"She's a widow," he inadequately maintained.

"So? She's not a strumpet, so I have to admit that I'm flabbergasted."

The admonishment stung. He and Charles were friends, but so much more. Their war experiences had forged a bond that went beyond family or class. Charles's comment underscored how outrageous his comportment was when viewed from the outside.

He knew better, and in a more sane state, would have restrained himself. Or would he have?

He'd never been so happy, and he wanted to blame his strident emotions, and poor choices, on a mixed jumble created by how his recovery had thrown them together. But what they felt for each other transcended time and space, was a passion so true and enduring that he wondered if their meeting hadn't been predestined.

Had all that transpired merely been a divine plan to convey him to this juncture? Had it been a lesson? A test? Had he passed or failed?

"What are your intentions toward her?" Charles prodded, then he must have read a clue in Stephen's expression, because he smirked with disgust. "I see: you have none."

"How could I?"

"How indeed?"

An awkward silence ensued, which was odd. They never quarreled, were of like mind in most discussions. They needed to change the subject, before they said something stupid, something irreversible, so he settled on, "What brings you here?"

"I've quitted Bristol Manor, and I shan't return."

"Why? Has someone upset you? It wasn't my father, was it? If so, I'll—"

"No. The earl was actually quite sensible. It's your sister, I'm afraid."

"Eleanor? What about her?"

"It seems you and I have both been short on moral judgment recently."

"You and Eleanor . . .?" He couldn't finish the indelicate query, but he wasn't surprised by the tidings. When they'd last visited, he'd speculated as to the depth of their relationship.

"Yes. I begged her to marry, but she wouldn't have me."

"Did she say why?"

"She *claims* it's because she's barren."

"You don't accept her explanation?"

"I'm not a fool. She's an aristocratic lady. She wouldn't stoop to having a crippled pauper as her spouse."

"You don't give her enough credit."

"Trust me. Her ability to birth a child, or not, had no bearing on her refusal."

"Everyone has always assumed she's infertile."

"*Everyone* is wrong. She's increasing, even as we speak."

"You're positive?"

"Very."

"What will you do?"

"I've requested your father contact me when the babe is born, so that I may have it and raise it. He's agreed."

"Oh, Charles—" Stephen sighed. He liked both of them so much, and he was heartsick at their impasse. What was the matter with Eleanor? Charles was a fine man, was all she could ever hope for in a husband. His finances were a problem, but hers more than made up for his lack, and their attraction was so blatant it was embarrassing.

Was she vacillating, due to their disparate positions, as Charles was insisting?

As the prospect spiraled to a conclusion, he paused. Wasn't their imbroglio an exact copy of his with Anne? What did the information imply about himself and his sister?

Were they snobs? Fickle? Inconstant? Was he inferring that Charles was good enough for Eleanor, but Anne wasn't good enough for himself? By what standard?

Charles had offered for Eleanor. Why was his situation with Anne any different? Shouldn't he do the same, even though he was certain it would be an idiotic resolution? Did he presume that Eleanor's reputation and virtue were more important than Anne's? Why? Because of *his* father? Because of *her* mother? It made no sense.

Anne's father was an earl, too, his own father's peer and equal. Gad, the two men were friends! Was Anne of less value because her father hadn't wed her mother three decades earlier? How could it possibly signify after all this time? Why should her parents' ancient history make his circumstance distinct from Charles's?

He was so confused that he couldn't sort out the troubling dichotomy. Men of his station didn't marry women of hers. It was an immutable fact. Any suggestion to the contrary was so outlandish that he couldn't process a response. It was like demanding he believe the sky was yellow or the ocean red.

His head began to throb.

"Why did you stop to see me?"

"To tell you that I'd proposed to her. I didn't want you supposing that I'd shirked my duty."

"You needn't have worried. I couldn't think badly of you."

"I asked her to wed, as my behavior required. What have you to say for yourself with Mrs. Smythe?"

"I don't know," he answered honestly. "I truly don't."

Charles studied him, his disappointment clear and painful

to witness, but though his umbrage was apparent, he didn't verbalize it.

"I'll be in London," he said.

"Where?"

"I'm not sure."

"Stay at the town house."

"No. I can't risk that I might run into your sister."

"Then, bunk yourself in the carriage house, with the stable hands. Wait for me until I arrive."

"When will that be?"

"Soon." The reply was deliberately enigmatic, but he couldn't be more precise, for if he voiced a date aloud, he would have to follow through, and he simply wasn't ready.

"As you wish."

Always loyal. Always allegiant. Charles turned and left, without a farewell, and Stephen went to the window and watched him ride away until he was a tiny speck on the horizon.

～ 16 ～

Camilla sat in the small office, uncomfortable in the chair that had been provided, and irked that her host hadn't been more courteous. In order to hide her identity and prevent recognition of her carriage, she'd arrived in a hired hack, but from her clothes and demeanor there was no question that she was a person of substance, and she should have been afforded more deference.

The fellow across from her didn't look competent, but he'd been highly recommended. He was short, burly and balding, and not very clean, but he had a crafty gleam in his eye, and he appeared to be strong, so hopefully he was the sort of ruffian to handle the job.

"How may I help you, milady?" He wasn't as fawning as she liked her underlings to be, but she couldn't be choosy. As the old adage went: when dancing with the devil, don't expect to encounter angels.

"This is a situation of some delicacy, Mr. McGee," she started, "and I've been apprised that you are precisely the man to assist me." She smiled, a feral smile meant to let him know that she was in charge, that she would be paying him and he shouldn't forget it. "Confidentially, of course."

"Of course."

"I have need for a woman to be prosecuted."

"For what crime?"

"Assault."

"Against whom?"

"Myself."

She blushed. Her chagrin and fury over the hideous incident at Mrs. Smythe's farm hadn't waned. If anything, it had grown more potent. She was the laughingstock of Bath, and she couldn't peek outside without being teased and having her name dragged through the mud. Derisive stories were being bandied, and she was the butt of crude, offensive jokes. People couldn't get their fill of recounting the battery, or how she'd been evicted, then denied future bathing privileges.

Declining to be cowed by the despicable tyrant, she'd returned to the spa several times, but the gate was locked, and there were guards patrolling the grounds, keeping Stephen in and others out. Herself, included. She wasn't certain, but she thought the sentries were Bristol footmen, which was an additional insult.

How could Stephen side with Mrs. Smythe? When Camilla had been snuggled in his bed, and the lunatic proprietress had barged in on them, he hadn't shielded her from danger, hadn't risen to her defense, hadn't so much as scolded Mrs. Smythe.

His dozens of slights had her fuming. How dare he! It was bad enough that he'd refused to allow her inside Bristol Manor, but to learn that he'd spurn her at Mrs. Smythe's emporium! That he would employ watchmen to prohibit her entrance!

Long ago, she should have quit the provincial hamlet and traveled on to London, but she wasn't about to give the impression that she'd scurried off in an embarrassed huff. Nor did she imagine her affairs would be much better in the city.

Many of her so-called friends had raced home, had embellished the details of the altercation to where it would be impossible to show her face in public.

For all the misery Smythe had caused, Camilla had vowed revenge, and she'd found the perfect method. Before Camilla was through, Smythe would lose everything, would be branded a felon and jailed, might even be transported to the penal colonies.

She garnered an enormous amount of satisfaction envisioning the tortures that were approaching for Mrs. Smythe. The only decision that remained was whether she should ultimately drop a hint as to who had orchestrated the downfall, or if she should forever let Smythe wonder as to who had devised her ruination. There was such pleasure in either scenario.

"Have you ascertained the identity of the individual who committed this attack?" Mr. McGee was inquiring.

"She's your neighbor. A Mrs. Anne Smythe. She runs a spa in the grotto behind her residence."

Her mention of Mrs. Smythe caught Mr. McGee's attention, charging the air with a new energy. He straightened, was more alert and interested in what she had to say.

"I'm acquainted with Mrs. Smythe, and it's difficult for me to accept that she would assault anyone, especially an exalted lady such as yourself."

He imbued the word *lady* with sufficient sarcasm to insinuate that he didn't think she was one, and his skepticism made her gnash her teeth. She'd married far above her station, and she never ceased to be ridiculed because of it, and she wasn't about to tolerate any scorn from such a lackey.

"The woman is quite mad, I swear it."

"What is it that she did?"

"I had gone to take the waters. It was my first appointment, and by accident, I went into her house, in search of the changing room. When she stumbled upon me, she became crazed, screaming and yelling, slapping me and pulling my hair." He looked so incredulous that she was compelled to declare, "I was lucky to escape with my life!"

"Were there any witnesses?"

"Dozens, but there's the rub, you see. I can't be linked to a scandal."

"No, we wouldn't want that."

His acerbity was grating, and she wouldn't put up with any insolence. As Mrs. Smythe was about to discover, commoners crossed Camilla at their peril. "I was informed that justice could be served without my being involved, but if you aren't clever enough to manage it . . ."

She began to stand, when he halted her, as she'd suspected he would. By all accounts, he had a criminal heart.

"A prosecution could be . . . arranged. For a price."

"How much?"

The figure he enumerated was so small that she nearly laughed aloud. He was a fool; she'd been prepared to pay much more. He needed a lesson in larceny! But then, everything was cheaper in the country—even the purchase of unlawful assistance.

"Pardon me for raising an indiscreet topic," he interjected, "but I've heard that Mrs. Smythe permits nude bathing. Did you observe any episodes of indecency?"

"Why are you asking?"

"I'm considering the manner by which Mrs. Smythe might be brought low. If I only had some *evidence*"—he paused to ensure she received his message—"that communal obscenity was occurring, I could examine the facility myself, without naming the source whereby I gleaned my proof. I'd proceed on a case of lewdness, without having to evoke the issue of assault, at all."

"As a matter of fact"—she was ready to play his game by whatever rules he concocted—"I beheld innumerable interludes of nudity." She leaned closer, pretending to be aghast.

"I'm shocked to confess that it goes far beyond therapeutic healing."

"In what fashion?"

"Her customers engage in perversion." Hah! The reprobate's brows rose to his hairline! Let him reflect on that piece of news! By the time she left, he'd be hard as a poker. "On the *sole* occasion I visited, women were touching each other's bodily parts and kissing on the mouth."

"Was it out in the open? Where any passerby could view them?"

"Yes. It was so foul that I wouldn't swim in the water for fear of what might happen to me. I'd been advised that it was a respectable establishment. Little did I know that it was scant more than a brothel for aberrant females!"

"Very intriguing. I'll have to investigate."

"Thank you." She proffered the cash he'd demanded, which would guarantee Smythe's demise, then she stood to go. "There's one more aspect to concern you."

"What is it?"

"Captain Stephen Chamberlin is currently her guest. You're familiar with him, I trust?"

Her alluding to Stephen had a strange effect. His eyes were flinty, his muscles tense.

"Yes."

"Rumor has it that he's developed a *fondness* for Mrs. Smythe."

"Really?"

"In light of his fascination, you should delay until he's in London, and far away from here. No need to court trouble." Plus, the longer the lag in McGee taking action, the further separated she would be from the event. There would be naught to connect her to Smythe's pending misfortune.

"You presume that I'm scared of Captain Chamberlin?"

"If you're not, you should be." Stupid oaf! "His family is very powerful. Should he learn of Smythe's plight, he would intervene on her behalf, and you wouldn't be able to fight him. She'd wiggle free unscathed, and I'd be tempted to believe I hadn't gotten my money's worth. We wouldn't want that, would we?"

Staring him down, she let him see how determined she was, how eager to have the situation resolved to her satisfaction. As her wrath could be formidable, he shouldn't blunder or thwart her. Amazingly, he matched her stare with such unveiled disgust and dislike that she could barely keep from squirming.

She had no doubt that he was dangerous, a cruel and callous villain, which made her glad in her choice of accomplice. He would be as diabolical as she would be herself, and he would serve her well.

"How shall I contact you when it's finished?" he queried.

"We shouldn't have to communicate. I've told you what I want, and you've been remunerated." She strolled to the door, desirous of making a memorable exit. "Just so we understand one another, I hate to be disappointed, so don't bungle it."

"I won't."

"Let's hope not. For your sake."

Smiling, she departed, pleased with her day's work.

"Good night, dearest Kate," Pru said, holding Kate's hand as they studied the house in the clearing, the moonlight casting eerie, sinister shadows.

"Good night, Pru. Be careful."

"I always am," but in spite of herself, she shuddered. It was just a building, wood and stone, an inanimate object constructed by her grandfather a half-century earlier. There was nothing evil or threatening about it, yet for some reason, it emanated with malignancy.

Shaking off the morbid impression, she decided it was the lateness of the hour, and their trek through the forest, that had her spooked. She was afraid of the dark, and even though she was with Kate, she was unsettled.

"Are you sure you won't change your mind?" Kate asked.

"I don't dare."

Kate had begged her to leave home, to move to Mrs. Smythe's farm, claiming that she could persuade Anne to let her stay, to give her a job. The prospect of earning a salary tantalized her, but she wasn't brave enough to acquiesce.

While she could muster the courage to sneak to the pool, to romp and pretend that what they were doing was normal, she couldn't jump from fantasy to reality. If she accepted Kate's proposal, she would have to admit that she was deviant, a grotesque anomaly.

She'd never speculated as to why men didn't appeal to her, why she'd never pestered Willie to find her a husband, but since meeting Kate, her untoward emotions made sense. She was attracted to women. They bewitched her, when men didn't at all.

Kate insisted there were many females like them who, lest they be caught and punished, concealed their shameful secret, and Pru suspected she was correct. She and Kate couldn't be the sole exceptions in the entire world, but that didn't mean Pru could take such a giant step. It was difficult to imagine herself in such a dubious existence.

Then, of course, there was Willie to consider. He would never allow her to live without his protection. To have his sister nearby and toiling for her room and board was a slight he would never sanction. He was a proud man, and if she forged ahead against his wishes, he would forcibly drag her away, and she wasn't about to bring his vengeance down on Anne and Kate.

"Promise me you'll think about it," Kate implored.

"I will, but I don't want to raise your expectations."

"I worry about you."

"Don't. I'm perfectly safe, and I'm cautious."

"I know you are, but I worry anyway."

Pru hugged her, cherishing her concern like a precious gift. No one had ever fretted over her before, and it was so marvelous that Kate was nearby, that she was in Kate's thoughts. It comforted her when she was lonely or sad.

"When will your brother return?" Kate inquired.

"Not for another three days, at least. I'll come tomorrow night."

"I'll be waiting."

Kate helped her climb the fence, and she waved, then hurried across the yard. The residence was quiet, the servants asleep. She crept in the rear door and up the stairs to her room, and as she tiptoed toward the wardrobe, she leapt with startled surprise.

"Willie McGee!" She clutched her fist over her racing heart. "You scared the life out of me."

Her brother was home! When he wasn't supposed to be! He was lounged in the chair next to her bed! How long had he tarried, angry and impatient for her arrival?

Frantic with dread, she struggled to remember how she looked—were her buttons fastened, her laces tied, her shoes on?—and to devise a plausible explanation as to where she'd been. She wasn't prone to insomnia, wasn't the type to wander outside. Her hair was tidy, plaited into a braid, but it was damp.

She compelled herself to act as casual as possible, going to the dresser and lighting the lamp, keeping busy, filling the frightening silence with chatter.

"What are you doing in here, sitting in the dark by yourself? And why are you home so soon? You were in London with your prisoners. If you'd apprised me that you were—"

He uncoiled from the chair, and there was such an air of menace surrounding him that she bit off her sentence. He wasn't tall, but he was bulky, and he towered over her.

"Where have you been?"

"I took a walk."

"Liar!" The word sizzled out of him, and he reached behind her and clasped her braid, yanking it. "Tell me! I would hear it from your own mouth."

"Nowhere, Willie. I've been nowhere."

"Your hair is wet. Why?"

"It's drizzling."

"Liar!" he repeated.

"Honestly! Cease your posturing! You're hurting me!"

He gripped the front of her neck, squeezing tight, tighter, making her squirm, making her panic. "I saw you."

"What are you babbling about?" He was choking her, and she pried at his fingers.

"I saw you with your freakish lover, with your repulsive Sappho."

He'd seen her with Kate? Oh, God! Her alarm escalated. "Willie, please—"

"Is that how you like it? From a woman? Or is she actually a man? I've often wondered. Does she have a cock in her trousers?"

"No, Willie, you're wrong. You're spewing nonsense."

"All this time, I assumed you were frigid. That you just weren't interested." His hand slithered to her breast, and he pinched the nipple until she cried out in pain. "What a pathetic strumpet you are. You finally spread your legs, and it's for a degenerate female!"

He slapped her, and she stumbled to the floor, smacking onto her knees. Terrified, she crouched down, rubbing her aching wrist. When she peeked up, he was clutching the leather strop with which he sharpened his razor. On many occasions, she'd experienced how proficient he was at inflicting appalling, scarring punishment in wielding it as a weapon.

She hated to show any fear, but she winced.

He hovered over her, stroking and petting the strop, then her breasts, in a manner that made her want to gag. She tried to scoot away, to escape, but she was trapped between the bed and the wall.

"I'm aroused from spying on you," he confessed. "I intend to coax your foul friend here, to my room. I'll have the two of you do it while I watch, then I'll join you. I'll have you both at my mercy."

Over the years, he'd abused her in many ways, but it had been physical, never sexual, and it hadn't occurred to her that he might try something so vulgar. How could she reason with him? He was mad in his fury, beyond persuasion, but there had to be a method whereby she could cajole him to sanity.

"Willie . . ." she beseeched, but the assertions required to plead her case wouldn't come.

In a flash, he ripped her gown, exposing her back, then he brought the strop down, cracking it across her bared flesh.

"Pervert," he seethed. "Filthy pervert."

He whipped it down, again and again, and she huddled into a ball, praying that the worst would pass quickly.

"What is it, dearest cousin?"

Robert entered the salon and shut the door, as Felicity spun toward him. She'd slipped away from her mother's musicale, wanting to be by herself as she read the post that had just been delivered, but he was so observant that he'd followed.

"Hello, Robert."

"You're upset. Has something happened?"

"I've received a letter."

"From whom?"

"Lady Eleanor in Bristol."

"Is it bad news?" He seemed excited that it might be.

"No. It's quite splendid." She steadied her smile, broadened it, urging herself to be glad.

"What does it say?"

"Captain Chamberlin is much improved and ready to be discharged from the spa where he's been recovering."

"How fabulous." He grimaced as if he were sucking on a pickle. "What are his plans?"

"He's returning to London, to establish himself at his father's town house."

"I see."

"Lady Eleanor has invited me to travel to Bristol, so that the two of us may retrieve him, then accompany him on his triumphant journey to the city."

"When?"

"As soon as I can prepare myself."

"Tomorrow?"

"Or the next day."

"When will you be back?"

"I'd guess a fortnight."

"Two weeks." Sighing, he came to her, took her hands in his. "How shall I persevere without your charming company?"

He kissed her on the cheek, then on the mouth. He'd done so several times now, and she kept waiting for it to become the moment of passion about which her married friends tittered, but no fireworks ignited, no spark flared.

Oh, she was so fickle! So erratic and irresolute! She was engaged! What was she doing, sneaking about in private parlors and dallying with her cousin? Why didn't she enjoy it? If it was more pleasurable, would it seem less sinful?

She was confused, perplexed about what she wanted. It was Robert, wasn't it? Then why wasn't she more thrilled by his amorous attention?

He was kind and gentle, and he needed her desperately, needed her support and strength, as she shepherded him through the murky waters of a musical career.

Yet, what of Stephen? He was gallant, brave, and he'd

endured so much. Wasn't he just as deserving of her energy, her optimism and vigor?

She was so bewildered over her choices, and she broke off the embrace and stepped away.

"Robert, we can't keep on."

"But I love you, Felicity! You can't demand that I desist. It's like asking the rain to stop falling."

"I'm betrothed. I betray Captain Chamberlin whenever we're alone."

"You can't go through with your marriage! Not after all we've meant to one another!"

He tried to clasp her hands again, but she wouldn't let him. Gliding to the window, she noted how the autumn leaves were orange and red, the flowers in the garden wilted with the onset of the season.

"I must proceed with the wedding. If Stephen will have me." Behind her, she could feel Robert bristle. Couldn't he understand how distressing this was for her? She needed sympathy and compassion, advice and counsel. Not chastisement!

What would people think of her if she announced that she didn't wish to wed Stephen? How could she unmask herself as such a vain, self-centered creature? Why, at the very mention of crying off, her mother would likely suffer an apoplexy.

"But what of our goals?" he wheedled. "We had such grandiose plans."

They'd frequently palavered, about his talent, about their villa on the cliffs above a quaint Italian village, where he would compose, and she would nurture his genius. In a thrice, their dreams had dwindled to ashes.

"I won't abandon you, Robert," she vowed. "Once I'm married, and the trust fund goes to Stephen, I'll be your patroness. You'll want for nothing. I swear it!"

Though she'd never discussed the matter with Stephen, she was positive he wouldn't begrudge her her fascination with struggling artists. Her giving Robert financial aid wouldn't be the same as their being together, but at least he'd have money to continue his work.

Such a boon was worth a great deal, but he was glaring at her as if he was angry, as if he might say something horrid about Stephen, or worse yet, about herself.

She couldn't bear to be admonished, not when she was so confounded about the future and what her role should be. She sustained her own wave of fury, and fleetingly, she wondered how he dared to be irritated with her, but she tamped down her vexation.

Robert loved her! He did! If he was irate, it was because of the pain he was experiencing over losing her.

"If you'll excuse me," she said, frantic to escape while she collected herself, "I must share the good news with Mother."

She hurried out and down the corridor before he could reply.

17

Stephen stood in front of the mirror, tying his cravat. Eleanor had sent a trunk of his clothes, and he'd gained so much weight, that they nearly fit as they'd been tailored. In his blue coat, white shirt, and tan trousers, he looked healthy and robust, with no lingering hint of how ill he'd been at the start.

Behind him, he caught glimpses of Anne. Quiet, morose, she was lost in a contemplation she had no intention of sharing. She was huddled on the bed, leaned against the headboard, her arms wrapped around her knees so that she appeared to be hugging herself, or perhaps, holding herself together.

He wasn't sure what had prompted his decision to depart. He'd been staring out the window at the colorful leaves, and he'd felt so stable and whole that he'd realized the moment was upon him. There'd been no lengthy rumination, no heart-wrenching deliberation.

Despite Anne's opinion, he'd never been an idle man, and with his recuperation, he was restless, impatient for a change. Though he had reservations about returning to the city, he was curious about his acquaintances, and ready to immerse himself in the social whirl.

On listening to his faltering explanation that it was time, Anne had been cheery and upbeat, not displaying any dismay, and he'd been annoyed at her nonchalance, which was stupid.

Would he rather have had her maudlin, weeping, begging him not to go? He grinned at the thought. While he would have gained some personal satisfaction from having her woe-begone, he wouldn't have wanted their last days to be doleful. Wasn't it better that they'd been merry, wild, extravagant? They'd philandered with a reckless abandon, had bathed and talked and fornicated as if there was no tomorrow, and for the two of them, there wasn't.

But now that the separation was nigh, he could detect her desperation, her anguish. She was shattered, sorrowing, her agony so extreme that she couldn't shield it, and it hurt to see how deeply she was grieving.

He should have grasped that she'd been hiding her feelings, that she'd feigned gaiety so that their final week would be a glorious adventure. He'd never forget a single detail of the interlude, would always recollect how close they'd been, how devoted and attached.

London would be so dull and dreary without her, and he'd considered imploring her to join him, to be his mistress, although he had no idea how he'd have supported her. His destiny was to marry money, and it would hardly be sporting that, in his initial act as a husband, he use his new bride's wealth to set up his paramour.

His musing launched a cycle of confused yearning, where he toyed with the notion of staying, which he could only do if he was willing to be dependent on her for every little thing. In his more morbid reveries, the concept didn't seem half bad.

You don't belong here, a voice rang out. *You have to leave.*

He knew the truth of the admonition, but that didn't make it any easier to bear.

A maid knocked, but Anne didn't move to answer her.

With a hollow expression, she continued to watch him, so he walked over, cracked the door, and peeked out.

"Yes?" he asked.

"Your sister and your fiancée have arrived, milord," the girl said. "They await you in the parlor."

Anne didn't respond, gave no indication of being upset that his betrothed was under her roof, but the tidings had to be a terrible blow. On numerous occasions, he'd informed her that there was no engagement, that there would be no wedding. What must she be thinking?

It was too late to fret, and strangely, he wasn't angry that Felicity had accompanied Eleanor.

Though he hadn't imagined he'd welcome her, he was glad she'd come. Her presence marked the shift that was occurring. He was in Anne's bedchamber—her convalescent, her lover, her friend—but when he exited into the hall, he would be crossing a sort of line, a line of inevitability and necessity, that would hurl him back to his old life, his prior existence.

Save for his marvelous memories, Anne would have no place there, while Felicity would be at the center. He wasn't certain that marriage to her was in the offing, but for now, she played a pivotal role.

"Is Mr. Hughes with them?"

"No, sir."

He hadn't heard from Charles, and he'd hoped that Eleanor would have reconciled with him, though in view of how stubborn she could be, it would likely never transpire.

"Thank you," he replied. "Please tell them I'll be down shortly."

She curtsied and left, and he accepted her deference as a symbol of the metamorphosis in progress. He'd ceased to be a member of the household, but was someone above it.

Turning, he gazed at Anne. She was a tragic figure, beautiful, silent, and so alone, and he went to her and took her icy hands in his, tugging her off the mattress and onto her feet.

"It's time," he stated.

"Yes."

As he pulled her into his arms, he was deluged by a tide of melancholy, which surprised him. When he'd envisioned their farewell, he'd predicted that he'd be somber, torn, but he hadn't expected this explosion of . . . of despair.

What was he doing? How could he cast her aside? Yet, Eleanor and Felicity were downstairs. The future dragged at him, like a rope hauling him to his fate, and he couldn't fight its steady draw.

"I never believed this day would actually arrive," he remarked.

"Nor did I."

Tears flooded her eyes, and her distress lit a spark to his own, igniting a pyre of disturbing emotion. There were so many things he'd never told her, so many thoughts he'd never uttered aloud. How had the end caught up to them so rapidly? Why hadn't he comprehended how dreadful it would be?

He cradled her face. "Don't you dare weep. I can't stand it when you're sad."

She chuckled, but it was an appalling sound that wrenched at his resolve and composure. "It will be so quiet after you go."

He'd pondered the same, brooding over the lull that would eclipse his world. She'd filled his waking hours with pithy conversation upon which he'd thrived. Who would he confide in when he had a vital secret to share?

"You'll be so busy," he teased, "that you won't miss me. In fact, after you reflect, I bet you'll be so relieved to be shed of me, that you'll be dancing in the yard."

The comment brought a tremulous smile to her lips. "You were a difficult patient."

"The very worst. Do you forgive me?"

"For what?"

"For my barking and snapping."

"Of course."

"I apologize for the trouble I caused."

"You weren't any trouble."

"Nonsense. I interfered with your business, I upset your customers. I'm sorry."

With a wave, she dismissed the ruckus he'd created. "The uproar will settle down. Don't worry about it."

He was positive that affairs would *settle* with his egress, and the idea was so depressing. Would she really miss him? With the pitiful legacy he'd bestowed, why would she? He'd conferred naught but inconvenience and misfortune, a few tumbles in her bed, a few romps in her pool. In the pending months and years, what reason would she have to recall him fondly?

He wished he had a gift for her, a personal and tangible memento, to remember him by, but nothing was appropriate or sufficiently special. She was so fine, so unique, and she meant so much to him, that he couldn't devise a present that adequately proclaimed his esteem.

He hugged her tight. "Will you think of me?"

"Every second, you bounder."

He had to release her, had to step away, but he couldn't force the ultimate break. Falling to his knees, he wrapped his arms around her and snuggled himself to her bosom, his chest flattened to her abdomen. As if he were a young boy, she riffled her fingers through his hair.

"I'd assumed it would be so easy to tell you good-bye."

"Foolish man," she chided.

"Do you know how much I love you?" Here at the last, it seemed important to remind her. Perhaps she'd finally be convinced.

"I've always known, even when you didn't recognize it yourself."

He drew away and peered up at her. "You're the best thing that ever happened to me."

"It's sweet of you to say so."

"Without you by my side, I'm not sure who I am."

"You'll recollect. Once you're home and surrounded by your friends and family."

Would he find himself again? He'd been lost for an eternity. How could he ever truly make it back to where he'd been before? "Are you certain you won't come with me? Kate could run the emporium for you, and we could manage to—"

She silenced him. He hadn't realized he was going to suggest the possibility, but it was essential that he ask, that she decline.

"You said it yourself: What would I do with myself in London? Sit around drinking tea all day?"

Had he been that cold? "You'd be with me. Would that be so awful?"

"But *you* wouldn't be with me. There are many others who have a higher priority." She referred to Felicity. "I'm aware that it's common for the women of your class to accept their men's dalliances, but I can't share you. It's simply not in me to be that gracious."

She raised him to his feet, and he studied her, memorizing every detail.

"May I write you?"

For a lengthy interlude, she considered, then shook her head. "No. We can't have any contact."

"Why?"

"Because I should be able to rejoice with you in the major events of your life, but it would hurt me too much, learning of your wedding, or the birth of your first child. There's some information of which I never want to be apprised."

He hadn't contemplated the kinds of letters he'd pen, and

she was correct. There would be no news he could impart. "I can't bear it that I'll never hear from you."

"I couldn't tolerate any other conclusion."

"This is *adieu,* then."

"It has to be."

Still, he couldn't move away. "If you ever need anything, no matter how minor, promise that you'll get in touch with me."

"I never will, Stephen."

"Anne . . ."

"You need to go. Lady Eleanor is waiting."

Undeterred, he urged, "Just send a message to Bristol. I'll be here as soon as I can."

Ignoring his plea, she countered with, "I've slipped a few recipes into your bag. Show them to your cook. You're continuing to heal on the inside, so you should eat one of my soups at least once a day."

It was as if they were talking in different languages, shooting off toward opposite universes. Her tears had overflowed and dripped down her cheeks. He leaned down and kissed her, gently, tenderly.

"Come downstairs with me. Eleanor will wish to express her gratitude, and I want to see you as we pull away." What a crazed request! Did he plan to gawk at her, like an infatuated lad, as Eleanor and Felicity watched?

"I can't. Don't ask it of me. I can't face them." She was the strong one, capable of severing their connection. She extricated herself from his embrace and walked away. "I love you, Stephen."

"I love you, too, Anne."

"Always remember."

"I will."

"Be well. Be happy."

"I'll try."

There was no more to say. Without glancing at her, he retrieved his bag and marched out. At the landing, he paused,
gazing down to the lower floor. He pictured the stairs as a
gauntlet, a road he had to travel before he could end up
where he was supposed to be. With each step, he was farther
away from her, and nearer to the parlor, and he felt as if one
door was closing, while another was opening, but he wasn't
frightened by the transformation.

The people and places on the other side were familiar,
comfortable, like a worn pair of boots, and he descended
slowly, needing to imprint the distance between her and his
future.

He entered the salon, but neither female noticed, and he
cleared his throat, making them both jump.

They rose, confused over how to acknowledge him, but
Felicity smoothed over the awkward moment, rushing to
him, hands extended in greeting. "My dearest Captain," she
gushed, "how dashing you look this morning!"

"Hello, Felicity."

Clasping her offered hands, he squeezed them, hiding his
disappointment that there was no spark, no tingle. He'd grown
so accustomed to the fire Anne generated, that he'd forgotten
how lackluster his attraction to Felicity was. Had he ever suffered any emotion other than an intense lust for her money?
Could there ever be more?

He shoved off the idiotic questions. As he hadn't exited
Anne's residence yet, it was inappropriate to be probing his
feelings as to matrimony. Later on, there would be plenty of
opportunity to ponder the tough issues.

"I must confess," Felicity bubbled, "that I hadn't expected
to have you so dapper ever again. You've amazed us all, you
magnificent fellow!"

Eleanor approached, too, but she appeared shaky and
weak, wan and pale. "Stephen! You've returned to your old
self. It's nothing short of a miracle."

Frowning, he kissed her cheek. "Are you all right?"

"Why wouldn't I be?" she snarled with more venom than was necessary.

"Have you been ill?"

"I've just had a bout with the flu. I'm still a tad under the weather."

"She's had it for weeks," Felicity whispered, brows raised for emphasis. "Her stomach has been plaguing her."

"I wonder if we should have Mrs. Smythe check you," he mused. "She might have a concoction to calm your digestion."

"I'm perfectly fine!" Eleanor maintained, forcing a smile. "Are you ready?"

"Yes," he replied, astonished by his burgeoning excitement. "Yes, I am."

"Will Mrs. Smythe be joining us?"

"No, she's very busy." He caught himself just before he stared yearningly toward the stairs.

"I had so wanted to thank her."

"Send her a note," Stephen advised. "With lots of cash in it. She's a mercenary at heart."

"I believe I will," Eleanor retorted. "She deserves a king's ransom for putting up with you."

"She definitely does," he concurred.

"Let's be off then. We've a tiring journey ahead of us in the coach."

"To London!" Felicity chimed, gesturing as if she were making a toast. "We'll take the city by storm! Like a column of medieval knights!"

Her enthusiasm was contagious, and in spite of himself, he echoed, "To London!"

He held out an arm to each lady, and they grabbed on, and as a trio, they promenaded outside. To hasten their trip, his father had provided them with his premium vehicle, and a team of six horses. A cadre of footmen stood by, eager to assist them, their gold buttons and black boots shining in the sun.

As the women were escorted up and arranged themselves on the plush seats, he tarried and accepted the congratulations of the men who had fretted over him. It was splendid to receive their felicitations, to observe their delight and relief.

While he imagined himself to be quite hardy, his legs were unsteady, his knee rickety, so he had the senior coachman help him in, and he relaxed, soothed by the customary smells of polish and leather.

They delayed as the servants fussed with the steps and the door. The interval might have been unpleasant, but Felicity filled it with blithe chatter, and for once, he was glad for her gibberish. She babbled on about parties that had been scheduled in his honor, soirees to which they'd been invited.

Everyone had been apprised that he was on his way, and all of High Society was prepared to shower him with a hero's welcome. There was even to be a supper at the palace. He'd hoped for a private return, and though he was irked that so many events had been scheduled without his being consulted, he didn't complain.

The driver cracked the whip, and the team lurched away. At the last minute, as they rounded the curve toward the main road, Stephen casually drew back the curtain and peeked out. He had a fleeting view of the side of the house, the window to Anne's room where he'd left her standing by the bed.

Foolishly, he'd presumed that she would be watching his departure, would perhaps even wave, but there was no sign of her. He dropped the curtain, reposed against the squab, and shut his eyes.

Anne huddled in the shadows so that, if Stephen glanced up, he wouldn't be able to see her.

She spied on the scene below, on the footmen who snapped to attention as Stephen advanced to the carriage, on his elegant sister and his beautiful fiancée.

In the period he'd been with Anne, she hadn't realized how disparate they were. When he'd arrived, he'd been so ill, had needed her so desperately, that he'd seemed a normal man, with strengths and failings like any other, and far removed from being the son of an earl. But as he and his companions climbed into the extravagant Bristol coach, something inside her shattered.

Over the summer, she'd convinced herself that Stephen was hers, that their differences were minor, that they were connected in a manner that transcended rank and station. She hated to concede how incompatible they were, but it was painfully clear that their disparities were irreconcilable.

The driver shouted out, and the six impressive horses struggled against the yoke as the wheels began to spin. Up until that moment, she hadn't truly understood that he would go. After all that had happened, how could he? What powerful lure was stealing him away? What could be more enticing than the love she'd had for him?

She'd wished him happy, but she hadn't been sincere. How could he achieve contentment without her?

The carriage wound toward the lane, and she couldn't bear to see it vanish from sight. She'd thought that, before getting in, he might have smiled in her direction, or that he might wave as he passed, but there wasn't so much as a flutter of the curtain, and his disregard made it appear as if he'd already forsaken her.

Her legs gave out, and she crumpled to the rug, a kerchief pressed to her lips to stifle her cry of dismay. She could hear the jingle of the harness, the clopping of the hooves, the creaking of wood and leather, but the sounds became more and more faint as the conveyance faded into the distance.

A dreadful quiet descended, like the pall that crept in with a death in the family. The house was still, bereft of the energy he'd imbued, the air stagnant without his bright presence to enliven the space. She'd suspected that the impact of his going would be immediate and striking, but she hadn't grasped the full depth of how terrible it would be.

An emptiness settled, her solitary, barren future stretching to infinity. This was how it would be without him, this hushed, mute world that he no longer inhabited.

She was so crushed that she felt as if her heart might quit beating, that if she prayed for it, her soul might leave her body. Her bones ached, her muscles spasmed, her head throbbed, as if she'd been afflicted with a grave malady.

She rested, she dozed. Once, when she looked up, the afternoon had waned, the sun set. It grew dark, and eventually, Kate came to check on her. She deposited a tray on the dresser, and lit the lamp, then she walked over and knelt down.

"I miss him," Anne murmured.

"I know you do."

"It hurts."

"I expect it will for quite a while."

"I can't believe he went."

"I wasn't surprised in the least," Kate asserted, though kindly. "He didn't belong here, Annie."

"No, I don't suppose he did."

"He has another life. We're not part of it."

"He'd have been better off if he'd stayed with me."

"I'm sure of it."

"I'm not sorry," she proclaimed. "Not about anything."

"You shouldn't be."

"Will he think of me? When he's forlorn or sad?"

"How could he not?" Kate posed. "Now, let's put you to bed. You'll feel more yourself in the morning."

"I doubt it."

Kate helped her up and guided her to the mattress. She was wobbly, worn, too fatigued to worry about disrobing or washing up. Kate poured her some tea, but she was too shaky to grip the cup, so Kate balanced it for her. She sipped, wrinkling her nose at the bitter taste.

"Laudanum?" she inquired. It was the elixir of the dying and the addicted. She detested it, and never used it herself for any reason.

"Just for tonight. It will ease your woe."

At Kate's firm insistence, she drank it down, then she lay on the pillows, but she couldn't abide the notion of being alone. The room was so large, so muffled, so dreary, without Stephen in it.

"Would you sit with me while I fall asleep?"

"Of course I will."

Kate blew out the lamp, and pulled up a chair, reached for her hand, and held it. The gesture comforted her, made it seem as if she was clutching a tether that linked her to all she cherished, all that was recognized and familiar. Ultimately, it would lead her back to how it had been before.

"It will get better, Annie."

"I know."

It was like old times, the two of them together, in her cozy home. Best friends forevermore.

The drug worked its magic. She closed her eyes and drifted off.

~ 18 ~

Kate stopped on the path, listening, waiting, hearing only the sounds of the forest. Sunlight dappled the leaves above her head, painting the ground a vibrant green.

"Pru," she whispered, but she received no answer, and she sidled nearer to the McGee fence.

Prudence hadn't visited in weeks, and Kate had assumed that Willie was at home, which would have precluded Pru's sneaking over. But with the message that had just been delivered from the McGees' stable boy, she was frantic.

Her heart pounded with dread and foreboding. She'd feared that something bad would occur. Willie reminded her too much of her deceased husband. He was a bully, a thug who enjoyed inflicting violence on others. She hated him, but recognized that he was dangerous and, as a female, she had to proceed cautiously. From her own experiences, she'd learned how little power a woman had against a man.

"Prudence!" she called more loudly, too worried to care if her voice carried through the trees.

"Kate!" The quiet appeal came from the bushes on her left, and Kate rushed toward them.

Prudence had collapsed next to a tree. Her face was battered, her eyes blackened. Her arm was on her lap, bent at an odd angle. She'd wrapped it in a towel.

Kate fell to her knees. "What did that bastard do to you?"

"He saw us, Kate. In the pool. He was spying on us."

"Oh, God."

"He was very angry."

"I can see that."

She ran her fingers across the jagged bone. "Your arm's broken."

"Yes."

"Anything else?"

"Maybe my ribs. It hurts when I breathe."

"When did this happen?"

"Several nights ago."

Kate sizzled with fury. All this time, Prudence had been in agony! What sort of knave would treat a dog so cruelly? Let alone his sister! Willie McGee was an animal who deserved to be shot dead in the yard like the rabid cur he was.

"Why didn't you send for me?"

"This was the only chance I've had. He's off on business." She started to cry, silent tears streaming down her cheeks. "My insides ache. He's been doing foul things to me. Terrible things. Don't make me go back there!"

"No. You can't. Not ever."

Kate wasn't sure what she should do. The ramifications of conveying Pru to Anne's, of requesting Anne to provide shelter and doctoring, could be dire. Considering Willie's stature and disposition, it was hazardous to intervene. Yet, she couldn't forsake Pru.

She would plead with Anne for assistance, but if Anne refused, Kate would devise another route, even if it meant terminating her employment. She would camp out in a ditch with Pru before she'd return her to such a horrid fate.

Then and there, Kate made a vow that Willie McGee would never lay a hand on Prudence again. She would defend Pru, or die trying, would murder Willie in his sleep if that's what it took to keep Prudence safe.

"We'll hide you at Anne's."

"It's the first place he'll look!"

"But he won't find you." Pru was so frightened by the prospect that Kate added, "I swear it, Pru. Trust me. Can you stand?"

"I don't think so."

"Then, relax, and let me do all the work. I'll be as gentle as I can."

She picked her up and rose, cursing when Pru flinched, but it was impossible not to jostle her, and she seemed to pass out, which Kate imagined was for the best. Hugging Pru to her chest, she cradled her as if she were a wounded bird. Determined in her mission, she marched straight to the house and in the rear door, depositing Pru in the servant's room that Captain Chamberlin had occupied for so many months.

If Anne allowed Pru to stay, Kate would conceal her more appropriately, probably in the priest's hole behind the pantry shelves, but for now, the bed was easiest.

Kate nestled her on the pillows, propping one under her injured arm, and covering her with a blanket. The movements roused her from her stupor, and she was disoriented and afraid.

"I'm going to fetch Anne," Kate explained.

"Don't leave me," Pru begged.

"I'll only be a second. Close your eyes and try to rest."

She went into the hall, steadying herself by inhaling slowly. She couldn't remember when she'd last been so angry, but neither Anne nor Pru should have to witness her outrage. Both women were suffering because of the men in their lives. Both needed protection, friendship, and compassion, and Kate had to be the stable center that held them together.

If she was lucky, Pru's appearance could be an unexpected boon. Pru required medical attention, and Anne could supply it, yet she was in no condition to utilize her healing skills.

With Lord Chamberlin's departure, she was bereaved, somber, and in mourning, as Kate had predicted she would be. Anne had never loved before, had never had the opportunity to abide the glories and miseries of passion.

She was like a ghost, so beaten down by heartbreak that she seemed to have shrunk in size, to have blurred and faded so that she was a shadow of her former self. Kate couldn't guess how long she would grieve, but she needed a reason to quit lamenting her handsome Captain. With a renewed sense of purpose, a task to take her mind off her woe, maybe she could muster the will to focus on the future instead of the past. Perhaps Pru's arrival would be a focal point to lure her out of her doldrums.

Kate located her in her room, perched on the mattress and staring out at the road, as if she could still see him going. When Kate entered, she glanced over but didn't rise, and Kate crossed the floor and pulled up a chair.

"You look distraught," she noticed. "Are you all right?"

"I have a favor to ask, but I won't be upset if you can't help me."

"What is it?"

"I have Prudence McGee downstairs."

"Why?"

"Willie's beaten her."

"How bad is it?"

"Very bad."

"Why would he?"

"Why would any man?" It was the infamy no one talked about, that no one addressed, for what a male perpetrated under his own roof was deemed to be his own affair, and others wouldn't question his actions or interfere.

"Prudence didn't mention what set him off?"

"No," Kate lied. She could never share her deepest, darkest secret with Anne. "He's done it to her before, but this time, it's worse. Much worse. She needs you, Annie."

"I know, Kate, but I'm so tired."

"Please? For me?" She was being unfair, pressuring Anne so that she couldn't say no, but she was desperate. "Just take a peek at her. I can handle her care myself, if you'll tell me what to do."

Kate was positive that once Anne saw Pru, and discovered the ravaging she'd sustained, she wouldn't be able to decline. She was simply too kind to ignore someone who was ailing.

"You're demanding too much of me."

"I can't turn her away. Where would she go? What would she do? I won't send her home."

"I realize that, but if she remains here, where would we keep her? Willie could have her forcibly removed. We couldn't prevent him. And then we'd be in trouble for aiding her."

Kate wanted to shake a triumphant fist in the air. If Anne was musing as to where they'd hide Pru, then Kate was on her way to victory. "I've figured out where to put her—while we ponder our next step."

Anne sighed. "I suppose it won't kill me to check on her."

"She's in pain, Annie."

"Bring my laudanum and the tea tray."

Anne walked to the hall, and Kate followed, assured that the two women she loved more than life itself would soon be on the mend.

Eleanor sat at her dressing table, studying herself in the mirror. A carriage rattled by on the street, a cool evening breeze rustled the drapes. The world continued to spin, common events transpired, while inside her bedchamber, the earth had tipped off its axis.

If she'd stood and strolled to the door, she was certain the floor would be tilted, and the impression of imbalance would have naught to do with her recurrent vertigo.

Could it be?

She gazed in the mirror. If such a momentous miracle had occurred, wouldn't there be some visible sign to indicate that she had been transformed?

Her personal maid had just left. The poor woman had been embarrassed but blunt, specifying that Eleanor hadn't had her courses, that there had been no pads for the laundress. Eleanor's frequent queasiness, which was most prevalent in the morning, had also been referenced.

The trusted servant had been with her since she was an adolescent, was a widow who'd birthed several children, and she recognized the symptoms of pregnancy, as Eleanor—apparently—did not.

Fortunately, she was too courteous, and too deferential, to have probed for details as to how it might have happened. In a succinct fashion, she'd dispensed the facts, then had exited as rapidly as she could, and Eleanor couldn't blame her. Who would welcome the dreaded responsibility of notifying their unwed employer that she might be scandalously expecting?

If her maid had deduced the truth, the servants probably all knew. While she'd presumed herself discreet, that her liaison with Charles remained a precious secret, the entire town house was likely brimming with speculation.

Were they all aware of her wanton adventure? How mortifying!

"Could it be?" she repeated aloud, murmuring the vital query to her reflection, a hand pressed to an abdomen that seemed too ordinary to be sheltering a child.

Charles had insisted she was increasing, but she'd refused to believe him. Why had she been so ready to renounce his allegations?

It would have been too agonizing to hope that he was correct, only to later learn that he'd been wrong. She'd wanted a child for so long, had beseeched and prayed, supplicated and sacrificed, but to no avail, and as she dawdled in the quiet, it was as if a voice spoke to her.

It's true. You know it is.

A tiny spark ignited, and it began to burn, brighter and hotter, warming her with the marvelous news.

A babe! She'd made a babe with difficult, randy, handsome Charles!

The reality was so bizarre that she couldn't process it, the notion so far-fetched, so fantastic, that she was teeming with a mixed jumble of supressed emotion. Was she glad? Terrified? Relieved? Shocked?

She couldn't decide, so what did she wish to do? Depending on how she chose to view her situation, it was either a blessing or the worst catastrophe imaginable. Which was it?

She peered at her thirty-five-year-old face, her rounded, mature shape, the wisps of silver in her golden hair. Most women her age were becoming grandmothers, and a smug smile slithered onto her lips, a serene joy creeping through bone and pore. When she recalled the snide remarks and hateful innuendo she'd endured, she could barely contain a giggle of glee.

A pox on their sorry hides! Despite how Harold had berated, how others had pitied and laughed, it hadn't been her fault. She'd merely needed a partner who could perform his portion of the job!

Hah! She'd shown them all!

Leaping up, she twirled in circles and danced a jig.

"I'm going to have a baby!" she sang over and over in an off-tune melody, delighted with the tidings.

At the window, she stopped and stared toward the mews. If she was about to have a baby, she ought to find herself a husband, and there was only one man who would do. But after all they'd been through, would he have her?

Stephen had hinted that Charles was lodging in the footmen's quarters over the stables—*just in case you were wondering,* he'd said—though if Charles was lurking in the barn, she hadn't crossed paths with him. If she might have privately pined away for a glimpse of him, or stupidly anticipated that he would seek her out, she'd regarded her yearning as misplaced idiocy. They'd had nothing to say to each other.

They hadn't conversed since that hideous night he'd interrupted their family supper at Bristol Manor. He'd announced their fling, then trotted off without a word of apology or good-bye, leaving her to explain and justify to her father and brother.

They'd ordered her to tell them about the affair, to confess if she was pregnant as he'd asserted. Why, Michael had actually had the temerity to ask if she'd like Charles murdered for what he'd done to her! To *her!* As if she were some fatuous girl, some innocent, who'd been led astray!

Was stubborn, headstrong Charles as angry as she? Or had he calmed to where they could parlay over this new circumstance? What would he do if she sent a message, mandating his presence in the downstairs parlor?

She laughed. He'd tear it up.

Well, she'd have to go to him. She'd swallow her pride, and propose on bended knee, for she was positive that she'd already received the sole offer she'd ever get from him. If she wanted him for her own, she'd have to grovel, would have to force the issue.

He had a strange code of honor, but at heart, he was a gentleman, and he wouldn't abandon a lady in distress. Before the hour was up, she would be engaged! By eleven on the morrow, she could be standing in front of the vicar!

Rushing to the wardrobe, she grabbed a shawl, as she

contemplated whether she should change her clothes into something more dramatic to befit the occasion, but she couldn't tolerate any delay. She raced into the hall and down the stairs.

As she reached the foyer, the door opened and Stephen came in. For a second, she considered taking him with her out to the stable, making him a witness or an accomplice, but she discounted the idea. If Stephen were in attendance, Charles would do whatever Stephen commanded him to do, and she had to garner Charles's acceptance without Stephen's assistance. He had to consent of his own accord and not because Stephen had pressured him.

"My goodness, Eleanor," he noted, "you're glowing. You must be feeling better."

"I'm so happy!"

"Where are you off to?"

"I'm about to speak to that rascal, Charles Hughes. He's deserved a piece of my mind, and I've decided to give it to him."

Stephen halted, frowned. "Charles?"

"Yes." He looked stricken, and she paused, a glimmer of alarm sounding. "What is it?"

"I thought you knew."

"Knew what?"

"He's gone."

"When will he be back?"

"He's not coming back."

"What do you mean?"

"He's off to try and link up with our old regiment."

She blanched. He would return to the Continent? To soldiering? Was he insane? He'd sacrificed a limb to the Crown. How much more could one individual be required to forfeit? Was he determined to kill himself?

"You're joking."

"No. He left yesterday."

"But he's crippled. How could they possibly allow it?"

"There are many chores he can manage besides fighting. And if he can't rejoin them, he'll sell himself somewhere else. There are many armies that would snatch him up."

"The man is a lunatic! A certifiable maniac!"

"He's proud, Eleanor. War is all he knows, all he's ever done. He feels compelled to earn his keep, even though he's maimed." Stephen rested a hand on her shoulder. "He couldn't stay here. Not when it was so clear that he wasn't wanted."

So . . . Charles must have mentioned their quarrel, or perhaps, Stephen had heard of it from their father. What was Stephen's opinion of her wild escapade? He wasn't the sort who would condemn or judge her, but did he believe her mad? Incautious? Reckless? Wise?

"Were you aware that Charles is a widower?" she inquired.

"Yes."

"Were you acquainted with his wife?"

"No. She died long before I'd met him."

"What type of husband do you suppose he was?"

"The very best," Stephen proclaimed without hesitation. "Why?"

"I was just curious."

"Any *personal* interest you'd care to share?"

He was much too pleased with his deductions, and she wished she had time to slap his cocky smirk off his face.

"Your moronic companion, Mr. Hughes, has no business hieing himself off to Europe."

"Really?"

"Yes. He has responsibilities here in England, primarily that he's about to become a father."

Stephen was a tad slow on grasping her intent, but as the significance sunk in, he grinned from ear to ear. "Are you saying . . .?"

"In which direction was that scoundrel traveling?"

"To Southampton. Some acquaintances of ours are mustering a ship to Portugal."

"I repeat: the man is a lunatic!" Stomping off, she started up the stairs. "If you'll excuse me . . ."

"Where are you going?"

"It occurs to me that I must take a sudden journey to the south coast. If anyone needs to contact me, I'll be at my estate in Romsey."

Before he could reply, she marched away and locked herself in her bedchamber, shutting him out so that he couldn't follow and enumerate all the reasons she was as deranged as Charles.

19

Willie McGee drove his prisoners' wagon to Anne's house and halted at her stoop. The yard was quiet, the property appearing sloppy and deserted. Her business had fallen off during Captain Chamberlin's stay, and it hadn't yet picked up, though Willie was unconcerned as to her loss of income or clients.

He had other, bigger plans for the erotic pool, and they had naught to do with Anne nursing the neighborhood invalids. He didn't give two figs about the elderly crones who sought her help. Let them expire! The mysterious grotto was wasted on them!

The magic of the water had been proven. How else could one explain the recent rash of carnality he'd witnessed?

His precious Anne had metamorphosed into a harlot, disposed to commit any foul deed. His own sister—circumspect, sensible Prudence—had soaked in it a few times, and had been transformed into a lesbian. That she could be stricken so horridly, and so quickly, underscored the presence of a dire alchemy.

The rumors were true. The pond changed ordinary people into raving, wild beasts, so intent on fornication that they would risk any hazard in order to copulate.

He still couldn't believe what he'd seen Prudence doing with that human cow she fancied, and as he climbed down from the box, he glanced around, wondering where she was. Without a doubt, she was hiding nearby, having sneaked to the feminine lair of abomination the moment he was away, but he was temporarily disinterested as to her whereabouts.

Later, he would deal with her, would ensure that she received sufficient discipline for defying him.

As he rapped on the door, his mind whirled with the revisions he would instigate posthaste. There were so many intriguing possibilities.

If the acreage was managed correctly, with the goal being maximum profit, he'd be rich, more affluent than any of the nabobs who flaunted their pilfered East Indian loot, more prosperous than the land-poor lords he was compelled to assist. He was eager to begin accumulating his fortune.

He would never allow females to avail themselves of the bewitched location. The havoc the spot had wreaked on Prudence provided ample proof of the pool's dangerous aspects. Males were better built to handle the stimulation, and they would be his customers, primarily the well-to-do, who would pay any amount to dip their wilting wicks.

After an experience or two, gentlemen would become obsessed. Like opium addicts, unable to resist, they would visit despite the cost, ready to cough up a bundle for the privilege of bathing.

The residence would be converted to one of ill-repute, where the prettiest, youngest girls would entertain his titillated swimmers. He'd arrange various frolics with the favorite strumpets, would schedule private parties, cater special events.

Through his policing activities, he was regularly thrown in contact with trollops, and he'd discovered that it was easy to coerce a female into behavior she'd normally refuse to attempt, if she was threatened with suitable punishment. Loss of a child, termination of employment, deportation, an asylum, were all perils he had no qualms about raising.

So many hideous prospects could be dangled to reduce them to quivering, begging lumps that it was almost humorous to learn how far he could push them. In particular, he relished those who started out adamant and strong, who thought they could withstand his tortures. It was amusing to bend them to his will, and he always succeeded, so he would have a constant flow of new talent to incite his guests.

He would promise the women protection from their criminal charges, and freedom from incarceration, if they worked for him. Flat on their backs! As he was a master at persuasion, they would all agree. The sole caveat would be that he enjoy the girls first. The other men would have to wait in line, would have to sample the wares after Willie had feasted.

Knocking again, he was rewarded by a maid ushering him into Anne's parlor. After studying the salon, assessing the furnishings, curtains, and rugs, he decided that the decor was too feminine and would have to be replaced. The expense would be covered by the remuneration Anne had obtained from the Chamberlins for tending her brave soldier.

She would forever rue the day she had reached so high above her station that she had shunned him for Stephen Chamberlin.

"Whore!" he muttered, and his fury was so vehement that he took many deep breaths, calming himself, not wanting Anne to have a hint of what was coming. Her future was winging toward her like a runaway carriage. She couldn't avert it, couldn't alter it. She could only hold on and float with the rising tide of despair that was about to wash her away.

Eventually, she showed herself. She was thinner, pale and wan at having been abandoned by her lover, but her looks hardly mattered. As happened with all the harlots he ravished, he would grow bored of her, but he would have the wenches in his brothel to keep him satisfied. Anne had a different role to play.

At the outset, he would ascertain which carnal antics she abhorred the most, and when she merited castigation, he would seek her out, would constrain her to perform those exploits she detested.

"Hello, Willie." Her smile was tepid, her welcome cool. "You haven't stopped in ages. What brings you by?"

He saw no reason to delay or skirt the issue with polite conversation. "Several times now, I've asked you to marry, but you've spurned me."

"Willie, please. We've been through this before, and you embarrass me by—"

He cut her off. "I won't listen to another repudiation."

"Then why are you here? Why torment yourself with this fruitless quest?"

"I have sworn out a warrant for your arrest."

"What?"

"I have a warrant for your arrest."

"Because I won't marry you?"

"No."

"Then on what grounds?"

He pulled out the document and commenced reading. "'Public Fornication, Nudity, Lewd Conduct, Encouragement of Homosexuality,' which by the way, is a capital offense, 'Illicit Sexual Intercourse, Inappro—'"

"That's the most ludicrous nonsense I've ever heard." Her mouth was gaping open and shut like a fish tossed on a riverbank. "Who's making these charges?"

"I am."

"On what evidence?"

"I've received numerous complaints as to the debauchery you permit, so I've been watching myself, and I've viewed rampant episodes of lechery."

Visibly shaken, she blanched. "How dare you! Get out! Right now!"

What a ninny she was! Did she suppose she could order him about? That she could snap her fingers, stomp her foot, and send him packing? She had no concept of the power he was prone to wield, the devastation he could wreak, but she was about to find out.

"I've been fond of you"—he ignored her command that he depart—"so I will give you a choice: You may marry me, and the accusations will disappear, as will the witnesses I have against you. Or you may proclaim your innocence, and endeavor to fight me." He paused, letting the gravity of her situation sink in. "Of course, if you're convicted, you'll be branded a felon. As a result, you'll lose your property, and your obscene business will be shut down. You'll be either imprisoned or transported, perhaps even executed if I produce a strong enough case."

She was bewildered by his malice. "Why are you doing this to me?"

"I proposed to you in good faith. I was prepared to honor you by allowing you to become my bride. Instead, you have prostituted yourself with Captain Stephen Chamberlin, and who knows how many others."

"This is about Captain Chamberlin?" At the realization that he'd exposed her repeated ignominies, her legs grew weak, and she collapsed onto the sofa.

"You have scorned me at your peril. *Your* punishment shall be that you will be my obedient, dutiful wife, where you will have many years to rue and repent your behavior. *My* reward, for suffering the shame and indignity you have heaped upon me, shall be the ownership of your precious farm, which will be mine as soon as we are wed."

"You will never coerce me into matrimony."

Her paltry display of bravado was entertaining. She had no idea how vengeful he could be. "Your compliance is of no consequence. Once we've had intimate relations—"

"I would never lie down with you. I'd kill myself first."

"Have I indicated that your consent would be required?"

"You . . . you . . . would rape me?"

She was horrified, and he chuckled. "After I've had my way with you, it will be easy to persuade the vicar that we must be immediately wed, that we've been swept away by passion."

"He'd never believe you over me."

"Wouldn't he?"

His composed assurance rattled her, and she scoffed. "This isn't the Middle Ages. He couldn't force me."

"He will do as I say." Of that fact, Willie had no doubt. He knew all of the vicar's dirty little secrets, especially his penchant for sodomy with boys. That fascinating peculiarity, coupled with the amount of money Willie donated to the parish, guaranteed that the minister would agree to whatever Willie requested.

"I'll write to Captain Chamberlin," she boasted. "He won't let you harm me."

"How will he protect you? He's in London. Even if you could post a letter to him, your fate will be sealed long before he could ever respond."

"He'll help me!"

"Will he?" Willie prodded. "Where is your fancy lord, Anne? You were quick enough to spread your legs for him, but he's gone back to his own kind. Why would he bother himself over you?"

The query halted her arguments. She must have been fretting, herself, over Chamberlin's decision to go, over his forsaking her for his other life. Was she really that stupid? Had she presumed that Chamberlin loved her?

"He didn't care about you," Willie admonished. "You were nothing to him."

"You don't know anything about us."

"Don't I? Your story is the most pathetic one in the land: poor, common country lass succumbs to sophisticated, dashing aristocrat. Are you assuming you're the only woman in history to be cajoled to indecency by a handsome blue blood?"

"No." She shook her head, denying his words and her new reality. "No. You're mad! I'm not about to take this from you." She jumped up, hurried to the window, and yelled, "Kate! Kate, come here! I need you!"

He grabbed her arm and slapped her, rendering a solid blow. Shrieking, she crumpled to the floor, her fingers pressed to her injured face.

He took advantage of her shock and prone position, flipping her onto her stomach and, with a cord he'd brought for the occasion, binding her wrists behind her. Though she fought and kicked, she was no match for his superior strength. She was cursing, calling for her employees, so he stuffed a stocking in her mouth, ending her diatribe, and he yanked her to her feet just as Kate rushed in.

"What the hell are you doing, McGee?"

Willie reached in his jacket and retrieved his pistol. "I am an officer of the court, and I am closing down this den of iniquity. Don't interfere."

"Let her go!"

"No. I have placed her under arrest."

"On what charge?"

"Too many to mention." He grasped the warrant from his coat and pitched it toward her, and it fluttered to the rug. "She is a whore, running a whore's house."

"You can't have her." As if she might dare clash with him, she approached.

"Who's to stop me?" She seemed to suppose *she* could, and she moved toward him again, so he aimed the gun and cocked the trigger. "You disgusting perverted Sappho! If you take another step, I'll kill you where you stand."

The threat intimidated her, and she froze. Anne was terrified, her eyes wide with alarm and panic. In their scuffle, her hair had fallen, and he clutched a fistful and dragged her toward the door.

"Should you attempt a foolish rescue," he warned Kate, "I will murder her instantly, and then I shall return to slay Prudence. You will have both their deaths on your filthy hands."

With that, he exited, hauling Anne as she continued to struggle, but as she was fettered, and a female, her skirmishing was for naught. He braced the rear hatch on his wagon, lifted her up, and flung her in, securely bolting it behind her.

Satisfied with what he'd wrought, he went to the driver's seat, climbed up, and cracked the whip as Kate and the other retainers scurried out to watch him race away. The horses neighed and lurched, then they were off, bound for the gaol he'd constructed in his pasture.

He smiled. Anne would have plenty of opportunity to consider her options, and with a bit of prompting, she'd see things his way. Even if she didn't, her destiny had arrived.

Camilla's coach slowed on the lane that led into Mrs. Smythe's property, and she peeked out. For once, the gate was open and untended.

She hadn't been able to glean any information as to what was transpiring at the bathing emporium. In her social circle, Mrs. Smythe was such a nonentity that no one recognized her name the few times Camilla had uttered it, so no one could apprise her of Mrs. Smythe's plight, and she was dying to know. Had McGee carried out the act for which she'd paid him?

Curiosity had been eating her alive, so she'd lowered herself to checking the details on her own. The venture was risky, but she had to verify the success of her machination.

She'd meant to pass by Smythe's entrance, to have a fleet

glance and travel on, but the unoccupied gate was like a magnet, luring her in, and she couldn't resist.

The driver helped her out, and she had him wait while she went to the door. Her knock was answered by a petite, middle-aged woman who was sporting a cast on her arm and two blackened eyes. The bruises had faded to yellow, attesting that she was on the mend but not completely healed.

My, my! Something interesting had definitely occurred! And it had involved fisticuffs! Her opinion of McGee blossomed to outright amazement. She wouldn't have guessed he'd have had the nerve.

"I'm Lady Camilla Warren," she proclaimed, intending to impress, and the underling dipped into a curtsy.

"Welcome, milady."

"I am a regular patron of Mrs. Smythe. I should like to utilize the pool. Is she available to assist me?"

"No, ma'am . . . that is . . . I don't . . ." Tiny, fragile like a bird, she looked as if a loud shout would bowl her over. She couldn't decide whether she ought to invite Camilla inside, and Camilla's hopes soared as to the likelihood of a bad conclusion for Anne Smythe.

"I don't have all day," Camilla snapped. "Is she here or isn't she?"

"Please come in."

She gestured, escorting Camilla to a parlor, then excused herself and returned with the lumbering, queer Miss Kate. Camilla wasn't aware of the Amazon's history, but she suspected it didn't contain any tidbits she'd want unveiled in public.

Were the freakish Kate and Mrs. Smythe lovers? If she was enamored of females, would Smythe have yielded to Stephen? Perhaps Stephen had reveled in a trio, or had titillated himself by observing as the women had at it.

The notion made Camilla want to gag. To think that he might lie down with this . . . this . . . cow! That he would

shun her for someone like Kate! It was an insult too great to
be borne.

"Where is Mrs. Smythe?" she demanded. "I can't get a
sensible reply from this half-witted abigail."

Kate bristled at the slur to her companion, but without
Mrs. Smythe as a shield, she wasn't nearly as brave or condescending as she'd been previously.

"She's not here."

"Where is she?"

"Ah . . . she's gotten herself in a spot a trouble."

"What sort of *trouble*?"

The pair flashed a silent communication, trying to deduce
how much to reveal. Finally, Kate admitted, "She's in a jam
with the law."

"The law!" Camilla feigned shock. "Well, I never! What
type of facility have I been frequenting?"

"It's a misunderstanding," the little bird chirped.

"Has she been arrested?"

"Yes," the giantess acknowledged, "and we were wondering if we could impose on you for a favor."

Camilla could barely refrain from laughing, and she
sniffed, sticking her nose up in the air. How dare these two
presume so much! But it would be amusing to hear their
plea. "What is this *favor*?"

"We need to contact Lord Stephen Chamberlin."

"The war hero of the Crown? The Savage of Salamanca?
What connection would he have to Mrs. Smythe?"

"They're acquainted, if you recall. She treated him during
his recovery, and he'd intercede on her behalf if he was notified of her difficulty."

"You don't say," Camilla mused.

"We need to write him, but neither of us ever learned
how, and even if we had, we're not certain how or where to
send a message. So we thought maybe you could . . . could
compose a letter for us?"

"I would be delighted," Camilla lied.

Kate led her to a desk, and Camilla penned a note to Stephen, drafting a genuine appeal in case either of the pitiful illiterates could read a few words, then she sanded the ink and folded the missive into thirds.

"I'm a friend of the Chamberlin family," she fibbed again. "I know exactly how to deliver this to him. If we're lucky, Stephen could have it by nightfall."

The fabrication was dangerous, as was involving herself in the situation, but she was giddy with her authority over them, so she was eager to hazard a slight intervention. What were the chances that Stephen would discover her link to the event?

And if he ever inquired as to a supposed letter, she could swear she'd passed it on. How could he prove otherwise? Was it her fault the post was so unreliable?

"Thank you, milady," both females gushed.

She swept out, not listening to the platitudes they spewed in her wake. Surely, Kate remembered Camilla and the tedious eviction Anne Smythe had ordered. Was she so stupid that she believed Camilla would aid her in her hour of need? What an idiot!

Rushing to the carriage, she bellowed to the driver, making it seem as if she was in a hurry. She clambered in without his assistance, then she relaxed, peeking out as they jerked away and rounded the yard, bound for the main road.

Smythe's small cadre of servants was dawdling on the stoop, gawking with pathetic, optimistic expressions, their misplaced trust apparent in their vapid stares. They were relieved, reassured, positive that a rescue was imminent, when no liberation would ever be achieved.

The driver took the corner so fast that they tipped on two wheels. She gripped the strap, giggling at the speed, at the peril.

Once they were on the lane, and shielded by the trees, she

reached for the *faux* letter, tore off a scrap, and flicked it out the window, sticking her head out to see the piece flutter to the ground. Then, she tore another and another, letting the fragments float on the wind. She kept on until the paper was ripped to shreds, taking extra long to release the last portion, receiving an incredible amount of pleasure as it drifted away.

"Good-bye, Mrs. Smythe," she howled to the deserted highway. "Godspeed on your journey!"

Grinning, she crawled inside, settling herself and adjusting her hair and bonnet.

"A fine day's work," she crooned. A fine day's work indeed.

~ 20 ~

Anne huddled in the halted wagon. Although she was terrified, she was focused on Willie and escape. They were at his farm, but when they'd arrived in the yard, he'd been waylaid by male visitors, so she'd been granted a reprieve.

Though she'd prayed for their assistance, and had kicked at the wooden walls of the box in which she was caged, they'd merely joked about what a rowdy prisoner Willie had captured. She'd been ignored, and he'd ushered them into his house, leaving her bound and frantic and grappling to break free, but to no avail. She couldn't loose her arms, although the stocking he'd stuffed in her mouth was now dangling, and she was near to spitting it out.

How long had he been detained by his callers? Minutes? Hours? Each second ticked by like an eternity.

Suddenly, noise erupted as, with boisterous farewells, Willie's guests departed. Then, he climbed onto the coach and they rattled off, traveling a short distance from his residence.

He tied the reins and leapt down, and she braced, ready to attack as he opened the door. If he was bent on rape, she had no intention of meekly submitting, so he would have difficulty following through.

She crouched down, hands trussed behind her back, as he raised the bar, as he pulled it away, and . . . she lunged at him.

At the last instant, she ejected her gag, and, hurling herself at him like a banshee, she let out a bloodcurdling scream.

"Bastard!"

"Holy Christ!" As he realized what she was about, he tried to jump away, but he couldn't avoid a collision.

Flying into him, she knocked him over, then she clambered to her knees, to her feet, but without the use of all her limbs, she was awkward and off balance. She attempted to run, but was too slow. Growling like a wounded bear, he scrambled after her, and he shoved her forward so that she landed with a painful thud. Smacking into the dirt, her cheeks and nose scraped across rocks and weeds.

After tackling her, he pinned her down, and she could feel the bones of his rib cage, the paunch of his obese stomach. Flattened to her bottom, she could detect his erect phallus. He was aroused by the violence, and she shuddered with revulsion. Up until that moment, what had transpired hadn't seemed real. She'd known Willie for ages, had considered him an odd duck, a bothersome, polite nuisance, whom she'd tolerated because he was her neighbor. When he'd placed her under arrest, the encounter had been bizarre, like a weird dream.

But to discover that he was sexually excited! She wanted to retch.

He was abnormal, perverted. She'd heard of men who reveled in brutality. Kate had insisted that her husband had been one of them, that he'd enjoyed cruelty for cruelty's sake, but the truth of Kate's admission hadn't registered. Anne's experiences with evil had been too limited.

Willie was dangerous, mad, capable of any foul deed. He might begin with rape, but he wouldn't stop there. Very likely, her life was on the line, and she was all alone in her jeopardy.

There was no one to rescue her, no one to ride up on a white stallion. Her brother, Phillip, was across the country at their father's estate in Salisbury, while Stephen was being feted in London. She had to save herself, had to employ every wile and deception she could contrive. By any means, she had to keep herself alive, had to buy herself time to flee.

As Willie hovered behind her, his fetid breath coursed across her ruined face. "Bitch! I could kill you for that!"

"Yes, but then you couldn't marry me. You couldn't put your greedy paws on my farm."

"Do you presume that marriage is the only way I can gain your property?" He laughed, a wicked, revolting chuckle that sent chills down her spine.

"Yes, and it shall never happen."

"Before we're through, you might just sign the deed over to me."

"Never!"

"Although I prefer matrimony. I want you forever under my authority and forced to do my bidding." Grabbing her by the neck, he grated her injuries into the sharp stones and twigs. "So proud! So strong! But you'll learn quickly enough."

"Brute! Monster!"

He laughed again, recognizing that words were her sole weapon, and as he moved off and yanked her to her feet, she peered around. They were out in the pasture, surrounded by trees and tall grass, where no passerby could observe them.

There was a small building in front of her, with a single door, a sloping roof, and under the eaves a few tiny slits for windows. It was his personal jail. Rumors had abounded as to its construction and use, but she hadn't actually believed the stories. How naive she'd been!

She assessed the structure with an enormous amount of dread, overwhelmed by the impression that if she went inside, she might never come out. She started to flail and shriek as he dragged her toward the threshold. It yawed like the gates of hell, a grotesque, black chasm that would swallow her whole, but try as she might, she couldn't alter their progress.

"Struggle as much as you like," he declared, relishing her inability to best him. "Yell, beg, plead. It won't do you any good."

She dug in her heels, but with no success. "Why aren't we at your home? I thought you wished to fornicate with me." If they were in the house, there'd be servants, would be more options. "Take me to your bedchamber. I'll go peacefully. I won't fight you."

"Maybe I want you to fight me."

"I'll do whatever you ask. Tell me what you'd like."

"What I would *like* is for you to languish in my little private prison. You'll be much more amenable once you perceive how miserable your life can truly be."

They were at the stoop, and he pushed her through, into a big chamber, with three cells, bars to separate the enclosures. It was dark, dreary, and she could smell sickening odors, of blood and fear and human torment, though it was empty of any other occupants.

At the far end, there appeared to be a torture chamber, complete with shackles, whips, and bludgeons.

How many people had he brought here over the years? Why had there been no hue and cry in the neighborhood? Were her acquaintances as oblivious as she had been? Perhaps others assumed—as had she—that any miscreant incarcerated in the sordid facility deserved his fate.

"Welcome to my gaol." He smiled. "I see that you're frightened. Splendid!"

She wiped away any expression. Though he was correct, and she was scared, she wasn't about to let him witness it. "I'm not afraid of you."

"You will be."

He tried to urge her in, but she relaxed her muscles, growing heavy so that he couldn't lift her, and he tussled with her shifting torso, battling to maintain his grip. He hauled her past the three pens, to the other side of the room, where his dastardly equipment awaited.

She continued to wrestle, but she had scant purchase, and he lugged her over, and spun her toward the wall. In seconds, he had her arms shackled, her legs splayed and chained at the ankles.

His body was mashed to hers, and he was sweating, his respiration labored, and she garnered some petty satisfaction in noting that he was winded, that her skirmishing had made it difficult for him to harness her.

Leaning in, he bit her nape and nibbled her ear. "We're going to have such fun, you and I."

"That's what you think."

"Hold your tongue." He reached for a riding crop, and he struck her alongside the head.

"No."

He hit her, harder, and she made no reply. "There," he crooned, "you're learning already. It will be so much easier, once you decide to obey."

"You can force me into anything"—she endeavored to sound bold, even as she hoped he couldn't detect that her knees were shaking—"but you'll never control me."

"Don't be too certain."

Clasping the neckline of her dress, he ripped it down the middle, so that her back was bared, the sleeves of the garment drooping, and he tugged down the fabric, exposing her to the waist. He wrapped himself around her and cupped her breasts, pinching the nipples until they hurt, and she swallowed down her need to beg him to desist.

She wouldn't grovel. Despite how vile it became.

"It's time for your first lesson."

"I'll never master it."

"I'm a patient teacher."

She glanced over her shoulder, and he'd retrieved a larger whip, one that had knots in the corded strands.

"For your cuckolding of me, by copulating with Captain Stephen Chamberlin, I sentence you to fifty lashes."

The switch crashed down, tearing into her flesh. She clenched her teeth until her jaws ached, refusing to cry out, declining to titillate him further with an overt show of agony.

His gestures were methodical, practiced, as if he regularly lashed people. He was adept, sure of his mark, and he thrashed her over and over. The pain was intense, and blissfully, she sank into a barren void, where she could feel nothing at all.

Charles ambled down the dock, hunting for the ship of which he'd been apprised the previous evening. He'd been up and down the wharves, but hadn't found the blasted vessel, when it occurred to him that he was in no hurry to locate it.

When he did, he'd book passage, and on the tide the following morning, he'd be off to America. Originally, he'd thought about traipsing to Spain, but in light of his exploits there, he couldn't bear to return. With the realization that Eleanor wasn't pregnant, there was no reason to dawdle, so he'd resolved to journey as far away from England as possible.

He'd heard tales of the young, wild country, that a man could have his own land, that there were opportunities around every corner. If a fellow couldn't make a fresh start in such a place, where could he?

Many of his distant Scottish relatives had settled in the Carolinas, and he imagined he could dig them up, could find some family.

The notion of being surrounded by kin was too dear to

contemplate, and as he gazed around at the busy harbor, at the bustle of the crowd, and the supplies being loaded and unloaded, he suffered a wave of melancholy. Except for the short period when he'd been married all those years ago, he'd never planted any roots, had never belonged anywhere.

He was tired of carrying on alone, of having no connections, no ties to bind. Perhaps it was his advancing age, or his depression over his maiming, that had him reeling, but he craved attachments, responsibilities, and obligations. His sojourn at Bristol Manor, his destructive affair with Lady Eleanor, had underscored how desperate he was for a few scraps of affection.

He was so pathetic! Lost, wandering, forlorn, with no one and nothing to call his own.

Down the pier, he observed the ship for which he'd been searching, and he was so despondent at having encountered it! The only bond he'd had in an eternity had been with Stephen Chamberlin, and once he climbed up the plank and stowed his gear, once the wind caught the sails and whisked him out to sea, he'd never see Stephen again, his last link with another human would be severed.

He would travel across the world, to another continent, a spot so exotic and distant that he might as well have been trekking to the moon. Could he do it? How could he not?

He'd been so positive that Lady Eleanor was pregnant, but no word had been delivered to verify his suspicions. Even after she'd arrived in London with Stephen, he'd tarried, hoping with each footfall in the yard that it was she, eager to inform him that she was having a baby, to solicit his forgiveness so they could begin anew.

What a wretched soul he was! While she'd been staying in the Chamberlins' grand mansion, he'd slept in his servant's bed in the barn, yet he'd been stupid enough to pray that she still wanted him, that she would brave those few steps, but she never had.

There was naught to do but leave, to tromp down the wharf, speak with the purser, and pay his fare. Resigned, saddened, he sighed and set forth, when a gilded carriage pulled out in front of him, blocking the entire lane from side to side.

"Bloody rich sod," he grumbled, and he was about to duck through the alley, when a man exited the vehicle.

He was nodding and whispering to whoever was sequestered inside, then he stared at Charles so intently that he shifted, uneasy with the scrutiny. Though the man was attired as a gentleman, with a hat and walking stick, the cane seemed more like a weapon than a dandy's adornment. He was muscled, rugged, a former pugilist, a bodyguard, or even a Bow Street runner, though why such an unsavory character would be looking for him was a mystery.

"Are you Mr. Charles Hughes?" he inquired as he approached.

"Yes."

"Formerly of the Fighting Hundred-and-First Regiment?"

"That I am."

"I'm Mick Rafferty. If you'll come with me, please."

"I don't *please,* Mr. Rafferty," Charles retorted. "What the hell do you want? And be quick about it. I've got business to attend."

"It's a matter of some delicacy. I'd rather not discuss it here on the street."

Charles grabbed a fistful of Rafferty's shirt. He might have one arm, but he was tough and fearless, and he wasn't about to have a stranger accosting him. "Start talking. Fast."

"Steady, my friend. No need to be surly." Not intimidated, Rafferty slapped him away. "I have a client who is considering filing charges against you."

"Charges? For what?"

"Breach of promise."

"Breach of . . ." He stopped. There was one family that

would raise such a fuss. Was this how they'd chosen to play it? To what end? What damages did they seek? He had no assets, so maybe they were angling for a pound of flesh.

A powerful nobleman such as Lord Bristol could have many punishments imposed that didn't involve cash remuneration. Imprisonment, flogging, deportation. A myriad of embarrassing scenarios careened through his head.

After all he'd done for Stephen, was this to be his reward? Was Stephen aware of what his father had set in motion? Was Eleanor?

He was so furious, he could have torn Rafferty in half.

Rafferty studied him. "I take it you're cognizant of the situation to which I refer, so I trust I won't be required to provide details."

"As I proposed marriage several times, and was consistently rebuffed, which promise—precisely—am I alleged to have breached?"

"I'm not privy to the facts, but I understand that there is some question as to the lady's reputation being tarnished."

Charles was aghast with outrage. "You can tell that horse's ass, Lord Bristol, to bugger off."

He'd meant to stomp away in a huff, but Rafferty halted him with a hand to his shoulder. "Let me make myself more clear: refusal to join me is not an option."

The lapel of his jacket was loosened, and Charles could view a concealed pistol. "What will you do?" Charles scoffed. "Shoot me?"

"I wouldn't push it, if I were you. It appears as if you're about to flee the country, and I've been well compensated to ensure you don't." He gestured toward the carriage. "My client is most insistent for the two of you to parlay. Shall we go?"

Charles was so incensed, he wanted to break something. There was nothing he hated more than bootlicking to a wealthy, arrogant prig such as Bristol, and he had a few cutting, terse comments he'd like to share as to the buffoon's pomposity.

"I'm anxious," he announced, "for the two of us to chat, as well. Lead on."

"A wise man."

"Shut up!"

He marched to the conveyance and climbed in. Another ruffian was present, and Charles seated himself, wondering if he'd ever meet the purported *client,* if these two lummoxes hadn't been hired to guarantee he vanished.

Well, if they were disposed to murder, they'd have to work for their money.

The coach left the harbor, then the town, increasing his worry that they would kill him. They rode in silence, Charles glaring at them, the two hoodlums glaring right back, and soon, they turned onto a manicured lane, lined with fruit trees and flower beds, and they reined in beside a formidable building that must have previously been a damned castle.

"Where are we?" Charles asked, when he was on the ground.

"It scarcely matters."

"It does to me." If he was about to meet his Maker, it would be nice to know the name of the location where it was to occur. As his kidnappers escorted him in a rear gate, and up a spiraling staircase, they encountered no servants, and he couldn't decide if they were sneaking in, or if the staff had been ordered to keep out of sight.

They entered a hall that was decorated with fancy paintings, ornate rugs, and fussy furniture, and they came to a carved wood door. His guards opened it and shoved him through.

"We'll be outside," Rafferty explained.

"For how long?"

"Until my client notifies us that our services aren't necessary," and he slithered away.

So . . . he wasn't going to be executed. Just talked to death! He couldn't determine which would have been the preferred conclusion!

Glancing around, he found himself in an elegant suite. The main salon was empty, but there was an adjacent room, and it was obvious that someone was inside. He stood very still, listening, trying to discern who it might be, and he was confused.

Lord Bristol wasn't the type to play games or dawdle. He would have jumped into the discussion without delay. So who was it? Sidling nearer, he could smell warm water and fragrant soap, perfume, powders, and other feminine accouterments. Who had summoned him to the lavish jail?

A female, certainly. But Lady Eleanor was the only woman of means with whom he was intimately acquainted. She wouldn't have . . .

His heart skipped a beat.

He went over and peeked in, and there she was. Eleanor, in all her spectacular, naked glory, was lounging in an elaborate bathing tub. Surrounded by the steam rising from the basin, she was mostly submerged, her legs bent so that her knees were sticking out. Her shoulders were exposed, as was her bosom, and the liquid lapped at her breasts, furnishing him with flirtatious glimpses of her nipples.

"Hello, Charles," she calmly greeted, as if they'd seen each other the prior day, with no intervening trauma.

"Lady Eleanor." He tipped his head in acknowledgment, but he wouldn't bow or show any other courtesy. He'd loved her, was passionately familiar with every delicious inch of her marvelous torso, and he wasn't about to prostrate himself before her.

"It's about time you arrived. I've been waiting forever."

She came up on her knees, the water rippling around her thighs, her entire front visible, and his nostrils flared, his phallus hardened, and he felt randy as a stallion about to mount his favorite mare. He didn't want to look at her, but he couldn't resist.

He evaluated her, noting that her breasts were bigger, the nipples enlarging. Her hips were wider, more curvaceous, her tummy rounded with a tempting bulge. The skin on her face was smooth and supple, her hair more lustrous than he remembered.

She was pregnant, in full bloom, radiant and aglow with pending motherhood. There could be no doubt, no denials, but though his spirit soared, and his mind whirled, he gave no outward sign that her condition had affected him.

"Your henchmen delivered me."

"And they did a very good job of it, too." She scrutinized him, focusing especially on his crotch where his cockstand tented his trousers. "I was so afraid they'd have to resort to fisticuffs."

Lately, he'd been so irritated, that he wouldn't have been adverse to a brawl, though with his infirmity, he'd have come out on the short end. "I'm here, at your bidding. What do you want?"

"Hmm . . ." she mused. "What *do* I want? Such a difficult question."

She lifted her dainty feet over the rim, and stepped onto the floor, droplets cascading onto the rug. Dripping, slippery, she approached, and he braced, fending off the rush of exhilaration he experienced by her proximity.

He would not be moved!

She slithered a finger into the waistband of his trousers, and pulled him to her so that they were pressed together, her damp skin moistening his shirt. Like a seasoned coquette, she ran her tongue across her bottom lip, wetting it, making it glisten.

Lust wrenched in his gut, and it was all he could do to keep from throwing her against the wall, and riding her. At the moment, a brutal, savage coupling would have suited him just fine.

"Have you missed me?" she queried.

"No," he lied.

"Not even a little?"

He didn't answer, scowling at her, maintaining an air of boredom and animosity. When she received no response, her wicked hand left his waistband and slinked around his flank to his buttocks, and she urged him closer so that their loins made contact. As she was nude, the only item separating them was the placard of his pants, and he was wild to rip at the buttons and take her.

But he said nothing, he did nothing, so motionless that he might have been a statue.

She raised up on tiptoe, and kissed him. "Are you still angry with me?"

"I'd have to care about you to be angry."

"Oh, Charles, don't be so vexatious." She kissed him again, nibbling and cooing, and so saucy that she was practically batting her lashes. "If I told you I was sorry, would you forgive me?"

"*If* you claimed you were sorry, I wouldn't believe you."

"I knew you'd be churlish." She sighed. "That's why I had help in fetching you. I didn't suppose you'd come if I asked politely."

"No, I wouldn't have." He pried her loose and set her away. "Now say what you've brought me here to say. Get the whole bloody thing off your chest so that I can go. I'm busy, and I have a thousand details to accomplish by the morrow. I'm leaving for America. Sailing with the dawn tide."

"Why?"

"There's nothing here for which I'd remain."

He yearned to have her know how desperately she'd wounded him, how crushed he'd been by her rejection. Before her, he'd lived a simple life, had carried on as a poor man ought, never pining for things beyond his ken. She symbolized the sole occasion he'd reached beyond his station. She'd made him dream and aspire to unattainable goals, and at her snatching them away, he'd felt as if the ground had been yanked out from under him, as if he couldn't find his balance.

He hated her for dangling herself before him. She was like a shiny star that would always be beyond his grasp, despite how fervently he tried to latch on to it.

"I'm sure you're anticipating your departure," she breezily stated, "but you'll have to cancel your trip. You see"—she came to him, once more, snuggling herself seductively—"I have an itch that needs scratching, and you're the only one who can relieve my suffering."

Is that what this was about? She'd had him abducted and forcibly conveyed to an isolated, hidden castle, merely so they could fornicate? The woman was mad as a hatter!

Hadn't she abused him sufficiently? Must she add cruelty to her list of sins? Didn't she realize that being in her presence was a torment worse than any he'd ever endured? It went beyond his war battles, or his near death and loss of an arm in Spain.

He was furious. At himself, for desiring her after all she'd said and done. But at her, too, for having the effrontery to flaunt herself, to feign a fondness that he wanted to count upon, but which had never been real.

She wanted to copulate? How dare she impose on him! How dare she deem him so weak, so irresolute! Though he was an individual of modest resources, he had his pride, and there were some mistakes he wouldn't make twice.

"I'd rather be castrated," he decreed.

Spinning on his heel, he strutted out. In a snit, he jerked at the door, having forgotten that his two jailers were lurking. They leapt to attention, blocking his egress, neither discouraged by his vicious frown. What he wouldn't give to have two useful hands! He'd beat the presumptuous pair to a pulp!

Behind him, Eleanor strolled up, and he glanced at her. She'd covered herself with a robe, and she was tying the knot as she advised Rafferty, "I'm having a spot of trouble convincing Mr. Hughes to stay."

"You had imagined you would, milady."

"Yes, so I'll need him restrained. Would you tie him to the bed for me?"

"With pleasure."

"What?" Charles gasped. His two guards advanced on him, and he bristled. "Don't even *think* about it."

"She's paying us a fortune," his nemesis replied, and Charles was positive the accursed knave's eyes were twinkling with merriment. "Don't fight it. You can't win."

Undeterred, they seized him and lugged him to the bed, and with a few quick knots, he was secured, trussed at wrist and ankle, like a Christmas goose, but not before it occurred to him that the cords had already been moored to the bedposts.

Had the insane shrew planned from the beginning to have him bound? Was there no end to her lunacy? Her treachery?

He didn't struggle against the bondage. What was the use?

"Thank you, gentlemen." She was so nonchalant that they might have been helping her across the street, rather than abetting her in her deranged scheme. As she checked the strength of the ropes, she chuckled, tickled with their work, then she ushered them out, turned the key in the lock, and approached.

"Now . . . where were we?"

She shed her robe, letting it slide to the floor, then she perched on the mattress, running her palms down his chest, his stomach, to his groin, where his disloyal cock swelled. She plucked at the buttons on his pants, and after several naughty flicks, revealed his privates.

Grinning, she took hold of him. "I know *you* are angry with me"—she leaned down, licked the crown, causing his abdominal muscles to tense, his balls to ache—"but your body and I seem to be getting on remarkably well."

"Bitch," he hurled, wanting to hurt her with the terrible word, but she wasn't insulted.

"I *am* behaving badly," she admitted, "but you'll have to bear with me."

As if he had any choice! "How long do you expect to keep me here?"

"Until the mood passes." She winked, relishing the control she wielded, reveling in her dominion over him. "Or until you forgive me."

Was that all it would take? "I forgive you. So let me go."

She waggled a finger, negating his false avowal. "You have to mean it."

"I do."

"Let's be certain, shall we?"

She eased him into her mouth, her teeth and tongue gliding over the sensitive tip, and he stared at the ceiling, wondering how he'd stumbled into such an impossible jam. And how was he to get himself out of it?

~ 21 ~

Stephen walked down the deserted hallway, glad to be away from the crush, even if it was for a few minutes. The ballroom was hot, crowded, and in the past weeks he'd grown weary of the handshaking, the pats on the back, and the congratulatory drivel. No one could talk about anything but war, when it was the sole topic of which he cared to be reminded.

As to his purported valor, he was gracious in accepting their compliments, but while another man might have been flattered and basked in the glow, he wished they'd desist.

Inside his jacket, he could feel the crackle of parchment that had just been delivered by royal messenger. Suddenly, he was a baron, a title and estate having been awarded by the King as compensation for his bravery under fire.

The investiture was scheduled a few weeks hence, in a fancy imperial ceremony at the palace. How would his father react? His brothers? At the notion of Stephen becoming a peer, his oldest brother, James, would likely laugh himself silly. Who could have imagined such an outrageous conclusion?

It was all so absurd. In Spain, he'd merely tried to save his sorry hide, and those of the soldiers who'd been trapped with

him. He felt himself to be an impostor, that he was the last
fellow on earth who should be lauded for courage, but he
wasn't so foolish that he would spurn the unanticipated boon.

His new estate was small, but it encompassed many acres
of productive farmland, and would provide a steady income.
With the stroke of a pen, his penury had been solved, yet he
couldn't find any joy in his windfall.

He stepped out onto the verandah and leaned on the
balustrade, inhaling the fresh night air and gazing up at the
stars. Behind him, the orchestra played a waltz, and dancers
chattered merrily as they whirled around.

If Anne could see him, what would she think? He was so
bored, but when he'd been sequestered with her, he'd been
champing at the bit, enthusiastic about reestablishing himself in London. Why? Where was the lure? What attraction
had been greater than the pleasure and contentment he'd
achieved with her?

He endeavored to remember what had been so vital, what
had spurred his rush to the city. This had always been his life.
These people—with their soirees, suppers, and receptions—
had formed the boundaries of his existence, but now that he'd
immersed himself, everything seemed so frivolous, so pointless.

Had he changed that much? Or was his dissatisfaction
due to the fact that he'd nearly perished? Perhaps his brush
with death had altered his perception of what mattered. He
craved more than parties, superficial discourse, and shallow associations, and he deemed it a fine thing that he'd received his barony. It meant he would serve in Parliament,
where he would be able to help those who were less fortunate.

What would Anne say? How would she regard his resur-
rection?

He sighed. It was ridiculous to moon over her, but he
couldn't get her out of his head. Their split had been so

abrupt, and so permanent, that it felt as if she'd died.

You could go visit her, a voice chided, cajoling him to do what he oughtn't.

She'd been adamant that their separation be immediate and total, and even though he knew a clean break was for the best, he'd repeatedly begun to write her, eager to inquire as to how she was doing, but he'd never finished any of the letters. She'd demanded that he leave her alone, but he couldn't quit pondering her, couldn't shake the impression that she was in trouble and calling out to him, that he should check on her welfare, which was ludicrous.

Anne was the most independent, self-reliant woman he'd ever met. She didn't need him!

Meandering along, he kept to the shadows. The patio was lined with open windows, and at one of them, two females were arguing. He halted, intrigued to discern that it was Felicity and her mother, Barbara.

He'd decided to marry Felicity. There wasn't any reason not to. She had an impeccable ancestry, and he was fond of her. If he wasn't especially thrilled with some of her character traits, his opinion didn't signify. He was thirty years old, and it was high time he settled down.

As he caught himself ruminating over how intensely passionate he'd been about Anne, on how differently he viewed Felicity, he cringed. He had to stop comparing them! Felicity had her own charms, her own appeal, and if he continued equating her with Anne, he'd drive himself crazy.

Felicity would be a worthy wife, and she would merit his devotion and esteem.

Though he was curious about their heated discussion, he'd planned to move on, when his name was injected into the ardent debate.

"What would you do?" Barbara was asking. "Would you embarrass Stephen? Would you shame his family and ours? Is that the sort of person I raised you to be?"

"No, but Mother, how can I proceed? It would be so wrong, so unfair to him. I don't love him."

"I wouldn't expect you to, so early in your relationship. True affection comes with familiarity. It's built up through acquaintance, habit, and routine. You'll have many years to fall in *love*."

"But you know how I feel about Robert."

Robert? Stephen stiffened, listening more closely. *Who the hell was Robert?*

"Yes," Barbara chided, "you've been boorishly consistent in extolling your cousin's virtues."

Stephen had a flash of memory, of a nondescript, blond sycophant, with an ingratiating nature that set Stephen's nerves on end. He was a violin player or some such talent, and adept at composing music, though Stephen couldn't describe much more about him.

She adored that sniveling, odd man?

Or half a man. The crude thought blasted by. He wasn't certain that Robert was attracted to women. He was very effeminate, and Stephen had pegged him a gay blade, but who knew?

On learning that she was enamored with her tepid beau, he should have been insulted, should probably have ranted and raved. Wasn't that what a proper fiancé would do? Shouldn't he sense something? Affront? Indignity? Hurt? At the very least, shouldn't his pride be dented?

In all actuality, he experienced very little emotion, save an enormous amount of relief. If her heart was elsewhere engaged, he could cut her loose. He didn't need her money anymore, and he was sure her struggling artist needed it very much.

Unencumbered, released from obligation, he'd be free. Free to go wherever he wanted, to do whatever he wanted. Free to . . . to . . . marry Anne . . .

The scandalous concept leapt into his consciousness,

wedging so dramatically that it all but bowled him over.

When he'd been with her, he'd convinced himself that their worlds were impossible to merge. But perceived from afar, the obstacles that had been paramount a month prior had vanished with the realities of his new situation.

The gilt had worn off London, and if he never came to town again, he wouldn't consider it much of a loss.

The estate bestowed on him was a few hours' ride from Bristol Manor in one direction, and a few hours to Anne's farm in the other. They were smart people. They could find a way to be together.

Inside, Barbara had risen. "I'm going to the ballroom," she told her distraught daughter. "You will remain here, until you've calmed. I won't have Stephen noticing your upset."

"Yes, Mother." At the subtle reminder that she'd have to spend the entire night smiling by his side, she looked as if she'd bitten into a rotten egg.

"I suggest you use the solitude to reflect upon your duty." Barbara strolled to the door. "When you return for the banquet, I demand that you have your attitude adjusted."

She exited and, irked and disconcerted, he brooded. So . . . he was Felicity's *duty*, was he? That comment, more than any other, resolved his dilemma. He wasn't about to progress to matrimony when the notion was so distasteful to her. Though he hadn't been excited about wedding her, he'd assumed that she was ecstatic. She always acted so optimistic and cheerful, when her conduct had obviously been a facade. If the prospect of being his wife was so abhorrent, he'd never force her into it.

With both of them pining away for someone else, what kind of union would they have? He didn't want a bride who was infatuated with another. Talk about a recipe for disaster!

He could split with Felicity, and before dawn, he could be traveling to Anne's, and suddenly, he was desperate to be off. The urgency that had been prodding at him started to prick like a burr under the saddle.

Would she be happy to see him? Would she welcome him with open arms, or would she laugh at his whimsy and send him packing?

He had to discover whether their connection had been as ardent as his recollection. Was it genuine? Or had it been an illusion created by the peculiarities of their circumstances?

An eagerness in his step, he raced into the house, so that he could liberate Felicity—and himself.

Felicity perched on the edge of the sofa, determined not to wrinkle her gown, a transgression which would further infuriate her mother.

Why couldn't she make the woman understand? With how confused and forlorn she'd been, she'd finally broken down and confessed her predicament, but instead of evincing any sympathy, her mother had railed as to Felicity's immaturity and foolishness, which had only left Felicity more bewildered. What was the benefit of being an heiress if she couldn't have her heart's desire?

Yes, she'd once been flattered by the idea of marrying Stephen, but she'd been so young when they'd begun courting, and in the interim, so much trauma had occurred.

Oh, she was so miserable!

Leaning forward, she rested her head in her hands, when the door's hinges creaked, and she stifled a groan, hoping it wasn't Robert. He'd insist that she repeat the conversation she'd had with Barbara, and every time she had to tell him how she couldn't alter her destiny, he became more depressed. He had a virtuoso's temperament, and his sensibilities were too delicate to weather such protracted torment.

"Felicity," a male voice murmured.

Stephen! Gad! What next! The accursed mansion had eighty-four rooms. Couldn't she have any privacy?

She vaulted to her feet, her composure firmly in place. No matter what, she couldn't let him detect how desolate she was. He—of all people—didn't deserve to suffer because of her capricious constitution.

"Hello, my dear, Captain. I was about to come locate you." She walked toward him, trusting he couldn't discern her fatigue, her agitation. "Are you enjoying yourself?"

"Very much," he replied.

"Good."

She halted. He was gaping at her strangely, and she was swamped by a wave of unease. What was he contemplating? He couldn't know about Robert! If he mentioned her cousin, she'd perish from mortification!

"I'm glad you're alone," he asserted. "I must speak with you."

As he locked the door and shut the window, her discomfiture increased. "It appears to be serious."

"It is."

He blushed, and she couldn't credit what she was witnessing. What had he done? In her disordered state, she couldn't tolerate any emotional upheaval. Why couldn't the blasted oaf be silent? They weren't married yet. She shouldn't have to be his confidante!

"Well . . . ?"

"This is so embarrassing."

"Just say it."

"I've been considering our engagement."

She gulped. "You have?"

"Yes, and I've been wondering . . . that is . . . ." He gulped, too. "Ooh, this is much more difficult than I'd imagined it would be."

"What is it?" she barked, weary of the suspense.

"So much has transpired since we were first betrothed. I've changed, and you've changed, too, I think."

"We have." At what was he hinting? Why couldn't he spit

it out? "But we've stumbled through! And we'll succeed!"

"That's just it. You see"—he cleared his throat, fussed with his cravat—"I no longer wish to *succeed*. Not with you, anyway." He winced. "I'm sorry. Was I too harsh in blurting it out?"

Too *harsh*? Her pulse pounded. "I expect I'll survive." She glared, concluding that if he dropped dead in the next second, she wouldn't mourn. "Are you breaking it off?"

"I guess I am."

"Why?"

"I've met someone else."

"What do you mean by someone *else*?"

He blushed a deeper shade of red. "I'm in love."

She was a tad slow on deciphering his precise message, and when it dawned, she was furious, though she couldn't figure out why. Hadn't she been yearning for a miracle like this to materialize? Wasn't this the answer to her prayers? Yet, *he* was tossing her over. *He* wanted to be free. After the indignity and abuse she'd endured from him the prior year, how the notion galled!

"You're in . . . in love?"

"I apologize. I didn't intend for it to happen. It just did."

"Is it anyone with whom I'm acquainted?"

"I don't believe so."

"Who is it?" She couldn't explain why it signified. This was her reprieve, her deliverance. Why concern herself with the woman's identity? She'd been rescued! She should be dancing in the streets.

"I was introduced to her when I was recovering."

A niggling memory plagued her, of the poised, beautiful widow, Mrs. Smythe, and the truth jumped out at her.

Mrs. Smythe had made a positive impression, had been autonomous in a fashion that had fascinated Felicity. She'd often pondered what it would be like to carry on so anonymously, to do whatever she pleased without the entire world going into a collective swoon.

On that last, poignant day, when she and Eleanor had retrieved Stephen and fetched him to London, Mrs. Smythe hadn't stopped by to make her farewells or to accept their accolades. At the time, her behavior had been rude, but with the excitement of their journey, Felicity hadn't thought about it again.

Why . . . she'd been too busy stealing Felicity's fiancé to mind her manners!

"Is it the proprietress of the spa?"

"It is."

What an insult! The bounder had chosen a female with no antecedents. A nothing and nobody who had no money or assets to offer as a dowry, who mixed tonics and brewed soups. Who . . . who *worked* for a living.

"Will you marry her?"

"If she'll have me."

Could there be any question? An individual as modest and common as Mrs. Smythe would grab at the chance.

"Is there some doubt?"

He smiled, cherishing a fond reminiscence, which had Felicity stewing. "She doesn't feel I'm much of a catch."

Why was he aware of Mrs. Smythe's opinion? Had he proposed before severing his commitment to herself? How discourteous! How disrespectful! How absolutely crass!

He was spurning her for a female who was so far below her station and situation! What traits did the sainted Mrs. Smythe possess that she, Felicity, didn't?

She was almost enraged enough to ask, when she recalled Robert. She could now have Robert, and she wouldn't have to hurt Stephen in the process. He would never have to know that she'd strayed. They could split amicably, and after a few months, she would announce her betrothal to her cousin, and it would seem perfectly normal. No brows would be raised.

There would be no scandal, no wedding to the wrong person, no marriage to a man she didn't love.

Why, then, was she so irate? So . . . so dissatisfied with the outcome?

"I don't suppose"—he interrupted her reverie—"that my decision is much of a surprise to you."

"No, it isn't." Which was an unadulterated lie. Never in her wildest dreams had she imagined he would cry off. Since his recuperation, he'd seemed happy with their arrangement, but she had her pride. She wouldn't let him ascertain how shocked she was.

"But before you give me your answer, there's one more detail of which you need to be apprised."

There was more? How could there be? "What is it?"

"A letter was dispatched to me this evening. From the palace." He paused for emphasis. "I've been awarded a title."

"For your military service?"

"Yes."

"The rank?"

"A humble baron, I'm afraid."

"You'll have a steady income?"

"It provides a small but prosperous estate that's not too far from my ancestral home in Bristol." He grinned, and his high spirits were really beginning to grate.

"How wonderful."

"The circumstance changes many things. If it makes a difference to you, we can forget this conversation ever occurred."

Wasn't he the consummate gentleman? As if she could forget his profession of love for another! If she forced him to the altar against his will, how miserable their lives would be!

Besides, his admission was irrelevant. She'd never aspired to being a nobleman's wife. Had she?

"No, it's of no import to me," she fibbed with a straight

face. "Is there anything else?" If he said *yes*, she'd hit him.

"I believe that about covers it."

With the worst of his confessions over, he looked calm and in control, almost as if he'd been confident she wouldn't fuss. Why wasn't he waiting for her to weep and wail?

What if she did emote? What if she refused to meekly accede to his scheme? If she fell to pieces, if she screamed and yelled and caused the biggest commotion London had ever seen, it would serve him right!

Instead, unruffled as she'd ever been, she inquired, "Are you sure this is what you want?"

"Very."

She nodded. "Once we go forward, you can't undo what we set in motion. I won't take you back."

"I realize that."

"How would you like to proceed?"

"I'll leave town, then your mother can circulate rumors that, since my return to health, our affection has waned."

He had it all planned out. How civil. How pragmatic.

She yearned to wring his neck.

"That will work," she blandly remarked.

"Will she be upset?"

Barbara would be so mortified that she might go into seclusion and never again show herself in public, but Felicity continued the pretense. "No. She'll be very understanding, once I've clarified everything."

"Should we find her and tell her?"

"I'll inform her tomorrow. When it's just the two of us."

"Are you certain you don't want me there?"

"I'm positive."

"Well then . . ." His chagrin visible, he trailed off.

"Well, then . . ."

"I appreciate your being so considerate."

She bristled with temper, but tamped it down. "Might I have some privacy?"

"By all means."

He appeared pained, as if he was eager to justify his conduct, or might say something even more horrid, and she prayed that he would hold his tongue. If he started spouting Mrs. Smythe's charms, or listing the reasons he'd picked her over Felicity, Felicity couldn't predict what she might do.

Thankfully, he left without shaming either of them further.

She listened to the quiet as it settled around her. Off in the distance, she could hear the orchestra playing a quadrille, a woman laughing in the garden.

There was a mirror on the wall, and she went to it, studying her reflection, trying to picture herself as Stephen saw her, as Robert saw her.

Pale, indistinct, she attempted to smile, to be glad for this rapid sequence of events, but she couldn't exude any joy, and she had no idea why she wouldn't.

Robert would be hers. The villa in Italy would be hers. She could utilize her fortune to become a major patroness of the arts, could live solely for Robert, the silent, unlauded force behind his genius.

She had a vision of herself, in the background, hovering in the shadows, the hidden impetus that spurred and fed his success. As if she'd been subsumed by him, she was invisible, not a separate individual, but merely an extension of his illustrious self, and the image didn't fit.

Be careful for what you wish. You just might get it.

The admonition swirled past, and she shoved it away, declining to pay it any heed. Bustling out, she distanced herself from any untoward thoughts.

Robert—her dearest, her darling—would be in the ballroom, searching for her, and she was anxious to share the marvelous news.

He would be elated.

~ 22 ~

Stephen reined in his horse at the entrance to Anne's farm. The gate was open, the residence appearing to be abandoned, and his sense of unease prickled, once again.

Why weren't there a dozen carriages parked out by the grotto, her rich customers enjoying an afternoon dip in the pool? Why wasn't she at work? Where were her patrons? Was she ill? Had she sustained an injury?

A thousand frantic thoughts scrolled past, but he pushed them away, refusing to panic until he had a reason.

Throughout his madcap journey from London, he'd been spurred on by the strangest feeling that Anne was in distress. As he'd put mile after mile between himself and town, the impression of foreboding had taken root, and he hadn't been able to shake it.

He'd told himself it was merely nerves, from his having jilted Felicity, from his going against the wishes of his family and hers. He'd broken away from all that was familiar, all that had formed the circle of his life. What man wouldn't be apprehensive?

Staring, he prayed to note any sign of activity, and the lack had him racing up the lane. He hurried to the door and rapped on it, knocking persistently before he heard foot-steps. Kate answered, which was odd. When he'd been stay-ing with them, she'd always been in the yard, gardening and puttering away at her projects.

"Kate, hello." He hoped his alarm wasn't obvious.

"Captain Chamberlin! You're here so soon! Come in! Come in!" She gestured to the front parlor, and as he marched by, she added, "I have to admit, I didn't believe that harpy, Camilla Warren, would deliver our letter."

Camilla had written to him? After the drubbing Anne had given her, he couldn't imagine she'd offer. "What letter?"

"You didn't receive it?"

"No."

"Have you spoken with her?"

"No," he repeated.

She stopped. "Then how did you know we needed you?"

"I didn't." Shrugging, he was confused by his burst of in-tuition. "I simply felt I should be here."

"And just in the nick of time, too." She called down the hall, "Pru, guess what? The Captain's arrived."

A petite, middle-aged woman bustled in, draped in an apron, a cast on her arm, bruises around her eyes. "Already? My goodness! That was fast."

Kate made introductions as he glanced about. There was an ancient rifle, a pistol, and some knifes on the table. The knives were dull and likely wouldn't cut a piece of meat, and the guns were old, rusty, and looked as if they'd explode if fired.

"What's happened?" he asked.

"Pru's brother, Willie McGee, has arrested Anne."

Anne had mentioned her fear of the villain. His knees buckled, and he sank onto the sofa. "On what charge?"

"Some nonsense about public indecency in the pool."

"Who would make such an accusation?"

"We suspect that Willie was spying on the bathers."

"With perverted intent?" He couldn't avoid the indelicate query. Matters had proceeded far beyond decorum.

"Yes," both females replied together.

"But we've talked it over," Kate clarified, "and we wouldn't be surprised if Lady Camilla had a hand in it."

"She's capable of treachery," he agreed, "but she's a coward. She'd never step forward to complain."

"Willie would do it for her," Pru asserted. "You see, my brother fancies himself to be an officer of the law. He assists the magistrate with various tasks, but it's been rumored that he'll do anything, if he's paid enough money."

It was possible that McGee was in league with Camilla, that he was acting to further her scheme. She'd want revenge for Anne's having humiliated her, and he should have realized that she might do something horrid.

He was furious with himself. How could he not have recognized the danger for Anne? His sole defense was that he'd been so in love with her, so distracted by his attraction, that he hadn't been focused on anything else.

A terrible calm flooded him, the sort that washed over him before a violent battle. His perception heightened, his blood pumped more swiftly, his heart pounded. He was like a wolf, a predator geared to strike, and others were wise to keep their distance.

"How long has he had her?"

"A few hours."

"Where would she be detained?" His mind was whirling with the supplies he would require, the assault he would initiate.

Pru responded, "We have a gaol in the field behind our house."

He was incredulous. How could such a thing be allowed? "The man has his own private jail?"

"He's operated it for many years."

"Without objection?"

"Only from the criminals he's incarcerated."

Which meant that there'd been no concern about who was held, or how they were treated, the general consensus being that a felon deserved his fate.

"Has no one ever questioned its existence?"

"Most in the neighborhood feel it's beneficial, what with Bath being so far away."

"Where is it located?"

"I'll show you," Kate proclaimed.

"No, you won't," he countered.

"I can save you time." Kate was mutinous. "Their farm is the adjacent property. It's quickest if we walk through the woods."

"I want my horse. In case I have to give chase." He went outside, marching so briskly that Kate and Prudence had to run to keep up. "Explain the details of the place to me."

They both chimed in with instructions about the position of the gate, the grounds, the buildings, the hidden jail.

"How about my pistol?" Kate inquired.

"I have two of my own." In case he'd been accosted by highwaymen on the road, they were loaded and easy to reach. "And a knife. A big one."

Seeming abashed, Kate gazed at him. "We were about to go after her ourselves. I wouldn't want you to think we let him have her without a fight."

At the notion of the pair confronting the madman, he could barely suppress a shudder. "Good for you, Kate, but I'm glad you didn't have the chance to intervene." He stared at the woods, wishing he had magical vision so that he could peer through the forest and detect what was transpiring on the other side. "Will he hurt her?"

"Absolutely."

As her evidence, Kate pointed to Pru, and he rippled with outrage. "Be prepared for anything, then, when I return."

"We'll take care of her. You just fetch her home."

"I will." Of that fact, he had no doubt.

He leapt onto his horse, wrenched around, and took off at a gallop.

Willie glared at the bed, where Anne was trussed at the wrists and the ankles. He was breathing hard, sweating from his exertions in tying her to the posts, and he wiped a hand across his lips, seething when he noticed that blood was oozing.

He'd had so much fun whipping her, had taunted and tormented her with the strop, but she hadn't begged him to stop. Not once. And other than a few whimpers, she'd scarcely cried out, which had deprived him of such enjoyment.

She'd fainted occasionally—at least, it seemed as if she had—and her stupors had extended the flogging, for when he meted out punishment, he liked his prisoners to be awake. He'd had to revive her, either with smelling salts or by tossing water in her face, but with the level of stamina she still possessed, he had to wonder if she'd ever really blacked out.

Had her display of weakness been a ruse? Was she trying to lull him into complacency?

Well, if she was, she'd definitely succeeded.

After her thrashing, he'd removed her shackles, expecting her to be beaten down, but she'd come around swinging, landing several blows that were so painful, he was worried his nose might be broken.

They'd struggled, kicking and wrestling, with Anne a worthy combatant, until he'd stunned her with a punch of his own, then he'd dragged her to the bed. As she'd regained consciousness, she'd been bound, and any hope of escape had been dashed.

"I'm going to kill you," he vowed.

"You sick bastard."

He slapped her, relishing how she flinched. "Shut your mouth."

"Sod off, you freakish—"

He slapped her again, more forcefully, and she was quelled, but she glowered at him with such hatred and malice that he was unsettled.

How did she persist with her impudence? Over the years, he'd disciplined many females, but their courage never lasted beyond the initial castigation. When they were routed physically, they were cowed mentally, grasping that defiance was futile.

But not Anne.

He smiled. Her endurance was thrilling, like a game. The more tenaciously she challenged him, the more he was entertained. How long could she persevere? How sweet would her capitulation be?

As he picked up a knife, her eyes finally widened with terror. He wouldn't cut her—not yet anyway—but she didn't know that, and it was amusing to have her supposing he would.

With the blade resting at her throat, he let her feel how sharp it was, how precise, then he drew it down to her waist, parting her gown to her feet, so that she was naked.

Studying her, he dawdled while her frantic imagination concocted various hideous scenarios. Her fear escalated to an alarming apex, and when her dread peaked, when he could smell her horror, he advanced on her, ready to prove who would be her lord and master.

He tugged off his shirt, and pitched it to the floor, then he preened, allowing her to see how brawny he was, how virile.

Resistance was idiotic! He was a man, and she was a woman. She *would* submit.

"Now," he crooned, sidling over, "we shall discover how tough you actually are."

"Don't touch me, you fat pig."

"Be silent!" He wasn't obese! How dare she say so! He was a robust, manly fellow, with a sculpted, masculine physique.

"You greasy, foul reprobate!"

He struck her, once more. Would she never learn to obey? How much fortitude did the accursed trollop have? "Desist! You can't win!"

"You swine, you degenerate, you . . . you—"

He prepared to clout her again, deciding that he should utilize something more terrifying than his fist, when a male voice sounded from behind him.

"Drop your hand, and step away from her."

He froze. He'd been so involved with Anne that he couldn't process what was occurring. Straightening, he spun around. The chamber was dark, and sunlight streamed in the open door, making it difficult to discern any particulars. Whoever had arrived was but an outline, a shadow.

"I said: step away from her."

Exuding bravado, he wasn't about to have some half-wit stumbling in and interrupting. "Who the hell are you?"

"Who am I?" the idiot hissed. "*Who* am I?" He abandoned the threshold and approached.

"You're trespassing and interfering, whilst *I* am a deputy magistrate, carrying out an investigation on a dangerous felon."

"An *investigation*?" He mulled the word. "Is that what they call rape and torture these days?"

"Be gone, you dunce! If you meddle in official business, I shall have to arrest you, as well."

"I would love for you to try."

The knave wasn't intimidated in the slightest, and he kept converging, his silhouette taking shape, the lamp illuminating his features.

"Captain Chamberlin . . ." Willie breathed.

"Yes. 'Tis I."

Was he hallucinating? He blinked and blinked, striving to clear his vision, but Chamberlin was really and truly there. A hulking, angry menace, he was a lethal assassin, renowned for his bravery and audacity under fire, a brute so vicious in battle that the enemy was reported to tremble at the mere mention of his name.

From where had Chamberlin come? What did he intend? He'd been in London for weeks. Before beginning, Willie had ensured as much. There was no way he could have been apprised of Anne's plight. No one knew of the plan except . . .

He fumed. That rich witch, Camilla Warren, must have set him up, but why would she? Save for the occasion she'd visited about Anne, he'd never met her prior.

"What are you doing here?" seemed the only pertinent question.

"Must you ask?"

They were toe-to-toe, and before Willie could react, Chamberlin lashed out, quick as lightning, and clutched him by the throat, yanking him off his feet so that his boots dangled above the floor. Willie was stunned by Chamberlin's power, his lithe, lean body. By all accounts, he was still recuperating. When had he grown so strong?

"Stop!" Willie was gasping, prying at the fingers that were shutting off his air.

"Tell me who put you up to this, and I won't kill you right away."

Chamberlin was contemplating murder? No, no. He had to be jesting! He had to be!

"Lady Camilla," he insisted without hesitation. Whether the shrew had betrayed him or not, it was too late to haggle over the details. He had no loyalty to the noblewoman, could care less what Chamberlin might ultimately do to her. His current goal was to mitigate the damage so that Chamberlin didn't fly into one of the frenzies for which he was famous.

"Excellent!" As though they were bosom buddies, Chamberlin nodded cordially. Without glancing away, he growled, "Anne, can you hear me?"

"Yes, yes. Stephen, is it you?" The bitch started to cry.

"I can't believe you came! I didn't want to hope!"

"How badly are you hurt?"

"He's whipped me, and hit me over and over, but he's had no time to do anything worse."

"Such a foolish, foolish man," Chamberlin murmured, and the hair on Willie's neck stood up.

Behind Chamberlin, someone else entered, and though the sunshine was intense, Willie could distinguish that it was the lesbian Amazon. She had a rifle propped over her arm.

"Is that you, Miss Kate?" Chamberlin queried without turning.

"Yes. I figured you could use some help."

"Untie Anne, cover her, and get her out of here."

"Will do."

As Kate set about her task, Chamberlin remained rooted to his spot, his grip not loosening. Anne was freed and escorted out, Chamberlin not observing any of it. His attention was glued to Willie, and despite how Willie shifted about, he couldn't lessen the tight hold.

The instant the two women exited, Chamberlin moved, lugging Willie backward, so rapidly that the motion made him dizzy. With a few deft gestures, Willie was shackled to the wall, imprisoned by his own instruments of torture. Splayed wide, his extremities were pinned, his bare flesh cutting into the rough brick.

How had Chamberlin accomplished the feat? Though his height surpassed Willie's, Willie had more girth, more muscle, and he was no stranger to brawling or fisticuffs. How had Chamberlin bested him? Was this smooth, graceful domination the root of his infamy? No wonder he'd conquered his foes with such ease!

Willie grappled against the restraints, as Chamberlin watched dispassionately.

"How does it feel to be on the other side?" Chamberlin goaded.

"Let me go!"

Chamberlin pretended to consider, then chuckled. "I don't think I will."

He riffled through Willie's straps and manacles, touching, gauging, deliberating, until he selected the cat-of-nine-tails Willie had used on Anne. Lifting the vicious weapon, he cracked it across Willie's face, slicing a deep gash.

"Bastard," Willie grumbled, as Chamberlin struck him repeatedly. The blows were precise, accurate, the lash scourging him with bruising force.

"I often had to flog disorderly soldiers in the army," Chamberlin explained. "I became quite adept. Wouldn't you agree?"

"Don't! Please!" There was a whine in his voice, but he couldn't keep it from slipping out.

"You're not nearly vulnerable enough to suit me." Peering around, Chamberlin saw the large knife with which Willie had taunted Anne. He picked it up, and in a thrice, rent Willie's trousers, shearing them to the ankles and tugging them away so that he was naked. The dagger just missed his genitals, the tip sliding past with a terrifying indolence that had his insides reeling.

Surely, Chamberlin wouldn't . . .

God, the concept was too horrid to ponder!

"Aah!" Willie shrieked as the blade glided by.

"Much better."

Chamberlin surveyed Willie's nude torso, then retrieved the whip and flailed him across groin and thigh, and his cock shriveled to a tiny nub. He writhed, pleading for mercy.

Kate returned, chortling when she witnessed Willie's predicament, and he flushed with shame, wishing he could jerk the chains out of the wall. If he could, he would rush across the room and beat her to a pulp! The perverted cow!

"You're a widow, aren't you, Miss Kate?"

"Yes, Captain."

"Look at this little worm." With the knife, he fondled Willie's withered rod. "It's not very dangerous, now, is it?"

Kate laughed, a sickening, female titter. "No, sir."

Chamberlin laughed, too. "Are you squeamish, Miss Kate?"

"Not a bit."

"Are you in a hurry?"

"It's frequently mentioned that I have the patience of a saint."

"Marvelous." He pointed to the bed, where Anne's stockings dangled off the mattress. "Bring one to me."

Kate fetched it. "Here you are, Captain."

"Thank you." His glare sent shivers down Willie's spine. "Will anyone miss you, McGee?"

"What?"

"Is there anybody to whom you'd like to leave a final message? If so, I'll deliver it."

"What the hell are you talking about?"

"I'll take that as a *no*." Willie opened his mouth to protest his treatment, and Chamberlin stuffed Anne's stocking into it. "I find it appropriate that you should choke to death this way."

Fuck you! You lousy prick! I'll kill you for this! The words screamed inside his head, but he couldn't speak, and he spit and sputtered, trying to emit his outrage, but to no avail.

Chamberlin raised the knife to eye level, guaranteeing that Willie noted the size and shape, and tested its sharpness by flicking his thumb on the edge.

"It will be very slow," Chamberlin claimed, "and very painful."

"No more than he deserves," Kate chimed in.

What? Willie silently bellowed. *What are you planning?* But he needn't have inquired, for the intent was clear.

He was about to be murdered! The truth of his imminent demise was written in Chamberlin's determined, resolved expression. The ex-warrior would slay him, in cold blood, on his own property! He'd get away with it, too! Who would suspect him? The entire world presumed he was in London. Even if there was a later hint that he'd been in the area, who would accept that the lauded hero would have been involved in something as sordid as a homicide?

No! No! You can't! Willie shivered, his bladder letting go, and he wet himself, his piss saturating his legs, the brine seeping into and exacerbating the sting of his welts.

"Say your prayers, McGee"—Chamberlin flashed an eerie, ghoulish smirk—"and take it like a man."

In a swift move, he stabbed Willie in the genitals. The dagger penetrated to the hilt, then he drew it upward with a twisting motion, ripping apart the middle of Willie's abdomen and chest.

It took several seconds for the pain to register, and when it did, Willie howled and retched, vomit gurgling from his stomach, but his gag blocked release of the disgorge, so he began suffocating on his own spew.

He peeked down, and he could see his entrails falling onto the floor. The sight was so bizarre, and so peculiar, that it didn't seem real. It was as if he'd floated out of his body and was viewing the spectacle from up above.

Chamberlin sidled away, not so much as a drop of gore staining his clothes, and he spoke to Kate.

"A Portuguese freedom fighter taught me this technique. Now all we need are some ants."

Unfazed by the carnage, Kate studied the wound. "It's a handy procedure—in the right circumstances. How long will he be able to endure it?"

"I'd guess an hour or two." Chamberlin went to the bed and wiped the blade on a blanket. "Can you stay with him? I'd hate to have him escape or be rescued at the last minute, and I must get Anne home."

"I'd consider it an honor to watch him."

"Do you know how to check his pulse to be certain he's dead?"

Kate pressed two fingers to her neck, indicating her knowledge. Chamberlin nodded and started toward the door.

"Should I bury him?" Kate asked.

"No. Leave him hanging for the maggots."

"With pleasure."

In tacit accord, they smiled, then Chamberlin sauntered out.

Kate followed him, and strangely, Willie cried out to her.

I don't want to be by myself! Come back! Come back!

He detested the idea of being alone, of departing the earth with no one by his side, and there was a specific irony in the fact that Kate would sit with him through his passing, though he couldn't focus on why it was absurd. A fog surrounded him, the light fading in and out, and he couldn't pay attention very well, but he was sufficiently cognizant to be relieved when she strolled in.

"It's just you and me, Willie," she said. "You and me to the end."

Bless you! Bless you! He was so grateful, he had tears in his eyes.

"Don't worry about Pru. I love her, and I'll take care of her for you."

She pulled up a chair and balanced herself on the two hind legs. Her mocking grin was the only object in his vision, and he concentrated on it, unable to see anything else.

❧ 23 ❧

Anne was crouched on the ground, leaned against the wall, and shivering so violently that her teeth were clacking. The sun was too bright, so she'd closed her eyes, although it occurred to her that they might be swollen shut.

She was conscious, but barely, having detached herself from what was happening so it was difficult to remember who or where she was.

The blanket in which she was wrapped did little to stem her quaking. It reeked of Willie and his jail, of panic and torment and murder.

Was Stephen inside? Or was she hallucinating? Had fear driven her mad? Had her mind snapped and conveyed her to another, better place? If so, she wasn't concerned. She preferred to be cloistered in her mental haven, rather than bound and gagged in Willie's prison.

"Anne!" The voice was male, insistent, calling her from the brink where she hovered. It couldn't be Stephen, yet it sounded like him. Stephen was in London, engaged to be married, the toast of the town, so she must really be crazed.

"Anne!" Like a pesky, buzzing fly, he refused to give her any peace.

He grabbed for her, but she didn't assist or resist. Every bone in her body ached, every inch of skin screamed in agony, so she couldn't help or hinder him in whatever he intended. Easily lifting her, he carried her in his arms, which was good because she couldn't have stood on her own.

She could sense a horse, could detect its heat and coat of hair, and, as if she weighed no more than a feather, he hoisted her up. Another person approached, and her pulse pounded.

Willie? Coming for her? No, it was Kate.

"Hold her steady, while I mount," the man told Kate, and Anne was relieved when Kate's hands rested on her thigh and waist.

She yearned to thank them for their kindnesses, to participate, or at least balance herself, but she felt as if she was made out of water, as if she'd melted and was invisible.

"You're all right now, dearie," Kate consoled. "Relax and let us take care of *you* for a change."

The man leapt up behind her, landing on the animal's rump. He cradled her, solicitous of her injured back, but nestling her to him all the same, so that she was secure and positive she wouldn't fall.

Was she free? Was she away?

She couldn't bear to hope, so she would float on a tide of dreams and prayers, would stay precisely where she was, until she found a reason to be somewhere else.

Speaking to Kate, he said, "As soon as the bastard dies, proceed straight to Anne's. Don't dawdle. And don't leave anything that might tie you to the affair."

"Don't worry about us. Willie and I will be fine."

"You're sure?"

"Yes. Now fetch her home. Prudence will be waiting."

He nodded, then kicked the horse, and it lurched away.

The wind was cool, bracing. The odors of autumn assailed her, and it seemed as if she might actually be outside and racing toward her farm. But if they never arrived in fact,

she could go there in her head. She could remain there in
perpetuity.

She was cognizant of the direction they were traveling,
knew each twist and turn of the road, recognized when they
entered her property, when they approached her residence,
but they skirted around it, moving across the yard to the
grotto.

Was it wishful thinking? Had she conjured up the cherished spot?

They stopped, and he dismounted, then he shifted her
weight, and she dropped to him, toppling so fast that her stomach tickled with the descent. The pressure on her wounds exacerbated some of the gashes. They were oozing, wet, sticking
to the blanket.

"Praise be! She's alive!" a female exclaimed. Pru. Yes,
sweet Pru. "And my brother?"

"Is about to meet his Maker. Kate's with him, but she'll
be here shortly."

"What can I do?"

"I'm going to bathe her. I'll need her robe, some soap,
and the softest towels you have."

"I'll get them."

Pru's footsteps faded away.

"Anne," he said, "it's Stephen. You're with me. I'm taking
you into the water. It might sting."

*I don't care! Just wash me! I want to be clean! Rid me of
this stench!*

She meant to say the words aloud, but she couldn't utter
them. Her mouth wasn't functioning.

He carted her across the grass, to the pool. Fully dressed,
he waded in, and soon, her heels were in the water, then her
feet, her ankles. Gradually, he squatted, lowering her into the
reviving warmth.

As she was submerged, she burned and spasmed, and he

linked their fingers, squeezing tight, as if he could absorb the pain.

"I've got you, Anne. I've brought you home." He sat on the bottom, with her on his lap, so that she was immersed to her neck. "You're safe."

"It . . . it hurts," she managed.

"Yes. I imagine it will for a long while."

Mustering her courage, she opened her eyes, though they were tiny slits due to the blows Willie had delivered, and Stephen was sitting with her. Not a chimera. Not an illusion. Or perhaps she had died, and this was her perfect version of heaven, herself sequestered at her farm, surrounded by the people she loved, and Stephen by her side forever.

Trembling, she traced the shape of his handsome, familiar face.

"You came for me." She was awestruck, overwhelmed with gratitude.

"Of course, I did, you silly girl." He raised her hand and kissed her palm.

"How did you know I needed you?"

"You were crying out to me, inside my head."

She started to weep, huge tears dripping down her swollen cheeks. "Promise me you won't leave."

"I won't," he vowed. "I won't leave you ever again."

Stephen hovered in the dark, watching Camilla's carriage, as her driver sneaked to the bushes to relieve himself.

Down the lane, under the hanging lamps illuminating the path, Camilla strolled toward him, having just exited a small soiree. Though the season in Bath was ended, she'd lingered with the last members of the Quality who hadn't left for town yet.

No doubt, she planned an uneventful ride to her next party, but she was about to be temporarily delayed. With her driver still occupied, Stephen crept from the shadows and climbed into her coach.

In his coat, he'd tucked a journal that he'd pilfered from Anne's desk. It was filled with numbers and notations, and it looked authentic, as did the entries he'd inserted for additional effect. If Camilla demanded proof for what he was about to relate, he'd be happy to disclose it—false though it might be.

For what she'd set in motion he'd like to kill her, to simply wrap his fingers around her slender throat and choke the life out of her, but rapid demise would be too easy. He wanted her suffering to go on and on, and he'd devised the ideal method by which to torment her for years.

Lounging against the squab, he folded himself into the dim corner, listening to the swish of her expensive gown, the glide of her fashionable slippers. The driver emerged, assisting her with the step, the door. As she clambered in, Stephen could smell alcohol on her breath, and he grinned. Intoxication would muddle her reasoning, would make her more likely to panic.

She wasn't expecting anyone to be lurking, and she'd seated herself before she glanced up and saw him. Since he was attired all in black, he was difficult to discern, and she jumped with alarm, emitting a muted squeal.

Leaning forward, he let her ascertain his identity.

"Lady Camilla?" the driver queried from outside. "Is everything all right in there?"

"Tell him *yes*," Stephen advised, "and that it will be a minute before you depart."

She pulled at the curtain and peered out. "Yes, Thomas. I'm fine. I tripped. Hold on a moment, would you?" Pasting on a smile, she regrouped, though it was obvious she wasn't pleased by Stephen's sudden appearance. "What a wonderful surprise. I thought you were in London."

"I returned."

"Marvelous. Bath has been so dreary, but I must say"—she assessed him, evidently thinking they might renew their liaison—"the scenery has definitely improved. Shall we retire to my house? We could have a nightcap."

"This isn't a social visit."

Simpering, she cooed, "We could make it one."

"I'd rather be attacked by bats than spend time alone with you."

"Honestly!" she bristled. "You don't have to be so rude."

"Rudeness is the only behavior you understand."

"What is so dreadfully important?" she huffed. "Why all this drama? If your intent is to hurl insults, you could have called on me tomorrow afternoon in my parlor."

"We shouldn't risk your servants eavesdropping."

"They're as discreet as any, but what could you possibly have to impart that I wouldn't wish them to discover?"

"I have some disturbing news that can only be shared in private."

If she had an inkling of what he was about to reveal, she concealed it well. "What is it?"

"There's been a murder."

"A murder! Why would you presume that I would have a connection to such a sordid incident?"

"I'm sure that's what the authorities would like to know—should any of the facts become public."

"Who was slain? It couldn't be anyone with whom I'm acquainted."

"Willie McGee."

At the mention of McGee, she flinched with shock, but she hastily shielded her reaction. "I've never heard that name before."

"It's funny that you haven't, when he considered himself to be your business partner."

"How did you arrive at such a ludicrous notion?"

"It's all in this diary he kept in his desk." Stephen held it up, letting her see the embossed cover, and he leafed to one of the faked pages. "He claims that you hired him to kill one of his neighbors—a Mrs. Anne Paxton Smythe."

"I didn't pay him to kill her! I merely—" Realizing what she'd admitted, she bit off the rest.

"Were you aware that Anne is the daughter of Edward Paxton?"

"The Earl of Salisbury?" She looked ill, her blush fading to a ghostly white.

"The very one. She's also my fiancée."

"She is not! You're engaged to Felicity."

"No, I'm not," he was delighted to pronounce. "So . . . she's about to be a Chamberlin, which will put her under my father's protection. And mine." He paused, allowing the implication to sink in. "It would seem that Mrs. Smythe has many powerful friends. Now about Mr. McGee—"

"What about him?"

"His records were very explicit. He was concerned about your motives, and he was convinced you were setting him up, in a double cross, to take the fall for Mrs. Smythe's death."

"That's crazy!"

"Is it? The details are all in here." He offered her the book, so that she could peruse it, but she didn't. "He maintains that if he's a victim of foul play, the authorities should question you. Why do you suppose that is?"

"I have no idea."

He snapped the journal shut. "You have one week to flee the country."

"How dare you demand as much! I won't do it, I tell you. I won't!"

"Won't you?" He smiled, a vicious indicator of his resolve. "McGee's body hasn't been found yet, but it will be very soon. If you are still in England when his corpse is located, I will turn this information over to the law. I have several witnesses who can place you at his property at some very inconvenient times."

"But . . . but . . ."

"I don't care where you go, just so it's far away from here. I have men watching you. They will report to me when you board ship. Should you decline to acquiesce, I will proceed accordingly."

"Everything you allege would be a lie."

"Would it? You don't know McGee? You were never at his farm? You never hired him?"

She fussed and stewed, her anger rising. "I'll fight you! I'll deny every aspect of your trumped-up story. It will be your word against mine."

"That's certainly your prerogative, but don't forget that the punishment for murder is hanging."

As though she could feel the noose tightening, she gulped and rubbed her throat. For an eternity, she glared at him, her malice palpable. "You bastard!"

"You shouldn't have hurt Anne, and in case you're inclined to repeat your folly, I plan to ensure that you never have the chance. Pray that she lives a long and healthy life. If anything ever happens to her, if she should become ill or suffer a convenient *accident,* I will hunt you down, no matter where on this earth you attempt to hide."

"You can't do this to me!"

"I already have." He moved to the door, the book clutched in his hand. "One week, Camilla, and you might want to hurry. The clock is ticking."

Exiting, he inhaled a huge breath of fresh air, liking how it cleared his head. Then, he sauntered off, thrilled with his night's work.

Eleanor took Charles into her mouth, and as she'd suspected, his hips responded. Even though he was trussed like a goose, he couldn't resist. She knew he wanted to come, that he needed to come, but he was so obstinate, he'd restrain himself forever just to spite her.

She abandoned his cock, and busied herself with his apparel, eager to have him as naked as she. With her pregnancy blossoming, her torso was on fire. She was in a lusty state, anxious for a fierce copulation, and she would persuade him to participate—or die trying!

"Where did you find your henchman?" he asked through clenched teeth.

"Mr. Rafferty?"

"Yes."

"I've known him for ages. He's Bow Street. I originally hired him to spy on my husband." She sighed. "You wouldn't believe what I learned."

As if he might inquire, a spark of interest glimmered, but he tamped it down. The intractable oaf!

"Aren't you worried that he'll tattle about what you're doing?"

"Oh, no. He's very discreet."

"If he blabbers, your precious reputation will be tarnished beyond repair."

"Maybe my character should be blackened a tad. Once a woman decides to keep a sexual slave—"

"A sexual slave!" His cheeks were red with fury.

"—her honor is shot to hell."

"I'm not about to be anybody's carnal captive. Especially yours!"

"I really don't think you have any choice."

"What if the servants gossip?"

"What if they do? They're *my* servants."

"This is your damned castle?"

"Yes."

"I might have guessed. Rich witch!"

"Stop complaining about my money. Imagine all the pretty baubles I can buy you with it."

She untied his cravat, and tugged the lengthy hem of his shirt out of his trousers, but it was in her way and hampering her enjoyment. Since she wasn't about to loosen his bindings, she couldn't draw it off, so she gripped the neckline and ripped it down the center, receiving an enormous amount of satisfaction at her raucous display.

She was such a desperate female! Her desire for him was so great that she felt she was a hazard to herself and to him. When he'd first arrived, she'd advised him that she had an itch for him to scratch, and she hadn't been joking. She needed him as she needed food to eat, or water to drink, and she would continue on until he forgave her.

"Unlike some people I know," he grouched, "I'm not wealthy, and I don't have clothes to waste. When this is over, you're going to pay for a new shirt."

She always forgot that he was an individual of limited means. He was too arrogant to be poor. "I'll buy you an entire wardrobe. Don't grumble."

What a wanton she'd become! Cursing profusely. Fornicating with enthusiasm. Having a person kidnapped off the street in broad daylight. What would she do next? Any exotic behavior was possible.

Like a greedy cat, she leaned down, and rubbed her cheek across his brawny chest, relishing his smell, his heat. She rooted to his nipple, licked and nipped at the tiny nub. Down below, his cock surged, growing even larger, and he was struggling so mightily to shield any reaction that she laughed. He was so hard for her, yet he was glowering at the ceiling, so detached that he might have been in another room.

Straddling his lap, she eased herself over the blunt crown, until he was impaled to the hilt. On her knees, she hovered over him, her hands on either side, her breasts teasing his lips.

She began to move, retreating, then plunging down, frantic to feel his length, his girth. Though it had only been weeks, it seemed as if they'd been separated for years, perhaps decades, and she couldn't get her fill.

Against his will, his body joined in, unable to ignore the blatant stimulation.

"Give over, Charles," she chided. "Let go."

"Never."

"Quit fighting it, and admit how much you still want me."

"You are so full of yourself."

He was at the edge. So was she. Another thrust. Another.

"Tell me that you love me, Charles."

"No."

Rigid, every muscle tense, he rose up into her, permeating her, as his seed spewed out. He came over and over, never achieving the pinnacle, and as his pleasure erupted, her own did, too. She soared with him, up and up, and as she floated down, he was watching her, wary, intense, and—apparently—unaffected.

He was so stubborn! She yearned to shake him!

She brushed a kiss across his lips. "Will you marry me?"

"No." He bucked with his hips, striving to toss her off, but he had no leverage. "If you're finished with your little game, you can release me."

She thought about refusing, just on general principles, but she decided to grant his wish. Proceeding slowly, she undid his ankles. She hated having the wild escapade end, but then, if he was too recalcitrant, she could shout for Mr. Rafferty. As she slackened his wrist cord, the notion had her grinning, and the moment he was free, he seized her, spun them over, and pinned her down.

"Don't ever do that to me again."

"What? Don't abduct you? Or don't tie you up?" She flashed a saucy smile. "I could agree to forgo another kidnapping, but I liked your bondage too much. I'm afraid I won't be able to resist."

"I ought to take a strap to you."

"You can't. You have to be extra kind to me."

"After this shenanigan, give me one reason why."

"Because I'm going to have a baby."

"As I informed you long ago."

"Don't you have anything to say?"

"Yes. Good luck finding a husband who will tolerate your nonsense."

His sustained pique finally set a spark to her temper. How much further did he want her to prostrate herself? Must she slice a vein and draw blood? "You are the most unbending, mulish, relentless bully that I—"

He cut off her tirade with a torrid, punishing kiss, but she reveled in it, wrapping her arms around him and pulling him close. She was grappling and biting at him, venting her frustration and anger, as he was venting his.

"I'm a man," he decreed, breaking off the embrace.

She batted her lashes. "I noticed."

"If I'm to marry, *I* do the asking."

"Well, if I waited for you to get around to it, I'd be a hundred years old!"

"*I* will rule in my family. *I* will be king. *My* word will be law."

"Yes, Your Majesty."

"I won't reside in some infernal castle."

"I have six other homes. You may have your pick. If you don't like any of them, we'll purchase something else. You may choose it."

"Christ!" he scoffed. "Aren't you listening? How could we wed? We have nothing in common. I'm modest and indigent, while you're . . . you're . . ."

Either he couldn't describe what she was, or he couldn't utter it in her company. "I'm what?"

He paused, then he slid off her and sat up. "No. I just want to go."

"Coward," she muttered to his back.

Infuriated, he whipped around. "What did you call me?"

"You're a craven coward." In a huff, she crawled past him and onto the floor, where she scooped up her robe and jerked it on, wrenching at the sash, seeking the fortitude provided by clothing. "I'm offering to make your every dream come true, but you're too scared to reach out and grab for it."

"I am not."

"Book your accursed passage to America! Slink off all alone! Spend your life by yourself, ruminating over what might have been. See if I care!"

As incensed as she, he stood up and adjusted his attire. His hot gaze sliced into hers, and she was so irate that tears welled into her eyes.

"Don't you dare cry," he barked.

"I'm sick to death of men telling me what I can and cannot do. If I feel like sobbing for a week, I will. You can't stop me!"

Her delicate condition had her overly excitable, and a wave of emotion swamped her, teardrops cascading down.

At witnessing them, he was enraged. "Dammit. Why did you do this?" He was scowling at her as if he really and truly hadn't a clue.

"You idiot! Don't you know? I want to be your wife. I want to give you a family who will cherish you. I want to use my fortune to alleviate your burdens, to ease your way so that you don't have to work so hard."

"I like to work."

Throwing up her hands in defeat, she growled, "Fine! Just bloody fine! Work yourself to the bone. Wallow in squalor and poverty for the rest of your days. Struggle till you take your last, exhausted breath." She marched to the door and flung it open. "Go! Go to America! Get out of my sight!"

Mr. Rafferty and his partner snapped to attention.

"Mr. Hughes is leaving," she explained. "Drive him into

Southampton. Deposit him at his precious ship so that he can board immediately."

"Are you sure, milady?" Rafferty queried.

"Yes. I don't have anything to *offer* Mr. Hughes that he deems to be important."

Perplexed, Rafferty evaluated the two of them, then shrugged.

"As you wish." He stepped toward Charles, ready to escort him out, and muttering his opinion of Charles's decision, "You crazy loon."

Charles halted him with a fierce frown. "Bugger off, Rafferty."

He shoved Rafferty into the hall, slammed the door, and stared her down.

"I won't live with your father."

"Am I forcing you to, you blasted ingrate? I told you: I own six houses!"

"I won't come begging to you for every penny."

"Upon signing the marital contracts, the income from three of my properties will be allocated to you. You can dispose of it however you like."

"I won't be some idle oaf, who has nothing to do."

"Toil till your fingers fall off, if it makes you happy. It's none of my affair."

"I've always wanted to breed horses. Thoroughbreds."

"Have I said you couldn't?"

"I'll need stock and stables, farms and employees. It will be expensive."

"Do you have any idea how rich I am?"

"No."

"Then, maybe you should propose, before you make me so angry that I change my mind."

"All right." He nodded. "I'll have you."

"You call that a proposal?"

"It's the best I can do on short notice."

Bristling, she almost retorted in the same rude, flip fashion, but her energy waned, her ire fleeing as rapidly as it had spiraled. She wasn't furious, but sad and discouraged. With such high expectations, she'd chased after him, had been so optimistic about the future they could build together. She'd convinced herself that she mattered to him, that once he saw her again, all would be forgiven and forgotten.

What a fool she was! Would she never learn? She didn't understand men, how they thought, what they craved. Hadn't her disastrous marriage proven what a failure she was at dealing with the male animal?

Sighing, she turned and went to the window, blindly studying the grounds. "When I was betrothed to my husband," she began quietly, "he didn't ask me, either. His father and mine signed some papers, and it was done."

She peered at him over her shoulder. "Since then, it's occurred to me that he didn't really desire the engagement, that I was so inconsequential to him, he couldn't be bothered."

"I'm nothing like your husband. I believe I've mentioned as much before."

"I realize you're not, but if you're serious about marrying me, I guess I need to hear you say why, and your reasons should probably have something to do with me personally. I won't let you break my heart. I'm wiser now."

He observed her, concealing his introspection, and her pulse thudded with dread. Just as she'd persuaded herself that he wouldn't profess his feelings, that her madcap pursuit had been a waste, he spoke.

"You're correct," he admitted. "I am a coward."

"Of what are you afraid?"

"I'm terrified that what you're posing isn't real, that it will be snatched away. Over the years, I've suffered horrendous loss, Eleanor—more than anyone should have to bear—and I can't endure more."

"I know," she concurred, "and it pains me to be reminded of how alone you've been."

"If I ask, and you accept, it's forever. I won't let you renege or back out. A promise means something to me."

"Have a little faith, Charles." She extended her hand, a lifeline, a tether that would bind them till death.

It hovered there, and he crossed the room, took it in his own, and knelt before her.

"I love you, Eleanor."

"And I love you, Charles."

"I'm not much of a catch—"

"I think you are."

"—but I swear to you that I will be a dependable, loyal husband. That I will watch over you, and care for you, that I will honor and cherish you, till my dying day. Will you marry me?"

"Yes, I will." She helped him to his feet and hugged him, confessing for the second time, "We're going to have a baby."

"I hope it's a girl, who looks just like you."

"Oh, you sweet man."

He was so stalwart, so strong and steadfast, and he would always be by her side, her best friend, her constant companion. She whispered a prayer, for her baby—but for Charles, too. She was so glad to have this chance, and she vowed to spend every minute bringing him peace and contentment, making him happy.

Serene, satisfied, she laid her head on his shoulder.

She was home. Home at last.

~ 24 ~

Anne rushed across the lawn, attired solely in her robe, her feet bare. She'd been sequestered in the house, lounging in her room like an invalid, and she was feeling restless, jittery, a bit wild.

It was a brisk, bleak autumn evening, a vivid indicator of the changed season. The moon cast ghostly shadows, the tree branches brittle with frost, the ground hard and ready for the snow and ice that would come with the onset of winter.

She could see her breath, and the lower temperature sliced into her skin. Up ahead, steam rose, clouding the grotto with mist and fog, so that it looked eerie, mysterious, and she raced toward it, anxious to ward off her chill, to be immersed in its warmth.

Shedding her robe, she stood, naked, arms raised, absorbing the cold. She stared up at the stars, pausing to give thanks for her blessings, for being alive to enjoy and treasure them. The frigid breeze lashed at her, and she began to shiver, so she walked down the ramp and waded in. The water swirled around her, heating her, welcoming her. It felt extra hot, like jumping into a boiling kettle, and she hissed out a breath.

Her wounds prickled and stung, but she forced herself through the acclimation, comprehending that the pain would pass, that the water would heal her. In a matter of days, most of her gashes were closed, the bruising faded, and she no longer doubted the peculiar qualities the spot was rumored to have. It had worked its magic on her, had rapidly stabilized her condition, and she wouldn't speculate as to how or why. She would simply be grateful.

Out on the lane, a horse approached, and she knew it was Stephen returning from Bath. She didn't know why he'd journeyed to the town, or what had occupied him to such a late hour, and she didn't intend to inquire.

Many events had occurred of which she didn't care to be apprised. Ignorance really was bliss.

Willie McGee had disappeared, and it was clear that Stephen, Kate, and Prudence were aware of what had happened to him, but they would never tell a soul. When they'd believed her asleep, she'd heard them whispering. They'd reached an agreement, a sworn pact that would endure till death.

She should have been insulted by their having a secret that excluded her, but deep down, she didn't need to have the particulars divulged. Any punishment leveled on the wicked, crazed maniac was fine by her, so long as he could never hurt anyone again.

Pru wasn't in hiding, but rooming with Kate in the cottage behind the barn. She was busy making the decrepit place habitable, planting flower bulbs, cleaning, and painting, which attested to her assurance that Willie wouldn't be back. Pru wasn't worried, so Anne wasn't either.

Her only regret was that she'd never had the wherewithal to muster neighborhood opinion against him. When she thought of what other women might have experienced due to his villainy, she felt ill.

She swam, waiting, and soon, Stephen marched across

the yard, the gravel in the drive crunching as he walked. Even in the dim light, it was easy to discern how tall he was, how lean and strong. Smiling, she remembered his plight when he'd initially been dumped on her stoop. It was difficult to conceive of him as the same fellow.

There was a vigor about him, an energy that floated out in waves. A dramatic incident must have transpired in Bath, which had been so climactic that his agitation hadn't waned during the lengthy ride home.

She wouldn't interrogate him as to what it was, for she was sure it involved his wrapping up of the calamity that had unfolded in Willie's pasture. With his typical curt efficiency, Stephen had supervised the mess, settling the affair so quietly and so completely that not a single rumor had circulated as to her having been taken prisoner. As far as her employees were concerned, naught had befallen her. Stephen had demanded their silence, and none of her staff would fail to heed his dictate.

Like an adoring gaggle of adolescents, they followed after him, so awestruck and charmed by his magnificence that, in their estimation, he'd assumed divine attributes. He was their hero, their champion, and he could do no wrong. Whatever he asked of them, they would gladly provide.

His gaze locked on hers, and butterflies coursed through her stomach. He'd been with her for less than a week, and throughout the period, she'd been so worn down that she'd done little but lie around holding his hand, unable to let go, scared that if she did, he might vanish.

After that appalling afternoon of terror, he'd sworn he would never leave her, and she distinctly recollected his vow, but since then, she hadn't pressed the issue, being too fatigued to learn what he'd actually meant.

Why wasn't he in London? What about his engagement to Lady Felicity? A thousand questions plagued her, but she steeled herself, as she always did, to live in the moment, to pathetically revel in whatever minor pieces of himself he chose to share.

As it was folly to pine away for impossibilities, she wouldn't beg for more than he could give.

A fiery gleam in his eye, he stopped at the bank and studied her. "You appear to be much improved, Mrs. Smythe."

"I am better."

"Good. Are you wearing any clothes under all that water?"

"No."

"I didn't think so."

Fully dressed, he tromped directly into the pond, and she laughed and shook her head. Despite his claims of penury, he certainly acted like a wealthy man with boots to waste.

He came to her and pulled her into a torrid kiss, his mouth on hers, their tongues sparring, the fabric of his garments rough and rubbing her nude torso. The embrace concluded, and he buried himself at her nape.

"I was so afraid for you," he admitted. "Afraid that you'd been too battered, that your mind might have—"

"Hush," she murmured. "Let's don't talk about it now." She couldn't discuss Willie's foul deeds. Not yet, anyway. Perhaps sometime in the future. Or perhaps never.

Leading her to the rocks, he seated himself on the ledge, and snuggled her on his lap.

"I have something to tell you," he stated.

For an instant, she stiffened, wary and alarmed that he was about to refer to the aftermath of her ordeal, or that he might mention his plans, that he was off to London or some such. She wasn't ready to consider the harsh reality, couldn't parlay over the details. At present, she wanted him with her, and she couldn't peer beyond that simple wish.

"And *I* have something to tell you," she injected, eager to forestall any sensational confessions.

"You first."

"While you were out, I received several surprising letters."

"From whom?"

"One was from your sister."

"Eleanor?"

"She's been trying to track you down."

"What's she up to?"

"She's marrying your friend, Charles Hughes."

"She finally relented! How wonderful."

Anne thought they were an odd couple—the elegant lady and the taciturn, maimed soldier—but who could predict where love would bloom? Look at herself and Stephen. There was no rhyme or reason to it.

"It sounded as if they're in a hurry."

He whispered, "She's having a baby."

"Well, that explains the rush! The ceremony is next week at Bristol Manor, and you're to be best man."

"There's nothing new in the distinction. I've always been the *best*."

"Vain beast!"

Swatting at him, she endeavored to conceal how hurt she was that he hadn't invited her to attend with him—not that she'd imagined he would, or that she would agree if he had. She tried to picture herself inside the grand mansion, being introduced to his ogre of a father, scrutinized by his two older brothers, snubbed by the servants who would accuse her of putting on airs.

The prospect was ludicrous, and she couldn't figure out why she persisted with such whimsy. She was a fool, a dreamer, a miserable, smitten ninny, intent on building castles in the sky.

"Who else wrote?" he inquired.

"My brother, Phillip. And . . . and . . . my father."

She couldn't quite process the development, and her

heart pounded from her communicating the amazing fact aloud.

"Really?"

"Yes."

Perceiving her trepidation, he counseled, "This is marvelous news. Don't be frightened by it."

"I'm not. It was just so . . . so unexpected." From the day her mother had moved them away, when Anne was three, her father hadn't contacted her, and she was spinning with the implications. "They're both getting married, too."

"Phillip *and* Edward? You're joking!"

"No."

"Who are the lucky women?"

"Phillip has snagged himself an aristocrat. Lady Olivia Hopkins."

"The devil you say!"

"Do you know her?"

"Yes."

"What's she like?"

"Very sweet, very bright, and pretty."

"And my father is marrying her cousin."

"Winnie Stewart?"

"Yes, that's her name."

"I can't believe it."

"They want me to come to Salisbury for the weddings, and to stay for an extended visit. They're going to be celebrating from now till Yuletide."

"I like their style."

"Lady Olivia and Miss Stewart wrote to me, too. With the nicest messages. They were so kind, so . . . so . . ."

She started to cry. The letters were so special to her, arriving as they had, when she was weary and forlorn. For so long, she'd been alone, as she would be when he left. It was reassuring to realize that there were others out there who cared about her, who might be friends.

"What's this?" He swiped at the trail dripping down her cheek.

"I could have a family again."

The declaration brought on a bout of weeping. She couldn't speak, couldn't clarify, and the sorrow of a lifetime gushed out until she ached with despair. Throughout the episode, he cradled her to his chest, stroking her hair, and patting her back. He was unruffled, content to tarry while she vented her woe.

As for herself, she was humiliated by her behavior, but she couldn't prevent the outpouring of melancholy. She was mourning for the little girl whose father had sent her away, but also for the adult woman she'd grown to be, the one who'd been stupid enough to love the wrong man, who would love him forever.

It was all so sad, so tragic.

Eventually, the tide ebbed. She was exhausted, and she collapsed onto him.

"Will you go to Salisbury?" he asked.

"I don't know. I can't see myself there. It would be so difficult."

She had the same vision as she'd conjured of herself at Bristol Manor. She would feel so awkward, would be so out of place.

"How about if I went with you?"

"As my what?"

She glowered at him. When they'd romped at her farm, they'd been afforded a substantial amount of privacy, but there was no way they could continue outside the confines of her property. She could never account for him to her father, her brother, their fiancées, or anyone else who might be curious.

He occupied no position that could be discussed in polite company. Previously, she'd been able to deal with the concept that she was merely his paramour, but with the catastrophe she'd recently suffered, her nerves were raw, her passions inflamed. She couldn't pretend that he didn't matter to her, couldn't feign indifference as to what he might do next.

In her current condition, courtesy was beyond her.

"What *would* I be?" As if the question was humorous, he grinned. "It does appear to be a month for weddings."

"There must be something in the air."

"Perhaps I should plan my own."

She gaped at him, her mouth falling open in stunned shock. How could he mention his union with Felicity? Had he no circumspection? No shame? Couldn't he discern how vulnerable she was? How defenseless? Why would he raise such a painful topic?

"By all means," she remarked bitterly. "Plan your own."

Anxious to swim away, she slithered off him. Tears were welling again, another round of sobbing about to inundate her, and she yearned for solitude as she shed them. He grabbed her, and though she struggled and fought, she couldn't escape.

"Calm yourself," he urged.

"No. I'm tired, and I'm angry, and I hate you."

"Are we back to that?"

"I don't think we ever left. Just go to London. Wed your precious Lady Felicity, and leave me be."

He laughed! The wretch! "I'm not marrying Felicity."

Lordy! Had he already found someone else? Very likely, he had a whole harem tripping over themselves. "Who then?"

"You."

She cocked her head, shook it. She couldn't have heard him correctly. "What?"

"I wish to marry *you*."

"Well, you can't, so quit being such a boor. It's cruel to tease me."

"Who's to tell me I can't?"

"The entire world. As you've so vehemently claimed."

"Since my jaunt to the city, my opinion of the entire *world* is a tad jaded." He fumbled under the water, dug around in his wet coat, and after much grubbing, he lifted his hand, a finger extended. There was a gold band slipped onto it, the ring jammed to his knuckle, and obviously intended for her. He wiggled it to and fro, and she followed the motion as if he was a mesmerist.

"What's that supposed to be?" Disdainful, incredulous, she was scared to attach any gravity to the object for fear of what it might—or might not—signify.

"Just what it looks like. A betrothal ring." He tugged it off and nestled it in his palm. "I realize it's rather plain, but it was the best I could find without traveling to London."

He'd gone to Bath to purchase an engagement ring for her? Was he mad?

"It's a fine piece of jewelry," she said noncommittally. "What sort of woman would crave anything more?"

"Let's see how it fits." He glided it onto her finger. It was snug, perfect, glowing as if it had always been there. "My dearest Anne," he began, "would you do me the honor of becoming my wife?"

Flummoxed and bewildered, she stared at him, trying to detect if he was jesting, but no one could be that callous. Especially not him.

"Why . . .?" There were a dozen interpretations to the query. Why would he? Why had he changed his mind? Why did he presume that their situations had been so drastically altered?

"Because I love you more than life itself, and I want you by my side forevermore."

Steady, true, earnest, his resolve settled on her like a benediction. "You're serious."

"Of course I am, you silly girl."

"But what about Lady Felicity?"

"Whilst I was away, she fell in love with her cousin."

"How fickle."

"I certainly thought so, although I was very glad. He can have her, with my blessing."

"What about your family?"

"They will adore you, as do I."

She pinched her wrist, wondering if she was dreaming, but she could definitely feel the tweak. She was conscious. She was alert. He'd actually proposed.

"So," he went on, "I should like to accompany you to your father's nuptials—as your husband."

"Oh, Stephen . . . oh . . ." She was beyond words, beyond comprehension.

"But there is one detail we need to consider before you reply."

Her heart thudded with apprehension. "What is it?"

"I was lauded by the King. For my military service."

"How?"

"With a title."

"Of?"

"Baron. It provides a small estate north and east of here. It's a day's ride. Maybe more. It's called Tetbury."

He was now a peer of the realm, donning a rank and station she despised. Did it matter? And what did it portend for herself? If she acquiesced to his offer, she would be a baroness, a member of the group inhabited by his beautiful, refined sister. Could she play the part? Did she care to?

"What you're really asking is whether I want to be your baroness."

"Yes."

"I'd be terrible at it."

"No. You'd be grand." He linked their fingers and squeezed tight. "Don't be intimidated, Anne. You can succeed wherever you focus your energies. I'm the living proof, so I have no doubts. And don't forget: half the blood in your veins is from your father. How long have your ancestors held the Salisbury title? Six hundred years? Seven hundred? You're from noble stock. More exalted than mine."

In the past, when she'd contemplated her father, it had only been the negative, the ways he'd maltreated her mother. She'd never reflected on her ties to the Salisbury line, had never pondered her pedigree, believing that her bastardry wiped out any assertion she might make to the contrary.

"Others will maintain that I'm not worthy, that you married far beneath yourself, and they'll snub you because of me."

"I'll kill any man who dares."

She snuggled herself to him. She was so conflicted! Wasn't this the answer to her prayers? He would be hers, would be hers permanently, but in her reveries, she'd pictured them at her farm, which she recognized had been a ridiculous delusion.

Was it a celestial test? A divine joke? She could have Stephen, but in exchange, she would have to forsake all that she cherished. It was so unfair.

"If I decline?"

"I won't let you. Anne, listen to me." He forced her to meet his gaze. "Although my new tenants will treasure your skills as much as the people here, we'd only have to be at Tetbury part of the year. And I would have to journey to London, to sessions of Parliament, but you wouldn't have to come to the city if you didn't wish to. Say *yes*, Anne. We can make it happen. I know we can!"

He was so sure, so optimistic, but there were so many obstacles. Had he truly weighed the hurdles?

"It's such an impulsive, frightening request." She trembled with the urge to give him the response he craved. Could she step out of her world and into his? She'd be like Cinderella at the ball. What if the clock chimed midnight and her fantasy crashed down around her?

"How could I convince you?"

"I don't think you can." She needed the opportunity to ruminate, to balance the benefits and detriments. To him and to
herself. She was greatly afeared that he was pushing for
something he ought not do.

He sighed. "The investiture hasn't occurred yet. If my ac-
quiring a title would cause you to refuse me, then I will graciously reject the distinction."

She blanched at the notion. "You'd relinquish your reward, just for me?"

"I would."

He'd scorn the King? Would waive his compensation?
For her? She couldn't let him. More than anyone, she knew
how much he'd sacrificed, and he deserved every reparation
that was presented.

"We could stay here some of the time?"

"Yes, and I've discussed the particulars with Kate and
Pru. They can handle the business during the periods when
we're away."

They had it all arranged! The scalawags!

"You're positive this is what you want?"

"I've never desired anything more."

"Swear to me that you'll never lament your decision."

"As if I could regret loving you!" Gripping her shoulders,
he shook her and repeated, "Say yes!"

Was she the biggest fool ever? Was it a mistake? An illusion? A colossal blunder?

She stared at him, sitting as he was in the pond, his
clothes on, the moon shining down, his devotion clear. She
twirled the ring. How could she deny herself this chance?
How could she ever pine for more?

Where he was concerned, she'd never had any willpower,
and she didn't know why she'd expected the current encounter to be any different.

"Yes, I will."

He looked eager as a schoolboy. "You mean it?"

"Yes, I will," she said again.

He let out a whoop that the neighbors could probably hear on the surrounding properties, and he whirled her around and around until she was dizzy with delight.

"Let's have the wedding night right now!" he decreed.

"Now?"

"This is where we met. This is where it all transpired. Can you imagine any place better?"

"No."

"Besides, the water is working its magic." He grinned. "I can't wait to have you."

He climbed onto the rocks, and he stuck out a foot, his boot dripping.

Pompous and arrogant as he'd ever been, he ordered, "Remove them. And be quick about it."

"Aren't you high-and-mighty, all of a sudden?"

"They call me *Lord* Tetbury," he announced. "When I'm feeling indulgent, I shall allow you to refer to me simply as Tetbury. At all other times, it shall be: my lord."

"Hah!" Shrieking, she slapped at his leg. "Never in a thousand years."

She writhed away, but not very fast. He caught her easily, wrapping her in his arms, and kissing her as if there were no tomorrow. He poured his affection into the embrace, and she could sense his joy, his exultation.

"I'm so happy," he declared.

"So am I."

"I want it to always be just like this between us."

"It will be."

But if their ardor ever began to fade, she could bring him home, to her erotic pool. The idea made her smile, as she envisioned them gray, aged, but Stephen still randy, still unsated, chasing her around the grotto like a lusty adolescent.

She reached for the placard of his pants and started to loose the buttons.

Hands on his hips, cocky as any rooster, he demanded, "What are you doing?"

"I thought we'd go for a swim."

"My dear Lady Tetbury"—he raised a brow and came closer—"I'm in the mood for a little more than swimming."

Deeper than Desire

CHERYL HOLT
National Award-Winning Author

With her family in dire straits, Olivia Hopkins reluctantly agrees to seek a marriage proposal from the aging Earl of Salisbury. But the plan goes awry when she finds an erotic volume in the earl's library. The book sets Olivia's body on fire. She simply cannot put it down—until she is caught red-handed by the Earl's devilishly handsome son Philip Paxton—a man who quickens her pulse and stirs her imagination with thoughts she's never dared entertain. Now, Philip lures Olivia into an electrifying affair that explodes into unbridled lessons of passion. But what begins as a rakish scheme soon becomes a genuine affair of the heart...

"Cheryl Holt demonstrates her phenomenal understanding of women's secret longings...With titillating and provocative narrative, she builds both the sexual tension and the romance to the point of eruption."

—*Romantic Times* on *Absolute Pleasure*

"A very sensual novel in the manner of Susan Johnson...Holt does an excellent job of raising one's temperature."

—*Old Book Barn Gazette* on *Love Lessons*

ISBN: 0-312-99282-3

AVAILABLE WHEREVER BOOKS ARE SOLD
FROM ST. MARTIN'S PAPERBACKS

Visit Cheryl Holt's Web site at: www.cherylholt.com

DTD 05 04

Complete Abandon

CHERYL HOLT
National Award-Winning Author

When the prim and proper Emma Fitzgerald storms the manor home of John Clayton, the new Viscount Wakefield, she feels more than justified fury. Having just inadvertently witnessed his lordship in scandalous dishabille with his London mistress, her blood pounds with outrage...and with a thrill she has never felt. The erotic image of his powerful flesh only heightens her determination to make this wicked rogue accountable for his actions. No woman has ever refused to be baited by him. And then Emma proposes a bargain worthy of his own insolence: In return for his kindness to others, she offers herself, never suspecting the consequences to her own heart...

"Cheryl Holt scores big with *Total Surrender*. Following in the erotic path set by Robin Schone, Lisa Kleypas, and Catherine Coulter, she taps into secret fantasies tied closely to a romantic love story."
—*Romantic Times* on *Total Surrender*

"Very well written...I would recommend it to those who like Thea Devine or the later books of Susan Johnson."
—*Romance Reviews Today* on *Love Lessons*

ISBN: 0-312-98460-X

AVAILABLE WHEREVER BOOKS ARE SOLD FROM ST. MARTIN'S PAPERBACKS

Visit Cheryl Holt's Web site at: www.cherylholt.com

CA 05 04

Absolute Pleasure

CHERYL HOLT

National Award-Winning Author

The lonely, never-married Lady Elizabeth Harcourt desperately longs for a distraction. She finds one when a chance encounter leads her to the lush studios of artist Gabriel Cristofore. Gabriel insists upon painting Elizabeth's portrait, vowing to do justice to her ravishing figure. But Elizabeth soon realizes that Gabriel's plans for her have little to do with painting—for his true passion in life is the art of seduction. But Gabriel is about to discover that some affairs cannot be so easily abandoned—especially when the heart of a rogue has been captured...

"With her well-defined characters, even pacing, and heated love scenes Holt makes an easy entry into the world of erotic romance...readers will enjoy *Love Lessons*."
—*Romantic Times* on *Love Lessons*

"Carefully crafted characters, engaging dialogue, and sinfully erotic narrative."
—*Romance Reviews Today* on *Total Surrender*

ISBN: 0-312-98459-6

AVAILABLE WHEREVER BOOKS ARE SOLD
FROM ST. MARTIN'S PAPERBACKS

Visit Cheryl Holt's Web site at: www.cherylholt.com

AP 05 04

Total Surrender

CHERYL HOLT

With the last of her family's possessions gambled away by her dissolute brother, Lady Sarah Compton has traveled to a country house gala for one last moment of grace and beauty. But she is unaware that the occasion is actually a notorious trysting event, where members of the aristocracy can indulge their every sensual fantasy and erotic whim. Nor does she realize that the striking man who has stolen into her bedroom is none other than Michael Stevens—a rake who gives and takes his pleasures boldly. When Sarah refuses to heed Michael's warning—to leave the house for her own protection—a powerful attraction grows, and soon, he longs to tutor the very proper Lady Sarah Compton in the art of passion...

"Cheryl Holt demonstrates her phenomenal understanding of women's secret longings...with titillating and provocative narrative, she builds both the sexual tension and the romance to the point of eruption."

—*Romantic Times* on *Absolute Pleasure*

"A very sensual book...I would recommend it to those of you who like Thea Devine or the later books of Susan Johnson."

—Romancereviewstoday.com on *Love Lessons*

ISBN: 0-312-97841-3

AVAILABLE WHEREVER BOOKS ARE SOLD
FROM ST. MARTIN'S PAPERBACKS

Visit Cheryl Holt's Web site at: www.cherylholt.com

TS 05 04

Love Lessons

CHERYL HOLT

A resolute spinster at twenty-five, Abigail Weston is nonetheless determined to see her cherished younger sister wed to a man of Quality. But Abigail's lack of experience with the opposite sex means that she cannot allay her sister's fears about the marriage bed—unless she takes bold steps to learn what the intimacy between a man and a woman entails. Yet the one man in London qualified to teach her awakens temptation Abigail never anticipated—to experience each whispered pleasure for herself...

"A lush tale of romance, sexuality, and the fragility of the human spirit. Carefully crafted characters, engaging dialogue, and sinfully erotic narrative create a story that is at once compelling and disturbing...for a story that is sizzling hot and a hero any woman would want to save."

—*Romance Reviews Today* on *Total Surrender*

ISBN: 0-312-97840-5

AVAILABLE WHEREVER BOOKS ARE SOLD
FROM ST. MARTIN'S PAPERBACKS

You can visit Cheryl Holt's Web site at: www.cherylholt.com